Printed in the United States of America

FEAR NO EVIL

America's War on Terrorism

Michael H. Cunningham

For two people who made me what I am.

My parents:
Absalom "Bill" Marion Cunningham
and
Mildred Elwilda (Watson) Cunningham

Ils ne passeront pas

INTRODUCTION

SPRING 2004

Ten months ago, July 2003, the terrorist attacks in America failed. All the protagonists—at least almost all—were either dead or in jail. The terrorist group, led by a few radical Salafists, was in shambles. Usayd was somewhere in Afghanistan. He was killing Americans and enjoying every minute. The group called "the triumvirate" (Aadil, Mubid, and Sabir) were in hiding in Arzew, Algeria, the city of their birth and the base of the previous operation. Correntine and Mubbaligh were amongst the missing. When the attacks on America began last July, they both disappeared. The streets of Arzew were full of rumors. Some said the couple was killed by the triumvirate for failure to successfully carry out the terrorist attack. Others thought they ran off to some South Pacific island to avoid capture by the authorities. No one really knew. Or at least no one was letting on. Sameenah, Mubbaligh's ex-lover before Correntine arrived on the scene, was also amongst the missing. Ten months ago, there was tension and anticipation in the air. Today, everything was calm and peaceful. This state of bliss was about to change.

PART I

CHAPTER ONE

Usayd did not want to return to Arzew. But like the good soldier that he was, he followed orders. When the triumvirate requested his presence, he immediately left the hills of Afghanistan and began his long trek home. Since a lot of people were looking for him, his travel had to be circuitous and clandestine. His arrival in Algeria would have to be especially secretive because the Algerian government had lookout bulletins posted all over the country. Government officials were paying close attention to the seaports and airports. Capturing Usayd would be a big prize and would ensure someone a promotion and the gratitude of the Algerian government.

It took Usayd almost a week to reach the seaport town of Beirut, Lebanon. His trek was not easy. He used all modes of transportation. Some times he rode on the back of a donkey. Other times he was able to hitch a ride on a motorized vehicle; once on a chicken-laden, dilapidated pickup truck and another time on a motorbike that belched thick black smoke the entire trip. He was robbed in Iran (or maybe he was still in Afghanistan, Usayd really didn't know). In Syria, he was accosted by guards along the border who accused him of being a drug smuggler. Usayd wasn't sure if these guards were official border guards, but he wasn't in a good position to argue with them. After taking a wad of bills from Usayd's backpack, the guards let him go. Usayd chuckled to himself as he left. The wad of bills was old Afghanistan money. The government had changed the currency of Afghanistan at least twice since this money was used. When the guards attempted to use the money, they would be in for a big surprise.

Eventually, Usayd reached the port city of Beirut. He looked up Bashir, an old friend from back home, and stayed at his apartment (ironically,

Bashir means bringer of glad tidings). Usayd was exhausted not only from his recent trek, but from fighting in Afghanistan. At the encouragement of Bashir, Usayd decided to stay several days in Beirut. He needed the time to rest, recuperate and replenish his body. While resting, Usayd could make travel arrangements for the rest of his journey.

The first day, Usayd never left Bashir's house. He mostly slept. When he was awake, Bashir fed him good food. After the first full day in Beirut, Usayd felt like a new man. He hadn't slept so much in almost a year. The food also nourished his body and spirit. The second day in Beirut, Bashir took Usayd sightseeing. As they walked the narrow streets of Beirut, Usayd took in all the sights. He couldn't believe how peaceful everything was. There wasn't the constant noise and commotion he was exposed to in the hills of Afghanistan. He scanned the sky for enemy planes, and then realized he didn't have to. He was out of the combat zone. He knew he was going to have to adjust to this new life outside of Afghanistan.

Bashir took him to a local restaurant for lunch. Before they ate, Usayd had a couple glasses of wine. When he felt the influence of the alcohol, Usayd panicked. He didn't like the feeling of not being in control. He was letting his guard down and this could get him killed. Usayd jumped to his feet and ran out of the restaurant. Bashir threw some money on the table and went after his friend. He found Usayd leaning against the building adjacent to the restaurant. Usayd's face was drenched in sweat and he was breathing heavily. His eyes were bulging out of their sockets and his hands were trembling. Bashir was scared and confused. He didn't know what was going on. Bashir placed his hand on Usayd's back and bent over to look into his face. As Bashir made eye contact with Usayd, he could see tears streaming down his face. Usayd was crying! Bashir began to panic himself. What was going on with his pal? Did someone poison his wine? That was impossible he thought, because he was drinking out of the same bottle. He wasn't suffering from any ill effects, so it couldn't be the wine. Then he realized, or more accurately, he suspected something else. Although Usayd looked fine outwardly, inside he was still all torn up. Drinking the wine triggered something in his head. Bashir wasn't sure what was going on, but he knew he had to get Usayd back to his apartment. He flagged down a cab and helped his friend climb in the backseat. They were back in the apartment within ten minutes. Bashir helped Usayd to bed. Within minutes he was asleep.

Usayd was awoken in the middle of the night by someone yelling. As he lay in bed staring at the ceiling, he realized it was himself yelling. He was having a nightmare. He was back in Afghanistan and American troops were pursuing him through a pass in the mountains. The faster he moved, the closer the Americans came. Just when he was about to be caught, the yelling awoke him. He shivered at the recollection. As he lay there thinking about the nightmare, Usayd realized he was soaking wet. He sweated so much during the nightmare, his entire body and the sheets he was laying on were soaked.

What is the matter with me? He thought. Usayd always slept through the night and seldom had nightmares. But, in the last few months, he was waking up in the middle of the night and he was having nightmares. After a few minutes, Usayd climbed out of bed. He looked at the clock on the night stand next to the bed and saw that it was 3:00 am—too early to get out of bed and wake up his friend. Silently, Usayd shuffled across the floor and entered the nearby bathroom. He turned the shower on and adjusted the water to real hot. As he stood under the cascading water, he felt his muscles relax. He was feeling human again.

He vigorously dried himself with a towel hanging behind the bathroom door and reentered the bedroom. After changing into a dry pair of pajamas, Usayd removed the wet sheets. Since he didn't have any clean sheets, he climbed back into bed and lay on the bare mattress. After all, he thought, he slept on far worse in the hills of Afghanistan. As he lay there, Usayd reflected on what was going on. Why was he incessantly hounded by these nightmares? He wondered if he had brain cancer or was he suffering from a stroke. The thought that what he'd been through the last year was causing these nightmares never crossed his mind. All the combat he'd seen, all the killing and dying, all the suffering.

The next time Usayd looked at the clock, it was a little after seven. While he was lying in bed wondering about all his nightmares, he fell back to sleep. He slept for almost three hours without interruption! Slowly Usayd crawled out of bed. As he was putting his pants on, he heard noise in the other room and then caught the smell of coffee wafting in the air.

A smile crossed his face. Bashir was up and by the smell, he was cooking breakfast. As Usayd shuffled into the kitchen, he was greeted by a beaming Bashir. "Good morning, sunshine," Bashir said, "Did you sleep well?"

"Great," Usayd lied, "How about you?"

Bashir ignored Usayd's question and asked him what he'd like for breakfast. Usayd said coffee and a piece of bread was sufficient. Even after several minutes of Bashir's pestering to eat more than just bread, Usayd stuck to his guns. He flippantly told Bashir if he ate too much, none of the pretty girls walking the streets of Beirut would look at him. Bashir told Usayd it didn't matter what he ate or didn't eat. He was so ugly none of the girls would look at him, fat or skinny. They both laughed hilariously as they sat at the kitchen table. Once seated, Bashir discreetly looked at his friend. On the outside, everything looked fine, but he knew, things must be boiling on the inside.

As they sat having breakfast, they reminisced about the good old days back in Arzew. Bashir and Usayd grew up in the same neighborhood. They went to the same school and played on the same soccer team. Their parents, brothers and sisters all knew each other. In fact, Usayd had a crush on Bashir's older sister when he was in his late teens. Usayd couldn't believe it when Bashir told him this same sister was now married and had five children. Where did all the years go? Usayd thought. Unlike Usayd, Bashir left Arzew seeking business opportunities. He first settled in Rabat, Morocco, but only lasted two years. The atmosphere was too stifling for him and business opportunities for foreigners were limited. Bashir heard nothing but good things about Beirut. The Lebanese welcomed foreigners and encouraged them to start new business opportunities. Bashir had been in Beirut ten years. He told Usayd he enjoyed every moment.

Bashir was a serious businessman, but there was also a fun side to him. He loved to party and date beautiful women, and Beirut was full of beautiful women. Because he had done well in business and invested wisely, money wasn't an issue with him. He was now in his mid-thirties and was ready to settle down. He had been dating a local girl for over a year and told Usayd he thought she was the one. In the near future he planned to ask this girl to marry him. As Usayd listened to his friend talk, he became reflective. He was also in his mid-thirties but didn't have anything like

Bashir did. Usayd was broke and the only girls he associated with were not of the type you brought home to introduce to your parents. But, that was the nature of his work. There wasn't any room in his life for a long term relationship with a woman.

Bashir interrupted Usayd's reflections by saying, "I've a great thought! Why don't you stay in Beirut and work for me?" Bashir told Usayd he needed someone reliable and trustworthy to help him in his import-export business. Sure, he could hire a local Lebanese, but the connection wasn't there. It wouldn't be like having someone from back home helping him. Bashir really didn't know what Usayd did for a living, but he had his suspicions. Usayd told him he'd been in Afghanistan for the past year, but he didn't say what he was doing there. Bashir wasn't about to ask either. He didn't have to. He knew Usayd's past and assumed nothing had changed. He suspected Usayd was still involved in the radical wing of the Salafist movement, only he didn't know how deeply involved Usayd was.

When Bashir offered him legitimate work in Beirut, Usayd was caught off guard. Never in his wildest dreams did he think of holding down an honest job. His life was so wrapped up in the movement; he never gave anything else a thought. But, the thought of working for Bashir intrigued him. It would be nice to have a normal job and perhaps even a family. After all, running around the world causing chaos and mayhem was taking a toll on him. How much longer could he keep up this hectic and danger-ous pace before he broke?—or worse. Look at him now. He couldn't even sleep at night without waking up from a horrible nightmare. Look at all the close calls he survived in Afghanistan. How much longer would his luck hold out? Maybe Bashir was right. Maybe it was the right time to change jobs. Usayd stared into his coffee cup as he continued to mull over Bashir's generous offer. But, something kept nagging at him. How could he leave the movement? It had been his life for so many years. How could he just up and quit?

Bashir broke the silence. "Well, Usayd, just don't sit there saying noth-ing. What do you think? Will you come work for me?" Usayd had a devil-ish grin on his face as he raised his head and looked Bashir in the eyes, "You bastard," he said. "What a tempting offer." Usayd explained to Bashir that he was most appreciative of his offer, but he just didn't know. Without saying what he was doing in Afghanistan, he told Bashir he loved his work there and was committed to seeing it through. But, if anything changed, he was definitely interested in Bashir's offer of employment. Bashir told him the offer would remain open and, if anything did change, all Usayd had to do was tell him. The job would be his. Bashir didn't want to pressure Usayd and decided to change the subject. "Well my friend, why don't we clean up and then we'll see the sites of sunny Beirut." Usayd slapped both his knees with the palms of his hands and smiled broadly as he said, "Sounds like a good idea."

CHAPTER TWO

Blenheim is located on the northern coast of New Zealand's South Island. The residents of the town of 30,000 enjoy hot, dry summers and moderate winters. Located in the middle of grape-growing country, Blenheim and the surrounding area are recognized for their fine wines and succulent cuisine. The residents of Blenheim are also known for their hospitality to strangers—no matter who they are.

Into this warm and friendly setting, Mubbaligh and Correntine (traveling under the assumed last name of Elias) arrived in the early part of 2004—six months after the failed terrorist attack on America. They both fell immediately in love with New Zealand and New Zealanders. They were so friendly and helpful, unlike the residents back home in Arzew. Arriving by plane in Wellington, the capital of New Zealand, in mid-January, Mubbaligh and Correntine had to find a place to stay. They entered the country on permanent resident visas, meaning they could stay as long as they wanted. But they had no idea where they wanted to live. During the Customs and Immigration processing allowing them into the country, one of the Customs Inspectors mentioned he was born in Blenheim on the South Island. Mubbaligh found this ironic. He had made many telephone calls from Arzew to realtors in Blenheim in the preceding months. Over the phone the area seemed idyllic to him. The Inspector recounted fondly his days growing up in the hilly, sunny region of Blenheim. Mubbaligh and Correntine enjoyed the inspector's tales of years gone by. Right there in the Customs office, they both decided Blenheim is where they would live. If the place was half as good as the inspector said, they knew they would be happy.

To reach Blenheim from Wellington, you could take an inter-island airplane hop or you could take the car-passenger ferry. The plane ride was less than an hour and ran every two hours on the half hour. The ferry was an all-day event and ran once a day, leaving at ten in the morning. Since "Mr. and Mrs. Elias" were in no hurry, they decided to stay in Wellington for a few days and acclimate themselves to their new country. They bought their ferry tickets for two days hence, before they took off to see the sights in Wellington.

Mubbaligh and Correntine were amazed how clean Wellington was. And the people were so friendly. Everywhere they went, the locals went out of their way to accommodate them. The first night they stayed at a well known hotel in downtown Wellington. They ate at a local restaurant. They enjoyed the local lamb with kumara (sweet potato) and had tea and pavlova for dessert. After dinner they took a short walk and were back in their hotel room by nine. As they were relaxing and discussing the events of the day, Correntine decided it was time to tell Mubbaligh. She was pregnant! She hadn't seen a doctor yet, but by her estimation she was three months along. Mubbaligh was ecstatic. He hugged and kissed Correntine. Correntine was so pleased to see how happy Mubbaligh was. She was afraid Mubbaligh might be upset because the timing was bad, moving to a new country and everything. That night when they laid their heads down to go to sleep, there wasn't a happier couple in all of New Zealand.

The morning of their scheduled ferry ride dawned bright and clear. As Mubbaligh and Correntine walked from their hotel to the pier, Mubbaligh could see the ferry boat off in the distance. She sat at the dock motionless. The sun was glistening off her upper decks. Sailors were busily moving about, preparing the ship for sea. As they approached the pier, the massive size of the ship impressed both Mubbaligh and Correntine. They expected to see a small inter-coastal ferry, not a huge ocean-going vessel. By the bow, Mubbaligh read her name—"South Sea Adventurer." He laughed at the name. How appropriate it was. They were indeed going on an adventure. Cars and trucks were already driving up a large steel ramp entering the bowels of the vessel. Passengers were lined up waiting to board. There had to be at least two hundred by Mubbaligh's estimation.

Mubbaligh and Correntine entered a large red brick building that had a prominent red and white sign displayed on the roof—New Zealand Government Ferry. They followed the signs to the check-in area and were met by a Customs Inspector as they approached the counter. "Good morning," the young female inspector said. Mubbaligh and Correntine were both struck by how pleasant and cheerful this government official seemed to be. Neither said anything to each other, but they both thought how different this greeting was compared to back in Algeria. The Algerian government officials were noted for their nastiness and greed. Nothing could be accomplished when dealing with Algerian government officials unless a bribe was offered. Make sure it wasn't too little because you could offend the official. If you did, you'd be waiting all day and even then you weren't guaranteed a successful outcome.

Mubbaligh and Correntine boarded the ferry and took seats on the upper deck amidships. After a half hour wait, the ferry slowly, but inexorably, backed out of the dock. A long blast followed by three short blasts from the ferry's whistle indicated she was backing down. When they cleared the headland, Mubbaligh detected a long slow swell coming from the east. The ferry began to rock from side to side. Correntine became queasy and Mubbaligh was concerned for her. Now Mubbaligh realized why the ferry was so big. The ride between the North and South Islands could be rather bumpy.

Eventually, Mubbaligh was able to find Correntine a comfortable recliner. He covered her with a thick quilt and sat down in a chair beside her. They were holding hands when Correntine slid off to sleep. Mubbaligh stayed by her side, looking out the ferry windows at all the other ships sailing through the harbor. Off in the distance, he could faintly make out a large, white ship. As the ship came closer, Mubbaligh read "U.S.Coast Guard" on the side of the ship. Sailors in white uniforms were standing at attention. Mubbaligh wondered why a United States ship was in New Zealand. On the stern in smaller letters Mubbaligh read "Southwind." He had no idea what this meant.

What Mubbaligh was looking at was the United States Coast Guard icebreaker "Southwind". She was headed down to Antarctica to conduct oceanographic and meteorological experiments. On her way there from the west coast of the United States, the Southwind stopped at many different ports. The purpose of these stopovers was to wave the American flag and to give her crew a bit of rest ashore. Calling on the port of Wellington was the Southwind's fifth stop on this voyage. The crew was really looking forward to liberty call. Wellington was considered to be an excellent liberty port by sailors in the Coast Guard.

Another thing Mubbaligh didn't know. The commanding officer of the Southwind was Captain Andrew Martell. Captain Martell, less than a year ago, was the commanding officer of the Coast Guard Cutter Spencer. At the time he held the rank of Commander. His ship, the Spencer, thwarted a terrorist attack on the city of Boston, Massachusetts by firing on a runaway LNG ship. The LNG ship, the Nautilus, was attempting to run a blockade of coast guard ships stationed at the mouth of the harbor. She wanted to get inside the harbor and blow herself up. If she succeeded, the devastation and loss of life would have been terrific.

Captain Martell took bold and decisive action to prevent this from happening. He ordered the gunners on the Spencer to fire on the Nautilus. They disabled the Nautilus' rudder. The captain of the Nautilus realized the futility of the situation and blew the ship up. The actions of Captain Martell earned him the rank of Captain. It also earned him the prestigious position of captain of one of the Coast Guard's newest and finest vessels. Mubbaligh was familiar with the Nautilus. He had been on her in Arzew just before she sailed to America. She was part of the terrorist plot he had planned. He didn't realize the role played by the captain of the ship he was watching sail by. If he had, shivers would have gone up his spine. So long ago and so many miles away, yet their paths crossed again in the far away waters of Wellington Harbor.

The rest of the cruise to the South Island was uneventful. After sleeping for a few hours, Correntine awoke feeling much better. The seas moderated and Mubbaligh and Correntine were able to sit out on deck and have lunch. As they ate, the sun shone on their faces and a gentle warm wind carrying the fragrance of flowers blew from the west. Mubbaligh and Correntine were more at peace than they had been in years.

The South Sea Adventurer cruised through the waters of the Tasman Sea at a pleasant fifteen knots. The captain expected to reach their dock at Blenheim on the South Island at 5:00 pm. Mubbaligh and Correntine spotted a couple of lounge chairs on the lee side of the ship. Feeling a little tired after lunch, they decided to read a bit and perhaps take a little nap. Soon they were enjoying a blissful sleep. They were awaken abruptly by an announcement over the ships public address system. The South Sea Adventurer would be docking in a little less than one hour. The purser requested all passengers to gather their belongings and be ready to depart the vessel. He asked all drivers to man their cars and trucks. This is it Mubbaligh thought, a new beginning—for the three of them. They walked to the ships railing and peered off into the distance. Rich, green hills under a layer of fluffy, white clouds awaited their arrival. Mubbaligh and Correntine looked at each other, embraced and kissed. A new life was awaiting them. They hoped all the troubles of the past were forever out of their lives.

CHAPTER THREE

The next few days were some of the happiest days of Usayd's life. He and Bashir rose early and, after a light breakfast, walked the few blocks that took them to the local beach. Usayd enjoyed soaking his tired body in the warm waters of the Mediterranean. One morning Hanifah, Bashir's girlfriend, joined them. She was a beautiful lady in her late twenties and by the way she carried herself, Usayd sensed her upbringing was quite unlike his. She had graduated from the Notre Dame in Paris, taking a degree in financing. After schooling in France, she returned to Beirut to work in her father's import-export business. Hanifah was easy to talk with and made Usayd feel comfortable. It was obvious to Usayd that the two were madly in love. Usayd was happy for his childhood friend. Someday, he thought, he might be as lucky as him.

Bashir, Usayd and Hanifah are Sunnis. Although they didn't practice their religion as faithfully as they should, they were still Sunnis. This fact mattered a great deal in Beirut. People lived in certain parts of the city based strictly on their religion. Christians lived in the eastern part of the city; Shias lived in the southwest part and the Sunnis occupied the west. Most major cities throughout the world are divided along similar demographic lines. If you lived in London, Berlin or New York City, it was the same. If you were of Italian descent, you lived in the Italian section. If you were Irish, you lived in the Irish section. If you strayed into a different part of the city from where you lived, you did so at your own peril. A fist fight or some other confrontation would likely ensue. In Beirut it was the same, only deadlier. If a Sunni strayed into the Shia district, or a Christian into the Sunni area, violence more than likely would occur. Although the lines of separation were invisible, they were there. If you wanted to keep peace, you had best know and respect the borders.

One night, Hanifah's father invited Bashir and Usayd to his house for dinner. When they arrived, they were warmly met by Hanifah at the front door. She looked her usual beautiful self. After giving Bashir a hug and kiss, she kissed Usayd warmly on both cheeks. Usayd couldn't remember the last time he had smelled a more beautiful woman. Shortly, they were joined by Hanifah's parents. When Usayd saw Hanifah's mother, he realized where Hanifah got her beauty. She was tall and lean and had the most beautiful smile. Her long black hair flowed gracefully over her bare shoulders. Even the way she walked fascinated Usayd. Every movement was so graceful and effortless, as if she was a model walking down a runway. Hanifah's father also impressed Usayd. He was tall, broad-shouldered and had a rough leathery face. Although dressed casually, he was obviously affluent. When Usayd shook his hand, he was impressed by his firm grip. Usayd suspected his life wasn't always so easy-going. Even the look in his eyes was captivating. This guy is not the type to mess with Usayd thought.

After introductions were over, Hanifah led the way down a long hallway. On both walls, Usayd viewed paintings, mostly seascapes. At the end of the hallway, two broad doors were opened wide. As they passed through the doors and stepped out onto a wide veranda, Usayd's breath left him. The view of the city and the Mediterranean Sea in the background was overwhelming. Never before could he recall such a magnificent sight. To add to the beauty, a warm fresh breeze was blowing in his face. Usayd was temporarily lifted from the past. All his troubles and concerns were gone, replaced by the beauty of his present surroundings. When a maid came by to take orders for drinks, Usayd respectfully declined. A glass of ice water was all he wanted. Bashir silently watched as Usayd declined a drink. He was relieved to see Usayd wasn't drinking. He didn't want another episode like the other day, especially in front of his future in-laws. After socializing for almost an hour, they went inside for dinner.

Once the meal was over, the men went back outside on the veranda to enjoy a cup of coffee and a fine Cuban cigar. The girls stayed inside looking at pictures from a trip to Europe Hanifah's parents had just returned from. Hanifah's father led the conversation by inquiring of Usayd what brought him to sunny Beirut. Usayd explained that he was on his way home to Algeria and was just passing through. He wanted to visit his old friend Bashir. When Hanifah's father asked where he had been, there was an uncomfortable delay in Usayd's reply. Finally he said, "Afghanistan, sir."

Hanifah's father's eyebrows distinctly rose at Usayd's reply. "Afghanistan?" he said incredulously, "What the hell are you doing there?" Usayd was quite uncomfortable and squirmed in his chair. Why the hell didn't I lie to him? he said to himself. Now what do I say? Usayd searched quickly for a reply. "Well, sir, I'm sort of freelancing," he said. "I'm into photojournalism and I figured where better to get some great pictures but the war in Afghanistan." Hanifah's father looked skeptically at Usayd. Bashir sat in silence. Neither of them believed Usayd. Hanifah's father directed the conversation into a different area.

About this time, the ladies joined them on the veranda. They engaged in small talk for the next hour or so. Finally Bashir said they had to go. He had early morning appointments and Usayd had to catch a ship. It was the end of a pleasant evening for all, but especially for Usayd. He had never been so relaxed in years—except for that one brief moment on the veranda. They were all standing in the driveway in front of the house. Hugs and kisses were passed all around. When Usayd shook Hanifah's father's hand to say goodbye, the father wrapped his arms around Usayd, giving him a big bear hug.

Hanifah's father looked affectionately into Usayd's eyes and softly said, "Usayd, there was a time in my life that I too was a photojournalist. It is a rough and dangerous business. Please be careful. I was able to get out alive, make sure you do too." Usayd looked in disbelief at Hanifah's father. Was he telling me what I think he's telling me, Usayd thought? Once again they embraced and the father said, this time for all to hear, "Usayd, when you tire of taking pictures, please come back to Beirut. I need a good man to help me in my business." Usayd was flabbergasted. Within the space of a couple of days, he'd been offered two good job openings. He was going to have to do some serious soul searching. Bashir drove slowly down the driveway as they both stuck their arms out the window and gave a final wave. What a night, Usayd thought.

CHAPTER FOUR

Back in Algeria, everything wasn't so rosy in the Salafist movement. Aadil, Sabir and Mubid, the leaders in the movement and better known as the "triumvirate", were furious. Not only did their plans to wreak terror on the shores of America go awry, the architect of the plans was missing. Mubbaligh and his girlfriend, Correntine, disappeared immediately after the failed plot. The triumvirate wasn't sure, but they didn't think anything nefarious happened to Mubbaligh and Correntine. But, they couldn't explain the couple's disappearance. One day they were walking the streets of Arzew, the next day they were gone.

Although the triumvirate was stymied, they promised themselves they would find the couple and find out why their well-laid plans had failed so miserably. In pursuit of this goal, they requested Usayd return immediately to Arzew. Usayd, the main planner of the terrorist plot against America before Mubbaligh came on scene, had been in Afghanistan for the past two years. He was actively involved with the Taliban in their pursuit to rid their country of all Americans. Usayd loved the fighting and killing. When word reached him that the triumvirate wanted him to return home to Arzew, Usayd was despondent. He loved life in Afghanistan. He was finally doing something worthwhile in his life—killing the much hated infidel Americans. He prayed the war would go on for many more years, allowing him to kill more Americans and their allies. But the order of the triumvirate had to be obeyed. Reluctantly he said goodbye to his Taliban friends and began the long voyage home.

The triumvirate was not idle while they awaited Usayd's return. When things settled down after the failed terrorist plot against America and the Algerian authorities began to relax their search for the perpetrators, the triumvirate began their search for the missing couple, Mubbaligh and Correntine. They were a couple, despite all the warnings of the triumvirate. The triumvirate knew Correntine was a CIA operative and they warned Mubbaligh about her when he started to see her. They told him she was CIA and was trying to infiltrate the Salafist movement. However, they wanted Mubbaligh to continue dating Correntine to see what she was up to, what kind of questions she asked Mubbaligh and what kind of information she was looking for. However, he had to be careful. Correntine was smart and could manipulate Mubbaligh into giving her valuable information about the upcoming terrorist plot. She knew Mubbaligh's weak point, his Achilles' heel—his lust for sex—and she was trained to exploit people's weak points. Mubbaligh didn't feel threatened by Correntine. He could handle her while satiating his desires for sex. Obviously, something went wrong, terribly wrong. The terrorist plot failed and the main protagonist, Mubbaligh, and his girlfriend were missing. The triumvirate was determined to find them.

The triumvirate began their quest to find Mubbaligh and Correntine by enlisting the help of Faarooq, a loyal Salafist follower living in Arzew. Faarooq began his hunt for the couple by visiting their old haunts. Dominique's was the first place on his list. Everyone knew Mubbaligh and Correntine frequented Dominique's on a nightly basis. Faarooq wanted to see if he could glean any information of the couple's whereabouts from the staff or customers of Dominique's.

As he entered the restaurant, Faarooq casually looked around the room at the patrons sitting at their tables. Most of the tables were filled, but there were a couple of tables with only one or two people sitting at them. No problem, he thought. As is the custom in Algeria, tables were shared by patrons not knowing each other. If a seat was available, the hostess would sit you there. No sense wasting an empty seat at a table was their common thought. As Faarooq was scanning the room, Maisa, the hostess, approached and welcomed him to Dominique's. "Good evening, sir. Welcome. May I seat you?" Faarooq smiled his disarmingly smile and replied, "Yes, please. May I have a seat on the other side of the room against the wall?" Maisa smiled pleasantly saying, "Certainly, sir, please follow me." As Faarooq followed Maisa through the maze of tables, he had no idea how fortunate he was. You see, Maisa was the cute, diminutive waitress Mubbaligh used to always flirt with whenever he visited Dominique's. Maisa had a secret crush on Mubbaligh and always enjoyed his visits. She hoped something would develop between them and was devastated when Correntine came into the picture.

As Faarooq approached his seat, he greeted the elderly couple already seated at the table with a friendly smile. They reciprocated and the gentleman motioned for Faarooq to take a seat. Faarooq noticed that the couple were already finished eating and were waiting for their check. Good, Faarooq thought. He wanted to be alone. He ordered a glass of wine from Maisa and asked the elderly couple if they would join him in an after dinner liqueur. The gentleman waved his hand and smiled. He told Faarooq and Maisa they were already out too late. They wanted to go home and prepare for bed. Faarooq acted disappointed, but secretly couldn't wait for the couple to leave.

When Maisa arrived with Faarooq's wine, the couple was just leaving. Now he could begin his investigation without any distractions. He thanked Maisa profusely for bringing him his drink and kidding asked her to join him. Maisa could feel herself blushing as she told Faarooq the owners would disapprove of such behavior. Faarooq feigned being hurt as he held his hand over his heart. They both laughed as Maisa slid away to assist another patron.

Five minutes later Maisa returned to take Faarooq's order. As they casually chitchatted about the items on the menu, Faarooq told Maisa a dear friend of his recommended Dominique's to him. He would have visited a long time ago but his job kept him quite busy and he didn't have the opportunity to dine out as much as he would like. But, now that he discovered Dominique's, he knew he'd be back. When Maisa inquired who his friend was, her breath was taken away when she heard his reply. "Mubbaligh?" she said. "Mubbaligh," she repeated. She hadn't seen or heard of Mubbaligh for at least a year. Now, suddenly, this stranger walks into Dominique's and brings him back to life. Maisa was visibly shaken and excused herself as she retreated to the kitchen.

Within a few minutes, Maisa reappeared, apologizing for her behavior. Faarooq shrugged it off, appearing unaffected by Maisa's reaction to hearing him mention Mubbaligh's name. In reality, he was ecstatic yet confused. Why did the simple mention of Mubbaligh's name conjure up such an emotional display by Maisa? He wasn't sure, but he knew he was going to find out. Trying to act as he forgot the whole matter, he nonchalantly ordered from the menu.

Maisa served his food a short time later. He ate in peace and was quite satisfied. When Maisa cleared the table and offered Faarooq a cup of Dominique's famous coffee, he readily accepted. Up to this time, there was no more mention of Mubbaligh. But, Faarooq had finalized his plan of attack. "Maisa, do you ever have a day off?" he inquired. "Yes sir," Maisa replied. "In fact, tomorrow is the start of a three-day vacation for me. I hope to spend as much time as possible with my friends at the beach." Maisa was attempting to be friendly to make up for her previous rudeness. Faarooq reached out and firmly, but tenderly, held Maisa by the wrist. "Maisa, I do not mean to interfere with your plans, but I must talk with you. Please meet me at the entrance to the park overlooking Lighthouse Point. Ten o'clock tomorrow morning. I want to have a brief chat with you and then you can be on your way to join your friends at the beach. It is not too far out of your way."

Maisa was scared and did not know what to do. An hour ago everything was fine. Then this stranger walks into Dominique's and starts talking about Mubbaligh. Now he wants her to meet him in the morning for a 'chat.' Strange thoughts went through Maisa's head. Did something happen to Mubbaligh? Was he hurt and needed help? She didn't know what was going on. Why did Mubbaligh disappear so suddenly without saying a word? Finally she made a decision. Although it would slightly interfere with her plans to go to the beach, she didn't see what harm could come out of meeting Faarooq. After all, it was out in the open and there would be plenty of people around. What harm could come out of it? More importantly, she thought, Mubbaligh might be in trouble. He might need her help. She had to go for that reason alone. With much trepidation in her voice, she told Faarooq she would meet him at ten o'clock. Faarooq smiled and slowly released Maisa's wrist from his grasp. He left money on the table to cover his bill, stood and walked out. Maisa was busy at another table and didn't see him leave.

CHAPTER FIVE

Faarooq was sitting on a park bench overlooking Lighthouse Point by 9:30. He was puffing on a cigar admiring the way the sun reflected off the calm waters of the bay. In the far off distance, he could see a large ship sailing out of the bay. He wondered where she was sailing to. Faarooq was mulling over in his mind how he was going to approach Maisa. Should he take the tough guy or good guy approach? He decided he could get more information from Maisa by acting as the good guy. He was going to act concerned for Mubbaligh's welfare and was only trying to obtain information from Maisa so he could find Mubbaligh.

Precisely at 10:00, Maisa came strolling down the park path. She was dressed in a long, black dress. Her head was covered by a large-brimmed hat. Over her shoulder, she was carrying a bag with a brightly colored towel. She walked right up to the bench and sat a respectable distance from Faarooq. She sat silently, her eyes fixated on the horizon. Faarooq spoke first. "Good morning, Maisa." He attempted to control his voice to make it sound as friendly and pleasant as possible. He was trying to put Maisa as at much ease as possible. "Good morning," Maisa replied. Faarooq didn't like the sound of her voice. Maybe this was going to be more difficult than he thought. After a short pause, Faarooq began. "First of all, I want to thank you for coming. I realize how difficult this must be for you. Let me assure you, I mean no harm. All I am trying to do is obtain information about the whereabouts of Mubbaligh. He is a close and dear friend of mine. I am deeply concerned about his welfare." Faarooq's words were comforting to Maisa. She began to relax a bit. She turned her head and looked at Faarooq and, in a softer tone of voice than before, asked him what he wanted from her. Faarooq felt he was making progress.

"Maisa, if you can provide me with any information about the where-abouts of Mubbaligh, I would be most appreciative. I am deeply concerned that something terrible might have happened to him." Maisa became alarmed. "What could have happened to him?" she demanded. "Who would want to do harm to him?" Faarooq was happy Maisa was so concerned about Mubbaligh. Maybe this wasn't going to be so difficult after all, he thought. Faarooq told Maisa that Mubbaligh and he were friends since childhood. They shared many pleasant memories growing up in the streets of Arzew.

Once they graduated from school, Faarooq went off to college and Mubbaligh stayed in Arzew working on the docks. Although they weren't as close as before, they still attempted to see each other whenever he returned home. Mubbaligh was like a brother to him, a brother he never had. Maisa listened intently to Faarooq's every word. He could tell by the look in her eyes that he was winning her over. He told her that a few months ago; he was told by another boyhood friend that Mubbaligh had suddenly disappeared. Supposedly he was seeing a woman of suspicious character at the time of his disappearance. He hoped and prayed this woman didn't do any harm to his friend. Faarooq feigned great concern and Maisa was convinced he only wanted to help Mubbaligh. She relaxed and decided to tell him everything she knew about Mubbaligh, as little as that was.

"Mubbaligh came into the restaurant quite frequently," she began. "At first he came alone. He was always the charmer. He was constantly flirt-ing with me and brightening my day. I had a crush on him and secretly always hoped he would ask me out, but he never did. He would go so far, but never crossed that invisible line. I became convinced he was married and just liked to flirt with other woman."

As Maisa spoke, she stared off into the distance. It seemed like she was in a trance. "Then one day, as he was having lunch, a woman I never saw before came into the restaurant. I sat her down at a table adjoining Mubbaligh. Before I knew it, they were sitting together sharing a bottle of wine. They acted as they were long-lost friends. To tell you the truth, I was devastated. Any chance I thought I had with Mubbaligh had vanished." Faarooq listened intently to Maisa's every word. "After that day, they always came into the restaurant together. Things were different between Mubbaligh and I. There wasn't anymore joking or flirting, at least not with me." They would sit all afternoon drinking wine, sometimes two bottles! Before Mubbaligh met this woman, he barely drank one glass. I guess I should have been suspicious of her, but I was trying to mind my own business. Besides, I had work to do."

Faarooq saw his opening. He asked Maisa if she ever overheard the couple talking about going away together or making plans for a trip. Maisa shook her head no. She told Faarooq she even attempted to have some-one else wait on their table. The pain seeing them together was too much for her. Suddenly Maisa sat erect and looked hard at Faarooq. "Wait a minute," she said, "there was one time." Faarooq stared back at Maisa; intently listening to Maisa's every word. "One day the two of them were really enjoying themselves. They had their usual two bottles of wine and then some. When they left the restaurant, the girl bumped into another table and knocked a glass to the floor. There was glass all over the place." "Well," she continued, "while I was sweeping up the glass, the girl wait-ing on their table came up to me and showed me some brochures they left behind. It was some kind of tourist material for Australia and New Zealand. I remember because I was fascinated with the pictures of the beaches and the huge waves."

Faarooq could have kissed Maisa. This was his first big break. Maisa told Faarooq they kept the brochures and gave them back to Mubbaligh the next time he came into the restaurant. He was only half-listening now. Australia or New Zealand, he thought. That's where the two of them are. Faarooq was having trouble concealing his excitement. He couldn't wait to tell the triumvirate the good news. Faarooq ended the conversation rather abruptly. He told Maisa he had taken up too much of her time. She should go off with her friends and have fun at the beach. Maisa told him she hoped she was helpful and it really wasn't any bother at all. She hoped the information she provided would help Faarooq find Mubbaligh. Departing, Faarooq kissed her on her cheek and thanked her. Maisa told him she would pray that he would find Mubbaligh. He assured her that he would pray for the exact same outcome.

CHAPTER SIX

Faarooq had a meeting with the triumvirate that afternoon. The triumvirate were the leaders of the Salafist terrorist movement. Not only were they the brains of the organization, but more importantly, they were the men behind the money. Aadil, Sabir and Mubid were their given names, but everyone in the organization referred to them as the triumvirate.

The triumvirate held meetings at locations of their choosing. They used to meet at the same apartment that they rented, but since the failed terrorist plot of a year ago, they constantly changed locations. They were much more careful now than they were a year ago. Obviously, government officials were wise to them.

Once Faarooq left his flat, he walked around the streets of Arzew for at least thirty minutes. He kept a close eye out to see if he was being followed. When he was sure he wasn't, he entered the building the meeting was to be held by way of a side door off an alleyway. This door led him into a dark, dank, musty-smelling basement. Once inside, he stood still to allow his eyes to acclimate to the darkness. After a few moments, he felt he was able to see well enough to proceed on. Faarooq took a back stairway up to the first floor. At the landing he turned right. A soft knock on a door signaled his arrival.

Immediately the door opened and Faarooq entered. Inside he was greeted by the three members of the triumvirate. They hugged, kissed and chatted. Aadil offered Faarooq something to drink, but he declined. He wanted to get right down to business. There was a large round mahogany table in the middle of an otherwise barren room. Around the table were four chairs. They all took a chair and pushed into the table. Aadil offered Faarooq a dark, thick cigar but he shook his head no. Aadil stuck one of these cigars in his mouth, lit a wooden match and held the flame to the end. Soon puffy clouds of smoke were swirling in the air. Aadil nodded to Faarooq and said, "Okay my friend, what do you have for us?" Sabir and Mubid sat silent, neither having said a word.

Faarooq told the group he wanted to give them a report on the progress he was making in finding Mubbaligh. He went on to explain his meeting with Maisa. Once he mentioned the travel catalogue for Australia and New Zealand, he could detect the change in them. They were more attentive and kept good eye contact with Faarooq. Sabir broke his silence, "So, it appears the rumors are true." Faarooq looked quizzically at Aadil. "I didn't tell you earlier Faarooq because I didn't want to influence your investigation," Aadil said. "But, we have received numerous reports that Mubbaligh has moved to New Zealand. He also brought that slut along with him." Aadil had special enmity for the girl that was supposedly traveling with Mubbaligh. Her name was Correntine and supposedly she worked for the CIA. Whatever was the truth, Aadil hated her because she tore Mubbaligh away from his niece, Sameenah. Aadil had visions of Mubbaligh and Sameenah marrying one day, until Correntine came along. Aadil wished harm on Mubbaligh, but he wished so much more misery on Correntine.

Faarooq regained his composure and proceeded with his report. He told them that he was quite certain Mubbaligh and this girl, Correntine, were in either Australia or New Zealand. But, to be sure, he wanted to conduct further inquiries. "What are your plans," Mubid finally broke his silence. Faarooq said he had some ideas and wanted to run them by the triumvirate. First, he wanted to conduct a thorough search of Mubbaligh's apartment. He knew this was already done, but he wanted to conduct a search himself. Secondly, he wanted to review the phone records of Mubbaligh for the last year that he lived in Arzew. He wanted to know who Mubbaligh called and where. This would be an easy task for Faarooq because he had a contact with the phone company. This individual would do anything Faarooq asked of him. Lastly, he was going to reach out to other contacts he had in both the Australian and New Zealand embassies. He wanted to know if Mubbaligh had applied for a visa for either country and, if he did, was it granted. The triumvirate was pleased with Faarooq's plans. They were satisfied that he was leading the investigation to find

Mubbaligh in the right direction.

Faarooq waited until the next day to search Mubbaligh's apartment. Although it had been almost a year since Mubbaligh had lived there, things were in pretty much the same condition as when he left. The triumvirate owned the apartment and let Mubbaligh live there while he was working for them. Before Mubbaligh, they used it as a safe house. The triumvirate was afraid the apartment was compromised; the Algerian authorities might have it under surveillance. Therefore, they were staying away from the apartment until they found out what was going on with Mubbaligh. Letting Faarooq search the apartment was risky, but the triumvirate decided the risk might be warranted. Perhaps Faarooq might find something that would point to Mubbaligh's whereabouts.

The mid-morning sun brightly illuminated the apartment as Faarooq entered through the front door. He was alone, armed only with a screwdriver, pen and paper, and a small flashlight. He began in the kitchen. The shelves were barren and only held a few glasses and plates. The refrigerator was empty, but for a few almost-empty bottles of wine. This guy lived a Spartan life, Faarooq thought. In the bedroom, everything was meticulously in order. There were still clothes hanging in the closet and underwear in the bureau. The bed was made. It appeared to Faarooq that Mubbaligh left unexpectedly, leaving pants, shirts, socks and underwear behind. A check of the bathroom confirmed Faarooq's beliefs. All of Mubbaligh's toiletries were still there: toothbrush, toothpaste, razor, after-shave lotion. Why wouldn't Mubbaligh take all these things if he had planned to leave? Maybe something nefarious did happen to Mubbaligh, he thought. Then Faarooq chuckled, or maybe that was the impression he was trying to leave behind. Mubbaligh knew people would search the apartment after he disappeared. Did he leave the apartment like it was to give people—the triumvirate—the impression he left unwillingly?

After searching thoroughly for almost an hour, Faarooq was confident the apartment was clean. He wasn't happy because he thought Mubbaligh would have slipped up and left something behind. That's when he hit pay dirt. When he pulled the cushions off the couch, he saw a shiny white piece of paper—the size of a sales receipt—partially stuffed in the back crease of the couch. He picked up the paper and attempted to smooth out the wrinkles with his thick, calloused fingers. As he did this, he noticed faint printing on one side. He squinted as he read, and then his eyes bulged. Barely legible, he could read *"Blenheim, New Zealand"*. A closer look also revealed a date, *January 29, 2003*. As he stared at the paper, it dawned on him what he was holding. It was a postal receipt for a package that was mailed from Arzew, Algeria to Blenheim, New Zealand on January 29, 2003. The paper said the package weighed 25 lbs.

Faarooq stood silently in the middle of the living room. In his hands, he was holding documentary evidence showing Mubbaligh had sent a package to Blenheim, New Zealand just a few months before the terrorist attack in America was to be carried out. Faarooq, still standing in the middle of the floor, gasped. "That son-of-a-bitch had it planned all along. He and that girlfriend of his were planning their escape months before the attack." Faarooq remained motionless as he thought out the whole thing. First of all, Maisa gave him travelogues belonging to Mubbaligh showing he had interest in New Zealand and Australia. Secondly, the triumvirate had been hearing rumors about Mubbaligh living in New Zealand. Now, Faarooq had evidence Mubbaligh was shipping packages to Blenheim, New Zealand. Although this was all circumstantial evidence, it wasn't painting a rosy picture for Faarooq. Softly closing the door to the apartment behind him, Faarooq scurried down the apartment stairs. He couldn't wait to tell the triumvirate what he found.

Faarooq was back in Dominique's that afternoon. Maisa was still on her days off, so another waitress seated him. He was sipping a glass of wine, reading the newspaper, when Yasir walked in. Faarooq saw him enter and gave him a big wave. Yasir walked over to Faarooq's table and they gave each other a big hug. Yasir was a friend of Faarooq's for many years and, although not a member of the Salafist movement, he was sympathetic with their cause. More importantly, he was the executive secretary for the economic minister of the New Zealand embassy in Algiers. When Faarooq called Yasir on the phone seeking information about Mubbaligh applying for a visa to enter New Zealand, Yasir told him he'd do some research and call Faarooq back.

After a couple of hours Yasir called. He had information to give to Faarooq but he wouldn't pass it over the phone. Thus, a meeting at Dominique's was made. Yasir and Faarooq shared a bottle of Dominique's finest wine and reminisced about the good old days. Once they ordered their meals, they began to talk in earnest. Yasir told Faarooq that both Mubbaligh and Correntine applied with the New Zealand Embassy for immigrant visas. Not only did they want to visit New Zealand, they wanted to emigrate there! Once the visa department reviewed their paperwork and interviewed both applicants, their immigrant visas were approved. Faarooq whistled softly and said, "Holy shit." Yasir quietly passed an envelope under the table in Faarooq's direction. Faarooq took the envelope and peeked inside and saw Mubbaligh's and Correntine's applications. Stapled to Correntine's application was her passport picture. Up to this time, Faarooq had no idea what she looked like; he never gave it a thought. But when he saw her picture, he was impressed. "Boy she's a beautiful young lady," he said to no one in particular. "French," Yasir whispered. "Mon ami," Faarooq coyly replied.

They ate their meal and talked about everything but Mubbaligh and Correntine. Yasir, quite naturally, was interested in world events. While working in the Algerian Foreign Affairs Department, he had been posted in many overseas countries. He found every country exciting but different. England was his favorite posting. Now, in the twilight of his career, he was content to be posted back home. Travel was fun, but the older he got, the harder it was. Yasir was instrumental in many successful Salafist endeavors throughout the world. He was able to furnish them valuable information. The movement owed him a lot and Faarooq tried to express how thankful they were. Yasir, the humble man that he was, dismissed the praise as nonsense. He was only doing things that could help his country and his fellow countrymen. Immediately after dinner, they left Dominique's. Yasir had a few hours of driving and Faarooq wanted to call on the members of the triumvirate. No longer did he only have circumstantial evidence. He now had cold hard facts. He was excited to let them know the good news.

When the triumvirate heard the news, they were ecstatic. Everything seemed to be coming together in the hunt for Mubbaligh and Correntine. They were satisfied that Mubbaligh was living in New Zealand. However, Faarooq had one more source of information he wanted to explore. The

Salafist movement had a contact that worked in upper management in the telephone company. He wanted to contact this source in the morning to see if he could furnish any information on Mubbaligh's phone records. Although the triumvirate thought this was unnecessary, they gave Faarooq the nod to pursue this line of inquiry. In the morning Faarooq would meet with his phone company contact. But for now, he was going home to go to bed. He was exhausted from the extraordinary events of the day.

Faarooq was up early. After a light breakfast of juice and toast, he was out the door. He expected the walk to the telephone headquarters building would take him less than twenty minutes. The walk through the morning streets of Arzew was refreshing for Faarooq. He walked at a leisurely pace, taking in all the sights. The streets of Arzew were a lot different today than they were when he was growing up, especially all the traffic congestion. Faarooq arrived at the telephone building shortly before 9:00am. He walked into the main lobby and headed directly for one of the elevators. He waited in line and soon the doors of an elevator opened. The elevator quickly filled and someone standing by the row of buttons indicating floor selections yelled out, "What floor people?" Faarooq smiled and yelled, "Nine please." Within thirty seconds he was walking off the elevator, walking down a corridor with rich, plush carpet, looking for room 935.

National Telephone of Algeria was written on the heavy glass door with ersatz gold lettering. Faarooq confidently swung the door open and walked into the foyer. At the reception desk, a pretty olive-skinned, long-haired brunette warmly greeted him. "Good morning, sir, how may I help you?" Faarooq smiled and said, "Good morning, I have an appointment with Mr. Farah." She picked up a nearby phone and dialed a few numbers. After a short conversation, she hung up the phone. She looked at Faarooq with a warm smile and told him Mr. Farah would be out to meet him shortly. Faarooq couldn't help staring at the receptionists teeth. They were gleaming white and perfectly aligned. Faarooq silently wished his teeth were like hers. Moments later, a side door opened and Mr. Farah walked out into the foyer. After a warm but professional greeting, Mr. Farah escorted Faarooq into the interior offices of National Telephone of Algeria.

Once they were behind the closed doors of Mr. Farah's private office, the two embraced. They each had a cup of coffee and amicably chatted. Eventually, Mr. Farah asked Faarooq what he could do for him. Faarooq explained the entire situation to him and asked if it was possible to track Mubbaligh's long distance phone calls for the previous year. Mr. Farah gave a sinister laugh and said, "So my friend, it appears you are still up to no good". Faarooq smiled and said, "Just trying to keep everyone honest." Mr. Farah laughed heartily and said, "Yes, that is good. But, who is going to keep us honest?" They both laughed. "Well, is it possible?" Faarooq queried impatiently. Mr. Farah tapped the top of his computer monitor that sat on the edge of his desk and said, "It is the 21st century, Faarooq. With these babies, we can do just about anything." Faarooq smiled broadly at this good news.

Within fifteen minutes Faarooq had more information than he could ever imagine. Mubbaligh had made at least a hundred calls to New Zealand in the last year before he disappeared. Many were to the New Zealand Embassy in Wellington. Probably regarding his visa, Faarooq thought. But, the majority of the calls were to a town called Blenheim on the South Island. The majority of these calls were to a company called Wither Hills Realty. "Bingo", Faarooq said. Obviously Mubbaligh was using this realty company to buy a house. What information! he thought to himself. Now he was certain beyond all doubt where Mubbaligh and Correntine had absconded to. All he and the triumvirate had to figure out was how were they going to best use this new-found intelligence. Faarooq asked Mr. Farah to print out all the names and phone numbers on his computer screen. Once he did, Faarooq took the copies and stuck them into an inside pocket of his jacket. He warmly hugged Mr. Farah and kissed him on both cheeks. "The movement owes you," he said. They shook hands and before Mr. Farah could mutter a word, Faarooq was gone.

He was in a meeting with the triumvirate shortly after noon. They all sat around the same table where they initially met and mulled over the information. There were many rumors about where Mubbaligh and Correntine had run off to, but now they had concrete information. The travelogues left behind at Dominique's were the first indication of their whereabouts. Then there was the postal receipt Faarooq found in Mubbaligh's apartment. The discovery of the immigrant visas for New Zealand was crucial. Now, the most recent bit of information, Mubbaligh's phone records, left no doubt. The two of them were living in New Zealand, most likely in the Blenheim area. The triumvirate knew where they were, the question was what course of action they should take.

Aadil was the first to speak. "You did an excellent job, Faarooq. More than we expected." Sabir and Mubid nodded their heads in agreement. Aadil continued, "Where do you think we should go from here?" Faarooq hesitated and then said, "Well, it all depends on what you gentlemen want. If you want to get rid of them, plans have to be formulated. It won't be easy." Mubid spoke in a rather harsh manner. "Why don't you think it will be easy?" Faarooq was taken aback by Mubid's aggressive tone. Faarooq was on the defensive and he wondered how he got himself in that position. "Well, I mean, New Zealand is a foreign country thousands of miles away. The logistics will be formidable," he stammered. "Nonsense," Mubid barked. "We have resources in New Zealand. We will utilize them to help us exterminate these two traitors." Mubid was telling Faarooq information he didn't know anything about. He realized he was at a distinct disadvantage. Maybe he should just keep his mouth shut, he thought.

There was a moment of silence before Aadil spoke. He confirmed what Mubid said. The Salafist movement had a cell in New Zealand. They were obviously a lot more familiar with New Zealand than any of them. Aadil agreed with Mubid about enlisting their aid to go after Mubbaligh and Correntine. But, Aadil thought it best if there was Algerian talent involved in the effort. He looked intently at Faarooq and said, "Faarooq, we would like you to go to New Zealand and coordinate our efforts. Your presence will be instrumental in the ultimate success of the mission." Faarooq was dumbfounded. He didn't mind tracking down the whereabouts of Mubbaligh and Correntine, but going to New Zealand to lead a hit team? He didn't feel qualified. He didn't have the expertise. Aadil, Mubid and Sabir stared at Faarooq. He saw no way out. Before he realized what he was saying, Faarooq acquiesced to their demands. He told them he would go and he would try his hardest to be successful. All three members of the triumvirate smiled. Aadil said, "That is all we are asking of you, Faarooq. Try your hardest and you will succeed."

CHAPTER SEVEN

Bashir drove Usayd to the Marfa section of Beirut, where the docks are, just as the sun was peeking over the eastern horizon. The ship that was going to take Usayd home to Algeria was looming in the background. Although the ship was not leaving port until 12:00, Bashir had to drop Usayd off early because he had an early morning meeting. They sat in Bashir's car for a few moments. Bashir assured Usayd his offer of employment was genuine and sincere. Usayd thanked Bashir and told him he would give the offer some serious thought. Usayd thanked Bashir for being so hospitable the last few days. He told Bashir he had a memorable time and he hadn't been so relaxed in a long time.

Finally, they both got out of the car. Bashir opened the trunk and took Usayd's bags out. He had two and they were both light. *Where are the cameras? Bashir asked himself.* Bashir put Usayd's bags down on the sidewalk in front of the terminal and faced Usayd. They embraced and held each other for a long time. Finally Bashir broke away. Tears were in both of their eyes. Bashir was thinking many things at the moment, but there was one thought he couldn't get out of his mind and it kept troubling him. Bashir was afraid this might be the last time he ever saw his boyhood friend. He thought something terrible was going to happen to Usayd. He kept trying to rid his mind of this thought, but it kept coming back. Usayd's infectious smile covered his face as he told Bashir, "Thank you my friend. I owe you." Bashir attempted to smile and said, "No, I owe you. I had a wonderful time the past few days. Thank you for coming." They hugged again. This time Usayd broke the hug. He bent over, grabbed his bags, turned and walked into the terminal building without saying a word. Bashir watched his friend disappear into the building, still driving those awful thoughts out of his mind.

Once inside the terminal, Usayd attempted to check-in his bags with the steamship line. After failing to find anyone to help him, a security guard told Usayd he would keep his eyes on Usayd's bags until someone from the steamship line arrived. Usayd thanked the guard, but said he better keep the bags with him. The security guard looked suspicious and Usayd feared his bags would be gone upon his return. He walked back out of the terminal into bright sunshine. He was hungry and wanted to find a restaurant. After walking several blocks, Usayd noticed a few trucks parked by the side of the road in front of a small but pleasant looking restaurant. Usayd walked in, placed his bags by a side wall and sat on a plastic stool in front of a copper-clad counter.

Shortly, a beefy guy with a pleasant looking face, wearing a sparkling white apron, was asking him what he would like to eat. Usayd ordered the obligatory cup of coffee with sugar and scanned the menu. Once the waiter returned, Usayd ordered a plate of foul mudammas with labneh and mankouche. He was finishing his cup of coffee when the food arrived. Usayd ate and had a second cup of coffee. He wasn't as much in a hurry as he was hungry. The waiter offered Usayd a third cup of coffee but Usayd respectfully declined. He paid his bill and was shortly back on the street walking towards the steamship terminal.

It had only been an hour since Bashir had dropped him off, but now the traffic was much heavier. Big diesel trucks belching thick black clouds of exhaust roared by as Usayd navigated his way back to the steamship terminal. Unlike before, the terminal was now a beehive of activity. Porters were scurrying about and a long line was forming at the previously empty check-in counter. Usayd took his place at the end of the line and patiently waited his turn. Shortly, a tall, thin balding man was motioning him to step up to the counter. Usayd presented his previously bought ticket and passport. The balding man scrutinized Usayd's passport and kept looking into Usayd's face. Usayd calmly stood his ground. Although the Algerian passport was fraudulently obtained, it was a good passport; all the visas were also good. It would be impossible to find any irregularity, Usayd thought. He stood there as nonchalant as possible watching the steamship clerk conduct his checks. When the clerk placed the passport under some kind of special light, Usayd became concerned. Usayd knew he had to do something and said, "What seems to be the problem? Are you having difficulty reading my passport?" Immediately, the clerk went on the defensive. "No sir," he said, "I was just checking the visa." Usayd sarcastically said, "I don't see any of the other clerks having any problems reading passports."

This is all Usayd had to do; he intimidated the clerk enough to make him self-conscious. The clerk hurriedly returned Usayd's passport and marked his ticket. Minutes later, Usayd was on his way to the boarding gate. Even though Usayd felt comfortable with his traveling documents, he didn't want to bring any undue attention to himself. If the clerk called for assistance, Usayd wasn't sure if his story would hold up against intense questioning. If the Lebanese Customs officials detected something was amiss, they could hold him in detention indefinitely. All he wanted to do was board the ship and be on his way. The triumvirate was impatiently waiting his return.

A few minutes before 11:00 an announcement was made over the terminal's public address system. All passengers sailing on the Lambros Y were directed to Gate 6A. Boarding would start within a few minutes. Usayd obediently complied and was at Gate 6A within minutes. Already a line was forming. Usayd estimated between two and three hundred people were sailing on the Lambros Y. Stevedores struggled to slide open the doors providing access to the ramp leading to the ship. Chips of grey paint fell off the doors as the stevedores finally were able to move them. Boarding began once the doors were completely open.

Usayd boarded about midway through the process. As Usayd reached the top of the ramp, he had a clear view of the entire ship. Usayd gave serious thought to turning around. The ship appeared to be in deplorable shape. Having grown up around ships, he knew a good ship from a bad one. This ship was one of the worst he had ever seen. There were two cargo holds forward of the center wheelhouse and two aft. The tarpaulins supposedly covering the hatches were frayed and disintegrating. Placed over the cargo holds to prevent water from entering, Usayd could see they were useless. Waves crashing on the decks of the ship would send seawater into the holds, thereby compromising the integrity of the vessel. Bilge pumps were designed to pump any water entering the hold overboard, if they were working properly.

When he saw the condition of the lifeboats, Usayd quickly forgot about the hatch covers. They were old wooden boats with little paint left on them. A couple were hanging unevenly from their davits. Usayd was sure the boats would sink if they were put in the water. A further glance of the rest of the vessel was even more disheartening. Rust was everywhere. The superstructure, where the crew lived and where the ship was navigated, was one large block of rust. Usayd estimated the length of the vessel to be about 350' and built about 30 years ago. Thirty years for a ship to be plying the seven seas required a lot of maintenance, especially in her later years. It was obvious, even to the uninitiated eye; little maintenance was performed on this ship. As Usayd stepped off the ramp and onto the main deck, he could see holes everywhere. He was afraid his foot was going to go right through the deck. Usayd couldn't believe what he was seeing. He hesitated for a moment and thought again of getting off the ship. Then the thought of the authorities ashore changed his mind. Whatever condition this ship was in, he was going to have to live with it.

Although they were scheduled to sail at noon, the ship was still tied up at the dock at 2:00pm. Finally, a little before 3:00pm, line handlers began to release the mooring lines attaching the ship to the dock. Usayd thought he could feel the vibrations of the ship's engine on his feet. A thick black puff of smoke rising out of the funnel confirmed to Usayd that the ship was underway. Slowly the distance between the Lambros Y and the dock increased. When the ship was about a hundred yards off the dock, the engines stopped. Usayd was enraged. He had to get out of Lebanon. The ship had to leave. The Lambros Y drifted slowly back in the direction of the dock. Suddenly Usayd could feel the familiar vibrating of the deck through his legs. The engines were running again. Slowly the Lambros Y inched forward. Within minutes water began to lap at her sides as she increased speed.

As the Lambros Y gained headway heading in a westerly direction, Usayd stood by the port railing amidships and viewed the city of Beirut as they passed. He had had a wonderful time in Beirut with Bashir and Hanifah, but it was time to leave. He was getting antsy and wanted to know why the triumvirate was calling him back to Algeria. As he gazed in the direction of shore, he recognized the International College on Paris Avenue in the distance. The last identifiable object he saw before he went inside was the lighthouse near the Goethe Institute. As he was staring at the lighthouse, he suddenly thought of Hanifah's father. Usayd was impressed with the man as soon as they met, but the events that transpired as they were leaving last night overwhelmed Usayd. Without saying so, Hanifah's father told Usayd he had been part of the movement at one time. He told Usayd he was a photo-journalist just like Usayd. They all knew Usayd was using the occupation of a photo-journalist as a cover; therefore Usayd took Hanifah's father's word as a signal. What was he trying to tell me? Usayd thought. Usayd shivered noticeably, and not from the cold. He decided he better go inside and familiarize himself with the ship.

A steward greeted Usayd as he entered the interior of the ship. He asked Usayd for his name and then looked it up on a list he had attached to a clipboard. "Ah, yes sir," he said. "Your cabin is 305. It is on the port side, one deck below. Please sir, follow me and I'll show you where it is." Usayd was pleasantly surprised with the steward's manners and professionalism. He expected the crew to be in the same shape as the ship. After a short walk and a climb down a flight of stairs, they were at room 305. The steward opened the door of the cabin and stepped aside. With a graceful sweep of his arm, he asked Usayd to step inside.

Usayd was impressed with what he saw. The room was immaculate. Nothing like Usayd had imagined! There was a large bed against one wall covered by a bright blue blanket. Two pillows wrapped in starched pillowcases lay at the far end of the bed. The walls were adorned with pictures, mostly landscapes. The floor was covered by what looked like brand new wall-to-wall carpet. Usayd opened the door to the bathroom and was met by more of the same. The shower, sink and toilet gleamed. A fresh, clean smell pervaded the entire area. Usayd looked at the steward and said, "What is your name?" "My name is Manuel," the steward said with a wide grin, showing his full mouth of bright white teeth. "Well Manuel," Usayd said, "this room looks so attractive. I thank you."

Manuel was bubbling over with pride. He told Usayd he had personally made up the entire room. It had taken him almost a whole day of hard work to make it look like it did. Manuel explained that he was the personal steward for ten people aboard the ship, to include Usayd. Whatever they needed, day or night, Manuel would be there to accommodate them. Usayd thanked Manuel and pressed some money into the palm of Manuel's hand. Manuel thanked Usayd, but told him it wasn't necessary. At the end of the voyage Usayd could tip him as much as he wanted, he didn't have to do it now. Usayd told Manuel he would take care of him at the end, but he wanted Manuel to have this money for now. Manuel grinned from ear to ear. "Please, Mr. Sir, allow me to show you more of the ship." Usayd smiled and said, "Right behind you."

Usayd was soon to learn the entire crew of the Lambros Y was as efficient as Manuel. All of the officers were Polish and the crew Philippino. The officers were polite and professional, but aloof. They had limited contact with the passengers and only professional contact with the Philippino crew. Manuel liked the officers but wished they were a bit friendlier. There were eight officers onboard and Manuel really didn't know any of them. The officers' contracts with the owners of the ship were a lot better than the crews. They served six months onboard and three months ashore. The captain only had to serve three months before he had three months off. The Philippine crew had far different contracts. They had to serve ten months and then had two months vacation. Their pay was far less also. Manuel told Usayd he was paid $250 a month from the steamship company. If he worked a lot of overtime and passengers tipped well, he could almost double his salary.

Usayd was shocked at how little Manuel made, but Manuel disagreed. He told Usayd that back home in the Philippines, $500 a month was extraordinary. In fact, you were lucky if you had a job back home. Manuel told Usayd that back home, he had a wife, several kids and a big house. He also had two servants to keep the house clean and to do all the cooking! Usayd was shocked at this incongruity. Onboard ship Manuel was a servant catering to passengers' every desire. Back home, Manuel had servants catering to him. Manuel said the only bad part of his job was being away from his family for so long. He was devoted to his wife and children and missed them terribly. But, if he didn't ship out, he wouldn't be able to find a job back home. He wouldn't be able to support his family. He had no choice but to go to sea.

Manuel showed Usayd the galley where he would be served all his meals while onboard. He explained the food was good and, if Usayd had anything special he wanted to eat, Manuel would arrange it for him. Next Manuel showed Usayd where the gym and library were. Although the gym was small, there was enough equipment to have a good workout. The library was amply stocked with good books and plenty of magazines, even if they were a couple months old. Off the gym, Manuel led Usayd into a misty, cavernous room. Usayd couldn't believe what he saw—a heated pool. Although it was saltwater, Manuel said most of the passengers loved swimming in it, especially after working out in the gym. Besides, you could take a hot shower afterwards. While chatting alongside the pool, an announcement came over the ship's public address system. All passengers were to convene on the mess deck for a required safety and indoctrination meeting.

There were almost three hundred passengers seated on the mess deck. Most sat at one of the many tables, but a few stood at the bar. After all the passengers were accounted for, the captain of the ship arrived. He went over the safety features of the ship and what the passengers should do if anything happened. He stressed that everyone should listen to the crew, more than likely their steward. Everyone was assigned a lifeboat and told where they could find a life preserver in an emergency. Next the captain wanted to discuss the itinerary of the Lambros Y. Their first port of call was Larnaca, Cyprus. The distance to Larnaca from Beirut was 110 nautical miles. Since the ship was traveling at 14 knots, they should be there in about 8 hours. The captain estimated they would be tying up at the dock at about midnight. Once secured to the dock, passenger and cargo operations would begin. No cargo was scheduled to be loaded and only fifty more passengers were expected to board. Once this was done, the captain wanted to sail immediately.

The next leg of the voyage was Valletta, Malta. The sailing distance was almost a thousand miles and he expected to arrive in seventy two hours. Finally, the last leg was Annaba, Algeria. This distance was about 350 nautical miles and the captain expected sailing time to be a little over 25 hours. All the passengers were intently listening to the captain. He appeared to be a no nonsense, all business type of guy. He spoke English, but some of his words were hard to understand. Then the captain's reserved style evaporated as a morning fog, but only temporarily. He joked that this schedule would hold if the ship's engines cooperated, the weather remained calm and dockworkers along their route didn't decide to go on strike. "However," he said as he rolled his eyes skyward, "we are prepared for any unexpected development." Then he smiled and said, "That is why we always keep the bar well stocked." Everyone laughed, some more haltingly than others. The captain wished everyone a pleasant voyage and excused himself. Most of the passengers remained on the mess deck, introducing themselves to each other. Not Usayd. He immediately went to his cabin. He had a lot of thinking to do before he arrived in Algeria. He was uneasy because he had no idea what the triumvirate wanted with him.

As expected, the Lambros Y passed the Larnaca Harbor sea buoy shortly before 11:00 pm. The lights of the inner harbor loomed brightly in the distance. The first mooring line was attached to shore a couple of minutes before midnight. Usayd was impressed with the captain's timetable. A gangway was set, attaching the ship to the shore, and passengers began to disembark. The ship's cargo boom began to strain as it lifted a heavy load of passenger's bags into the bowels of the ship. The night was warm and the wind was nonexistent as Usayd watched the crew run around attempting to make everything happen all at once. Within three hours, they were done. Everyone going ashore was gone, cargo was loaded and all embarking passengers were onboard. As the stars twinkled brightly overhead, the Lambros Y severed her connection to shore and headed seaward. Valletta, Malta was a thousand miles and three days away, if the engines didn't fail and the weather cooperated.

Usayd was asleep shortly after climbing into bed; he was tired from a long day. The last thing he remembered was listening to the gentle noise of water rushing along the outer hull of the ship. The next three days passed slowly. The weather was warm and sunny with only a light wind. The seas were calm. Life at sea always falls into a routine. Sleeping, eating, reading and chatting with your fellow passengers were the normal activity for the day. For those athletically inclined, the gym and pool offered brief periods of respite. Usayd didn't do much socializing. He kept to himself unless he didn't have a choice but, even then, he was a man of few words. Usayd preferred to stay in his cabin and read. He went to all the meals, but as soon as he ate, he left the mess deck.

Often he would walk around on deck after meals, digesting his food and enjoying the solitude. The gym and pool was a distraction, but the usual crowds aggravated Usayd. Almost every night, he woke up while in the middle of a nightmare. He had hoped these nightmares would disappear, at least lessen, but they didn't. He thought of taking medication to help him sleep, but he didn't want to be under the control of any drug. The drinking incident with Bashir in Beirut was still fresh in his mind.

On the second day of the voyage, while sailing under cloudless skies south of the island of Crete, the passengers and crew of the Lambros Y witnessed an awe-inspiring sight. It all started out with a few jets flying low over the Lambros Y shortly before the noon meal. As the afternoon progressed, more and more jets could be seen flying in the vicinity. Just before dusk, a huge armada of ships came into view. At least one aircraft carrier and fifteen other types of ships were clearly visible from the deck. A passenger queried one of the officers as to these ships. He told the passenger that the ships were part of the United States Navy sixth fleet. They were conducting a naval exercise with other NATO units in the Mediterranean Sea. The Lambros Y was skirting the outer edge of the security zone and should be clear of the area by dusk.

As the officer was explaining the presence of these ships, six fighters were circling directly overhead. Another group of fighters approaching from the north pounced on this first group. For the next hour, passengers watched in amazement as these two groups of fighters engaged in a mock dogfight. Soon all the action was left astern and the Lambros Y was sailing by herself once again through the calm waters of the Mediterranean. Most on board quickly forgot about this American naval force, except for Usayd. He was incensed to see these Americans running around the Mediterranean, acting as if these waters were theirs. He reminded himself that this is why he was fighting, to rid the entire Mid-East of these infidel Americans. As he went to bed that night, deep inside he knew he could never accept Bashir's offer of a job. He still had a lot of unfinished business to attend to and, reviewing the events of the past few hours, it looked as if his workload was increasing.

It was mid-afternoon on the second day out of Cyprus. The Lambros Y had just passed the midway point between Cyprus and Malta. The ship was running fine, the weather was beautiful and all the passengers were enjoying themselves. Usayd was sitting on a bench at the stern of the vessel. Not many other passengers strolled so far back aft; Usayd was by himself, exactly the way he liked it. Usayd had his face to the sun, enjoying the warm rays. Unexpectedly he jumped, something had startled him. As he quickly turned his head, he saw Manuel, his steward, approaching. Usayd suspiciously eyed Manuel. "Good afternoon, sir," Manuel quipped. "Are you enjoying the afternoon sun?" Usayd was annoyed. He was seeking solitude. He didn't appreciate the steward hunting him down asking meaningless questions. "I was," he said with a bitter tone in his voice. "What do you want, Manuel?" he impatiently asked. Manuel told Usayd he was out for his usual afternoon walk and happened to bump into Usayd. As he was saying this, he was looking all around. Usayd detected nervousness in Manuel's mannerisms and in his guarded language. Usayd became suspicious and went on alert. He was ready to spring into action at a moments notice.

Once Manuel was assured that no one else was around, he looked directly into Usayd's face. "Sir, I am always supposed to keep my mouth shut. It is the company's policy. If they found out I am talking to you, I could be fired. Please understand me. But, I feel I must tell you." Manuel had Usayd's full attention, but as he listened to Manuel, he kept looking around the immediate area. "Tell me what?" Usayd asked. Again, Manuel looked all around. "Mr. Usayd," he said in a low but clear voice. "This morning I was cleaning my assigned cabins on the third deck. As I was coming out of the cabin adjoining yours, I saw a man exiting from your cabin, cabin 305. I thought it was you and said good morning. When the gentleman looked at me, I saw it was someone besides you. This stranger quickly turned his head and ran down the passageway in the opposite direction."

Usayd was stunned. His cabin door was always locked. Who could have been in his cabin? "Are you sure?" he asked Manuel. "Are you sure it was my cabin?" He asked Manuel if he could have possibly made a mistake and had the cabins mixed up. Secretly, this is what Usayd was hoping for because, if someone was in his cabin, that meant there was someone onboard following him. It meant that people knew who Usayd was and they were keeping an eye on him. They were doing even more than that; they were breaking into his cabin and probably searching his personal belongings. Usayd was reflecting on the ramifications of what Manuel had told him. Suddenly he realized he better let Manuel go. He didn't want other people, especially the people watching Usayd, to see them talking together. Manuel could be in jeopardy if they thought he was helping Usayd. Usayd looked at Manuel and said, "Manuel, thank you so much for telling me this. But now you must go. I will explain everything later." Confused and hurt by the way Usayd dismissed him; Manuel did what he was told to do.

After Manuel left, Usayd reflected on what he had just been told. True, it was possible this was a random act. Someone was breaking into cabins looking to see what they could steal. This was a possibility, but Usayd thought it was too much of a coincidence. More likely than not, Usayd thought, someone onboard the Lambros Y knew who he was and broke into his cabin looking for information. Whoever they were, they were good because Usayd couldn't detect any signs that someone was in his cabin. If Manuel didn't tell him, he wouldn't have had any idea. Now that he knew someone was onboard the same ship as him and snooping around, Usayd had to be careful. He wasn't sure if it was one guy (or lady) or more. Whoever it was, they might only be following Usayd or they might wish him harm. Usayd was going to have to change his tactics. His long walks around the ship by himself would have to stop. He was going to have to go on the defensive.

Then it struck him. If people onboard the ship knew who he was, how about the authorities in Algeria. Were they waiting for him when the Lambros Y docked in Annaba? If they were, Usayd would be grabbed before he even set foot in Algeria. All of a sudden his well laid plans were unraveling before his eyes. What should he do? Within a little more than a day they would be in Malta. A day after that they would be in Algeria. He had two days to make a plan. In the meantime he was going to have to be careful. People were lurking around the ship wishing him harm. Being forewarned by Manuel gave Usayd the edge he needed. He was going to have to think fast while keeping his left hand high.

For the rest of the trip to Malta, Usayd was suspicious of everyone. If someone looked at him for a second too long, Usayd became suspicious. He was never the talker, but now he became a virtual recluse. He spent more and more time locked up in his cabin, thinking of a plan that would get him safely back to Algeria and the triumvirate. Eventually, Usayd came up with an idea. He was convinced the authorities would be waiting for him when he arrived in Algeria aboard the Lambros Y. Therefore, common sense told him he wouldn't be on the Lambros Y when she docked in Annaba. He was going to have to jump ship in Malta. But he was going to have to be real careful. He was going to have to evade whoever was onboard the ship watching him.

Was it possible? Usayd wasn't sure, but he knew he didn't have any other option. If he stayed onboard the ship and sailed into Algeria, he would be arrested, jailed and probably killed. For a second Usayd recalled standing on the gangway surveying the Lambros Y as he boarded the ship back in Beirut. He entertained the thought back then of not sailing on the ship. She looked like a death trap to him. But the alternative of going back into Beirut didn't appeal to him either. There was danger on both fronts. Now he wondered if he had made the right decision.

CHAPTER EIGHT

The Lambros Y arrived in the outer harbor of Valletta, Malta in the early morning hours. Usayd was wide awake observing everything. He watched as the tugs came alongside and nestled the ship alongside the dock. After the ship was secured to land, discharging of cargo and passengers began. The sailing time for the Lambros Y was posted on the chalkboard in the galley, 1:00pm. Usayd had to do something before then, only a few hours away. He finished breakfast and went back to his cabin, thinking how he was going to get off the ship undetected. While he was sitting in a chair by his cabin desk, there was a knock on his door. Usayd stepped to the door and asked who was there. Manuel responded that he had the clean sheets that Usayd had requested. Usayd never requested clean sheets; he knew Manuel wanted to talk with him.

Carefully Usayd opened the door and let Manuel in. As Usayd thought, Manuel had a suggestion and possible plan. Manuel knew who broke into Usayd's room and who was keeping an eye on him. If Manuel could distract this man for five minutes, Usayd could depart from the vessel undetected. Usayd agreed but wondered how this would be possible. Manuel told Usayd not to worry about that, he just wanted Usayd ready to leave the ship at precisely 11:30. He told Usayd that he couldn't carry any luggage; he had to walk down the gangway acting as he was going ashore for a walk. Usayd thanked Manuel for his help, but was a bit suspicious. He asked Manuel why he was helping him. They didn't know each other, and there was no reason for Manuel to put himself at risk helping a stranger.

Manuel looked at Usayd with a confident, assertive look in his eyes and said, "Sir, you are an intelligent man, but you don't know everything. I have sailed all around the world and I have seen much human misery. I am not sure what your cause is, but I know they are trying to stop you. I have had family members back home in the Philippines disappear in the middle of the night. I am helping you in their memory, so what happened to them doesn't happen to you." Usayd believed what Manuel said. The fire in his eyes, the conviction in his voice was compelling. Usayd shook Manuel's hand and thanked him. Manuel dismissed Usayd's thanks and told him to be ready; he would only have a minute or two to act.

Shortly after 11:00, Usayd was on deck exercising, walking the deck from bow to stern. He timed it perfectly to be by the gangway at 11:30. He was no more than fifteen steps away when the ship's fire alarm sounded. Bells were ringing throughout the vessel. Crewmen began running in all directions. As planned, Usayd casually walked down the gangway. When he reached the dock, he walked between an area of small warehouses and disappeared into the shadows. He was ashore unnoticed!

Anticipating jumping ship in Malta, Usayd had called Aadil in Algeria for help and advice. Aadil told him if he could get ashore unmolested he should proceed to a safehouse on the outskirts of Valletta. Aadil gave Usayd the address and name of the contact. Acting on Aadil's directions, Usayd headed for the safe house. Luckily, the safehouse was close by and Usayd had no problem obtaining directions from the locals. After a short fifteen minute walk, mostly uphill, Usayd approached the house. He saw an old man chopping wood in the side yard. Usayd approached him and asked if he was the owner of the house. When the man said yes, Usayd told him he was the man from the sea. Immediately, the old man dropped his axe and hugged Usayd. The strength of his hug impressed Usayd. The old man immediately brought Usayd inside the house. There to meet them was the old man's wife. She was expecting Usayd and had a big pot of lamb stew simmering in front of an open fireplace.

Usayd and the old man sat at a rough-hewn table and feasted on stew and black bread. Usayd was relieved to be off the ship and in the presence of friends. Not much was said between the three of them as they ate, but the feeling of trust pervaded the room. Usayd wondered what this old couple's connection was to the Salafist cause, but soon dismissed these thoughts. It didn't matter, all that mattered was that he was safe and with friends. After their meal, the old man led Usayd to a side room. He told

Usayd this was his room for as long as he stayed in Malta. The old man wasn't sure how long that was to be. All he knew was that he was told to take care of Usayd, and make him safe and comfortable. If anyone asked who this new visitor was, they were to say Usayd was a nephew of a deceased friend. Usayd knew Aadil was working on arrangements to get him back to Arzew. All he had to do was be patient and enjoy the old couple's hospitality. Within a few days, word reached Usayd via a man on a bike. The message was short and cryptic. Usayd should expect a visitor in a day or two.

Two days later, the visitor arrived. The man was of medium height, but had a barrel chest and thick, hairy forearms. He was wearing a bright, flannel shirt, sleeves rolled up over his elbows, and black, leathery pants. Atop his head was a yellow stocking cap. When Usayd met him in the front yard of the old man's house, the visitor introduced himself as Captain Papadopoulos. Usayd liked him immediately. There was something about his smile and the twinkle in his eyes that exuded confidence and authority. The captain told Usayd he had a fishing boat tied up at the town pier. He pulled into Valletta Harbor ostensibly for fuel and ice. In reality he needed neither. He pulled in because he had received a call from a mutual friend. This mutual friend asked Captain Papadopoulos to pull into Valletta and pick up Usayd. The captain wasn't sure why, but he knew it was best to ask questions later.

By law, he could only tie up for the maximum of six hours. If he stayed longer, he would have to pay costly customs fees. Since he didn't want to do this, he asked Usayd to pack his bags so they could debark. Usayd hurried inside, grabbed his coat and was back outside within seconds. The captain laughed when he saw Usayd reappear. "Traveling light, I see." Usayd ignored his remarks. He hugged the elderly couple and pressed some money in the old man's shirt pocket. He kissed the wife's cheek and could feel her warm tears upon his cheek. Turning, he said, "All right, let's go." Just before Usayd and the captain disappeared over the hill, Usayd turned to look back at the house. The elderly couple was still standing in the yard, watching Usayd walk down the road. Usayd waved and was gone.

As they approached the town dock, Usayd saw the boat. She was 100 feet at most, built of wood, with nets hanging over her sides. The wheelhouse was aft and forward was an entrance that led below. In between was a large hatch leading below to the fish bins. She was old, but in good shape and powerfully built. Her hull was painted black and topsides was a combination of red and green. Usayd followed the captain onboard and nodded to the four crewmen waiting on deck. The captain began barking out orders. He wanted all lines taken in and ordered the mate to slowly back the boat into the channel. Immediately, they jumped into action.

As the last line came onboard, the stern of the boat gracefully arced into midstream. Once there, the mate threw the gear into forward and pushed the throttle ahead. A puff of smoke billowed out the stack and Usayd could smell the familiar exhaust from a diesel engine. Imperceptibly, the fishing boat increased speed. Soon they were leaving the inner harbor and approaching the breakwater. It was less than an hour before they were in the open sea. Usayd was standing on the open deck just forward of the wheelhouse. He could feel the movement of the sea in his legs and the wind on his face. He was deep in thought when Captain Papadopoulos' voice bellowing from the wheelhouse awakened him, "Come inside before you're washed overboard," he said.

The pleasant smell of varnished wood greeted Usayd as he entered the wheelhouse. The captain and mate had unlit cigars dangling from their mouths as they discussed their heading. The captain's was dark, thin and short, the shape of a cigarette. The mate's was dark, thick and long. As they were talking, Usayd looked around the wheelhouse. Everything was tidy and clean. The brass shined and the windows were bright and clear. Above the large wooden wheel used to steer the boat, nailed to the bulkhead, was a piece of finished wood with the name of the boat neatly painted in red and green, PEGASUS. Usayd chuckled a bit when he realized he wasn't aware of the name until then.

Once the captain agreed on the proper heading to Algeria, he turned his attention to Usayd. "Come," he said, "let us go forward and have lunch. Are you hungry?" He was opening the door of the wheelhouse as he talked. Usayd followed close behind. He and the mate waved to each other as he left. When they were walking forward Usayd heard the mate yell something through the open wheelhouse window. He wasn't sure what he said because of the noise of the waves breaking against the side of the boat.

However, he knew it wasn't complimentary by the captain's response; his middle finger waving in the now stiffening breeze.

The galley was in the forward part of the boat. Access was gained by a set of stairs pitched at a 45 degree angle. Protecting this set of stairs from the wind and broaching sea was a small wooden shack. As they entered this shack and began to climb down the stairs, Usayd could smell something good cooking. Once he reached the galley deck, he saw the cook slicing a big slab of beef. Usayd was hungry and the smell made him hungrier. The captain and Usayd took seats at a bench that ran lengthwise to the boat. The bench was attached to a thick piece of mahogany used as the main dining table. Deep depressions marked the edges of the wood, causing Usayd to wonder how many meals had been served on the table. As they sat, the cook served plates of beef with rice and carrots. Usayd devoured his meal while listening to the captain amicably talk between heaping mouthfuls of beef. The captain told Usayd that the trip home to Algeria might take 36 hours, if they were lucky. The Pegasus could only go between 9 and 10 knots at best, and the distance to Algeria was almost 350 miles. However, a low pressure system was sweeping across the Mediterranean. Unfortunately, the path of the low and the path of the Pegasus intersected somewhere off the coast of northern Africa. The captain and the mate attempted to adjust the Pegasus' course so they could avoid the brunt of the storm, but anything could, and probably would, happen. In the meantime, the captain said Usayd would be sleeping in his cabin on a spare couch.

Immediately after lunch, Usayd went to the captain's cabin to take a nap. Thick woolen blankets and a lumpy pillow had been placed on the couch for Usayd. He took his shoes and socks off and wrapped himself in the blankets. Within moments he was asleep. After sleeping for some time, Usayd dreamt he was flying through the air. His stomach was upset and he thought he was going to vomit. Then he hit something hard. Usayd tried to focus his mind on what was going on. Where was he? Was he asleep? Then reality set in. He was sound asleep until the Pegasus rode up on a huge swell and then violently slid down the backside of the sea. It was this action that bounced Usayd off the couch, landing him hard on the deck. Then the vomiting began. Usayd attempted to reach the captains toilet, but the boat bouncing in every different direction all at once prevented him from doing so. He threw up all over the captain's carpeting.

The low that Captain Papadopoulos had warned Usayd about was on top of them. Winds were howling out of the northeast between 40 and 50 knots, building seas to almost 30 feet. The Pegasus was a good solid boat, but 30 foot seas carried a lot of power. Usayd attempted to stand, but another wave hit the Pegasus broadside. He was picked up and literally thrown against the far bulkhead. Usayd had been to sea before on numerous occasions, but he had never experienced weather like this. The entire boat was shaking and creaking and Usayd feared the Pegasus might be broken apart. He struggled to the cabin door on his knees, attempting to locate a crewmember to find out if the Pegasus was indeed sinking. As he groped in the dark for the door handle, a thought flashed through his mind. He should have stayed on the Lambros Y. Running the risk of being captured by the Algerian government would have been better than sinking in the middle of the Mediterranean on an old creaky, stinky fishing boat.

After struggling along a narrow passageway, Usayd found a door with light beaming through the side. He thanked the spirits for delivering him from hell. When he opened the door, the warm air meeting him felt comfortable and reassuring. Once his eyes adjusted to the bright light, he realized he was in the wheelhouse. The same mate he had met before lunch was still at the wheel. Behind him and seated on a high wooden stool was Captain Papadopoulos. The captain was reading a magazine and chatting with the mate at the same time. Usayd felt like he had just entered another world. Moments ago he had thought he was on a sinking boat; in the wheelhouse all was calm. In fact, they barely noticed when he stumbled into the wheelhouse. Finally the captain looked at him and said, "What's the matter, can't sleep?" Usayd couldn't believe what the captain just said. Can't sleep? He thought the boat was sinking and he was going to die. Who was concerned with sleep? The mate was a bit more sympathetic with Usayd's plight than the captain. He told Usayd it was a bit rough, but within twelve hours they should be out of the worst of it.

All of a sudden, Usayd began retching again. He didn't have anything left in his stomach to throw up. He retched his guts out while on his knees in the wheelhouse hanging onto a pipe that ran along the side wall. As he was being sick, Usayd felt as if he was going to pass out. While in a semi-conscious state, he felt strong arms picking him up from under the armpits. So this is how it feels like when you die, he thought. In reality, Captain Papadopoulos saw how sick Usayd was and came to his aid. The captain half carried and half dragged him back down the passageway from where he came. But this time the captain put Usayd in his own bed. He even adjusted the shifting boards along the outside of the bed, preventing Usayd from flying out. Once Usayd was secured, the captain went back to piloting the Pegasus. The semi-comatose Usayd fell into a deep sleep.

When he awoke, Usayd was confused by his surroundings. Slowly, as he lay in the captain's bed, he was able to recall the events of the past few hours. The wind was still blowing, but the sound was different than before. The intensity of the howling had seemed to lessen. Even the seas felt different. Although the Pegasus was still rolling heavily, the motion was less severe. Usayd swung his legs out of bed and sat on the edge for a few moments. Yes, the motion of the boat was a lot different than before. He was no longer being thrown from one bulkhead to another; Usayd was able to stand with little difficulty. Once he put his shoes and socks on, Usayd left the cabin to return to the wheelhouse. Captain Papadopoulos was still there, reading the same magazine of a few hours ago and chatting aimlessly. The mate was gone, replaced by the boatswain. Usayd nodded to both and walked to one of the forward windows. He could see waves occasionally break on deck, but the water harmlessly rolled off and over the side. Before, the seas were continuously breaking on deck. It was so severe the Pegasus looked more like a submarine than a fishing boat. The mate knew what he was talking about when he said the storm would abate within twelve hours.

When Sabir, acting on behalf of the triumvirate, contacted Captain Papadopoulos and asked him to pick up Usayd in Malta, the captain readily agreed. He had done work for the triumvirate before and everything always went as planned. The captain wasn't exactly sure what the triumvirate was up to. But, the pay was fantastic and it was in cold hard cash. The captain's instructions were specific. He was to arrive in Valletta Harbor, pick Usayd up in the safe house and then transport him to a point on the chart 10 miles off the Algerian coast. At this point on the waters of the

Mediterranean, the Pegasus was to meet a small Algerian fishing vessel. Usayd was to be transferred to this second vessel and they would transport him into a prearranged port in Algeria.

The plan sounded simple, but this time the captain encountered problems. First of all, the storm had delayed the Pegasus' arrival by almost a full day. Delays on the high seas were expected, but a full 24 hours was out of the ordinary. Captain Papadopoulos needn't worry, because the smaller fishing vessel hadn't even left her dock. The storm passing directly over Algeria was so severe; the rendezvous boat had to wait to get underway until the weather abated. When the Pegasus finally arrived at the meet point, they couldn't find the second boat. They scanned the horizon with their binoculars only to see seagulls diving for the remnants of fish lying on the ocean surface.

Captain Papadopoulos was afraid if he loitered in the area too long, an Algerian patrol boat or aircraft would spot him. They might become suspicious and decide to board and search the Pegasus. If they did, Usayd would be found and everyone would be in serious trouble. The Algerians were known to be rather ruthless to people breaking the law, especially if you were a foreigner. Smuggling people into the country was an especially egregious act.

Therefore, Captain Papadopoulos decided he better take the Pegasus further offshore, out of reach of the Algerian authorities. He scanned the horizon one more time. Still seeing nothing, he checked his radar. At maximum range of 26 miles, all he could see was the fuzzy Algerian coastline. Seeing the coastline and all the inherent dangers it represented sent shivers through the captain's body. Without raising his head from the radar cover, he told the boatswain to steer due north, directly opposite the direction of the Algerian coastline.

They steered in this direction at a leisurely 5 knots through the afternoon. Come sunset, the captain turned the Pegasus around and headed back towards the coast. Just before midnight, the Pegasus was approaching the meeting point. All eyes strained to identify the boat they were supposed to meet, but still nothing. As Captain Papadopoulos finely tuned the clutter setting on his radar, he identified a faint blip heading in their direction. Slowly the blip on the radar screen became bigger and brighter, but they still couldn't visually see the boat.

Finally, when the blip was within a mile of the Pegasus, someone on the port wing yelled out that he could see a boat approaching. The boat was running without any lights, making a visual sighting almost impossible until they were close. Captain Papadopoulos slowed the Pegasus to bare steerageway and made a lee on his starboard side. The smaller fishing vessel understood what Captain Papadopoulos was doing. Maintaining radio silence, he slid his boat under the stern of the Pegasus and stealthily laid his boat along her starboard side. Without tying up, both boats gently drifted alongside each other. Usayd had already said his goodbyes. Within a minute he deftly stepped from the Pegasus' boat deck onto the bow of the other vessel. After a quick wave of his hand, he was gone, swallowed up by the darkness of a moonless Mediterranean night.

Once the other boat was clear of the Pegasus, Captain Papadopoulos ordered the boatswain to steer a course to the northeast. He was hoping to be back on the fishing grounds to the west of Malta by noontime. Even though the triumvirate paid the captain good money for transporting Usayd, they were still fishermen and had to make their catch. As they settled on their course, the boatswain was relieved on the wheel by the mate. After a brief chat in the wheelhouse, both the captain and the boatswain went below to get some well deserved sleep. The events of the past 36 hours had drained them. Although they wouldn't know for some time, it was lucky Usayd jumped ship in Malta. The Lambros Y was met by Algerian authorities when she arrived in Annaba. A contingent of at least thirty customs people boarded and searched the Lambros Y. The first cabin they searched was 305! When they didn't find Usayd there, they ripped apart the entire vessel. They were furious when they realized Usayd had some how given them the slip. Finally, after being onboard for almost six hours, the boarding team departed. When they left, they brought a "passenger" with them—the man Manuel saw leaving Usayd's cabin. It appeared the customs officials had plans for him.

CHAPTER NINE

Life in New Zealand was even better than Mubbaligh or Correntine ever imagined. They were so happy they decided to settle in the town of Blenheim. Mubbaligh already knew a little about the town from his calls to realtors before they left Arzew. After listening to the Customs Inspector talk about his boyhood home, they were convinced; Bleinheim would be their adopted home.

Upon arrival, their first order of business was to find a house. Miraculously, they found their dream house the first week of house hunting. But, to be sure, they elected to rent the house for one year with an option to buy. They didn't want to jump into anything too quickly, only to regret their decision later on. The house was made of stucco and was painted pink with bright yellow shutters. There were three bedrooms, a bath, living room and a large modern kitchen. In the front of the house was a screened in porch. Because the house was almost at the top of a hill, they would have an unobstructed view of the ocean as they sat on the porch. In the back of the house was a large fenced in yard. The grass was greener than either one of them had ever seen before. Correntine was convinced this was the house. She wanted to buy the house on sight, but understood when Mubbaligh suggested they rent with an option to buy. Whatever, she thought, all she wanted to do was move in. She was excited and anxious to start decorating, especially the baby's room.

After settling on a house, Mubbaligh had to concentrate on finding a job. He still had plenty of money stashed away from his drug smuggling days, but he preferred leaving the money in the bank. He wanted to start this new life on an honest footing. If he needed the money in the bank, he could always withdraw what he needed. Secretly, deep down inside of him, Mubbaligh was hoping someday he could take that money—all of it—and donate it to a charity, probably for little kids. He never discussed this with Correntine; he kept these thoughts to himself. Donating the money to a worthy cause, to people who needed it more than him, might make him feel better. It might help purge some of the guilt that was always gnawing at him. He wasn't sure if it would work, but he knew he wanted to do it if at all possible. But, time would tell. For now, he wanted to find a legitimate job that would provide for Correntine, the love of his life, and their new arrival.

Since Mubbaligh had years of experience working in the shipping industry (although most of that experience was illegal), he decided to try his luck down on the waterfront. He wasn't looking for manual labor, more white collar. After visiting several steamship offices without any luck, Mubbaligh called on the Maersk steamship office located on Violet Street in the heart of the bustling harbor. The Human Resources officer who interviewed Mubbaligh was impressed with his qualifications and experience. Coincidentally, an opening for a steamship agent had just occurred due to an early retirement. Mubbaligh seemed qualified for this position, and he told Maersk he would take the job if it was offered to him. The human resources officer told Mubbaligh they had several other applicants to interview, but between the two of them, she was going to talk with the general manager and recommend they hire Mubbaligh. She told him they should know within a couple of days.

When Mubbaligh left the Maersk office, he was excited. He wanted so much to start a new life with Correntine, a life where he didn't have to constantly look over his shoulder. As promised, he received word in two days. He was to begin work the beginning of next week. That night he and Correntine had plenty to celebrate: new country, new home, new job and soon, a new baby. What a difference from a year ago.

Until all the paperwork for their new house was processed, he and Correntine were living in a bed and breakfast in the center of town. The place was pleasant, but they couldn't wait until they moved into the house. Mubbaligh began work the following Monday. His first impression of his new employer was positive. Upon arrival, he was introduced to the entire Maersk staff—almost thirty people. Next, the Human Resource officer that interviewed him explained the entire list of benefits he was entitled to. Mubbaligh was speechless. Never in his entire life was he offered so many benefits and entitlements. Paid vacations? He never heard of such a thing. Paid sick time? What's that?

Mubbaligh now had a legitimate job with real benefits, but he also had many responsibilities. As a steamship agent, Mubbaligh had to coordinate all the shore side activities for ships Maersk represented arriving in the south island. He had to hire a pilot to navigate the ship into the harbor, tugs to assist the ship in docking and line handlers to tie the ship up. Mubbaligh's work was just beginning once the ship was docked. Not only did he have to hire longshoremen to offload the ship, but he had to look after the personal needs of the crew. Medical and dental appointments were scheduled in advance and, if anyone was signing off the ship, travel arrangements had to be made. These were only his primary responsibilities. He was to soon learn there were many secondary responsibilities he was required to look after.

Blenheim was the busiest port on the south island, but Mubbaligh had to cover two additional, less active, ports. In all, Mubbaligh could be working up to five vessels per week. He would be working all hours of the day and night, holidays and weekends included. The pay and benefit package was fine, but the workload justified Maersk's apparent generosity. While Mubbaligh was away on business, Correntine made preparations to move into their new house. She went shopping for curtains, wallpaper, paint and furniture. In between, she made an appointment to see a doctor. As she thought, Correntine was a little over three months pregnant. The doctor estimated June 26 as her due date. So far, she hadn't experienced any morning sickness or bizarre cravings. In short, everything was going fine. They were settling in to their new country, and the adjustment period was virtually painless.

Mubbaligh and Correntine moved into their new house as planned. Correntine kept house and prepared the baby's room while Mubbaligh quickly established himself as one of the south island's top steamship agents. The work was easy, Mubbaligh thought. All he had to do was dedicate himself to his new profession and everything fell in line. When Mubbaligh was off, he enjoyed many quiet days in their new home. He liked working in the yard the most. All the neighbors were friendly and constantly offered Mubbaligh and Correntine help. By the time the baby was due, they both felt comfortable in their new environment. As each day passed, the memories of the chaotic and scary times in Algeria began to fade. It was about the same time as Correntine was giving birth when things began to change. Faarooq had arrived on the island, and he wasn't planning a long stay!

Faarooq had been dispatched to New Zealand by the triumvirate. They wanted him to eliminate Correntine and Mubbaligh. If the two were not eradicated, the Salafist movement would lose face in the international community. To help Faarooq in this endeavor, the triumvirate contacted a Salafist cell on the island. It was a small group, but they would be able to provide Faarooq with invaluable local knowledge. Unlike Mubbaligh and Correntine, Faarooq decided to fly from Wellington on the North Island to Woodbourne Airport on the South Island. He was on a mission and wasn't about to waste a whole day on a slow-moving ferry. When Faarooq arrived at the Woodbourne Airport, he was met by two native males in their early thirties. Once he collected his bags, they escorted him to their car parked in the airport parking garage and whisked him away. Faarooq sat in the back while the driver maneuvered through the streets of sunny Blenheim. While he was being driven to a safe house less than 10 miles south of the airport, Mubbaligh was driving Correntine to Mercy Hospital. Her water broke and the contractions were coming fast.

CHAPTER TEN

Faarooq wasn't exactly sure how to handle this situation. He was briefed in Arzew what to expect upon his arrival, but he was still tentative. They arrived at the safehouse in the early evening. From what Faarooq could see, the house was rather innocuous and blended in with the rest of the neighborhood. The inside of the house was bright and clean. Faarooq's bedroom was Spartan at best. There was a small bed against the far wall and a stand-up dresser in a corner. The near wall had a long rectangular window at about eye level. Faarooq had never seen a window like this and thought it strange. By the foot of the bed, a door led into a private bath. Faaroq began to unpack his clothes. As he was finishing unpacking, one of the guys that picked him up told Faarooq they would be eating in a few minutes. Faaroq hadn't eaten all day. Airport food didn't appeal to him.

The kitchen was as Spartan as the rest of the house. Faarooq's attention was concentrated on the aromas that he smelled as he entered the room. There was a rather heavy woman standing in front of the stove, using a wooden spoon to stir the contents of a large black pot. She turned and smiled as he entered, exposing wide gaps in her front teeth. Faarooq smiled back and then saw the other two sitting at the table. They waved at him to sit and Faarooq obliged. "Lamb stew," one of them said. He must have recognized the quizzical look on Faarooq's face. Faaroq was nodding his approval when the woman set a large bowl on the table in front of him. Angus, the one who first spoke, introduced Matilda to him. Faarooq stood and reached out his hand. "Nice to meet you Matilda," he said as they grasped hands. Her shake was firm and solid. Faarooq suppressed a laughter as their eyes met. All he could think of was the song "Waltzing Matilda". Obviously this Matilda didn't do much waltzing, he thought.

Even though she was overweight and had gaps between her front teeth, Faarooq thought that at one time she must have been a pretty woman. Her smile was pleasant and her eyes twinkled when she said, "Nice to meet you, sir." She turned and filled two more bowls with heaping helpings of lamb stew. Flynn, Angus' partner, kept his head down and stayed to himself. Faarooq thought he was a rather odd fellow. For the next ten minutes the three of them ate in silence. Matilda left the room after serving them. Faarooq made the decision halfway through eating his bowl of stew. When they were done eating, he was going to convene a meeting in the living room.

Flynn was the only smoker amongst the three, but he smoked enough for all of them. Before he was done with one cigarette, he was lighting another with the butt of the previous one. They sat around a coffee table situated in the middle of the room. Faarooq sat on a couch on one side of the table while Angus and Flynn sat on chairs on the opposite side. Faarooq sized up the other two and then began. He asked Angus and Flynn what they knew about the upcoming operation. Were they aware why Faarooq was in New Zealand? Surprisingly, Flynn was the first to speak. He told Faarooq they were instructed by their leader to help him in any way he wanted. They knew there was going to be violence and killing, and they were comfortable with this. That is why they volunteered. Angus sat silent, but nodded his head in agreement. So far, Faarooq was comfortable with their response.

Faarooq went on to explain the purpose of their mission. They were going to kill a man and a woman who were traitors to their cause. This couple had betrayed the movement, causing many to lose their lives. If they didn't respond by killing them, the Salafist movement would lose respect throughout the world. They had no choice. Angus and Flynn nodded their heads in agreement. "Now," Faarooq continued, "we have to develop a game plan. We must figure how to kill them without getting caught." Once again, Angus and Flynn responded with a nod of their heads.

The mission was clear, now they had to work out the details. Faarooq was pleased when he found out that Angus and Flynn had already done some research on their targets. According to them, Mr. and Mrs. Elias were living in the Sunny Hurst section of Blenheim. "Whoa," Faarooq said, "Who the heck is Mr. and Mrs. Elias?" They both smiled, Angus spoke. "Mr. and Mrs. Elias is the couple you refer to as Mubbaligh and Correntine." Farrooq was stunned and taken aback. These two characters who Faarooq considered to be a couple of country bumpkins had really done their research. Faarooq had no idea Mubbaligh and Correntine had changed their names. Maybe he better do some listening instead of talking, he thought to himself. "Please, go on," he said. "Tell me everything you know about, ah, Mr. and Mrs. Elias."

Flynn slowly raised his head and began to speak. He told Faarooq that he and Angus had been following Mr. and Mrs. Elias for the last two months. Initially, their surveillance was hit or miss. When they had the opportunity they would follow the couple. If they didn't have the opportunity, they wouldn't. Everything changed about a month ago, sometime in late May, he thought. They were told to increase the level of scrutiny. In fact, they were told to conduct surveillance around the clock. Obviously they couldn't conduct 24 hour surveillance, but they did as much as they could. Certainly a lot more than two months ago. The results of their surveillance were quite conclusive. Mr. Elias was working as a steamship agent for a world renowned steamship line, Maersk Steamship Company. He traveled extensively between the three ports on South Island. However, most of his work—maybe seventy percent—was done in the port of Blenheim.

While Mr. Elias was off working, Mrs. Elias spent most of her time sprucing up their new house. Their observations had her concentrating on the baby's room. Faarooq immediately stopped Flynn. "The baby's room?" he said. "What baby are you talking about?" Flynn smiled, the first time Faarooq could remember, and continued. He told Faarooq that Mrs. Elias was quite pregnant. In fact, their contact at Blenheim General called them as they were driving to the airport to pick Faarooq up. Mrs. Elias was being admitted to the hospital as they spoke. Her water had broken and the time between contractions was decreasing. She was about to have the baby. Faarooq was flabbergasted. He knew so little, while it appeared that Angus and Flynn knew everything.

Flynn continued. The couple was renting the house in Sunny Hurst with an option to buy. According to the realtor (not only do they have an inside contact in the hospital, but also with the realtor) money wasn't the issue. It appeared Mubbaligh had plenty of money. She was just as confused as anyone why they opted to rent, but she felt reluctant to delve any further. Faarooq was just as confused. He knew Mubbaligh was rolling in dough from his drug smuggling days. He was going to have to figure out why Mubbaligh didn't outright buy. Flynn said that Mr. and Mrs. Elias were friendly with all their neighbors but mostly kept to themselves. Occasionally they went into town to watch a movie or to have dinner, but most of their activities centered around their home.

Faarooq was impressed with Angus and Flynn. Their leg work was top notch. They had covered everything. The outward appearance of the two had a lot to be desired. They were both in their mid twenties and of average height and weight (5'8", 175lbs). However, things went downhill from there. They both dressed terribly and they smelled. Their body odor was highly offensive. Faarooq wondered when was the last time either had taken a bath—or at least a shower. Their hair was matted and greasy and their teeth looked horrible. However, the two of them had collected enough information to make Faarooq's job easier. Consequently, he wasn't going to have to spend a lot of time in New Zealand. This made Faarooq happy because the longer he stayed, the greater the chances became that he would be caught. Now, all he had to do was digest all this information furnished him by Angus and Flynn. Maybe he would have to garner a few more pieces of information, but not much. Once he was done going over all the intelligence, he could formulate a plan. Once his mission was accomplished, he could get the hell out of New Zealand and get back home to Arzew—where he belonged. During this briefing, Correntine delivered a baby boy. Mubarak, named after Mubbaligh's long-deceased father, was born on the evening of June 26, 2004.

CHAPTER ELEVEN

While Faarooq and his co-conspirators were in the planning stage, other important events were happening not only in New Zealand, but in other parts of the world. In Arzew, Algeria, Usayd had finally arrived back home. After a few days rest, he planned on meeting with the members of the triumvirate. He was utterly exhausted from his travels and his close brush with being captured. He tried to rest and get some sleep, but his recurring nightmares kept hounding him. In Langley, Virginia, Headquarters of the Central Intelligence Agency, intelligence specialists were hard at work evaluating newly acquired information.

Less than a week ago, the Middle East bureau of CIA Headquarters received intelligence from one of their field agents operating in Algeria. The information was sensitive and considered highly reliable. The field agent providing the information had worked in the field for a number of years, and his dispatches were thorough. This most recent dispatch was no exception. If what he was saying was true, immediate action had to be taken because lives were at stake. Even more importantly, the lives of a CIA operative and her family were in jeopardy.

As the intelligence specialists pored over the field agent's report, they attempted to find any inconsistencies or inaccuracies, but they couldn't. The report was rock solid and was deemed to be "actionable information", a code word within the agency meaning an immediate response was required.

As usual, most information the CIA and other law enforcement agencies receive comes from individuals seeking revenge, money or some special favor. In this case, it was a special favor. The source of the information would take the breath away from anyone who knew him and his supposedly unquestionable loyalty to the movement. But, as happened so many times in the past, blood proved thicker than "the cause".

Mr. Yasir, the executive secretary for the economic minister of the New Zealand embassy in Algeria, had assisted the Salafist movement many times in the past; providing them sensitive information that he had access to became a routine matter. He did it out of a sense of obligation to his country. However, over the course of the last several years, he became disillusioned. The movement was using and, most recently, abusing him. After he gave Faarooq the information about Mubbaligh and Correntine receiving New Zealand immigrant visas, he felt they didn't adequately protect his anonymity. The movement—specifically Faarooq—talked too much about how easy it was to acquire information from the New Zealand embassy. Whenever he had a glass too much of his favorite wine, his lips loosened and he talked freely about sensitive matters.

Mr. Yasir wasn't sure if he was becoming paranoid, but he felt people within the embassy knew he was the leak. This feeling began shortly after he provided the information to Faarooq about Mubbaligh and Correntine's whereabouts. He sensed he was being left out of embassy meetings that he usually attended. Often while talking on his desk phone, he could hear faint clicking sounds. Certainly this could be blamed on Algeria's inferior phone system, but he never heard the noises before. Driving home at night was also disconcerting. He always took different routes and on several occasions he was sure he detected that he was being followed. Even at home he thought he saw cars parked in the neighborhood keeping an eye on his house.

Mr. Yasir loved Algeria. He and his wife were devout Muslims and they raised their three children accordingly. Now he had grandchildren and they were being raised in the faith. He couldn't imagine living anywhere but in Algeria. But, things were different now. The government had become radicalized and less tolerant of its citizenry. However much the country changed, Mr. Yasir never imagined that he could possibly move somewhere else. Now he was scared. Had his involvement with the Salafist movement jeopardized himself and his family? Was the government suspicious of him and ready to act? Mr. Yasir wasn't sure what to do. He wished that he had never heard about the Salafist movement. He wished he never heard the name Faarooq. But, it was too late now. He did what he did. Now was not the time for lamentation. It was time for action. He had to do something to protect himself and his entire family. What was he to do? When he came to work one morning and found items on his desk rearranged, he knew he was under suspicion. They were on to him and they were getting closer by the minute. Mr. Yasir knew he had to do something and he had to act quickly, otherwise he would lose everything.

They met in the Revolutionary Park for National Heroes located in the center of Arzew. As usual, Mr. Yasir was early. As he waited for his contact, he casually strolled amongst the statues of national heroes. He thought it was so ironic; he was in the presence of all these national heroes, many of them giving their lives for their country, and he was about to betray what they fought for. He was deep in thought when a voice from behind startled him. Mr. Yasir quickly turned and faced the caller. He was shorter than Mr. Yasir, dark complexion with a thick, black mustache and wore rimless glasses on a large, hawk like nose. His short fuzzy hair perched on a large head gave him an intimidating appearance. The black shiny running suit he was wearing concealed his bulky frame. His white sneakers gleamed in the sun. The gentleman reached out his hand and said, "I am Mr. Laham."

Working in embassies the majority of his adult life gave Mr. Yasir access to many contacts, including the CIA. When he called the CIA's secret number in Algiers to arrange a meeting, they told him to meet a Mr. Laham in the Revolutionary Park at noontime. They knew the park would be crowded with people on their lunch break so the meet would not look conspicuous. Also, he was given a code name to identify himself—Mr. Youssef.

"Mr. Youssef" took Mr. Laham's hand and shook it firmly. It was if that simple handshake was locking him into a deal with the devil. "Yes, good, I am Mr. Youssef. And you are who?" Mr. Laham repeated his name for the wary Mr. Yasir. Once the code names were vetted, Mr. Laham escorted Mr. Yasir to a park bench opposite a six foot long cement statue of a large fish; water was flowing from the fish's mouth, splattering noisily on the cement ground. Mr. Laham was using this noise to drown out their conversation from any listening devices that might be nearby. He wasn't sure if this was a set up and was taking all precautions. Mr. Yasir knew what he was doing and realized Mr. Laham had been in the park before, perhaps for meets exactly like this. Once settled on the park bench, the two chatted for a few minutes. Mr. Laham was continuously scanning his surroundings. Finally, in a low menacing voice, he asked Mr. Yasir what he could do for him. Mr. Yasir's moment had arrived. Could he, would he, go through with it? Could he rat on a fellow Algerian, a long-time friend, to the hated American CIA?

Mr. Yasir cleared his voice, looked around him, and looked into Mr. Laham's eyes. He began, "I have some information I think you would be interested in having. It involves the possible murder of a couple of people, one who is supposedly on the CIA's payroll." Mr. Laham's ears perked up when he heard about the possible murder of a CIA employee. He was paying close attention as Mr. Yasir continued. "You know where I work and you know I have access to a lot of sensitive information. While discharging the responsibilities of my position, I came across this information. But, before I go any further, I want to make a deal." Mr. Laham knew this was coming. He was interested in what the deal was: money, revenge or some other special request.

Mr. Yasir began a lengthy monologue. He told Mr. Laham that he felt, no he knew, the Algerian government was on to him. He wasn't sure how, but they knew he was secretly giving the Salafist movement sensitive information. Recently, he realized he was being followed and his phone at work was tapped. It was only a matter of time before they arrested him. Mr. Yasir said he could accept being arrested, but he was concerned for his family, his wife, his children and their children. Therefore, he wanted a guarantee that if he gave up this information, the CIA would spirit him and his entire family safely out of Algeria. He wanted to settle possibly in a neutral country in Europe, perhaps Switzerland or Lichtenstein.

Mr. Laham viewed a young couple as they walked by the park bench. Lovers, he thought, but maybe not. Mr. Yasir continued, "If you guarantee me safe passage for me and my entire family, I will divulge the name of the CIA official. But, I must have a guarantee." Mr. Laham told Mr. Yasir that he was sure he could provide safe passage for him, but the entire family was not possible. Mr. Yasir jumped to his feet. He was in a rage. "What are you, a fucking idiot? Do you think I will leave without my family?" Laham was playing a much used game that the CIA had mastered over the years. *Promise them nothing and then they'll be happy with something.* He was playing with Mr. Yasir, seeing how far he could push him. He found out by Mr. Yasir's reaction. "Settle down, settle down," Laham said. "Let me think about it." Mr. Yasir settled down but he was still in a rage. *Who was this CIA guy he was dealing with? Leave without his family?* Mr. Yasir was getting scared. He was beginning to regret ever going to the CIA. But, it was too late. He had exposed himself and now he was going to have to go through with it. He only hoped he could cut a good deal. He had to, for the sake of his family.

After much discussion and wrangling, Laham compromised, but with a proviso. The information Mr. Yasir said he could provide had to be one hundred percent accurate and it had to be a life and death situation for a CIA employee. If not, the deal was off and the CIA would not spirit anyone out of the country, not even Mr. Yasir. More than likely, transportation, false documents and money to get them started in a new country would be provided. According to Laham, Switzerland or Lichtenstein were realistic choices. Both countries had been receptive to the CIA's request in the past. But, he again cautioned Mr. Yasir, the information had to be exactly as he said. If not, the CIA would walk away from the whole matter. Mr. Yasir thought for a moment and realized he had no choice. "Okay," he said, "here's the deal."

For the next hour, Mr. Yasir recounted his story to Laham. He told him how he had provided the Salafist movement secret government information in the past, on numerous occasions. He was never worried or concerned before, but after this most recent transgression, he was terrified of being caught and arrested. He was worried more for his loved ones than for himself. He was in his sixties and had led a good life. If he was imprisoned or killed by the Algerian government, that was the price he had to pay. But, he was so afraid harm would come to his family, especially the children. The thought was driving him crazy. He had to get them out of the country before he was exposed.

Laham patiently listened. He was convinced Mr. Yasir was for real. He was too desperate to be otherwise. Finally, in an attempt to have Mr. Yasir give him the information, he said, "I promise you I will do everything possible to honor my promise. Anything can happen, however. But, I have always been successful in my previous endeavors." He continued, "Please tell me what you know. If someone's life is in danger, we'll have to act immediately. Then we'll start making arrangements to get you and your entire family out of harms way." Mr. Yasir felt it was time to tell all.

Mr. Yasir explained what his position was within the Algerian government. He had held numerous positions during his career, but now as an executive secretary, he had unfettered access to top secret intelligence. The Salafist movement knew this and exploited his position. Therefore, when they came to him in the most recent past to ask him for a minor favor, he thought nothing of it. After all, checking to see if someone was issued a visa was of minor significance. However, this time something went wrong. He wasn't sure what happened, but he was convinced the Algerian government knew he was a leak. Maybe he should have been more careful when he realized why the Salafist's wanted the information. When he told the Salafists the couple they were inquiring about was indeed issued visas to immigrate to New Zealand, they were ecstatic. When the Salafists told him they were going to send a hit team to New Zealand to kill the couple, he was surprised. When he was told the couple were CIA agents, he was stunned. That is when he should have realized he had to be careful. After all, messing with the CIA was bad business. But, he remained complacent and that is how he got himself into the situation he was in.

Mr. Yasir told Laham that Faarooq was the Salafist member who was going to lead the hit team. He also gave him Mubbaligh and Correntine's name. When Laham heard the entire story, he knew it was the real deal. He knew because he was familiar with the Mubbaligh/Correntine case. He knew they skipped town after the failed terrorist attack on America. He also knew the Salafists were looking for them and would kill them once found. This was a big break for the CIA. They too were looking for Correntine, but for other reasons than the Salafists. Laham kept his emotions in check, but he couldn't wait to file a report on this newly acquired information. In fact, he would be making an oral report before the formal written report; the information was too time sensitive to do otherwise.

Laham told Mr. Yasir he would be acting on this information immediately. He told Mr. Yasir to sit tight and be patient. If any problems arose, he was to call the special CIA number. Laham also told Mr. Yasir to try to stick to his normal routine. The information he was providing the CIA was crucial. Therefore, travel arrangements for his entire extended family would be given the highest priority. Laham had secured vital intelligence for the CIA. Mr. Yasir had secured a new future for his family—if everything went as planned.

CHAPTER TWELVE

While Mr. Yasir was in Arzew exposing Faarooq to the CIA, Faarooq was on the South Island in New Zealand finalizing the assassination plot with his co-conspirators. Faarooq wanted to get the job done as quickly as possible; the less time in New Zealand the better. He never really even wanted to be there, only going at the request of the triumvirate. But, unfolding events would not be cooperating with Faarooq's plans. Correntine's birth of Mubarak went smoothly enough, but complications soon set in. Mubarak's lungs weren't fully developed and the doctors wanted him to stay in Blenheim General until they were sure he was out of danger; a week or two at the most. Even though this was disappointing news to Correntine and Mubbaligh, fate was shining down on them. Unknown to the new parents, Faarooq was planning on killing them when they returned home from the hospital with the baby. Faarooq wouldn't harm the baby, but he was planning on shooting Mubbaligh and Correntine with a 9mm handgun furnished by Angus, silencer included. Since Correntine insisted on staying in the hospital with her new-born son, Faarooq's plans were put on hold. Sure, he could kill Mubbaligh as he slept at home alone, but he wanted both of them. The waiting game began.

Angus' contact at Blenheim General promised to keep him posted about Mubarak's anticipated release date. In the meantime, they had no alternative but to wait. Faarooq updated the triumvirate on the status of events on the South Island and they concurred with Faarooq; killing Mubbaligh was only ridding themselves of half the problem. They wanted both of them dead. They wanted to send a message to the entire world; if you cross a Salafist you will die, plain and simple.

Idling away the hours and days was hard for Faarooq. He mostly stayed in the safe house and read. At least once a day, usually several times, he went over his assassination plans. They were simple enough. Once Mubbaligh and Correntine came home with the baby, they would wait a day or two. He assumed Mubbaligh and Correntine would be having visitors welcoming home the new baby. Faarooq didn't want to have witnesses. After a day or two, when life settled down for them, Faarooq planned to act. Angus and Flynn would drive the cars. Angus was to park at the rear of the house while Flynn would pull up to the front. Faarooq was to be with Flynn. As soon as both cars were in position, Faarooq would go to the front door and ring the door bell. Mubbaligh and Correntine would assume he was just another well wisher. As soon as one or both of them came to the door, Faarooq planned on shooting them with his 9mm semi-automatic. The silencer would make the gunshot virtually noiseless. If only one of them came to the door, Faarooq would enter the house and shoot the other one. He would leave the baby alone. As soon as the killings were done, he would exit the house and get in the car parked out front. Flynn would slowly drive away with Angus following them. He really didn't need the second car but wanted to use it for backup. If someone witnessed the event and identified one car, they could ditch it and drive away in the second vehicle.

Faarooq's plan seemed flawless, but he still kept looking for holes. He didn't want anything to trip them up. He questioned Angus and Flynn about the cars, Were they traceable? Angus assured Faarooq they were not. The vehicles and plates were stolen months ago and the vehicle identification numbers had been removed with acid. Maybe after days of research the police could figure something out, but by then the three of them would be long gone. Faarooq would be back in Algeria and Angus and Flynn would be gone—wherever that might be. Faarooq seemed satisfied. While Faarooq waited in the safe house, Matilda faithfully cooked all his meals. Frequently she would make trips to the local bookstore to buy him books. He enjoyed history books, biographies and especially books on local history. However, the hours passed slowly for him. He sensed if his stay was too long, something bad would happen. The authorities would somehow be tipped off. But, what could he do? He had to wait for Correntine and Mubbaligh to get out of the hospital and settle in at home.

The wait was not so uneventful for Angus and Flynn. Being single and in their twenties, they were full of life. Spending hours bar-hopping in downtown Blenheim was a daily occurrence for them. Womanizing naturally followed. Angus was the extrovert and for some reason never had a problem meeting girls. Flynn was the introvert and followed Angus' lead. They usually had simple fun and never really got in any trouble. However, one night Flynn, of all people, caused a scene that attracted the attention of the police. Flynn was sitting at an outdoor bar with Angus. The two of them were carrying on with a couple other patrons about a local soccer match. In the middle of the discussion, Flynn decided he had to use the men's room. As he slid off his seat, his foot became caught in the stools crossbar. His momentum carried him forward. As he was falling to the ground, he grasped for anything in sight. Unlucky for the gentleman sitting next to him, Flynn grabbed hold of his shirt. Both of them landed on the ground with a big bang. The man had a full glass of beer in his hand when Flynn pulled him down. The glass flew threw the air, spilling beer on a couple other patrons. The glass smashed on the ground, spraying others with glass splinters.

The policeman walking by at first thought there was a fight. Then he realized Flynn had a little too much to drink and fell off his bar stool, creating the ensuing havoc. However, just in case someone complained later on, the policeman asked for Flynn's driver's license. He copied Flynn's name, date of birth and address, then told Flynn he better be going on home. Angus grabbed Flynn's arm and escorted him out. They could find a men's room someplace else.

When they arrived home, Matilda recognized their inebriated state and fixed them a quick supper. As they were eating, they told Matilda what happened at the bar. Faarooq was in the living room sitting on the couch. He was engrossed in a recently purchased book, but was half listening to the conversation in the kitchen. When Faarooq heard the policeman copied Flynn's driver's license, he went nuts. He jumped off the couch and stormed into the kitchen. Yelling as he ran, he called the two just about every four letter word in the book. Faarooq was furious because this is exactly what he was afraid of; attracting the attention of the police. Even though this appeared to be a minor incident, he didn't want any contact with the police whatsoever. He knew there was always a chance the police could stumble upon something innocently, compromising their entire mission. Angus and Flynn saw how mad Faarooq was and that tempered their outlook considerably. After Faarooq was done venting, he walked back into the living room. However, he was too upset to read. He didn't like the incident with the police. He hoped his recent bad feelings weren't coming to fruition. He couldn't wait for Mubbaligh and Correntine to get out of the hospital. He wanted to complete the mission and get back home.

CHAPTER THIRTEEN

Thankfully, the next morning Angus received the word. Baby Mubarak was being discharged. Mubbaligh, Correntine and the baby should be home by early afternoon. Faarooq was ecstatic; finally they could implement their plan. That afternoon Faarooq drove by Mubbaligh's house several times. Sometimes Faarooq took either Angus or Flynn, sometimes he went alone. Each time they drove by the house, well-wishers were either coming or going, exactly as Faarooq thought. The following day, there was much less activity at the house. Faarooq drove by about mid-morning and noticed two interesting facts. The main door to the house was always open. A white screen door (sans glass paneling) was in place, allowing the fresh ocean breeze to blow through the house. This was good, Faarooq thought. He could shoot right through the screen door without the sound of breaking glass alerting neighbors that something was wrong.

Even better, he noticed how the rising sun shone directly on the screen door. Anyone standing inside the house looking out would be blinded by this sun. While driving back to the safe house, Faarooq decided that tomorrow was the day. At exactly 10:00 am, he would walk up to Mubbaligh's front door bearing a large wrapped gift. Beneath the gift, he would be holding his 9mm handgun. Whoever came to the door would be shot. He was hoping they both would appear. The quicker it was done, the better. He also hoped for a bright, shining day.

Faarooq was restless all night. He slept little, thinking of the following morning's execution. He was satisfied that everything was covered. If all went as planned, he would be on the 2:00pm Qantas flight flying home to Algeria via Singapore. This thought comforted him. All three were up early. Faarooq splashed water on his face and brushed his teeth. He dressed in the same clothes he wore the day before. He could change when they returned. He placed his suitcase on his bed and packed the clothes he intended to wear on the plane on top.

Entering the kitchen, he saw Matilda serving Angus and Flynn scrambled eggs and ham. The aroma of coffee filled the room. He declined breakfast and asked only for a cup of black coffee. Silently they sat at the table, everyone in their own thoughts. Faarooq kept looking at his wristwatch. When 9:00am approached, Faarooq broke the silence. "Angus, Flynn, what do you think? Are you ready?" In a surprisingly cheerful mood, Flynn responded, "All set boss. Let's get the show on the road. We have dates with a couple of hot chicks tonight. We don't want to be late." Faarooq was a bit perturbed by Flynn's carefree response. He was hoping for a bit more reserved reply. He thought of rebuking Flynn, but decided now was not the time. He looked at Angus saying, "How about you Angus, all set?" Angus looked up from his coffee cup and said, "Yes, Faarooq, we are ready." Faarooq took one last sip of his coffee, and then said "Let's get going."

After Faarooq placed the baby's gift in the back seat, he climbed in the front passenger seat next to Flynn. That is when he first smelled the alcohol. Flynn had already been drinking! Faarooq was enraged, but kept his mouth shut. They were committed and it was too late to make changes. Faarooq only hoped Flynn was capable of driving. As he sat in the passenger seat, he watched Flynn's shaky hand put the keys in the ignition. Soon the engine roared with energy. Flynn backed the car out of the driveway onto the side street. They waited for Angus to do the same. Angus' car remained motionless. Finally, Angus got out of his vehicle and looked at Faarooq, arms in the air, shoulders shrugged. "Won't start," he yelled. Faarooq and Flynn got out of their car and walked down the driveway. As they approached Angus' car, Faarooq said, "Open the fucking hood!" The three of them stuck their heads under the hood, looking for any obvious source of trouble. Faarooq slid his hand along the battery cable leading to the starter. Everything was connected properly. But, when Faarooq gave the cable a tug, the end connecting to the starter fell off. "What the fuck," Faarooq said. Then it happened.

At first Faarooq thought kids were throwing rocks at them. They were slamming off the house, the side of the car and a few even hit him. The windshield shattered and glass was flying everywhere. Faarooq was pissed. He was going to break someone's head over this. Then the sizzling sound started and within seconds they were wrapped in a thick, dark cloud of smoke. One breath of the smoke told Faarooq it was tear gas. Immediately he started to choke. Tears welled up in his eyes and his nose ran uncontrollably. He tried to run out of the smoke but ran right into the side of the house. Faarooq was gasping for air. He knew if he didn't get out of the cloud of tear gas soon he might suffocate. Desperately seeking fresh air, he made one more attempt. This time he ran into the side of the car. The impact knocked him to the ground. He was done fighting, his air passage was closing. Just as Faarooq thought he was losing consciousness, he felt his legs and arms being lifted in the air. Faarooq didn't care anymore. He knew he was dying.

The next thing Faarooq remembered were two figures looking down at him. They were talking, but their words were unintelligible. Faarooq thought they were Martians. He wondered what was happening to him. Had he died? Then slowly reality set in. The "Martians" were human beings with gas masks covering their faces. He hadn't died but he felt like he had. The two men wearing the masks flipped Faarooq on his side. They were groping his entire body. Faarooq felt his 9mm handgun slipping from the small of his back. Then he cried in pain as his arms were twisted behind him. He felt his hands go numb as handcuffs were strapped to his wrists. Once again he was lifted in the air. This time he was deposited face down on the street, the smell of tar mixing with the tear gas. Next he felt heavy pressure between his shoulder blades. Someone was standing on his back. Faarooq gasped for air and attempted to twist free. Someone hit him hard on the side of the head. As he began to lose consciousness, he heard others yelling and crying in pain. What's going on?

The "Martians" were members of New Zealand's Special Air Service (NZ SAS), an elite anti-terrorism unit. The SAS was comprised of roughly 300 army troops, all highly motivated and subjected to some of the best training in the world. It is said that for every 100 applicants for this elite force, only one will successfully graduate from the grueling nine-month training and wear the coveted beret of the unit. Designed as a clandestine unit, the majority of New Zealand's over 4,000,000 population have never heard of the SAS. However, they have been around for years and have a highly decorated history. They fought in the deserts of North Africa in WWII, chasing Rommel's tank force all the way to the fateful battle of El Alamein. After WWII, they fought Communist forces in the jungles of Malaya and Borneo. In Vietnam, they fought bravely for several years alongside their American allies. In Kuwait and later Afghanistan, they were involved in intense fighting, but always staying out of the limelight. They worked mostly reconnaissance behind enemy lines and suffered proportionately high losses. On the home front, their mission was anti-terrorism, training daily to defend their country against any terrorist threat. Their response to this most recent threat was a tactical decision for the New Zealand government.

Acting on the information furnished by the CIA in Langley, the intelligence branch of the SAS was able to track down Faarooq and his co-conspirators within hours. Two teams were assigned to follow them wherever they went. Another team was assigned 24 hour surveillance of the safe house. Faarooq, Angus and Flynn couldn't move without a pair of SAS eyes watching them. Every time Faarooq drove by Mubbaligh's house, he was followed closely by one of several SAS vans. If Faarooq had made a threatening gesture, he would have been immediately neutralized. In fact, the incident at the open bar with Angus and Flynn had been orchestrated by the SAS. The gentleman sitting next to Flynn was a member of SAS! Flynn didn't accidentally catch his foot on the rung of the bar stool, it was caused by this SAS soldier's strategically placed foot. Although the SAS thought they knew who Flynn was, they wanted to get a positive identification. Against this elite, professional force, Faarooq, Angus and Flynn had little chance to succeed.

Within minutes, all three were unceremoniously dumped in the back of an armored vehicle and whisked away. They were still suffering from the effects of the tear gas. Unsurprisingly, the SAS members riding in the van with them showed little concern or empathy. As the armored vehicle sped away, other members of the anti-terrorism unit raided the house. They didn't think anyone else was inside besides Matilda, but they had to be sure. Also, they were looking for any incriminating evidence for prosecutorial purposes. Matilda was overwhelmed with fear when at least a dozen black-clad figures ran into the house, brandishing deadly looking machine guns. She backed up against the kitchen sink and put her hands over her face. She trembled uncontrollably as she heard people running from room to room, intermittently yelling "clear, clear."

Once the house was thoroughly searched, the leader of the team approached Matilda. He told her the three men living in the house were bad people. He knew she wasn't aware of that. The leader suggested Matilda pack her bags and get the hell out of there. The less she knew the better. He also cautioned her to keep her mouth shut. If she didn't, she could become entangled in legal proceedings and could even face jail time. Matilda had trouble catching her breath. She indeed had no idea what was going on. Fifteen minutes later, Matilda was walking out the front door of the house, toting her cloth-covered suitcase. The SAS search team followed shortly after. One of them had Faarooq's airplane ticket in hand. He didn't think Faarooq would need it. Besides, it was evidence.

Woodbourne Airport on the outskirts of Blenheim was the civilian airport servicing the South Island. Few people knew Special Air Services occupied a building at the end of the main runway. Faarooq, Angus and Flynn were taken there directly after they were arrested at the safe house. Each one was put in a separate cell in the basement. During the course of the next three days, each was subjected to intense questioning. The meals were meager and infrequent, barely enough to keep them alive. Angus and Flynn were easy to break. They told their interrogators everything they knew, which wasn't much. Faarooq behaved differently. He was stubborn, belligerent and wouldn't tell the SAS interrogators the time of day. Finally, they had enough of Faarooq's arrogance. Even after some severe beatings, Faarooq wouldn't talk. If it was up to the SAS, they would have killed him and disposed of his body in the Tasman Sea. However, the CIA officers on site said they couldn't do that. Instead, Faarooq was going to be taken to Guatanamo Bay (Gitmo), Cuba, where the United States was holding several hundred other terrorist suspects. As for Angus and Flynn, even the CIA didn't care what happened to them.

Early the following morning, while it was still dark, Faarooq was put on a Royal New Zealand Air Force C-130. He was bound, shackled and blindfolded. Surrounded by CIA agents and Special Air Services Team #10, Faarooq was placed on the floor in the middle of the plane. He was flying more like cargo than a passenger. It was a long flight and Faarooq didn't receive much attention by his handlers. Every so often they checked to see if he was still breathing, but that was it. Late in the afternoon, the coastline of the Philippines was visible through the side windows of the aircraft. The airport in Manila was less than an hour away. Once the plane landed, everyone deplaned except for Team #10 and Faarooq. In the fading light, giant fuel trucks pulled up alongside the C-130. With help from the crew, fueling operations began. The CIA agents went inside a small terminal to make some phone calls. They had to keep their superiors apprised of the situation. Faarooq was a big grab, and a lot of high ranking officials in Washington wanted constant updates on his status. Inside the plane, Team #10 attended to Faarooq's needs. They let him go to the bathroom in a five-gallon plastic bucket and fed him a can of cold hot dogs and beans from their c-rations. All the time, several members of the team had their weapons trained on him.

After being on the ground for a little over an hour, they began the second leg of their journey; Manila to Okinawa, a tiny island in the middle of the Pacific Ocean. The flight was uneventful and they landed in Okinawa a little before midnight. Everyone was exhausted from the long, bumpy, noisy flight. Meeting them on the tarmac was a fresh contingent of escorts consisting of five CIA agents and approximately thirty United States Marines. They were to baby-sit Faarooq until travel arrangements were finalized for his trip to Guatanamo.

The next evening, a giant C-141 waited on the taxiway for Faarooq's arrival. Within minutes, a military bus escorted by numerous military police cars pulled to the rear of the plane. Several Marines escorted Faarooq, still in shackles and handcuffs but not blindfolded, onto the plane. Onboard they were met by another escort team that would take Faarooq all the way to Guatanamo. Once the transfer was complete, the giant C-141 lumbered down the taxiway and waited at the beginning of runway 240 for clearance from the control tower. Once clearance was received, the pilot gave full power to all four of the giant C-141's engines. Soon she was airborne and adjusting her heading for Guatanamo, Cuba. The scheduled non-stop flight was estimated to take fourteen hours.

This is the official version of what happened to Faarooq, but if an inquiry was made by an interested party, no record would be found. In fact, according to the U.S. and New Zealand governments, they never heard of Faarooq, Angus or Flynn. No raid was ever conducted by New Zealand's Special Air Service on a safe house in Blenheim. There never was, nor will there be, any record of Faarooq being detained in Guatanamo.

Both governments would plead complete ignorance and would never change their story. What was the fate of Angus and Flynn? They have never been seen or heard of again.

Mubbaligh and Correntine were informed when the threat on their lives was over. However, they both knew they would have to remain vigilant for years to come. The Salafist movement had a long memory. Even though their efforts were thwarted this time, they could always come back for another try. In the meantime, Mubbaligh and Correntine were enjoying being new parents. Mubarak was a healthy baby and they looked forward spending many happy years with him. With any luck, some day they might be blessed once again with a baby brother or sister for little Mubarak.

CHAPTER FOURTEEN

Once Usayd landed in Algeria, he slowly made his way back home to Arzew. This was the easiest part of his long voyage. His surroundings were familiar and the people were his people. No longer was he a foreigner in some distant land. Now that he was home, however, he had to be careful of the authorities. They were still looking for him and must be fuming at him for giving them the slip off the Lambros Y. When Usayd reflected on that incident, a smile crossed his face and he chuckled. "Fuck them," he said out loud.

After bumming a couple of rides from passing truckers, Usayd found himself on the outskirts of Arzew. He was at a gas station that had a little diner attached. What was best, the local bus traveling to Arzew stopped at this diner. Since the next bus wasn't due for another hour, Usayd decided to have something to eat as he waited. He enjoyed his first meal back in Algeria. He didn't realize how much he missed the local cuisine. Even in Beirut, although the food was delicious, it wasn't the same as back home. After eating, he stepped outside and sat on an old wooden bench. The sun felt warm on his face and before he knew it, he was asleep.

They were closing in on him and the faster he ran the closer they came. His entire body was trembling. He couldn't let them capture him. The sound of the bus' air brakes startled him awake. He jumped to his feet, arms raised in a defensive posture. What the fuck? He thought. Then he realized he was having the same recurring nightmare. When are they going to stop? When? He asked himself. Once he got himself together, he stood in line to board the bus. There were only six others in front of him so the wait was short. Once onboard, Usayd sat back in his cushioned seat and enjoyed the scenery as the bus sped into town.

Usayd wanted so much to stop by his mother's house. After all, it had been over a year since he saw her. But he was afraid the authorities were staking out the house. He assumed they weren't complete morons. Even though he wanted to see her, he decided he best stay away. He could make arrangements later to see her, but going to her house, especially now, was too dangerous. He had no alternative but to go to a safe house Aadil had suggested. He could relax there and slowly unwind from the hectic schedule he had been keeping for the past year. Aadil and the other members of the triumvirate had done an excellent job setting up safe houses throughout Arzew. Usually they were small apartments located in an innocuous apartment building. They were clean and comfortable, and were well stocked with food and reading material. Of utmost importance, there were always multiple exits out of the building. If the authorities caught on that the apartment was a safe house and decided to raid it, whoever was living there at the time could escape to the roof, through another apartment or down an adjoining hallway—if they were warned of the raid and had time to escape.

Usayd arrived at his assigned safe house as the sun was setting over the city. The view from his living room window was breathtaking; he had forgotten how beautiful a city Arzew was, especially compared to some of the filthy, rat-infested places he'd been in recently. He walked around the apartment, checking everything out. He was pleased at what he saw. When he opened the door to the refrigerator in the kitchen, he was pleasantly surprised to find a six-pack of Heineken beer, his favorite. He smiled because he knew this was a personal gift from the triumvirate. In their subtle way, they were thanking him for a job well done. For the past year he'd been roaming the hills and valleys of Afghanistan and Pakistan, seeking out and killing Americans. He was in some of the toughest fighting yet. Obviously when they met face to face, the members of the triumvirate would express their gratitude, but until then this was a small token of their appreciation.

He grabbed a bottle of beer and searched for a bottle opener, a glass wasn't necessary. Once he opened the beer, he walked out into the living room and flopped on the couch. He removed his shoes and placed his feet on the glass-topped coffee table. The six-pack went quickly. Usayd was actually getting a little tipsy. He could remember when he drank a lot more than six beers with no effect on him at all. The old days he thought. When he was on his fifth or sixth beer, Usayd began to reflect on the past. He had been through a lot, too much. How much more could he take? He asked himself. Not too many other people had seen as much fighting as he had and were still alive. Was he crazy to keep it up or did he have some kind of death wish? Then Bashir's offer of employment popped into his head. The more he thought of it, the more he liked the offer. Yes indeed, maybe it was time to get out of the killing business. Maybe it was time to get a normal job and settle down. Who knows, maybe he would even get married and start a family. Shortly, these pleasant thoughts lulled Usayd into a deep, well deserved sleep.

As usual, the same haunting dream disturbed his sleep. He was just about to be captured by the Americans when his own yelling woke him. At first he didn't recognize where he was. Once he did, he sat on the edge of the couch and stared off into space. Sweat was dripping down his face and his hands were shaking. He knew he had to do something. These dreams were occurring more frequently, and they were becoming more intense. Initially, he thought he had some kind of terminal illness, but the recurring dream told him it had to be related to the war. Then it struck him. Could it be that medical condition they call PTSD? Usayd wasn't even sure what the letters meant, but he knew it had something to do with seeing too much combat, too much fighting and dying. Somehow all the traumatic events he had witnessed in the past year or so might be causing these nightmares.

He was confused, depressed and lonely. He had to do something about these dreams or else he was going to go crazy, if he wasn't already at that point. Then he made the decision, in the morning he was going to see a doctor. He had to find a remedy for all these nightmares. He couldn't stand it any more. Then he made another decision, even bigger than the first. He was done with the Salafist movement. He was done with all the killing, dying and suffering. He had given enough. In the morning, after seeing a doctor, he was going to call Bashir to see if his offer of a job was still open. All of a sudden, it felt like the weight of the world was lifted off his shoulders. Usayd stood up from the couch and went into the bedroom.

After taking a shower, he climbed into bed. He was looking forward to the morning. He couldn't wait to see the doctor and talk with Bashir.

In the morning, Usayd had a hard time making a doctor's appointment. He had to call a friend who had a connection in the medical field. This friend made a couple of calls and was able to secure a 1:00pm appointment for Usayd with a prominent local psychiatrist. Things are the same in Arzew, Usayd thought. You had to have a connection to get anything done. The doctor's office was located less than a mile from Usayd's apartment. He felt like walking and taking in the sights so he left his apartment shortly after noon.

He couldn't believe how much the city had changed since he'd been gone. There was construction work going on all over town. Old buildings were being razed and new ones were sprouting up. The car traffic on the roads seemed to have increased also. People were bustling about going in every different direction. The sleepy town Usayd left over a year ago had suddenly awoke. He was happy to see people working but he missed the way it was. He was uncomfortable with the changes. Then the realization struck him. Yes, obviously Arzew has changed dramatically, but he has changed too. That's why he was going to see the doctor.

The receptionist in the doctor's office was pleasant and helpful. She assisted Usayd in filling out all the necessary forms. Once that was done, she told Usayd to have a seat and the doctor would be with him shortly. Over an hour later, the doctor's assistant stepped into the waiting room. She looked at him and called his name in a tentative and questioning manner. Usayd stood, nodding yes with his head. She showed him to an examination room and told him the doctor would be right in. As he waited, Usayd looked around the room; it wasn't a typical examination room. The room had a comforting appearance with a pine-scented smell permeating the air. The walls were decorated with numerous oil paintings, all quite expensive looking in Usayd's limited knowledge of paintings. The furniture consisted of many soft cushioned chairs and a couple of sofas. The typical doctor's desk was missing.

As Usayd was looking for the bed he assumed he would be laying on during the interview with the doctor, a side door opened. A tall, dark-complexioned man dressed in a three piece suit walked into the room. He walked up to Usayd and introduced himself, "I am Doctor Assad, how are you?" Usayd immediately liked the doctor. He exuded a warm, comforting feeling, exactly what Usayd needed in his present state of mind. He was quickly put at ease by the doctors soothing mannerisms. "Fine doctor," Usayd said, but his eyes betrayed him.

They talked for the better part of an hour. The doctor would ask Usayd a leading question and then sat back and listened. Usayd surprised himself how talkative he was, but it felt good to let his inner feelings out. The more he talked the more he wanted to say. He told the doctor about the recurring nightmare and his feelings of loneliness, depression and isolation. The doctor listened without making a sound. Before Usayd knew it, his time was up. He had been talking for almost an hour, but to him it seemed only minutes. The doctor told Usayd he wanted to schedule a few more meetings; Usayd agreed. Then he looked at the doctor and said, "What is going on with me, doctor? Why am I feeling like I am? Why do I have this constant nightmare?" Doctor Assad patiently listened to Usayd, and then he spoke.

"Usayd, you have undoubtedly been through a lot. Seeing killing and combat over a long period of time will have a detrimental effect on the mental state of just about anyone. You are suffering from what you have endured over the last year. It is called trauma, thus—post traumatic stress disorder. Granted, everyone is affected differently. Some people suffer PTSD from one episode of trauma. It doesn't even have to be war-related. Others don't suffer at all from months of exposure to heavy fighting. Our minds work differently. I am not surprised at all with your condition. You have seen too much for too long not to be suffering; however, not to worry. Hopefully, after working together, we will be able to lessen the ill effects it is having on you. With a few more sessions and a prescription of the right drugs, I hope to have you feeling better. As to those recurring nightmares, maybe we can have them go away forever." Dr. Assad's words were comforting. No one had ever talked to him like this doctor did. It felt good and gave Usayd some hope. After scheduling another appointment with the receptionist, Usayd left and went directly to the local pharmacy to fill his prescription. He was anxious to get on the road to recovery.

Usayd put his promised call to Bashir on hold because he had a more important promise to fulfill; he wanted to see his mother. Aadil had made all the arrangements for Usayd. In a different safe house than the one he lived in, Aadil arranged for Usayd and his mother to spend the evening together. He even had a catered meal for them. Usayd was ecstatic to see his mother. Not only was she his mother, but she was also the only living relative Usayd had. Everyone else was dead. Usayd's mother was in her early 70's but was in excellent health. At 5'8", she was taller than the average Algerian female. Even though she was retired from her teaching career, she still volunteered her services at local schools a couple days a week. Extremely smart and articulate, she was also an astute observer of human behavior. She was never told what Usayd was doing out of the country, but she had strong suspicions. Usayd always made up fictitious stories about how he was working for different construction companies all over the world; she didn't believe a word he said. She took the opportunity that night to persuade Usayd to find a different line of work. She wanted him to find something in Arzew so she could see him more often.

Usayd's mother's pleas tore at his heart. He did intend to get out of the business he was in, but there wasn't any chance he could settle close to his mother in Arzew. The authorities would have him arrested within a week. If he took Bashir's offer to work in the import-export business in Beirut, maybe he could have his mother come live with him. After all, she didn't have any binding family ties in Arzew. All that was for tomorrow, he thought. Tonight he wanted to enjoy his mother's company. They spent the rest of the evening reminiscing. Usayd loved to hear how things used to be when Algeria was a colony under French rule. His mother told Usayd how his father was always a thorn in the side of the French. He never killed anyone or blew anything up, but he was a master of sabotage. Many a French vehicle was incapacitated by sugar in the tank or their four tires slashed. Usayd laughed when he heard these stories. Now he realized how he became what he was, he was just like his father, but a bit more sinister.

About 10:00, Usayd decided they better call it a night. His mother looked tired, and he had a big meeting with the triumvirate first thing in the morning. It was going to be an important, watershed meeting when Usayd told them he was done. His days of fighting, killing and maiming were a thing of the past. They'd have to find someone to replace him.

CHAPTER FIFTEEN

Usayd awoke bright and early after sleeping peacefully through the night. He hoped it was because of the medicine the doctor prescribed, but he also thought seeing his mother helped. He was happy to see that she was healthy and in good spirits. He was looking forward to the new day for many reasons. He was anxious to see his friends on the triumvirate; it had been a long time. He considered them all to be his good friends and appreciated how they took care of his mother while he was away. But, he was mostly looking forward to the new day because he was going to declare his intentions. He was done working for the Salafist movement. He was going to accept Bashir's offer of work in Beirut. Soon everything would be in the past. With the assistance of counseling and medicine, he hoped those terrible nightmares would disappear. Usayd had a lot to look forward to as he walked the streets of Arzew on the way to his 10:00am meeting with the triumvirate.

He arrived at the apartment exactly on time. Waqas, the triumvirate's bodyguard, was the first to greet him. He wrapped his beefy arms around Usayd's chest and squeezed tightly. Waqas picked Usayd off his feet and spun him around in the air. The two of them were smiling, laughing and hollering. Standing around a large mahogany desk located in the middle of the living room were the members of the triumvirate—Aadil, Mubid and Sabir. They were laughing heartily as they watched Waqas manhandle Usayd. Waqas was never known for his gentleness. It was lucky for Usayd that he was on their side. Waqas was known for giving a somewhat less friendly greeting for people who weren't. As Waqas surrendered to the law of gravity and returned Usayd's feet to the floor, the members of the triumvirate approached. In turn, they all hugged and kissed Usayd and welcomed him home. After their displays of affection were over, Aadil insisted they have a seat around the table. In the center of the table were two big carafes of coffee with all the condiments. Also, there was a silver tray with a pile of pastries. Usayd's mouth watered when he saw the pastries. It had been a long time since he had a good cup of coffee and one of his favorite pastries.

As he was reaching for an empty cup, he saw someone walk into the living room from a side bedroom. It was Sameenah! Usayd jumped from his chair and ran over to her. They embraced and held each other tightly. Tears flowed down both of their cheeks. It had been such a long time; Usayd didn't realize how much he had missed her. By the way Sameenah was acting, she felt the same way. Eventually they released each other. They held hands and looked into each others eyes. Then they embraced once again. As they were showings their signs of affection, the triumvirate sat uncomfortably around the table. Eventually Aadil took the ever-present black cigar from his mouth and spoke, "Okay you two, enough. You can get together later. Right now the coffee is getting cold and we have pastries to eat. Please, sit." Aadil's remarks broke the ice. Usayd and Sameenah started to laugh and the others soon joined in.

They sat next to each other, often holding hands under the table. Usayd served Sameenah her coffee and pastry while she stared at him with a broad smile on her face. Aadil, Sameenah's uncle, saw the look in Sameenah's eyes and was pleased. It had been a long time since he saw her so happy. The last time was when she was with Mubbaligh, but that was a long time ago, and Aadil didn't want to think of unpleasant times. He quickly washed those thoughts from his head and concentrated on the present. In between mouthfuls of food, Aadil puffed on his cigar and blew smoke rings in the air. Usayd laughed at this display that he so fondly remembered from past meetings. The bantering went on for awhile. No one brought up plans for the future and surely Usayd didn't mention his anticipated resignation. Everyone was having too good of a time—especially Sameenah and Usayd—to spoil things with serious talk.

But, once again, Aadil took control when he affectionately looked at his niece and said, "My dear, I must ask if you'd mind leaving us now. We have some important business to discuss and we don't want you around distracting us with your beauty. Some more than others!" His last words were addressed directly at Usayd. Sameenah stood, acting insulted, as everyone laughed. Usayd stood and held her hands in his. Unexpectedly, they kissed each others lips and then she was gone. Usayd heart was beating rapidly. He wasn't sure if it was because of Sameenah's presence or what they were about to discuss.

Once Sameenah left the room, Aadil started the conversation. He told Usayd how much they all welcomed him back. His absence in the day-to-day activities of the Salafist movement was sorely missed. They knew the last year was tough for Usayd. All the reports they received from the Afghanistan-Pakistan region praised Usayd for his leadership, loyalty and bravery. They knew he was in some heavy fighting and acted fearlessly in every instance. But now his services were needed in Arzew, the center of the movement. Plans had to be made to carry out terrorist attacks on the western world, specifically America. Usayd's role in the development of these plans was vital, that is why they called him home from the front. As Usayd sat listening to Aadil's words of praise, he squirmed in his seat. He was feeling more uncomfortable by the minute. He had come to this meeting to tell the triumvirate he was quitting, not to listen to Aadil tell him he was to be the cornerstone of a new terrorist plot. Sweat broke out on Usayd's forehead and all of a sudden he felt like he was going to become sick. The room began to spin. Usayd held the arms of his chair tightly and tried to concentrate on Aadil's words, but it was no use.

He jumped out of his chair and ran to the nearby bathroom. He slammed the bathroom door and dropped to his knees in front of the toilet. Immediately he began to throw up. His head felt like it was going to explode; the pressure on his temples was excruciating. He retched so hard, there was a time he thought he was going to pass out. Between bouts of throwing up, Usayd laid his head on the cool bathroom floor. The coolness brought relief to his throbbing head. As he lay on the floor he thought of the predicament he was in. He wanted out of the movement and the triumvirate were getting him deeper involved. "Please leave me alone." he moaned. "Please, please, let me go." Exhausted, he fell into a gentle sleep. The knocking on the door woke him. It was Waqas checking to see if he was all right. Usayd told Waqas he was fine and he'd be right out. "It must have been something I ate last night," he told the concerned Waqas. Usayd stood at the washbasin and threw cold water on his face. He looked at himself in the mirror, "What do I do?" he murmured to himself out loud.

When Usayd returned to the living room it was obvious they were concerned for him. Aadil suggested they hold the meeting later, but Usayd said no. He wanted to stay and get what he had to say off his chest. Usayd looked at the three older gentlemen sitting around the table, cleared his throat and said, "Gentlemen, I have something important I must tell you." Sabir pulled his chair closer to the table and Aadil placed his cigar in an ashtray. Mubid looked directly at Usayd with pathos in his eyes. Usayd continued, "Gentlemen, I come to you in a confused state of mind. I have experienced more horror in the last year than you can imagine. My body might be in one piece, but my mind is all scrambled. I can't sleep at night and I have to concentrate real hard even to perform a simple task."

Usayd paused, sipped from a glass of water Waqas had placed on the table in front of him, and then continued. "Honestly, I came here this morning to tell you that I was finished. I quit." No one stirred. They were all transfixed on Usayd's every word. He continued, "But now, you are asking me to take on an even bigger assignment. I am honored and humbled by your confidence in me, but I don't know if I can do it. I don't know if I WANT to do it." Aadil picked up his cigar out of the ashtray and began blowing smoke rings. Somehow seeing the all too familiar smoke rings comforted Usayd. He didn't know why. Perhaps it reminded him of the less hectic and more halcyon days of the past. He wasn't sure. He attempted to continue but couldn't. Waqas, the brute that he was, sat beside Usayd and wrapped him in his arms. Everyone had tears in their eyes.

It was obvious the meeting was over. Usayd was in no shape to continue. Aadil motioned for everyone to leave. As they were walking out the door, Aadil grabbed Waqas by the shirt and said, "Waqas, you stay and keep an eye on Usayd. Get him to bed and stay with him. Whatever you need, call me. I'll get in touch with Sameenah and have her come back. Maybe she can fix something for him to eat. Understand?" Waqas, in a gruff but gentle voice said, "Don't worry about a thing boss. I'll take care of him." Satisfied, Aadil followed Sabir and Mubid out of the apartment.

Waqas was in deep thought when he heard a soft knock on the apartment door. As expected, it was Sameenah. As she walked by him, Waqas saw the concern on her face. "How is he?" she whispered. Waqas closed the door, following Sameenah into the apartment. "He's sleeping," he said. "I have been checking on him regularly. A couple of times I heard him talking in his sleep, but otherwise he has been peaceful." Sameenah walked to the bedroom where Usayd was sleeping and gently opened the door. She peeked in and saw him lying in the middle of the bed with a comforter covering him. Sameenah began to cry. She felt so sorry for poor Usayd. None of them realized what he had really been through. As she stared at the lonely figure in bed, she made a solemn promise to herself. She was going to help Usayd mend, whatever it took. He had given so much and that is the least she could do. As she closed the bedroom door, she felt better. Now, once again, she had a cause for living.

Sameenah's mother died when she was two years old. Her father, a sailor, went to sea one day and never returned. Aadil, Samennah's maternal uncle, took care of Sameenah while her father was at sea. When it was obvious he was never going to return, Aadil adopted her. Sameenah treated Aadil as if he was her father. She was always respectful, loyal and thankful for all he had done for her. In return, Aadil would do anything to make Sameenah happy. He and his wife were never blessed with children of their own, so Sameenah was really special to them. When Aadil's wife died suddenly, Sameenah and Aadil became closer than ever. They only had each other in the whole wide world.

Aadil was protective of Sameenah since childhood. But, as she grew older and became a young lady, his protectiveness grew. Everyone knew if you messed with Sameenah, you were messing with Aadil, and this is something you did not want to do. Perhaps that is why Sameenah never married, men were afraid to date her seriously in fear of incurring Aadil's wrath. After all, she was a beautiful woman: tall, olive skin, jet black hair, a beautiful figure, intelligent with a great personality. Or perhaps Sameenah was afraid of leaving Aadil, her security blanket for the past thirty years. Whatever the reason was, she was still single at the age of thirty- two.

Over a year ago, despite Aadil's strenuous objections, Sameenah became involved with Mubbaligh, a man devoted to the Salafist movement. Sameenah was smitten by Mubbaligh, but Aadil thought otherwise.

He had met many men like Mubbaligh in his life and he didn't want him to have anything to do with his adopted daughter. Mubbaligh was a staunch Salafist supporter, and the key architect for the 2003 terrorist attack on America. Although his credentials were impeccable, he was a drinker and womanizer. Two traits Aadil would not tolerate. However hard he tried, Aadil couldn't control Sameenah's affection for Mubbaligh. The two of them were inseparable for months. Every ploy Aadil used in an attempt to thwart their relationship failed. Then one day, as soon as it started, it ended. Sameenah literally threw herself on Mubbaligh, but he spurned all her advances. A couple of times he was tempted, but he always told her to go away. Sameenah was devastated. She went into severe depression and her friends were concerned for her mental health. Aadil was even afraid she might hurt herself. All their attempts to help her work her way out of this depressed state failed. She became more isolated as time past and gradually her friends began to fade away. Only Aadil, Waqas, Mubid and Sabir stood by her.

If Mubbaligh wasn't in charge of the upcoming terrorist plot in America, Aadil would have killed him. Mubbaligh was lucky that Aadil put the mission before any personal considerations, even his precious niece Sameenah. Then when Aadil discovered Mubbaligh dropped Sameenah for Correntine, a known CIA agent, mission or not, he decided to kill Mubbaligh. If the other members of the triumvirate didn't intercede, Mubbaligh would have been killed. Everyone knew Waqas was willing and able to carry out the act. Eventually Aadil calmed down, but he would forever hold Mubbaligh in low regard. When the 2003 American terrorist plot led by Mubbaligh failed miserably, the triumvirate looked to Mubbaligh for answers. The problem was, they couldn't find him—or Correntine. The two of them simply disappeared off the face of the earth.

Initially, Aadil and the other triumvirate members thought the authorities had grabbed the two. Slowly information began to filter down to the triumvirate that something else was going on. Mubbaligh and Correntine might have slipped out of town to begin a new life in a different country. This is when Aadil requested help from Faarooq. When Faarooq called from New Zealand and said they had Mubbaligh and Correntine in their crosshairs, Aadil was delighted. His hopes were soon dashed.

They never heard from Faarooq again and could only imagine something terrible had gone wrong. All their inquiries with their sources in New Zealand came up negative. Knowing how the New Zealand Special Air Services operated, this was a bad sign. They were notorious for clandestinely carrying out heinous acts when their government's interests were at stake. Even high ranking government officials were often ignorant as to what the SAS was doing.

Aadil regretted not killing Mubbaligh when he had the chance. Now, not only did he spurn Sameenah and cause the terrorist attack in America to fail, he was responsible for the disappearance and probable death of Faarooq and his two co-conspirators. Aadil was more determined than ever to kill Mubbaligh, but once again he had to put his desire on hold. Other concerns merited his immediate attention. New terrorist plans had to be formulated rapidly before the Salafist movement lost credibly in the eyes of their peers throughout the rest of the world. Also, Usayd's welfare was paramount in his mind. He still wanted Usayd to lead the new terrorist initiatives, but he wasn't sure if Usayd could. If he couldn't, they would have to find a replacement. In the meantime, he wanted to make sure Usayd received all the help he needed.

Aadil's feelings and sentiments were a mirror-image of Sameenah's. Usayd's reappearance in her life gave her renewed vitality and strength. Usayd was her raison d'etre. She was always infatuated with Usayd, but nothing ever developed. He was constantly busy with the movement and when he wasn't, he hung out with a different crowd. Things seemed to be different now. Being separated for over a year seemed to be the reason. When they met that morning at the meeting something happened between the two of them, something clicked. It was spontaneous and unexpected, but genuine. For the past year, Sameenah had suffered in silence. The hurt from the sudden breakup with Mubbaligh remained all that time. But suddenly, her anguish and struggles disappeared when she saw Usayd. She felt like a woman again; her life had a new beginning. Sameenah prayed that Usayd felt like she did. She knew he had to. One thing she knew for sure, she would do everything within her power to help Usayd through his most recent struggles. Whatever happened after that, she could only speculate.

CHAPTER SIXTEEN

Usayd took life easy for the following week. Sameenah was constantly by his side, taking care of his needs. Gradually Usayd began to mend. He flushed the medicine the doctor gave him down the toilet because he didn't think it was doing him any good. He would confront his problems face-to-face, like a man. He didn't need counseling by a psychiatrist who had no idea what he'd been through. After a few days, Usayd moved back to his apartment, but not before Sameenah went on a shopping spree. She stocked the refrigerator and shelves with all his favorite foods. She even bought some Heineken. To brighten up the apartment, she bought several colorful rugs and a couple of paintings for the walls. She placed flowers strategically around the apartment in an attempt to uplift Usayd's spirits. After being home for a few days, Usayd mentioned to Sameenah that he was going to talk with Aadil and the other members of the triumvirate. He'd been thinking a lot lately, and he decided he was going to try staying with the movement. Bashir's job offer would have to wait. He was feeling stronger all the time and wanted to stay in Arzew close to his mother. Usayd asked if Sameenah could relay his wishes to Aadil. Sameenah was excited that Usayd had decided to stay in Arzew. With any luck, maybe something would develop in their relationship.

The triumvirate was ecstatic when Sameenah told them Usayd had decided to stay with the movement. Aadil, the gentleman that he was, first inquired about Usayd's physical and mental health. He wanted Usayd back in the worst way, but he didn't want to compromise his health. Sameenah told her uncle that although Usayd wasn't in perfect shape, he was much better than before. He would have to go slow at first and they could monitor his progress. While caring for Usayd, Sameenah conducted some research on the internet about "PTSD." She learned what caused this mental condition and what the best treatment was. Her reading and research gave her the confidence making her feel comfortable she could help Usayd confront his demons. Although she wasn't a doctor, her just being there for Usayd was a big step on the road to recovery.

Usayd and the triumvirate met ten days after their first meeting. Sadly, they still had not heard from Faarooq. He and his two co-conspirators simply vanished off the face of the earth as if they had never existed—classic modus operandi for the New Zealand Special Air Service. Everyone understood Usayd's condition and treated him with the utmost respect and consideration. At first they sat around and chatted cordially. Waqas was in the kitchen, cooking eggs and brewing coffee. Sameenah was running around making sure everyone had enough to eat, always keeping an eye on Usayd. After an hour or so, Aadil, still smoking one of his dark-black cigars, directed the conversation to business. He asked Usayd if he had any thoughts on what would constitute an effective and dramatic terrorist attack on the United States. Aadil stressed that the same three criteria of the previous terrorist plan was still in effect; the attack had to be simple, doable and symbolic.

Usayd cleared his throat as he rose to his feet. He stood ramrod straight, accentuating his six foot plus frame. His eyes casually scanned his audience as he began to speak. Usayd told everyone he assumed he was being called back to Arzew from the Afghanistan battlefield to develop some kind of terrorist attack. Therefore he had indeed given the matter plenty of thought. He had three suggestions for the triumvirate to review, but he personally had already decided on a course of action. But, of course, it was up to the triumvirate to make the final decision. First of all, Usayd said, they could use parasitical devices attached to the bilge keels of ships. These parasitical devices, more commonly called "torpedoes", were plastic pipes usually six inches in diameter and ten feet long, capped at both ends. The pipes were attached to the bilge keels (fins protruding from the side of ships beneath the waterline to help prevent the ship from excessively rolling) of unsuspecting ships by divers using large C-clamps. Inside the pipes were enough explosives to blow a big hole in the side of the ship, easily sinking the vessel with the associated catastrophic results. Death and environmental and psychological damage would be ensured.

These "torpedoes" could be affixed to the bilge keels of vessels load-ing petroleum products in the local harbor of Arzew. Acquiring explo-sives and finding divers to perform the task would be easy. Exploding the devices in foreign ports would be accomplished by remote firing devices. Colombian drug cartels had been successfully using this method for years to introduce cocaine into the United States. The only difference, they used divers to recover the cocaine once the ship arrived into the United States. Usayd could tell by the look in their eyes that Aadil and the others liked this idea. However, Usayd went on to explain, there were drawbacks to this plan. Usually they would know the destination of a ship loading in the port of Arzew. If a ship was loading a cargo of petroleum for the United States, they would attach a "torpedo" to the bilge keel. However, ships would often be diverted from their original port of destination. While at sea, captains would be notified by the owners of a change in orders. Instead of a port in the States, the ship could be diverted to Europe, Asia or someplace else. Consequently, they would have a ship sailing around on the high seas with their explosives attached to her bottom. It could be months, if not longer, before the ship sailed into an American port. In the interim, the C-clamps could loosen compromising the integrity of the "torpedo."

Usayd recounted a story about a ship sailing from Maracaibo, Ven-ezuela to Miami, Florida. While passing through the Windward Passage, the ship ran into some rough seas. The seas were pounding the vessel from dead ahead. Although it was a rough and uncomfortable ride, the ship was never in any danger. Off the coast of Florida, as they were approaching the outer harbor of Miami, the mate on watch heard an unusual banging from somewhere down below. He sent several seamen to investigate, but they couldn't find anything. After consulting with the captain, they deter-mined the noise had to be coming from the outside of the hull. They had absolutely no idea what could be making this noise, but once they reached port they would have a diver investigate. When the ship arrived at their assigned pier at Dodge Island, they saw a dive team standing by on the dock. As soon as the ship was secured, the dive team came onboard and began preparations for a dive. Within an hour a diver was in the water.

After roughly forty-five minutes, the diver surfaced off the port beam of the ship. In his possession was a ten foot section of PVC plastic pipe, six inches in diameter. The crew of the tanker threw the diver a line. Once the diver secured the line to the pipe, they hauled it on deck. Becoming suspicious, the captain ordered everyone away. He told the mate to call the port authorities and ask them to respond to the ship.

Within five minutes, Miami CET (Contraband Enforcement Team) was onboard. These individuals are highly trained United States Customs Inspectors dedicated to enforce the drug laws of the United States. Once they saw the pipe, the inspectors knew what was going on. They removed the cap at one end of the pipe. Sure enough, their suspicions were correct. The pipe contained over fifty pounds of almost pure cocaine. After interviewing the captain, they realized what happened. The pipe was a "torpedo" that was affixed to the bilge keel of the ship by divers while she was loading in Maracaibo. They must not have tightened the C-clamps properly, because they worked loose when the ship hit the heavy weather on the way to Miami. One of the clamps was actually missing, leaving the pipe dangling from the bilge keel. As the ship sailed through the ocean, the motion of the water rushing by the hull kept banging the pipe against the ship. Although they were lucky this time, sadly most "torpedoes" arrive successfully at their destination.

Usayd told the triumvirate this story to balance out his presentation. "Torpedoes" did work, but there was an element of risk. The ship used in his illustration only had to sail from Venezuela to Florida, a relatively short distance. Could a "torpedo" survive a sea passage in the North Atlantic, especially in the notoriously bad weather experienced in winter crossings? Also, what would they do if the ship was diverted to another port? As Usayd left this question dangling with the triumvirate, he hit them with another possible problem. Who would they have on the other end to ignite these "torpedoes" full of explosives? Wouldn't this cause a logistical nightmare? After 9/11, the United States really tightened up their immigration policy. Would it be possible to place enough people in the States to accomplish the mission? Suddenly, the gleam in their eyes began to fade. They realized "torpedoes", although it sounded like a good idea, might not be as feasible as they first thought. Aadil silently chuckled to himself as he stared at Usayd. He knew he'd made the right decision when he called Usayd back from the Afghanistan front. There was nobody better than him.

After a short bathroom break, Usayd proceeded to the second option—swallowing/packing explosives. "Swallowers" and "packers" were a phenomenon of the last quarter of the twentieth century, Usayd told Aadil, Mubid and Sabir. Aadil stoically listened to Usayd while Mubid and Sabir squirmed in their seats. *What the hell are swallowers and packers? They thought.* Usayd told his audience that the science of swallowing and packing drugs was perfected by the Nigerians and Ghanaians of northwest Africa. Surely citizens of other countries had their share of swallowers and packers, but Nigerian and Ghanaians perfected the process. Mules, the name given to people who swallowed or packed the drugs, actually had to be trained on the intricacies of the process. Usayd told them because he didn't think swallowing explosives was a viable option for their plans; he wouldn't go into all the details.

However, packing was a different story. In the past, it was not uncommon for packers to vaginally or anally insert three to five ounces of drugs. This fact was well documented by countless stories on TV news and newspapers all around the world. U.S.Customs had a plethora of experience with packers. So, Usayd rhetorically asked, what prevented them from putting explosive-packing suicide bombers on planes? There wasn't a body scanner or metal detector in existence that could detect a passenger carrying explosives in one of their body cavities. All three members of the triumvirate were intrigued by what Usayd was telling them—including the usually staid Aadil. Sameenah was standing in the doorway listening. She gave Usayd a broad smile and a cute wink of the eye. Aadil caught Sameenah out the corner of his eye. Finally, he thought, Sameenah has found a bright, intelligent man that seemed to deeply care for her.

Usayd sipped from his glass of water and continued. He said that once the suicide-bomber was on the plane, all he had to do was sit back and act like any other passenger. Once the plane was in mid-flight, he would visit the bathroom at the rear of the plane. Locked in the bathroom, he could remove the explosives from the body cavity. Inside the explosive would be a small blasting cap and a short wire. When the time came, all he had to do was connect the wire to a dedicated connection on the cell phone; pressing a special code would cause the phone to ring, igniting the blasting cap which in turn would ignite the explosive. Strategically placed against the outside wall of the bathroom, the explosion would blow a huge hole in the plane. Most likely critical cables and controls would also be severed, rendering the plane uncontrollable. The likelihood the plane would plummet to the ground was great. When the flight was over American territory—hopefully a major city—is when he should blow the explosive. This way, not only would he take down the plane, but countless people on the ground would die also.

They were stunned with this scenario. Taking down a plane over a major American city? Who could ask for anything better? But, as usual, there were drawbacks to the plan. Could they find enough volunteers to carry out this suicide mission? Could the people who did volunteer complete the training? What were their chances of successfully navigating through airport security? Would they hold up under the expected intense interrogation or would they fall apart and divulge sensitive information, compromising the entire project. What if they hesitated at the last minute? These were all valid questions that Usayd asked. The triumvirate didn't have any answers. All of a sudden, the perfect terrorist scenario fizzled before their eyes. Indeed, there were serious concerns with this scenario that appeared to be overwhelming. Now they understood why Usayd didn't like this second plan. They sat patiently, eagerly waiting to hear the plan Usayd did endorse. But, they would have to wait a bit longer. Samenah insisted they take a break for lunch and nobody was about to argue with her.

After the lunch break, they got back to business. Everyone wanted to hear all about the third scenario, Usayd's first choice. Usayd began by describing some of his experiences fighting in the mountains of Afghanistan. He held the soldiers he fought with—and against—in high regard. Not only was the fighting intense at times, but the conditions were brutal. Most of Usayd's fighting was up in the mountains at high elevation. The weather was often cold, windy and snowy. He grew close to most of the soldiers he fought with, but especially a Pakistani named Kheazai. As in all armies of the world, nicknames are often used to address each other.

Usayd never knew why, but Kheazai's nickname was "Sleazy." The name couldn't be further from the truth in this instance. "Sleazy" was an honorable and brave soldier. He never slacked off and always volunteered for the riskiest assignments. As they fought for months alongside each other, a bond formed between the two of them. They enjoyed each others company and were constant companions. One day "Sleazy" told Usayd he was going home, he was leaving the battlefields of Afghanistan. Usayd was devastated; he was losing his closest friend. Although Usayd was devastated, he fully understood when "Sleazy" told him why he had to leave.

"Sleazy" was born in Islamabad, Pakistan, but at an early age his family immigrated to Frankfurt, Germany. His father found work at a trucking company on the outskirts of town, a place called Bad Homburg. Eventually, after working in the trade for fifteen years, his father and uncle opened their own freight terminal. They operated a huge warehouse and had a fleet of trucks. Primarily, their business was international. People who wanted to ship freight overseas came to them. At the warehouse, they would consolidate several different shipments going to the same country into one big forty foot sea container. The United States, Australia and Canada were the most common destinations. Once they had a full container, they trucked the container to a seaport for exportation—usually Antwerp, Belgium.

Business was brisk and they were doing quite well. However, "Sleazy's" father's health was deteriorating. Years of smoking three packs of cigarettes a day had caught up to him. He was suffering from emphysema and couldn't work anymore. Consequently, they needed help running the business and wanted "Sleazy" to come home and lend a hand. "Sleazy" had no choice but to return. However, the fire was still burning in the pit of his stomach. If he ever had a chance to fight and kill the infidels from the west, he'd jump at the opportunity.

This brought Usayd to the crux of his story. His friend, "Sleazy", had intimate knowledge on how international cargo was transported. Better still, he controlled a small segment of this process. He had unfettered access to the cargo after the shipper dropped the freight off at his warehouse. He could manipulate the cargo any way he wanted without anyone knowing. Simply put, "Sleazy" could slip something in cargo destined for overseas without being detected. Drugs, money, explosives or even a dirty bomb were within the realm of possibility. Usayd was getting the triumvirates attention; they were riveted on his every word.

Then Usayd told them the best news yet. "Sleazy" had a cousin who lived in Boston, Massachusetts. This cousin was in the same type of business as "Sleazy." He was the lead warehouseman in a cargo terminal on the Boston waterfront. Only in America they called them container freight stations (CFS). The point Usayd was making in case someone didn't understand, "Sleazy" could arrange for legitimate cargo to be shipped from his warehouse in Bad Homburg, Germany to his cousin's warehouse in Boston, Massachusetts. They could exploit the situation by putting something in this legitimate cargo that only they had access to. Usayd's audience was transfixed. They had already dismissed the first two options and were focused on Usayd's third option. The possibilities were boundless. If they did everything like they should, it was possible to utilize "Sleazy" and his cousin's positions in the cargo business to introduce into America anything they wanted—like a dirty bomb!

As in the first two options, they waited to hear about the drawbacks of this plan, but there really weren't any. If Usayd was able to get his hands on a dirty bomb, he was sure he could clandestinely ship it from Germany to the United States undetected using "Sleazy" and his cousin as his contacts. Exhaustive planning, tight security and utmost secrecy would be required to ensure success, but Usayd knew they could pull it off. He looked around the room and saw a lot of consensus. Usayd's presentation had made converts out of them all. Aadil was the first to speak. "Usayd," he said, "finally, I think we have a plan that will work." Sabir, quiet most of the day broke his silence, "Now young man," he said, "we want you to go home and get some rest. Go home, have something to eat and go to bed. We'll talk more tomorrow." Usayd thanked them, smiled and left the room. Sameenah was waiting for him with outstretched arms. They hugged, she whispered something in his ear and then they were gone. They all had had a long day.

PART II

CHAPTER SEVENTEEN

Boston, Massachusetts has some of the finest law enforcement personnel in the entire country. Three agencies in particular were led and staffed by highly motivated personnel. The U.S. Customs Port Director in Boston was Sebastian Auvil. He was born in 1949 in Parsons, West Virginia. His father was a lawyer and then a judge, but he grew up in a middle class, blue collar environment. There were no airs in the Auvil home. If you wanted something you worked for it, plain and simple. Auvil attended public schools in Parsons, graduating from Parson High in 1967. After a semester of lackluster performance at West Virginia State, he dropped out of school and enlisted in the United States Army. He scored high on the battery of aptitude tests the army gave at indoctrination and was offered any job he wanted. Without hesitation, Auvil picked the infantry. He came from a family with a long history of military service, so picking the infantry seemed natural to him. After basic training in Fort Dix, New Jersey, Auvil was shipped off to the swamps of southern Georgia for jungle training. His training company spent most of their time in the field learning the art of war. After two months of exhaustive and grueling training, almost his entire company received orders for Vietnam.

Auvil survived the horrors of war, but came back a changed man. He stumbled around for a few years working at several different jobs, eventually marrying and having three kids. But his life seemed so different from his peers. Something was missing. He couldn't put his finger on the problem, but he knew it was there. He wasn't sure why, but one day he decided to apply for a job with U.S. Customs. To his astonishment, they hired him. Within a month, he found himself back training in Georgia. He was a member of Basic Customs Inspector class 414. After graduation, Auvil was assigned to the southwest border. He roamed the deserts of Arizona and Texas for several years. He applied himself and studied hard for promotional tests. Gradually he ascended to the upper ranks of management. His assignments varied and required frequent moves. Family life suffered and eventually a divorce was the only option. In the spring of 2004, Auvil was offered the coveted job of Port Director in Boston, Massachusetts. He accepted the offer and began packing his bags—once again. His adventure in Boston was about to begin.

After acquainting himself with his staff, Auvil ordered a threat assessment for the Port of Boston and the surrounding area. While personnel were involved in this task, he went out into the field to meet the troops on the front line. He knew these men and women were the backbone of the service. If you treated them well and with much deserved respect, they would more than reciprocate. Informally, he asked the troops how everything was going. Most of the responses were positive, but a few malcontents blew off some steam. Auvil always was able to deftly handle any situation that crossed his path. One time an inspector at the airport complained about the people working in the regional office. Auvil temporarily transferred the inspector to the office he was complaining about. Within a few weeks the inspector was back working at the airport; he never again complained about the regional office.

He was always solicitous of people's opinions and ideas. When he asked the troops where they thought the highest threat of a terrorist attack might occur, they said the seaport. They felt that since 9/11, the increase in security in the airport environment had been sufficient to thwart another terrorist attack. However, the seaport was different. According to the troops, there were still major holes in security in the seaport environment, especially regarding sea containers. They told Auvil the volume of sea containers imported into the Port of Boston was overwhelming the force that staffed the seaport. They thought something should be done about this obvious threat. Auvil thanked the troops for their opinions and promised them he would look further into the matter.

About a week after Auvil's airport visit, the staff assigned to conduct the threat assessment for the Port of Boston had completed their assignment. Their briefing to Auvil was exhaustive. According to their report, the whole seaport was at risk. On their list of potential areas of concern were: the numerous cruise ships arriving at the Black Falcon passenger terminal in South Boston; the Liquefied Natural Gas ships arriving in the port every week, and the countless tankers coming into the port carrying hundreds of thousands of barrels of petroleum products. Auvil was taken aback by their report, but they weren't finished. They saved the worst for the last. Their concern for the safety and integrity of the thousands of sea containers that passed through the port on a daily basis took priority over all their other concerns. What they had determined after a week of intense work matched what was told to him last week by the group of inspectors in his impromptu meeting at the airport. Obviously there was a problem concerning sea containers. Now that the problem was identified, he was determined to find a solution.

Sebastian Auvil's counterpart in Boston for the United States Coast Guard was Captain John Lynch, Captain of the Port. Captain Lynch's upbringing was similar to Sebastian Auvil's. Lynch was born in 1950 in New London, Connecticut. His father was a Chief Torpedo man in the United States Navy assigned to a submarine stationed in New London. His father had been in the Navy for almost fifteen years when John was born. Having seen a lot of action in WWII (his sub, the Redfish, had sunk two Japanese carriers) he knew the value of discipline. This trait he applied not only on subs, but at home. Lynch and his siblings had best behave and be respectful or they would incur their father's wrath. After twenty years of faithful service, Lynch's father retired from the Navy. A week after retirement, he joined the civilian work force at the submarine base in New London.

John Lynch and his brothers and sister attended public schools in New London. When John was in the eighth grade, his class went on a field trip to the Coast Guard Academy, only a few miles from their school. John fell in love with the school. He was in awe of all the midshipmen walking swiftly from one building to another, stacks of books tucked under their arms. The field trip inspired John to study hard in school. One day, he told himself, he too would be a midshipman at the Academy. He excelled at New London High, taking advanced courses in the sciences and mathematics. Calculus, chemistry and physics were his favorite subjects, exactly what he would need at the academy. In the fall of 1966, when he was in the beginning of his senior year at New London High, John was conditionally accepted at the academy. If he kept his grades up and continued to play football and baseball, John would be accepted into the academy's class of 1971. John and his parents were ecstatic. Not only would he be receiving a free education, but he was staying close to home.

From the beginning, John loved every day at the academy. Academically, he excelled, ranking in the top ten percent of his class. Although a knee injury kept him off the gridiron, he was an able member of the sailing and baseball teams. In his junior year, John went on a two month cruise aboard one of the Coast Guard's 378 foot cutters. When he returned to the academy, he had his mind made up; he wanted to serve aboard cutters, "the big white ones." Because of his class standing upon graduation, John was able to get his first pick. He was assigned to the United States Coast Guard Cutter Morgenthau, a 378 foot cutter out of Kodiak, Alaska.

For the next thirty years John spent the majority of his time at sea, interrupted by only a few brief shore assignments and a two-year stint at Harvard for an advanced degree in public policy and administration. In the late fall of 2003, the Commandant of the Coast Guard called John and asked him for a personal favor. He wanted John to come ashore and take the Captain of the Port job in Boston. The mayor's office was causing a big stir about the LNG (liquefied natural gas) ship transiting Boston Harbor and the Admiral needed a good man to deal with the sensitive political situation. John didn't want the job, but when the commandant asked you to do him a personal favor you didn't really have a choice. The fact that the commandant promised there might be a promotion to admiral in the not too distant future lessened the pain.

As soon as John took over in Boston, he started making changes. First of all, to the commandant's delight, he diffused the volatile atmosphere with the mayor's office. John invited the mayor to dine with him at the Coast Guard base in the North End. After eating, John took the mayor and his entourage for a boat ride in Boston Harbor. John showed the mayor everything the Coast Guard had implemented to lessen the danger when an LNG transited the harbor. The mayor was impressed with John's presentation and felt more comfortable about the LNG passing through the waters of Boston Harbor; however, he vowed to continue his efforts to ban all LNG arrivals into the port. But, the mayor was appreciative of John's efforts and assured John he'd work with him in a constructive manner in order to provide maximum safety for the citizens of Boston and the surrounding towns.

John's next major initiative was an attempt to foster better working relationships with his sister agencies, specifically the FBI, Customs and the Massachusetts State Police. After numerous meetings, John felt he was making headway, but the feeling of "turf mentality" still existed, although not as widespread as in the past. U.S.Customs and the State Police were the most receptive to working together. In fact, a decision was made to open an office at the Coast Guard Base manned by representatives from all three agencies. The FBI declined to participate. Supposedly there was an issue about security. John was disappointed, but he was satisfied with the headway he did make. He hoped in the future he could convince not only the FBI, but other agencies, to participate in this joint venture.

About six months after John became Captain of the Port, just about the same time Sebastian Auvil was appointed Port Director for Boston Customs, Major Leo Williamson took command of Troop F of the Massachusetts State Police located at Logan Airport. The major had over thirty years on the job and was a highly decorated trooper. Like Auvil, Williamson was a Vietnam Veteran, having served with the 101st Airborne. When he was discharged from the army in 1970, he took advantage of the GI Bill and attended school at the University of Massachusetts/Boston. While he was studying history in school, Williamson took every civil service test possible. He preferred a job on a police department, but knew he'd take whatever job that came along.

In addition to going to school and taking civil service tests, Williamson worked part-time on one of the many party boats in Boston harbor. He liked this job because it was on the water and he got to meet a lot of pretty young ladies. Eventually, he received a call from the State Police. He was selected to attend the next class of state police recruits that was scheduled to begin in the fall of 1973. Williamson had to make a choice. If he accepted the job, he'd have to drop out of college. He didn't want to do that because he loved school, but if he declined the job offer, he might never be asked again. After consulting with his father, a retired longshore-man, Williamson decided to take the job. He never regretted the decision.

The six months of training at the State Police Academy was pure hell. He swore some of the drill instructors were trying to kill him. From early morning to late at night they were kept on the move. Usually the first half of the day was dedicated to physical activities. Williamson had been through jungle training and jump school in the army, so he was prepared for the academy, but many weren't. The first week at least ten recruits quit. As the training progressed, more and more dropped out. Although physically demanding, the academy equally demanded every recruit be mentally tough. The drill instructors posed impossible problems to the recruits, just to see how they reacted. Many crumbled under the pressure. The academic requirements were also demanding. Not only did the recruits have to learn all the laws that they were going to enforce, but how to apply them in a common sense manner.

Midway through the training Williamson began to excel. The drill instructors noted his leadership skills and realized he was going to be a top notch trooper. What really impressed the drill instructors was how Williamson always tried to help his fellow recruits. On long arduous runs, Williamson often fell back to help the last cadet make it over the finish line. While studying for an upcoming exam, he would tutor others who were having a hard time. Williamson always gave of himself. It was never about him, but about the entire class.

After six months of intense training, graduation was days away. The entire academy staff met and evaluated the class. Over fifty percent had dropped out or were kicked out. Unanimously, they picked Williamson as the outstanding recruit. Academically and physically, he was far above all the others. On a clear, crisp afternoon in the spring of 1974, Williamson graduated from the academy. The hell was finally over. He was assigned to the night shift at the Topsfield barracks. For the next three months he would ride with a veteran trooper. After that, he would patrol the highways of northeastern Massachusetts in his own assigned cruiser.

After a couple of years working out of the Topsfield barracks, Williamson transferred to the Essex County District Attorney's office as a fledgling detective. For the next twenty five years Williamson worked on some of the biggest criminal cases in the Commonwealth. Working with the Drug Enforcement Administration and United States Customs, he was involved in some huge drug busts. Time consuming surveillances and wire taps were his specialty. He was methodical, patient and had a sixth sense on what the bad guys were up to. Everyone who ever worked with him enjoyed the experience. As he developed into a veteran trooper, Williamson began to advance in rank. He was promoted to sergeant and then lieutenant. As a lieutenant, he was assigned to the barracks on Cape Cod as a shift commander. He enjoyed working with the younger troopers, but didn't like responding to all the accidents on the highways. He yearned for the days when he chased drug dealers through the neighborhoods of Boston and Lawrence.

A promotion to Captain sent him to the Foxborough Barracks as the commanding officer. At the time, the Foxborough barracks wasn't performing as well as the other barracks throughout the state. This would soon change under his leadership. Within a year traffic fatalities had plummeted and drug arrests had skyrocketed in his area of responsibility. He developed excellent working relationships with the local police departments. Jointly, they organized outreach programs and visited all the local schools at least twice a year. Because of his hard work, Williamson was recognized by the community leaders on several different occasions. After leading the Foxborough Barracks for two years, Williamson was once again recognized by his superiors. He was promoted to the rank of major and given command of Troop F, Logan Airport. The stars were lining up perfectly.

CHAPTER EIGHTEEN

During the first six months of 2004, Coast Guard intelligence had been receiving unconfirmed reports from numerous sources regarding possible terrorist activity in the Boston area. At the admiral's weekly briefing, concern was raised that not enough attention was being given to these reports. The admiral agreed and ordered Captain Lynch to convene a meeting of all the different federal, state and local law enforcement agencies in the Boston area. The admiral wanted to throw a large net out to see what he could catch. After a lot of work by Captain Lynch and his staff, a June meeting was scheduled. At least fifty different agencies were expected to attend.

The meeting was scheduled to convene at 8:00 am Friday at the Coast Guard Base in Boston. Because parking was restricted due to construction, the Coast Guard asked if attendees could car pool or take public transportation. Needless to say, no one paid attention to the Coast Guard's request and a traffic logjam ensued. At 8:30am, a half hour after the scheduled start, people were still streaming into the meeting hall. While they waited for the meeting to start, most grabbed a cup of coffee. Sebastian Auvil was on his second cup when Major Williamson walked up and introduced himself. The two chatted for a few minutes when one of them mentioned being in the service. To their astonishment, both had served in Viet Nam with the U.S.Army, Auvil with the Americal Division and Williamson with the 101st Airborne. Not only that, they were both infantry and they had both fought in the Que Son Valley, a deadly area of mountains between DaNang and the Laotian border. Immediately a bond developed between the two. They had both risked their lives in a faraway land over thirty years ago; now they were standing side by side drinking coffee at a Coast Guard base.

As the two were engrossed in conversation, Captain Lynch was attempting to get the meeting underway. Over the microphone, he asked everyone to take their seats. Auvil and Williamson complied. They walked over to a row of folding chairs and took the first two seats. As the others were slowly finding a place to sit, they continued their conversation in a low voice. Finally, Captain Lynch brought the crowd to order. Williamson and Auvil stopped talking and directed their attention to the captain; they both knew they'd be continuing their conversation later, probably over a couple of cold beers in the officer's club.

The meeting finally started about 9:00 am and was over just before noon. As Captain Lynch said, the purpose of the meeting wasn't to talk about specifics. He only wanted to get everyone together and talk generalities. Based on this meeting and discussing what areas of interest people had, the captain was going to organize smaller groups that could meet on their own and report back to him. As usual, some people were more interested than others. However, by the end of the meeting, Captain Lynch was satisfied with the results. He had penciled in six areas of concern with at least six names assigned to each area. Once he returned to his office, he would polish up the list and then email a copy to all participants. Not bad for an initial meeting.

As the meeting broke up, Leo Williamson and Sebastian Auvil stood off to the side and continued their previous conversation. They started to discuss going to lunch when Captain Lynch walked by. The captain smiled and said, "Looks to me as if you two are making plans to get in some trouble." They all started to laugh. Sebastian asked Captain Lynch where in the area he would recommend having lunch. The captain thought for a second and said, "Depends on what you want to eat and how much you want to spend. If you like shrimp scampi, follow me. I'm on my way to the officer's mess and I'd enjoy your company. I'll even buy." Leo and Sebastian smiled and nodded their heads. "Sounds good to us," Leo said, as they followed the captain down the hallway.

The three of them talked throughout the meal. It was as if they were old buddies that hadn't seen each other in years. As they were discussing their backgrounds, Leo told the captain that he and Sebastian had both been in the army and fought in the same area of Viet Nam at slightly different times. When the captain learned that Leo and Sebastian had fought in the area west of Danang called the Que Son valley, a broad smile crossed his face. "Guys," he said, "you're not going to believe this, but I too was near Danang but on a ship. I was stationed on the cutter Hamilton, a 378 footer out of Boston. We used to steam up and down the Viet Nam coast providing naval gunfire for the infantry. You guys were a little earlier than me and you were on the ground, but I was there also." None of them could believe that they all had served their country so many years ago at virtually the same place. It was as if some outside force had arranged this chance meeting between the three of them.

They were almost done eating, when an officer interrupted. The commandant had called looking for the captain and wanted a call back as soon as possible. The captain rose, wiped his mouth with his napkin and dropped the napkin on his plate. "Well guys," he said, "I can't tell you how much I've enjoyed myself. To have lunch with a couple of old warriors was indeed a pleasure. Thank you." He started to leave and then turned back and said, "Guys, do you mind if I call you next week? I'd like to get together again and maybe form some kind of working group comprising all three agencies." Leo spoke first, "Absolutely, John, I am sure both Sebastian and I would love that." Leo turned to Sebastian as he was talking. Sebastian's head was nodding up and down. "Thanks," the captain said. He turned and started walking away until Sebastian's voice stopped him. "By the way, John," Sebastian said, "you're wrong. It's three old warriors." A lump formed in the captain's throat. He didn't say anything, he couldn't. He swallowed hard, waved and walked away.

As promised, John called the following week. The first call went out to Sebastian. John suggested they get together for lunch that Friday. After checking his calendar, Sebastian said he was free. John suggested they meet at noon at the No Name Restaurant. Sebastian, not being from Boston, didn't realize the No Name Restaurant was the actual name of a restaurant. The ensuing conversation was pretty comical. "That's fine, John," Sebastian said, "where shall we meet?" Taken aback a bit, John repeated himself. "I said the No Name Restaurant. What are you going deaf?" Sebastian was confused. "Okay, where do I find this no name restaurant?" he asked quizzically. "Down the fucking fish pier, where the fuck else?" John said.

Then John realized Sebastian, being an out-of-towner, had never heard of the No Name Restaurant. He began to laugh when he realized the confusion. He explained to Sebastian that the name of the restaurant was really called the No Name Restaurant and it was located on the fish pier in South Boston. Now it was Sebastian's turn to bust ass. "How the fuck am I to know that a place called the No Name Restaurant is really the name of a restaurant. You people in Boston are really fucked up. You're so stupid you can't even think up a proper name for a restaurant." They both were laughing when John said, "Hey Sebastian, fuck you. See you then and by the way, you're buying." He hung up the phone, laughing at the ridiculous conversation.

John's next call was to Leo over at Logan Airport. Leo picked up the phone after the first ring. He told John he'd be delighted to have lunch with them on Friday. When John told Leo about his previous conversation with Sebastian, Leo started to laugh and said, "What did you expect, John? Sebastian is a fucking hick from the hills of West Virginia." They both started laughing. Leo said, "Okay, I have to run. I'll see you guys Friday. Let's hope the hick can find the place."

CHAPTER NINETEEN

The three of them arrived in the parking lot within minutes of each other. Leo pulled up in his shiny, black unmarked cruiser with an array of tiny antennas on the roof. Sebastian was right behind him, driving a white van with the name "U.S.Customs" broadly displayed in blue letters on both sides of the vehicle. John arrived seconds later. He was sitting in the back of a shiny new black Mercury Marquis, his aide driving. When the vehicle stopped, the aide jumped out of the car and opened John's door. As John climbed out of the back seat, he eyed the two of them staring at him. He knew what was coming. Leo and Sebastian waited until the aide jumped back in the vehicle and drove away. Then they let lose. "Are you shitting me?" Leo said. "Can't you fucking drive yourself?" Sebastian chimed in. John felt embarrassed and didn't have a rebuttal. He didn't bother trying. All he could think of was to change the venue. "Fuck you guys," he said. "Stand around a parking lot with your head up your ass if you want. Me, I'm going to go eat." He started walking towards the restaurant. There was a lot of muttering under their breaths as they followed.

As he walked up the long flight of stairs to the dining room, Sebastian gawked at all the pictures of famous people hanging on the walls: politicians, movie stars, world leaders, athletes. Gus, the owner of the No Name, was in each picture along with the celebrity. "Holy mackerel," Sebastian said to no one in particular, "this guy knows everyone." As they reached the landing on the second floor, Nick, one of the waiters, rushed up to them. "Major Leo," he said, "how nice to see you again. Please come in." "Can Nick sit you at a fine table by the window?" he asked. As Nick escorted them to their table he chattered nonstop. He wanted to know who Leo's friends were and where were they from. Nick made Sebastian and John feel right at home.

As they sat at their window table, Nick passed out greased stained menus. Sebastian rested his elbows on the table to read the menu and almost caused a catastrophe. The legs of the table sat unevenly on the floor. The pressure from Sebastian's elbows caused the table to flip to one side. If it wasn't for Leo's fast reaction, the full pitcher of ice water sitting in front of him would have wound up in his lap. Nick sheepishly laughed saying, "Be careful of the tables, some of them aren't too steady on their feet." They all laughed.

Nick took their orders and said he'd be back in a flash. True to his word, Nick was back within seconds bearing a big plate of garlic bread and three bowls of steaming fish chowder. John was about to protest, because none of them had ordered chowder, when he saw Leo raise his hands palm outwards. "Not to worry guys," he said, "this is standard treatment every time I come in here." Leo went on to explain that the restaurant loved to see police and other public officials eat at the No Name. It was as if their presence was giving an official stamp of approval to the place. The No Name especially loved to see the state police come in. They were the local law enforcement agency policing the piers and would always respond immediately if there was any trouble at the restaurant. Gus, the owner, made sure his staff took care of them because he never knew when he'd need their assistance. He looked at it sort of like an insurance policy, although Leo said they would respond in the same manner no matter what kind of treatment they received.

While waiting for their meal, Leo gave Sebastian a tour of the harbor from the vantage point of their table. First there was the airport across the harbor, planes landing on runway 4R and 4L every couple of minutes. Leo explained how Logan Airport was actually made from three islands: Bird, Apple and Governor. All three islands, but especially Governors, were razed when the airport was built. Additionally, thousands of trucks over a period of years hauled tons of fill to complete the process of building a top-notch airport. John had never heard this story and was impressed with Leo's knowledge. Going to the east, Leo pointed out several lighthouses that were visible on the horizon. First there was Deer Island Lighthouse, now barely worthy of the name. The old structure was torn down and replaced by a small metal conical-shaped structure only half the original size. Deer Island marked the northern entrance to Boston Harbor.

Traveling along in an easterly direction, marking the southern entrance to the harbor, was Long Island Light. Perched atop a hill at the edge of Long Island, Long Island Light was still in its original condition. In between Deer Island and Long Island Light, but further out to sea, was Boston Light, the oldest lighthouse in the country and the only one still manned; the rest of the lighthouses being automated by the Coast Guard to save manpower and money. Leo explained how Boston Light was burned to the ground by the British when they evacuated the port of Boston on March 17, 1776. Both Sebastian and John were appreciative of Leo's tour. Sebastian, being a new guy on the block, knew nothing of Boston's maritime history. He was fascinated listening to Leo's wide breadth of knowledge of the local area.

John was a bit embarrassed because Leo was even teaching him a thing or two. Continuing his tour, Leo pointed out where Anchorage #1 and #2 were located and what their significance were. Anchorage #1, located inside the harbor close to the airport, was used exclusively to anchor small ships and barges while they waited for a pier to free up. Anchorage #2 was located further out by Deer Island Light. Big ocean-going ships, usually tankers, anchored there because their draft was too deep to enter the harbor. They would have to discharge (lighter) part of their cargo into barges, decreasing their draft, before they could proceed into the inner harbor. While Leo was elaborating on the lightering process, Nick arrived with their food. As interesting as the tour was, it would have to wait. The scallops and full-bellied clams had priority.

Leo and John were used to eating seafood, but not Sebastian. Obviously, he had eaten seafood before in his travels, but not like the seafood the No Name served. Sebastian especially liked the scallops dunked in the rich creamy tartar sauce. Eating full-bellied clams were also a special treat for him. He had had clam strips before, but never clams with bellies. He thought they were delicious. As Sebastian stuffed himself, Leo and John looked on with awe. They couldn't believe how much he was eating. Obviously Sebastian didn't know they always serve you more than you can eat at the No Name, but this time maybe they didn't. Once they were finally done eating, Nick cleared the table and offered them dessert. They all passed, even Sebastian. After paying the bill (yes, Sebastian paid) they walked outside to their cars. It was still early in the afternoon and none of them had anything pressing to do, so they decided to drive over to the state police office at Black Falcon Terminal to have a talk.

Black Falcon Terminal is located on the Reserved Channel opposite the Conley Container Yard. Hundreds of passenger vessels visit Black Falcon every year, mostly during the summer and fall months. In the days of WWII, thousands of troops left for the European battlefields from here when it was called the Boston Army Base. In the ensuing years, the Army Base evolved into a light commercial zone with many art studios. The transition didn't go as smoothly as the city officials hoped. There were always money problems and conflicts between competing interests, but eventually the area turned into a vibrant section of the waterfront. Recently, a few local breweries opened outdoor cafes on the site; offering beer drinkers a pleasant venue to drink their favorite beer. Today, thousands of people flock to the area to enjoy the usually sunny summer days with the cool, clean air blowing in from the sea. This was the destination for Leo, John and Sebastian, but there wasn't going to be any fun in the sun for them. It was time to get down to business and develop a good strategy to protect the city of Boston from any possible terrorist attack.

CHAPTER TWENTY

About the same time Usayd was weaving his way back home to Algeria from the Afghanistan front, Sebastian, John and Leo, some of Boston's finest, were meeting at the Black Falcon Terminal. Although none of them had been directly involved in the attempted terrorist attack on New England the previous year, they had all studied the scenarios and had learned many important lessons. First of all, just about everything was subject to an attack. Obviously Logan Airport was of prime concern, but measures were already underway to strengthen security there, as in all the airports throughout the country. It was the seaport they were concerned about and they wanted to give their undivided attention to it.

From studying last year's failed terrorist attempt in Portland, Maine, they knew the terrorists were targeting large ocean-going tankers carrying upwards of 250,000 barrels of petroleum products—aviation gas, #2 home heating oil and gasoline for motor vehicles. Sinking a loaded tanker in the harbor would devastate the local ecology, have a shattering effect on the local economy and psychologically numb the community. Boston had tankers entering and leaving the harbor on almost a daily basis. The risk was high.

In Bar Harbor, Maine the terrorists attempted two acts of violence. First, they tried to hijack the ferry running to Nova Scotia. If the hijacking was successful, their plans were to ram the ferry into the side of a passenger ship anchored in Bar Harbor. If they succeeded, loss of life would have been high. The adverse economic effect on the cruise line industry would be catastrophic. Boston had ferry boats transiting the harbor by day and night. Hundreds of passenger ships visited the city yearly. Again, the risk was high.

In Portsmouth, New Hampshire, terrorists attempted to hijack an LPG (liquefied petroleum gas) ship and ram it into a nuclear submarine moored at the Portsmouth Naval Shipyard. Thankfully, the attempt was thwarted, but if successful, a nuclear holocaust was possible. Just the LPG blowing up on the Piscatagua River, in the middle of Portsmouth, would have resulted in a major loss of life. Boston had weekly arrivals of LNG (liquefied natural gas) ships, just as dangerous as LPG ships.

In Boston, there were three simultaneous terrorist attacks last year. Terrorists attempted to blow up a cruise ship by having a couple posing as passengers carry two suitcases loaded with plastic explosive onboard. The cruise ship was tied up less than one hundred feet from the state police office where they were holding their meeting. When Leo, John and Sebastian, realized this, the gravity of the situation really hit home. This wasn't a mock exercise they were conducting; it was the real deal. At the same time the couple were carrying explosives aboard the cruise ship, a runaway LNG was attempting to enter Boston Harbor. If it wasn't for the gallant efforts of the coast guard, Boston would have had an LNG ship blow up in the inner harbor with the resulting devastation and loss of life. In addition, a container ship was entering Boston Harbor destined for Conley Container Terminal. Fortunately, at the last moment, the coast guard and customs realized there were several high risk containers onboard. They diverted the container ship back to sea. Upon investigation, explosive-laden sea containers were found onboard and were offloaded at sea onto a barge. The barge carried the containers further out to sea where the state police safely blew them up.

From studying these past cases, Leo, John and Sebastian knew the situation was critical. The enemy was knocking on their front door and it was up to them to do something about this threat. Ignoring the threat wouldn't make it go away. The mood was somber in the state police office as the three of them contemplated the best course of action. Sebastian spoke first. He told his two companions that it was time for them to get innovative; they had to forget about all the old practices that were used. They had to come up with new and effective measures to counter the terrorist's plans. The old rule book just didn't work anymore. They had to write an entire new game plan; otherwise the bad guys would win and he would be damned if he'd let that happen. John and Leo agreed with Sebastian. They knew how critical the situation was and they knew it was up to them to figure something out which is why their superiors put them in the positions they were in. It was time to develop a global strategy that would knock the terrorists off course. The three of them wanted to develop a grand strategy that the rest of the country would want to emulate. They were excited to get to work and they were confident they could get it done.

As they were talking, John realized something that might be the key to all their plans. The three of them talked as if they were one unit, because they were. That was the secret! All the anti-terrorist efforts in the past had been conducted separately by numerous different agencies. Oh sure, they would all get together occasionally under one umbrella like the JTTF (joint terrorist task force) but their true allegiance always went back to their own agency and not to the task force. In John's mind, this mindset had to stop. The turf mentality handbook had to be burned and thrown away. If everyone came together and truly dedicated themselves to the task at hand, no terrorist plot would have a chance to succeed. They all knew how difficult that might be, so John suggested the three of them set an example for all others to follow. When the other agencies saw how successful they were, they'd want to jump on board. Leo had a broad grin on his face as he listened to John's sound advice. How simple and yet how true, he thought. He was willing to give it a try and he knew Sebastian would jump on board also.

Their plans were rather simple. They knew what threats lurked in the shadows of Boston Harbor by studying the terrorists past practices. Armed with this knowledge, they would attack these threats jointly. Teams would be set up with members from all three different agencies; customs, coast guard and state police. The forces would complement and not compete with each other. It was a novel idea, but they were sure it would work. After much discussion, four areas were deemed to be of highest concern: ship searches, container inspections, intelligence gathering and patrols on the water. Each agency had varying degrees of competency in each area. Team leaders would be designated and the entire operation would be supervised by the three of them. On paper their ideas looked good and they all were anxious to give it a try. As their initial plans developed, they would keep the practices that worked and discard the ones that didn't. Eventually they would have a grand strategy to address the terrorist threat at the Boston seaport.

Since they wanted their efforts to be intelligence driven, their first priority was to establish a sound and credible intelligence unit. All three agencies supplied three individuals each to staff this unit that they decided should be located at the coast guard base in the North End. The intelligence unit would spearhead what the other three units did. One of their functions was to assess the risk of every anticipated arrival in Boston Harbor. The unit would decide what ships should be boarded before she entered the port and what ships could be allowed in without a pre-inspection. This decision was usually based on where the ship was coming from, and if there was any derogatory information on any of the crew members. If the intelligence unit decided a ship should be boarded offshore, before she entered the port, they would contact the team leader of the ship search team. Once the ship search was completed, the team leader would complete the circle by informing the intelligence unit the results of the search.

The same procedure was set up for container examinations. The intelligence unit would review the paperwork for all inbound containers coming into the port. Based on country of origin and any derogatory information they might have—or simply a hunch—the intelligence unit would refer containers to be inspected to the team leader of the container inspection team. This team leader would utilize all available tools to ensure the container was safe before they released it into the commerce of the country. X-ray trucks, bomb sniffing dogs and a slew of inspectors were at his disposal for this purpose. Once again, after the inspection was completed, the team leader would inform the intelligence unit of the results.

The patrol was the fourth unit comprising their grand strategy. The patrol would act in concert with the intelligence unit, but would have more flexibility than the ship search or container units. Comprised mostly of coast guard patrol boats and supplemented by state police boats, their responsibility was to patrol Boston Harbor and the surrounding waters, looking for any suspicious activity. The officer in charge of each boat would communicate and coordinate their activities with the intelligence unit. Patrol was given a lot more flexibility than the other units because

it was assumed the officers in charge of the boats had intimate knowledge of the area waters. By letting them conduct random and sporadic
patrols, they might discover nefarious activity. However, they were always
answerable to the intelligence unit and would respond to their requests
in a timely fashion.

Overseeing the daily operation were four shift commanders, assuring
every shift would have someone in charge. Each agency would participate
in providing shift commanders. Finally, the three of them—Leo, John and
Sebastian—would be in charge of the entire operation. They all assumed
equal authority, equal direction and most importantly, equal responsibility.

CHAPTER TWENTY ONE

It wasn't long before this new strategy was put to the test. The intelligence unit became aware that an LNG ship coming from Algeria was due to arrive in the port within a few days. Algeria was considered to be a country less than friendly to the United States; however we needed their natural gas. Consequently, we had to let their ships into the port, but with stipulations. The team leader of the intelligence unit, an experienced United States Customs Inspector with over thirty years of maritime experience, decided they should board and search the LNG while she was still at sea. Based on all the recent developments and intelligence reports, this seemed to be the prudent course of action to take. After conferring with the shift commander, the decision was made; the ship search team was directed to board and search the LNG ship that was due to arrive in the port within the next couple of days.

Tuesday morning dawned bright and clear; the water of Boston Harbor appeared as a pane of glass, indicating not a wisp of wind, confirmed by the listless American flag hanging from the flagpole in the middle of the parking lot of the Coast Guard base. Perfect weather for a boarding at sea, thought John McDonough, team leader of the ship search team. John was a ten-year veteran of the United States Coast Guard. In those ten years, he had been stationed all over the country and on several ships. He had studied hard at his boatswain rate and had risen quickly through the ranks. He made the rank of Boatswain Mate First Class after only six years in the Coast Guard. Last May he took the service wide examination for chief. Just last week he received the results of the test, he scored high and was number forty-nine on the list. His promotion to chief was assured, probably within the next year.

John was proud of himself and attributed his success to hard work. He was pleased Captain Lynch picked him to be the team leader of the ship search team. Obviously, the captain had a lot of confidence in his ability to entrust him with such an important position. John was determined not to let the captain down. With any luck, he might be able to stay as team leader even after he made chief. He hoped so because he, his wife and three little girls had just relocated to Boston after having served three years in Alaska on a buoy tender. He and his wife wanted to give the girls a bit of stability in their lives. Besides, they were both from New England and their families lived in the area. They thought it would be nice if they could spend some time with them when John was off duty.

As John approached the small-boat pier, he could see the rest of the team gathered at the top of the gangway leading to the port quarter of the Flying Fish, an 87 foot coast guard patrol boat. There were four customs inspectors, four state troopers and two coast guardsmen. The ten of them, led by John, comprised the boarding team that was assigned to board the Aldebaran, the LNG ship due to arrive outside Boston Harbor at 10:00am. Lying in the water on the other side of the Flying Fish, John saw two small state police boats patiently waiting to get underway. On these two boats rode the state police dive team, led by Corporal Spellman. John strode up to the group and wished everyone good morning.

Once he determined that everyone was present, he directed the team to board the Flying Fish; it was time to get underway. Just as they were singling up their mooring lines, a state police cruiser with K-9 in big white letters stenciled on the side, sped up to the dock. Once stopped, the trooper climbed out of his vehicle. "Sorry I'm late," he yelled, "I was tied up with a bomb threat on a train in South Station." John McDonough didn't care if the trooper was a little late, he was happy to have the K-9 team along. They were a valuable asset to have when searching a ship, especially one as big as an LNG.

Once the K-9 team was safely onboard, the captain of the Flying Fish maneuvered his boat away from the dock. The state police backed their boats out of the way, allowing the Flying Fish some sea room. Once the Flying Fish was clear of the pier, the captain gradually brought her speed up to fifteen knots. At that speed, he estimated they would be on scene just as the Aldebaran was dropping her anchor in Broad Sound, the outer edge of Boston Harbor. As they sailed through the calm seas, with a state police boat on either side and slightly astern, the boarding team went inside to go over all the last minute details.

They had all conducted ship searches before, but never before as a team. McDonough wanted to make sure they were all on the same page. The meeting was short and as they broke up, McDonough and Tom, the state police dog handler, stayed behind to chat. Harvey, a two year old German shepherd, kept pacing in circles even though he was on a short leash. Tom told McDonough that Harvey was still pumped from searching the train in South Station. He assured McDonough that he'd be calmed down by the time they boarded the LNG. McDonough, having worked with the state police K-9 units in the past, wasn't concerned.

When the Flying Fish turned the corner at Deer Island Light, the captain brought her around on a northeasterly direction; soon they were entering the North Channel, the gateway into and out of the harbor. With the aid of a set of powerful binoculars, the lookout on watch scanned the horizon directly ahead of the path of the Flying Fish. When abeam of #7 buoy, he thought he saw a smudge on the horizon. After adjusting his binoculars, he looked again. This time he clearly identified the object, it was the LNG. "Ship off the starboard bow. Distance four miles," he said in a firm, confident voice. "Looks like the LNG." The captain looked through his own binoculars in the direction the lookout stated. Sure enough, there she was. "Good job, son," the captain said. "Thank you for keeping a sharp lookout."

Although he didn't show any reaction, the captain's words meant a lot to the young lookout. Although he was only a lowly seaman, the lowest rank onboard the Flying Fish, he tried hard to contribute to the boat. The captain's words assured him that he was. After referring to a chart taped to the chart table and making a few mental calculations, the captain realized he'd have to reduce the Flying Fish's speed if he intended to meet the Aldebaran just as she dropped anchor. "Reduce speed to ten knots," he said to the helmsman. "Aye, Captain, ten knots it is," the helmsman immediately replied. Satisfied everything was going as planned, the captain climbed into his chair and stuck an old beaten up pipe into his mouth.

Unconsciously, he sucked on the stem of the pipe as he stared off in the direction of the LNG. He wasn't focused on the LNG however, his mind was somewhere else.

It was almost a year ago to the day when the captain had the encounter with another LNG, the one the terrorist's had hijacked. He was the Chief on the Coast Guard Cutter Thunder Bay out of Rockland, Maine at the time. Along with the Thunder Bay, two other coast guard cutters attempted to stop the runaway LNG from entering Boston Harbor. Everything they did failed. Finally the cutter Spencer fired her 3" guns at the ship's rudder and propeller, attempting to disable the ship without endangering the volatile cargo. The plan worked; in fact it worked too well. The terrorists knew their plans were doomed; they would never reach the inner harbor. So they did what they had come to do, only a bit early. They blew the ship up in the outer harbor. Barely a scrap was found of the ship and certainly there were no survivors.

His pipe hitting the steel deck of the wheelhouse brought the captain back to the present. Before the captain could bend over and pick it up, the seaman already had the pipe in his hands. "Here you go sir," the seaman said. "It must have slipped out of your hand." The captain, feeling old and tired, attempted to thank the seaman. "Thank you again, son," he said. "You're doing one helluva job." The seaman turned and resumed his lookout duties.

The time was exactly 10:00am when the LNG Aldebaran dropped her anchor in 100 feet of water, two miles to the southwest of Nahant Headlands. Slowly, she swung on her anchor, propelled by an outgoing tide. The Flying Fish approached from astern, monitoring the activity at the bow of the vessel. When she was 100 yards from the ship, the captain ordered the small boat with its human cargo launched. The Flying Fish, like all of the 87 footers, had a unique way of launching their small boats. In the old days the small boat was raised off her cradle on deck and lowered over the side by a crane. Once the boat was in the water, you had to climb down a Jacob's ladder and jump into the usually bouncing boat. This was always a tricky maneuver and required close attention. Many bruises and an occasional broken bone resulted from the endeavor. Consequently, when the 87 footers were designed and built, the coast guard had a boat ramp installed on the stern of the boat. The small boat rested on this ramp until launch time. When it was time to put the boat in the water, the stern, or transom, of the 87 footer was raised in the air by hydraulic pumps. The small boat, with the passengers sitting down and hanging on, slid down the ramp and into the water. Many compared the experience to a water ride at an amusement park.

Since there were twelve people—and a dog—boarding the Aldebaran from the Flying Fish, the small boat had to make two trips. Once the small boat was alongside the Aldebaran, everyone stood and stepped off onto the accommodation ladder. Luckily, the sea was calm and everyone made it onboard safely. Once on deck, they spread out as planned and ushered the crew onto the mess deck. As this was happening, McDonough went to the bridge to talk with the captain and explain what was going on. The captain, a man in his early fifties, fully understood and promised his complete cooperation with the search team. McDonough and the captain reached the mess deck just as the last crewman arrived. Now that the entire crew was accounted for, the ship search could begin. Two teams consisting of four people per team left the mess deck to begin their search. McDonough and one customs inspector stayed to guard the crew. The remaining two members of the search team were assigned to work with the state police divers as they searched the outer hull of the ship. Their responsibility was to assist the divers in any way they requested, but mostly it was to tend to their lines.

After a two-hour search, both teams reported back to McDonough on the mess deck. John was pleased with their results, especially the K-9 team. For the first time searching together, he thought they did a thorough job. As they were relaxing on the mess deck, John went out on deck to check the status of the dive teams. Both teams had been in the water over an hour and were almost done with their search. They began at the bow of the ship and worked towards the stern, making sure there weren't any foreign objects attached to the hull. Once they arrived at the stern section, they gave special attention to the sea chests, an area known to be used by drug smugglers to hide contraband. If they could hide drugs there, they could also hide explosives. While John was still on deck, the first dive team surfaced and swam over to one of the dive boats. Within minutes, the other dive team did the same. Over the radio, Corporal Spellman told John the dive was complete. Both teams reported negative results.

Having completed their first successful ship search, John was ready to leave the ship. He called the Flying Fish and requested they send the small boat to pick them up. Fifteen minutes later, they were all back onboard the Flying Fish and headed back to the coast guard base. When the Flying Fish tied up to her assigned dock, Captain Lynch was waiting for them. He jumped onboard and personally thanked the entire team. He stressed how important of a job they were doing and how proud he was of each and every one of them. Knowing they hadn't eaten since earlier in the morning, Captain Lynch ordered the coast guard galley to prepare a meal for the team. When he told John hot meals were waiting for them at the galley, the team was impressed. They all left the Flying Fish together, headed towards the galley. Captain Lynch was smiling as he watched them disappear into the nearby building. He was pleased with the initial phase of their new strategy. Things were coming together just as they hoped.

While McDonough and his team were searching the Aldebaran, people were watching from a distance. Captain Lynch, not expecting any trouble but being ready if there was, had one of the shift commanders send the patrol team up to Gloucester the day before to board the Coast Guard Cutter Grand Isle, a 110 foot patrol boat home ported in Gloucester. He asked the captain of the Grand Isle to get underway and shadow the Aldebaran as she approached landfall. He didn't want the Grand Isle to make contact or be seen by anyone; he wanted covert surveillance. Captain Lynch wanted to see if any other boats attempted to make contact with the Aldebaran before she anchored. In the past, it was known that some ships coming into port would rendezvous with fishing boats offshore and discharge drugs and stowaways before they were boarded by government officials. Captain Lynch wanted to see if the Aldebaran was involved in this type of activity. He also wanted the Grand Isle to be a backup for the boarding team and the Flying Fish. If anything went wrong with the boarding, he would have more resources on scene to deploy in a moments notice. Keeping this part of the plan secret was necessary to ensure the integrity of the operation.

After the search of the Aldebaran was complete and the Flying Fish was steaming back into port, the Grand Isle departed the scene. There was an oil tanker due into Salem Harbor later that evening and Captain Lynch wanted the Grand Isle to pull surveillance on that ship also. According to the intelligence unit, the ship was coming from Colombia, South America and had been involved in shady activity in the past. According to their records, there was a cocaine seizure off the ship five years ago and as recently as a year ago, stowaways were found hiding in the engine room in the port of Houston, Texas.

As the Grand Isle steamed out to sea to intercept the tanker, the captain of the Grand Isle, Lieutenant Chris Martin, called Captain Lynch on his cell phone to give him an update. Captain Lynch was pleased with the results of the entire operation. The intelligence unit had done their homework by detecting two possible sources of trouble. The ship search team and the patrol team responded to these areas of concerns and performed admirably. Members from all three different agencies worked smoothly together. After Captain Lynch hung up from talking with the captain of the Grand Isle, he placed a call to his partners, Leo and Sebastian. He wanted to tell them the results of today's activities; he was sure they'd be pleased also.

CHAPTER TWENTY TWO

As all this activity was going on offshore, the container inspection team was hard at work inspecting containers at Conley Container Terminal in South Boston. Since the attack on the World Trade Center in New York City in 2001, inspecting containers took on a whole new importance. According to the latest intelligence, Al Qaeda was going to attempt to smuggle a dirty bomb into America via a sea container. Based on this intelligence, U.S.Customs bolstered their workforce at all the seaports and armed them with new and innovative equipment. One of the most valuable pieces of equipment was the X-ray trucks. These trucks were state of the art, equipped with the latest technology. Since acquisition, the aim of U.S.Customs was to x-ray every imported sea container before it was released into the commerce of the United States. By using the x-ray truck, it was possible to actually "see" into the sea container without opening the doors. This method expedited the release of containers and greatly enhanced security. Also attached to the truck was a radiation detector. Each sea container was "sniffed" while it was being x-rayed. By using this equipment properly, it was virtually impossible for a dirty bomb to get by the team.

Boston was more fortunate than other seaports because they had two trucks. Always keeping one truck at the port, the container inspection team was able to take the other truck on the road. Port Director Auvil instructed the team to visit other small outlying ports to help them in their law enforcement efforts. Frequent visits to New Bedford, Massachusetts and Portsmouth, New Hampshire resulted in an increase in security along the coastline. While traveling between these ports, the container inspection team often pulled into truck stops along the highway and conducted impromptu container examinations using the x-ray truck. Truck drivers were usually less than pleased by these examinations, but the presence of Massachusetts State Troopers on the team prevented them from becoming too vocal.

Although no dirty bombs had been found, drugs were detected in the tractors on several occasions, resulting in arrests of the driver and seizure of the drugs. The Port Director was pleased with the initial results of the container inspection unit. He felt the security of the port had increased dramatically since the inception of their new strategy. Also, the "officer presence" factor was invaluable. By keeping the container inspection team moving about, the bad guys would always have to be on their toes. Not a bad side effect of their master strategy to keep America safe.

While part of the container inspection team was on the road, the rest of the team remained at Conley Container Terminal x-raying containers coming off a ship that arrived that morning from Bremerhaven, Germany. All was going well until late in the afternoon. Larry, the most experienced operator of the x-ray truck, detected an anomaly in the center of a forty-foot container. On the x-ray screen it looked like a white mass about the size of a shoe box. From past experience, Larry knew it was probably a block of Xerox paper, but they had to make sure because in training, they learned that Xerox paper looked exactly like plastic explosive. They told the driver pulling the container to pull off to one side. Two members of the team opened the doors to the container with the intention of climbing into the container to verify what the anomaly was. When they opened the doors and looked into the container, they were confronted with boxes piled to the ceiling. They knew right away it was impossible to examine the container on the pier. They would have to have the container moved to the container freight station (CFS) to be stripped.

A call to Shawmut Freight Terminal, the CFS where Customs stripped all their containers, brought the usual instant response. Joseph, the lead warehouseman, answered the phone. Joseph was well known to U.S.Customs, having worked with the inspectors for at least ten years. He always went out of his way to accommodate whatever requests Customs made. Keeping the warehouse open late at night or on week-ends was unusual, but if Customs asked, Joseph made it happen. Within moments of Joseph receiving the phone call to pick up the container and transport it to his CFS, he had a trucker on the road. An hour later, the container was backed up to the loading platform. Because it was so late and half the container inspection team was gone, Larry asked Joseph if he'd mind waiting until the morning to strip the container. As usual, Joseph said there was no problem. He'd make sure the container was secured for the night and he'd see the team in the morning.

The following morning, Larry sent three members of the container team to Shawmut Freight Terminal to determine what the anomaly in the container was. As expected, it was four packages of Xerox paper stuffed in a box with office supplies. Even though it was a false alarm, the inspection proved that, if they had a problem with a container, they had a feasible plan in place to address their concerns. When Port Director Auvil was briefed on the activities of the container team for the last couple of days, he was pleased. While part of the team was out on the road helping other ports, the rest of the guys were in Boston x-raying containers. Both facets of the operation were having encouraging results, confirming Auvil's beliefs that this part of their new strategy was also working as planned. Upon further reflection and evaluation, Sebastian, John and Leo were convinced that all four units comprising their new strategy were meeting their expectations. They all felt comfortable that they were prepared for any possible challenges that might confront them in the future.

PART III

CHAPTER TWENTY THREE

The summer of 2004 was one of the rainiest in Sleazy's memory. Every morning began with a heavy, dark cloud cover and worsened as the day progressed. Rain usually arrived by early afternoon, often lasting for several hours. The temperature was below normal, necessitating wearing jackets to stay warm. Many talked about global warming and what kind of affect it was having on the environment. They were confused because they thought global warming *warmed* the earth. Sleazy's father's container yard at the freight terminal on Homburger Landstrasse in the Bad Homburg section of Frankfurt was like a swamp; mud and water everywhere. The truckers plodded through the container yard, making a mess when they came inside the office dropping off their paperwork. It wasn't their fault; there wasn't anything else they could do.

Sleazy's father was spending more time in the hospital than at home, constantly requiring treatments to help his breathing. When he was home, he was on oxygen and required constant monitoring. Sleazy was able to hire a live-in nurse, but his father still required much of his attention. To make matters even worse, the trucking business was at its worse in more than twenty years. Sleazy had to lay off a couple of warehousemen because business was so slow. He would often jump in and work the warehouse floor, but his time was limited and he could only do so much. Between the weather, his father's poor health and the dismal state of business, Sleazy was often despondent. He felt helpless in his current situation. Often he wished he never came back home to Germany when his father called. He wished he stayed in Afghanistan fighting those sons-of-bitches Americans. At least there he was doing something productive. The only bright spot in his life was his girlfriend-of- three-months, Sonja. She was always there for him to brighten his day, in spite of all the depressing conditions surrounding him.

Sleazy was lying on his back, in a puddle, in the middle of the container yard, looking up at a blocked fuel line on one of his tractor-trailers, when he received the call. The static on his cell phone made hearing almost impossible, but he thought he could hear Usayd's cheery voice yelling on the other end. As he slid out from underneath the truck, his cell phone dropped out of his oily hands and fell into the puddle he'd just been lying in. "Son of a bitch," he cried, as he reached out for the phone. He shook the phone and wiped it on his wet shirt and then put it up to his ear. Remarkably, Usayd was still on the line and this time his voice came through loud and clear. "Sleazy," he yelled, "how the fuck are ya?" "Good," Sleazy replied, "How is my friend the mountain man?" referring to the time they had spent together in the mountains of Afghanistan. "Good my friend…" Usayd said, and then there was silence. Sleazy looked at his cell phone as he held it in the palm of his hand. Green gooey sludge eked out between the keys, forming a puddle at the base of his thumb. "Mother fucker," he cried, as he threw the phone aimlessly in the air. Sleazy was pissed. He had finally heard from a buddy from his past and, what happens? They get disconnected.

Sleazy was muttering obscenities when he realized he had another cell phone with the same number in his truck. Quickly, Sleazy plodded through the mucky water to the other side of the yard where his truck was parked. As he opened the truck door, he could hear the spare cell phone ringing. Sleazy jumped in the driver side door and reached for the glove compartment. A second later he had the phone up to his ear, "Hello! Hello!" Sleazy was yelling. "What the fuck are you yelling for?" Usayd said laughing. Sleazy was so relieved that they had reconnected. If they hadn't, Sleazy would have gone crazy. Usayd was like a brother to him. Sleazy made a conscious effort to get his voice under control. "How are you my friend?" Sleazy asked in a finely modulated tone of voice. "That's better," Usayd said. "I'm fine," he continued, "How is your father's health?"

Sleazy and Usayd exchanged pleasantries for a few minutes and then Usayd got down to the crux of his call. Usayd told Sleazy that he and his girlfriend, a woman named Sameenah, were going to be taking a trip to

Europe in the next week or two. He wanted to know if Sleazy was going to be around and, if so, did he feel like having visitors. Sleazy read in between the lines and knew exactly what Usayd was saying. Yes, maybe he was coming to Europe with his girlfriend for a visit, but other things were on his mind also, other things that the two of them had discussed while fighting in the mountains of Afghanistan.

"Sure I'll be around," Sleazy said, "tell me where and when and I'll be there." Usayd was confident Sleazy would be receptive to his visit, but hearing his approving words made him feel good. "Should be sometime late next week," Usayd said. "I'll call you again when I have a confirmed flight." "Sounds good," Sleazy said, and then they hung up. Sleazy sat in the driver's seat of his truck, staring through the rain-splashed windshield off into the distance. He knew what the visit was all about and he knew it wasn't a social call. The time had come. What they had talked about months ago in the snow-peaked mountains of Afghanistan was now coming to fruition. He was excited and scared at the same time. He was excited because he knew if they pulled off what they had planned, they'd do some serious harm to the American infidels. He was scared because if they failed, he'd lose everything, possibly even his life. His concern was for his family, especially his father. Who would take care of him and the struggling business if things went bad?

On Monday of the following week, Usayd made the promised call. He and his girlfriend, Sameenah, would arrive at the Frankfurt am Main airport at 6:00pm on Friday on the Lufthansa flight coming direct from Algiers, Algeria. Sleazy told Usayd that was great news and he was excited to see him. He promised Usayd that he and his new girlfriend, Sonja, would meet them at the gate in the Lufthansa terminal. After they hung up, Sleazy reflected on the ramifications of Usayd's visit. He knew Usayd was coming to Germany to discuss business.

Months ago, in Afghanistan, while they were fighting the infidel Americans, the subject first came up. They agreed it would be a great idea, indeed an honor, to be responsible for an act of terrorism against the Americans. It was when they discussed the matter further on later dates that the idea of planting a dirty bomb in freight came up. On paper it seemed simple. If they were able to get their hands on some radioactive material, making a dirty bomb would be simple; all they had to do was add maybe five pounds of C-4 and a blasting cap. The delivery method was assured because when you owned a freight terminal in Germany, and had a strong contact in another freight terminal in America; moving freight between the two places was easy.

Sleazy and Sonja arrived almost three hours early at the airport. He didn't have any difficulty leaving work early. Even when they were busy, Friday afternoons was always the quietest time of the week, and they hadn't been busy for months. Sonja was "in between jobs" as she told everyone. Sleazy didn't think she actually ever had a job, unless you consider hustling drinks from American GI's a job. For years Sonja worked the bars of downtown Frankfurt, earning a commission off drinks GI's bought her. She called them drinks, but usually it was nothing but sparkling water. The GI's would buy Sonja, or one of the other girls hanging out at the Frankfurt bars, a drink in the hope a friendship would develop between them. The lonely, far-from-home soldier would always lose out on the deal. In spite of the girl's promises to leave the bar with him after 'only one more drink', he would leave by himself—frustrated and broke.

Sonja made a decent living for many years plying her trade, until Sleazy came along. It was just over three months ago when Sleazy dropped in on one of these downtown bars just across the street from Frankfurt's main railroad station, the Hauptbahnhof. All he wanted was a quick beer because he was dropping off a piece of freight across the street and had to get back to the freight terminal to pick up another delivery. Well, when Sonja snuggled up beside him, rubbing his arm, asking for a drink, it was love at first sight. At least that is how he tells the story. Others think Sonja saw him for what he was, a real sucker, and she jumped at the opportunity and latched onto him. Whatever the case may be, they had been together ever since, and they both seemed like they were enjoying themselves.

The Lufthansa terminal was the most modern of all the terminals at the airport. Built only a couple of years ago, the designers had passenger comfort in mind when they put pen to paper designing the place. Soft, comfortable chairs were located throughout, especially in the drinking and eating areas. Drinking concessions were conveniently located to attract as many people as possible, usually by big windows overlooking the busy runways, offering a panoramic view of the airport. At one of these drinking concessions, Sleazy and Sonja dropped in to await the arrival of their friends from Algeria. When the rather shapely waitress asked them what they'd like to drink, Sonja ordered an apfelwein and Sleazy asked for a Shultheis beer, in the bottle. Although Henninger beer was the beer of Frankfurt, Sleazy had developed a taste for Shultheis on one of his many business trips to Berlin. Ever since, that is the only beer he drank. The two of them sat, drank and enjoyed the soft, mellow music that was piped into the terminal over the airport's public address system. Every so often, the music would be interrupted by the announcement of an aircraft arrival.

When it started to get close to 6:00pm, Sleazy attempted to listen more closely to these announcements, although it seemed to be more difficult than when they first arrived. Sonja was completely oblivious to everything but one thing, the glass she was holding in her hand containing her precious glass of apfelwein. As soon as she drank half the glass, she started waving at the waitress to bring her another. Even in Sleazy's rather inebriated state, he realized she was drinking a prodigious amount of alcohol. Once when she had to visit the ladies room, she walked into a nearby table, spilling drinks all over the floor. Her matter-of-fact attitude dismissed this faux pas out rightly and she continued on to the ladies room as if nothing had happened. Even though Sleazy bought the table another round of drinks, he was embarrassed and couldn't wait to hear the announcement over the public address system of the arrival of Usayd's flight. Finally, a little after 6:00 pm, the flight was announced. "Lufthansa Flight 444, arriving from Algiers, Algeria will be arriving at Gate 6A. Baggage claim will be carousel 3." Sleazy immediately stood and put his hand under Sonja's arm, gently persuading her to stand. As they walked out of the bar, Sleazy held firmly to Sonja's arm and guided her between the tables. One accident a night was enough for him.

They stood just outside of gate 6A, awaiting the arrival of Usayd and his girl friend, Sameenah. Sonja was uncertain on her feet, causing Sleazy some concern. He had wanted to take Usayd and Sameenah out on the town once they arrived, but now he wasn't sure what to do. But, he realized, he was the one to blame. He kept buying her those glasses of apfelwein. The loud whining noise told them that the plane was pulling up to the gate.

Slowly, passengers began to appear. About halfway through deplaning, Usayd walked up the ramp leading from the plane, arms interlocked with a tall, dark-haired, beauty. Sleazy whistled softly when he saw her while Sonja remained oblivious of her surroundings. Usayd and Sleazy hugged, slapped each other on the back and kissed each others cheeks. Eventually, Usayd introduced Sameenah and Sleazy introduced Sonja. Remarkably, Sonja came to life and actually appeared coherent.

After claiming their bags, the four of them walked out to Sleazy's car parked in the adjoining parking lot. Usayd and Sleazy walked together and chatted. Sonja and Sameenah followed close behind, carrying on as if they were life-long friends. Sleazy was happy they were getting along. A while ago, he thought he was going to have to take Sonja home and put her to bed. Once they were in the car and driving off the airport, Sleazy asked if anyone was hungry. He received a resounding yes from all three. Good, Sleazy thought, he had just the place for them.

The Top of Frankfurt is a high class restaurant located in the downtown area of Frankfurt by the Main River. The restaurant is on the top floor of a thirty story office building and revolves on its axis once every hour. The locals say you know it is time to leave when you see the same sights out the window more than once. The restaurant is well known for its steaks, seafood and top-notch service. They were in front of the building in less than an hour. Sleazy gave his keys to the valet and they walked inside. After a swift elevator ride, they stepped out into the restaurant. They were all struck by the beauty and pleasant ambience.

The maitre'd sat them at a table by the window, followed closely by a waiter asking if they'd like something to drink. Sameenah asked for a glass of white wine. After looking at the wine list, Sonja gave the waiter a pleasant smile saying, "I'd like a glass of water with a lemon twist please." Sleazy was afraid the others heard his sigh of relief. He was happy Sonja wasn't drinking; he couldn't handle another row with her. After Sleazy convinced Usayd to have a bottle of Shultheis beer, they sat back and continued their conversation. They all had a pleasant time together and enjoyed their meal. About 10:00pm, after the restaurant's second go around since they were there, Usayd said it was time to go. He and Sameenah had had a long day and they were exhausted.

In the morning, Usayd and Sleazy were the first ones awake. Sleazy was in the kitchen when Usayd walked in, wiping sleep from his eyes. Since the girls were sleeping, this was a convenient time to talk; but Usayd insisted they go outside just in case Sleazy's house was bugged. He trusted Sleazy beyond a doubt, but they had gone too far to take any unnecessary risks. Once outside, Sleazy and Usayd walked casually down the sidewalk adjacent to his house. Usayd was smoking one cigarette after another, blowing foul, acrid smoke in Sleazy's face. Sleazy was surprised because he never saw Usayd smoke before.

The weather had finally broken and the morning sun felt good on their faces. Usayd did most of the talking, while Sleazy listened intently to his every word. Usayd told Sleazy they had finally obtained the radioactive material they needed to make a dirty bomb. The triumvirate had bought 1 kilogram of a substance called caesium-137 from the black market in Belorussia. Supposedly some disenchanted, unemployed professor had access to the material at a university in the capital city of Minsk. He was willing to sell the material to the triumvirate—through a third party, of course, for $100,000. He insisted on American dollars because, according to him, the Euro was worthless and was going to collapse within weeks.

The exchange was scheduled to occur in Berlin the next day. Usayd and Sameenah were scheduled to fly out in the morning. They were supposed to meet this third party at a coffeehouse called Rex opposite the church on Kurfurstendamm. Usayd looked quizzically at Sleazy. When Sleazy began to say something, Usayd shook his head and said, "Wait!" Sleazy was taken aback by Usayd's abruptness, but he kept his mouth shut. Usayd said he was told to give this third party the money and then leave. Arrangements would be made to ship the caesium-137 to a fellow professor, who taught astrophysics at Marburg University, a school two hours away by car from Frankfurt. This is when Sleazy would get involved in the plans.

Usayd stopped walking, lit another cigarette, looked at Sleazy and said, "So, what do you think?" Sleazy hesitated and then said, "What do I think? I think you're a flying fucking idiot, that's what the fuck I think!" Usayd was stunned; he never expected such a rebuke from his friend. Before Usayd could say anything, Sleazy continued. "You are telling me that you are flying to Berlin in the morning to give $100,000 in cold, hard cash to someone you've never met before; someone who is PROMISING to send a kilogram of celium or cerium or whatever you call the fucking stuff. I think you're a fucking nut." Sleazy took a breath and continued. "Why don't you make things easier on yourself and just give me the money, because you're never going to see the money again or the shit you think you're buying." By this time Sleazy was really in a rage. He couldn't believe how stupid this whole plan was. Obviously, he thought, the whole deal was a classic rip-off. There was no nutty professor or radioactive material for sale. Some slick rip-off artist heard that someone was looking for radioactive material and cooked up this grand scheme of events. The triumvirate, in their haste for revenge, fell for the ploy and was about to lose $100,000.

Usayd stood still in the middle of the sidewalk, silently listening as Sleazy ripped him apart. As Usayd listened, he realized how stupid the plan did sound; but supposedly the triumvirate knew what they were doing. Don't blame him, he was just the messenger. Sleazy had just about vented all his rage, when he thought of something else. "And, by the way," he said, "how the fuck .." Sleazy suddenly stopped; it felt like his head was going to burst. His face was beet red and he began shaking. Usayd saw that his friend was really upset and tried to calm him down. "Okay, Okay," Usayd said, "maybe we should talk to the triumvirate some more about this. Maybe you are right. Maybe this plan is a little fucked up." Sleazy's eyes bulged out of his head. "Fucked up," he said, "I'll tell you what's fucked up."

A mother with two little children walked by, as they stood glaring at each other. They both forced a smile and wished the mother a good morning. Usayd even waved at the kids. Once they were beyond listening range, Sleazy continued his tirade. Now, however, his emotions were in control. Sleazy was not only concerned that they being scammed by a con artist, but he was afraid this could be a set up by the authorities. He envisioned Usayd and Sameenah meeting this third party in Berlin, giving him the money and then being arrested for trying to procure weapons of mass destruction. Usayd stared at Sleazy. Sweat broke out on his forehead, yet he felt a chill run through his body. Usayd had never thought of such a scenario, but he now realized how plausible the idea was. All of a sudden, his plans didn't seem too sound after all; thanks to Sleazy's critique. It was now obvious that before they went any further with their plan, a call to the triumvirate was warranted. Maybe they had acted in haste.

Later that morning, Usayd placed a call to the triumvirate in Arzew. Waqas answered the phone and told Usayd to hang on. Shortly, Aadil picked up the phone. "Hello, hello," he said rather impatiently. "Usayd, is that you?" Aadil was not pleased with this phone call because it could only mean problems. When Usayd left Arzew, he was given explicit instructions on what to do. He was only to contact them if something went wrong. Again, Aadil yelled hello into the phone. Usayd swallowed hard. His mouth was dry as sandpaper. "Yes, Aadil, it is me," he said sheepishly. "What is wrong?" Aadil yelled, "Why are you calling me?" Usayd was already regretting making the phone call. Why didn't he just go ahead and do what they told him to do? Why was he questioning them? Because Sleazy didn't think it was a good idea? Who the fuck was Sleazy? Who cares about losing $100,000? They had plenty of money. $100,000 meant nothing to them.

Usayd swallowed hard one more time and then began to speak. He told Aadil the concerns that arose once they started to think about the plan. He told Aadil that to him and Sleazy, it didn't sound like a good idea to give this guy the $100,000. It sounded like a rip-off and they'd never see the money again or the radioactive material. Additionally, Usayd told Aadil, this whole plan could be a set up, a sting operation by government authorities. Had he thought of that? Usayd queried Aadil. Aadil listened patiently, but he was fuming inside. Finally, when Usayd finished talking, Aadil asked him if he was done. When Usayd said yes, the fireworks began. "Listen you dumb son of a bitch," Aadil said, "I'm not asking for any of your cheap advice. I told you what to do and that is what I want done. Tell that shithead friend of yours to mind his own business and keep his fucking mouth shut. He's putting ideas in your head and you're stupid enough to listen to him." Usayd felt humiliated as Aadil yelled at him. He wished he never made the call.

Aadil continued his tirade, "Did it ever occur to you two morons that we checked this professor out? Well, for your information, we did. He is totally legit! That is why I told you what to do. Now you're questioning me?" Usayd couldn't wait for the conversation to be over. He knew he was going to Berlin in the morning. What a mistake the phone call was. Aadil wasn't done, however. He still had a few words of wisdom for Usayd. "Now," he said, "this is what I'd like you to do. Shut the fuck up and do what I told you to do. If you dare even think of calling me again, I'll personally come up there and drive my foot so far up your ass you won't be walking for a fucking week." Usayd felt humiliated. He was ready to strangle Sleazy for putting him up to making the phone call. Aadil continued, this time his voice was calmer. "Now, are there any more questions? If not, I expect you and my niece to be on that plane to Berlin in the morning. Understood?" Usayd said he understood and began a feeble apology. It was too late. Aadil had already hung up.

Sleazy took them to the airport in the morning. Sonja was too tired to get out of bed. Although they were still close friends, the incident about the phone call yesterday had put a damper on their visit. Now all Usayd wanted to do was complete the mission and get back to Arzew. He had some making up to do with Aadil. Sameenah tried to console Usayd, but nothing she said or did helped. He had to come face to face with Aadil to make amends. As they were sitting in the airport waiting to board their flight, the three of them drank coffee and ate hot apple muffins. Usayd told Sleazy that once they arrived in Berlin, he planned to take a taxi to their hotel. Precisely at 3:00pm, he and Sameenah would walk into the Rex Café and order a drink. From there it was up to the third-party to initiate the contact. Once the money was passed, Usayd would receive all the particulars regarding the transfer of the radioactive material. Usayd promised Sleazy he'd pass this information on to him as soon as possible. If everything went well, they should be home in Arzew the following afternoon and if things didn't go well? They decided not to think about that scenario.

There was a deathly silence amongst the three. They knew they were committed to Aadil's plans, but none of them felt too comfortable. The silence was broken by the announcement of their flight. Lufthansa flight #35 for Templehof Airport, Berlin was ready for boarding at Gate #3. Usayd and Sleazy hugged. After all they had been through; they hoped this wasn't the end.

Neither of them had ever been to Berlin. They were struck by the beauty of the buildings and the busy activity on the streets. Usayd was amazed to see that war damage was still evident in some parts of the city. In fact, the church just opposite the Rex Café was missing its steeple because of allied bombing. *Over sixty years ago*, Usayd thought. It was amazing. As they entered the Rex, Sameenah held Usayd's arm and attempted to act as nonchalant as possible. She was scared, knowing that if this was a set-up by the authorities, they could be arrested. They sat at the bar and ordered two Schultheis beers. Usayd thought of Sleazy when the bartender put the bottle in front of him. They were sitting at the bar, sipping on their beers, when a pleasant looking gentleman approached. He commented on their selection of beers and then challenged Usayd to a game of fussball. Realizing this was more than likely their point of contact, Usayd readily accepted the challenge. Sameenah followed the two as they went into a back room to play Germany's favorite barroom game.

After playing a couple of games, Usayd losing both, they sat in a booth drinking a couple more beers. Dieter, the name this gentleman used to introduce himself, was a great conversationalist and wanted to know all about Usayd and Sameenah. As Usayd began to make up the story of his life, Dieter reached into his pocket and produced half of an old German five mark note. He slid the paper across the table in Usayd's direction. Usayd reached into his pocket and produced the other half of the five mark note. Usayd put the two halves together, they matched perfectly. He slid the halves across the table to Dieter. Dieter inspected the two halves and smiled. He reached his hand across the table and shook Usayd's hand and said, "Welcome to Berlin."

The transaction went rather swiftly. Usayd gave Dieter the dark leather briefcase he was carrying and Dieter gave Usayd a small, bulky envelope. Neither one of them looked at the contents. They had one more Shultheis and then it was time to leave. As they were walking out the door, Dieter laughingly asked Sameenah if she would allow Usayd to return to the Rex the following day; he had to practice his fussball game. Sameenah tried to play the part of a loving wife, as she nervously said, "Only if he does his chores." They waved as they bid farewell and walked in different directions.

For the rest of the afternoon, Usayd and Sameenah walked around the city, acting as tourists. They stopped at one of the bratwurst stands and ordered a couple of weiswursts mit brot (veal sausage with bread). Sameenah didn't care for the sausage and gave hers to Usayd. Usayd especially liked the sharp mustard. Once the sun started to settle, they went back to their hotel and stayed in their room for the rest of the night. Usayd felt comfortable that all went well. If it was a set up by the authorities, he felt they would have been arrested by now. First thing in the morning they were up and on the way to the airport. They couldn't wait to get on the plane back to Algeria. Usayd kept the envelope safe in his sport jacket pocket; he kept feeling for it to make sure it was safe. Their plane departed Berlin on time.

Usayd and Sameenah sat back in their seats and prayed for an uneventful trip home. As Usayd reflected on the past few days, he was rather pleased with the results. But, he had learned one valuable lesson—when Aadil told you to do something, don't question him. Sameenah must have sensed from Usayd's body language that he was being introspective. She grabbed his hand and brought it to her chest. Then she leaned over and kissed his cheek, whispering how proud she was of him. Usayd was more at peace then than he had been in a long time. He had finally found a woman he was totally in love with. With a smile on his face, Usayd closed his eyes and drifted off to sleep. Sameenah continued holding his hand and planned on holding it for some time to come. Eventually, she too nodded off.

CHAPTER TWENTY FOUR

They didn't wake up until the plane was on final approach. Usayd was amazed when he looked out the airplane window and realized they were almost home. He couldn't believe they had slept almost the entire flight. Waqas was at the airport to meet them. In spite of his rough exterior, he was a beautiful sight to see for both of them. Claiming their bags took only a few minutes; soon they were in a car being whisked through the streets of Arzew. Waqas was rather chatty during the drive, quite unusual for him. Usayd tried to feel him out about what kind of mood Aadil was in but Waqas didn't take the bait. He remained silent on matters relating to his boss. In less than thirty minutes, the car pulled alongside the sidewalk in front of the building where the triumvirate held a lot of their meetings. This is it; Usayd thought to himself, it was time to face the music.

Aadil gave Sameenah a big hug and kiss as she entered the apartment. Usayd stood sheepishly in the background, nervously waiting his turn. He knew he was in for a good ass-chewing. When Aadil was done greeting Sameenah, he turned and looked squarely in Usayd's eyes. "What's the matter with you?" he said to Usayd, "you look like someone just kicked the shit out of you." Usayd didn't know how to respond; instead of being yelled at, Aadil was attempting to comfort him. Then Aadil started to laugh, a deep laugh from deep down in his gut. Usayd remained motionless, not sure what to do. Then Aadil explained. "Okay, Usayd, I know why you are nervous, but not to worry. Yes, I was mad at you the other day, but it's over. I apologize for yelling at you and ask your forgiveness." Usayd began to relax, but remained wary, as Aadil continued to explain. Aadil said he understood why Usayd and Sleazy questioned giving the money to an unknown person, but they should have had more faith in Aadil. Didn't they realize he thoroughly checked out the situation before he risked losing $100,000? Now, in the safety and security of being with friends, Usayd realized his mistake. But, in Frankfurt, Germany, his thought process was working differently.

Aadil saw how badly Usayd felt. He was humiliated and ashamed of himself for questioning Aadil. Seeing Usayd in this condition made Aadil mad at himself. He had no right to humiliate Usayd, not after all he had been through. Aadil stepped forward, wrapped Usayd in his arms and said, "I deeply apologize to you Usayd and humbly seek your forgiveness." Usayd felt the compassion and sincerity in his voice. Usayd smiled and said, "Forget it, it's over. We all learned something out of this, especially me. It's over and let's forget about it." They were smiling as Sameenah walked up to Usayd and gave him a big hug. What was even more revealing, Usayd returned the hug and gave her a kiss on the forehead.

"Okay," Aadil barked, "enough of this sweet talk bullshit. Let's get down to business. What do you have for me, my friend?" Usayd reached in to his inside jacket pocket and pulled out the envelope. He passed it over to Aadil as they both walked over to the table in the middle of the room. Aadil motioned to Usayd to sit. As he sat opposite Usayd, he slid over his box of cigars, telling Usayd to take one. He wasn't a smoker, but for some unknown reason he took a cigar. Aadil leaned over the table and held a match to light Usayd's cigar. As he sat there puffing away on his cigar while Aadil read the letter in the envelope, Usayd caught Sameenah's eye. She was sitting with Waqas on the couch staring at him. As their eyes met, Sameenah had a mock face of disgust on her face and wagged her finger at him. Usayd shrugged his shoulders, smiled and pointed his finger at Aadil, as if it was his fault. They both started to laugh.

After reading a few minutes more, Aadil looked up at Usayd. "Very well," he said, "this is pretty straightforward. The question is; how well do you trust this friend of yours, Sleazy?" Usayd knew where Aadil was coming from. Sleazy was to play a vital role from this point forward. If Sleazy couldn't be trusted, if he might crack under pressure, now was the time to say something. Otherwise, he might compromise the entire operation. Usayd looked Aadil straight in his eyes and said, "I trust the man with my own life." Aadil saw the intensity in Usayd's eyes, the passion in his voice.

"Well," he said, "that's good enough for me. If you say we can trust the man, then we can trust him. I have no right to question your word. After all that you two have been through, you probably know him better than his own mother." They sat in silence for a moment, each puffing on their cigar; Aadil reflecting on his next move, Usayd patiently awaiting his orders.

Aadil took a puff on his cigar, leaned his head back, and blew a couple of perfect smoke rings. Usayd was admiring how he did this when Aadil began to speak. He told Usayd that he was going to be the contact, and only contact, they had with Sleazy. No one else would communicate with him. This way there wouldn't be any confusion in relaying orders. Aadil had seen in the past what confusion could result when too many people were involved in relaying commands. Aadil wanted to keep everything simple to avoid any such confusion. Usayd nodded his head in agreement.

The first thing Aadil wanted to relay to Sleazy was when and where to pick up the shipment of caesium-137. According to the letter, a professor of astrophysics in Marburg University, a Professor Schwartz, would receive a package from Minsk in a week or so. The professor received packages from universities in Minsk on almost a weekly basis. He was involved in a joint venture with Minsk universities, and other European universities, so receiving numerous shipments in the mail was not unusual at all. In this package would be their shipment of caesium-137, intermingled with an assortment of laboratory supplies. Aadil referred to a notebook and said, "That means the shipment should be in the hands of the professor the first week of September." Usayd mentally calculated the days and then nodded his head in agreement. "So," said Aadil, "let's set the 5th of September for the date of pickup. Would you contact your friend to see if this date is amenable to him?"

Usayd nodded yes and began to stand. "Hold on," Aadil said, "there is more." Aadil said that the kilogram of caesium-137 would be packed in a grey lead canister to prevent a radiation leak. When Sleazy arrived at Marburg University he was to go to the Physics Department in the Heller Building and ask for Professor Schwartz. He should identify himself as a graduate student from Frankfurt University and say he was sent to pick up an atomic scale for his school. The professor would be expecting this story and would release the package to Sleazy. Once he had the package, he was to return to his father's freight terminal in the Bad Homburg section of Frankfurt and secure the package. In a few days he would receive further instructions.

Aadil thought for a few seconds and then said, "Okay, Usayd, I think that's it. Notify your friend immediately and let me know if this plan is fine with him. If it is, I'll contact Berlin and make sure our stories match." Usayd stood and left the room. He had a bit of trouble calling Germany, but eventually he got through. Sleazy understood his instructions and told Usayd he didn't see any difficulties. He would drive one of his father's trucks to Marburg, pick up the piece of freight and return to Frankfurt. He did this type of work almost every day. Nothing was out of the ordinary, and he felt sure he wouldn't draw any attention. As soon as Usayd hung up the phone, he marched into the other room and told Aadil the news. Aadil was pleased and said he would call Berlin to make sure everything was understood on their end.

CHAPTER TWENTY FIVE

Sleazy was up before dawn. Sonja, as usual, remained in a deep sleep. He would have liked to take her for the ride, but he thought twice. It was best to leave her home, just in case something happened. Her company would have made the trip more enjoyable, but he couldn't see getting her involved. If people started asking questions at a later time, who knows what she would tell them. The last few months were quite pleasant for Sleazy, but more recently, Sonja started to get on his nerves. She drank too much, and then she started running with the mouth. When he first met her, Sleazy didn't realize the depth of her problems. Now that he did, he wished he could get rid of her, but he didn't know how. But other times he could ignore her drinking and enjoy her company. The relationship was baffling to him and he wasn't really sure what to do. One day he loved her, the next day he wanted to get rid of her. Oh well, he thought, it was best to put this problem aside for the day. He had more important matters to address.

He put on a pot of coffee and warmed his thermos; it was at least a two hour ride to Marburg. While waiting for the coffee to brew, Sleazy made himself three eggs with sausage and potatoes. He figured if he was on the road by 7:00, he'd be in Marburg by 9:00. He gave himself an hour in Marburg and figured he should be back on the road heading home by 10:00. If all went well, he'd be back in his father's freight terminal by lunchtime, but he'd spent too much time on the road to expect everything to go as planned. While eating his eggs, Sleazy reflected on what he was about to do. Up to this point, everything was just talk. Once he took off for Marburg, he was committed. There was no turning back. But he realized he had made the commitment a long time ago. This latest event was just expressing his feelings in a different way. Instead of fighting the American infidels on the battlefields of Afghanistan, now he was going to fight them on their own home ground. He was satisfied with the decision that he had made and was looking forward to carrying out their plans. Even if he had second thoughts of backing out, he knew he never could. His friendship and loyalty to Usayd prevented any possibility of that choice.

Armed with a full thermos of hot, black coffee, Sleazy was on the road a little before 7:00am. The traffic was light as he maneuvered his truck through the narrow streets of Bad Homburg. Although the distance to Marburg was only 100 kilometers, most of the driving would be over similarly narrow streets. There wasn't any major highway connecting the two cities. That was fine with Sleazy; he preferred driving on the back roads. As he drove along, Sleazy was uncharacteristically disconnected from the unfolding events. This behavior was highly unusual for him; usually he was focused in on whatever he was doing. Sleazy was conscious of his ambivalent attitude and wondered why he felt as he did. He brushed off these thoughts because it was confusing him and making him feel uncomfortable. He just wanted to enjoy the nice, pleasant ride through the countryside. Perhaps if he better psychoanalyzed himself he might have realized his attitude could be a defense mechanism against the possible danger that confronted him. It was easier to detach himself from the reality of the situation than to face the possibility of the dark consequences that might result from his actions.

Before he knew it, Sleazy was approaching the outskirts of Marburg. He could see off in the distance several tall church steeples nestled in amongst countless stucco houses. What a beautiful city, he thought. Although Marburg was close to Frankfurt, this was Sleazy's first visit. He silently promised himself that he would return some day, hopefully under more pleasant conditions. Who knows, maybe he'd even bring Sonja. The streets were narrow and hilly, requiring Sleazy to pay close attention to his driving. While he negotiated the sharp turns, he also had to be on the lookout for signs showing him where Marburg University was. As he approached the center of town, signs began to appear showing directions to the university. After ten more minutes, Sleazy found himself in front of Heller Hall. He wasn't exactly sure how he got there, but he was there.

After breathing a sigh of relief and relaxing for a few minutes, he decided it was time to go inside to meet the professor.

He had a breathtaking view of the surrounding hills as he approached the main door of Heller Hall. He stopped for a moment and absorbed the view. What a place to go to school. Sleazy never had the opportunity of furthering his studies after high school; after seeing Marburg University, he realized what he had missed. He pulled the huge oak door open and stepped inside. The place was eerily quiet and smelled of polished wood. Directly in front of him was a directory of names and room numbers. Sleazy's eyes scanned the board and settled on the S column. Halfway down the list he saw the name Schwartz—Room 312. Sure, third floor, he said to himself. Probably no elevator either, he muttered. He was right on both counts.

The professor's office was on the third floor and there wasn't an elevator. The trek up the old granite stairs gave Sleazy the opportunity to view the rest of the building. The iron handrails were solid, yet ornately illustrated with delicate-looking flowers interspersed amongst the vertical railings. When Sleazy reached the third floor landing, he had to stop and catch his breath. Once he was breathing normally, he walked down the corridor; his eyes scanning the doors, looking for 312. He could hear his footsteps echoing off the ceiling when he spotted a massive door with golden numbers inscribed exactly at his eye level. They must have known I was coming, he joked to himself.

He paused in front of the door and then gave a strong, assertive knock. Silence. He knocked again. This time a voice from within told him to enter. Sleazy had to strain the muscles in his right arm to open the door. As he pushed the door aside, he looked inside, expecting a massive room in proportion to the door. Instead, he was met by a room no bigger than an average size bedroom. Sitting at a desk in the middle of the room was a gentleman of middle age wearing a three piece suit. Long graying hair drooped down over his forehead and partially concealed his left eye. Hanging from the right corner of his mouth was an unlit meerschaum. "May I help you?" he queried. "Yes," Sleazy said, "I'm a graduate student from Frankfurt University and I've been sent up here to pick up an atomic scale."

His initial disinterested facial expression was soon replaced with a look of glee. "Please come in," he said. "Please have a seat." Sleazy didn't like him from the start. He seemed deceptive and calculating. But, what did he care. All Sleazy wanted to do was pick up the package and get the hell back on the road to Frankfurt. "How was your trip?" the professor said. "Fine, fine," Sleazy said. In his head he was thinking other things. *What the fuck does he care? He doesn't know where I really came from and it's damn sure I'm not going to tell him.* The professor sensed Sleazy wasn't making a social call. He realized Sleazy was all business. He was on a mission and wasn't in the mood for any socializing. "Well," he said rather nervously, "your scale is locked in a closet on the first floor. Shall we go there?" Sleazy nodded in the affirmative, stood and waited as the professor walked around to the front of his desk, his hand in his jacket pocket fumbling for what Sleazy assumed were the keys to the closet.

Sleazy followed the professor in silence as they walked back down the granite stairs. The building appeared to be empty except for the two of them. Just before they reached the door leading outside, the professor stopped in front of a black metal door. While he fumbled with a combination lock, the professor muttered incessantly. Sleazy was getting spooked by this guy. After several attempts, the professor unlocked the combination lock. He then reached in his jacket and produced a large bronze key. With one swift motion, he inserted the key in the keyhole and twisted; the door popped open. A light automatically came on when the door opened. Inside the room, sitting amongst wooden and cardboard boxes, sat a cold grey metallic canister. Sleazy knew that was it as soon as he saw it.

The professor grabbed a clipboard off a shelf as walked into the room. Sleazy was right behind him. "You must sign first," the professor said in a rather authoritative voice. Sleazy felt like telling the professor to fuck off, but thought better of it. He just wanted to grab the canister and get the hell out of there. The place really bugged him. Sleazy grabbed the clipboard and scanned the attached sheet. There was a column for printed name, signature and company represented. The last column was easy, but he had to think for a second about the name. Then he thought about his boyhood chum he used to play soccer with. He neatly printed Hans Winkler and then scribbled the signature. The professor looked at the signature and then looked up at Sleazy. He could barely conceal the sneer that was unfolding across his face. He knew Sleazy was lying, but what could he do. Sleazy ignored the professor and went to retrieve the package. When he attempted to pick the box up, he thought he was going to have a hernia. The professor seemed to enjoy Sleazy's obvious discomfort. As much as Sleazy hated to do it, he had to run out to the truck to get the two-wheeler. When he retuned, the professor was standing in the same spot. This guy is really strange, Sleazy thought, as he slid the two-wheeler under the box. Soon he was rolling the two-wheeler down the sidewalk to his awaiting truck. He couldn't wait to get back on the road; he thought the professor and Heller Hall deserved each other.

Sleazy was back on the road shortly after 10:00am. The ride home was uneventful, but the traffic was a lot heavier than earlier in the morning. It was just noon when he pulled into the container yard in Bad Homburg. He didn't want to unload the package while other people were around, so after ensuring the roll-down back was locked, he went into the house to see what was for lunch. Sonja was up by now and, anticipating his arrival, was cooking bratwurst and beans on the stove. She was in a pleasant mood and greeted Sleazy as he walked through the door. This is the part of Sonja he loved. She could brighten his day and take the load off his shoulders and make him feel as if everything was going to be okay. But it was the other times that were confusing. When she was in a foul mood she could be a real bitch. Sleazy wondered if she was bipolar or just a screwed up drunk. Whatever, he thought; he was too tired to try to figure her out.

While Sonja was fixing lunch, Sleazy grabbed a Schultheis out of the refrigerator and sat down at the kitchen table. He was happy as to what transpired this morning. Their plans had just jumped one giant leap forward. Now that they had the radioactive material, the next step was planning how to deliver the package to America. Sleazy had his ideas and he planned on telling them to Usayd when he called later that night. He had time for one more beer before his lunch was served. Sonja sat down at the table as he ate and they had an enjoyable talk. In spite of all her faults, Sonja never pried into Sleazy's personal business. She knew he was involved in more than moving freight, but that wasn't any of her business. Sleazy was providing her a comfortable life and that was all she was looking for. It was much more than she had in the past and it sure beat working the bars downtown. After eating, they talked a little more and then Sleazy decided to take a nap. He was exhausted from getting up so early and driving all day. He asked Sonja to make sure he was up by 5:00pm. By that time all the workers in the warehouse would be gone and he could lock the package up in the high security room without anyone seeing him. After that, he expected a call from Usayd. Sonja asked him if he'd like her to join him in bed, but he declined. All he wanted to do was catch some sleep, he was tired and the couple of beers he had relaxed him.

As soon as Sleazy hit the bed he was asleep. The next thing he knew he heard Sonja calling him. He was dreaming, but the voice wouldn't go away. Then someone was grabbing his shoulders. Sleazy jumped and hit Sonja in the face. Luckily it was just a glancing blow to the side of her head. Sleazy realized he wasn't dreaming; it was Sonja waking him as promised. Sonja was whispering in his ear and massaging his shoulders and back. After apologizing, he jumped out of bed and got dressed. It was a little after 5:00 pm. Sleazy walked out into the container yard and jumped into his truck.

After backing the truck up to the docking platform, he jumped out and walked inside. As he hoped, the warehouse was empty. He slid the warehouse door open and then opened the truck's back door. Sitting in the middle of the floor of the truck was the lone package, exactly where it was when Sleazy last saw it. He grabbed the two-wheeler and slid it under the package. He effortlessly rolled the two-wheeler across the warehouse floor, through a doorway and into a back room. Once there, he unlocked a wire-meshed cage they called "the high value cage." This is where they stored shipments of high value, usually jewelry, gems, expensive coats, guns and the like. If they left goods of value out on the warehouse floor, they would eventually be stolen. He knew from past experience; thus, the purpose of the cage. Sleazy and his father were the only ones who had keys. Once the package was secured, Sleazy locked up the warehouse and parked the truck. He went back inside the house; Usayd should be calling within the hour.

The phone rang as Sonja and Sleazy were enjoying a pre-dinner drink. As expected, it was Usayd. When Sleazy told him all went well and the package was locked up, safe and secure in the warehouse, he could tell by the sound in Usayd's voice that he was pleased. This was a major hurdle that they had just overcome and now they were on to the next step. Usayd told Sleazy that the members of the triumvirate would be pleased when they heard the good news. Sleazy didn't even know the members of the triumvirate and he couldn't care less about what pleased them. All he cared about was his friend, Usayd. If Usayd was happy, he was happy. Be damned with the triumvirate. Usayd began talking about the next steps. How were they going to transform the caesium-137 into a dirty bomb by adding an explosive? After that, how were they going to secretly ship the dirty bomb to Sleazy's cousin, Joseph, the lead warehouseman at Shawmut Freight Terminal in Boston, Massachusetts?

Sleazy listened patiently for awhile and then interrupted his friend by saying, "Listen Usayd, excuse me for interrupting, but I have a few ideas." Sleazy went on to explain that all he really needed was the explosive—possibly four pounds of C4—to convert the caesium-137 into a dirty bomb. The transportation to America part he had already figured out. Usayd chuckled as he listened to his friend's ideas. Son-of-a-bitch has been doing his homework, he thought. Sleazy explained how his father had signed a shipping contract with the U.S.Army a few years ago. Thousands of soldiers were stationed throughout Germany, often times accompanied by their families. Consequently, the army was constantly arranging to have their personal and household goods shipped from and to the states. What better way, Sleazy thought, but to intermingle their dirty bomb with the household effects of a soldier returning to the states from a tour of duty in Germany? Who would suspect? Usayd thought. What a good idea.

He was amazed how Sleazy took such a monumental problem and minimized it to a small, everyday concern. Sleazy told Usayd it might take a few weeks to consolidate enough freight that was going to Boston, but he was sure it could be done. Usayd just shook his head as he listened, then said, "You bastard, Sleazy, you're trying to take my job away. If I tell the triumvirate all the work you are doing, they'll realize they don't need me. They'll fire my ass." Sleazy laughed. "Fuck them," he said, "you take the credit, I don't give a shit. I'm only doing this for you, my friend. I don't give a shit about those morons." It was Usayd's turn to laugh. He thought that although Sleazy was a great operative, he sure could polish up on his social skills. Usayd told Sleazy it looked like they had everything worked out. He would brief the triumvirate and then get back to him. Sleazy said okay and he'd be having a couple of Schultheis beers while he waited. Usayd was laughing as he hung up the phone.

Usayd called the next day. He said the triumvirate was delighted about the most recent events. Regarding the future plans, they were in complete concurrence with Sleazy. They couldn't think of any way to improve his plans. Lastly, Sleazy should expect a shipment of C4 explosive within the next few days. The delivery would be coming from within Germany. Even though Sleazy said he couldn't care less about the triumvirate, he took pride in knowing they unanimously approved his plan. Not bad for the son of a warehouseman he thought. To celebrate, Sleazy took Sonja into downtown Frankfurt. They had a wonderful time, but in the morning they paid the price. At least Sleazy did. When he got up to go to work, he had such a bad hangover he thought he was going to die. Sonja's hangover didn't bother her; she slept right through it.

CHAPTER TWENTY SIX

Sleazy continued going to work each morning as if everything was the same. Freight came into the warehouse; freight went out of the warehouse. Truckers were coming and going all day long. Business was slowly improving and Sleazy thought he might have to hire another warehouseman. A package addressed to him was delivered to his house a few days after his conversation with Usayd. The contents were what he had requested. Now that he had everything he needed, all he had to do was wait to get enough Boston freight to fill a twenty or forty foot container. He knew it wouldn't be long.

Down the street from Sleazy's father's warehouse were two old WWII German Army camps that the U.S. Army took over after the war. They renamed the camps—Kaserne in German—Drake and Edwards Kaserne. Home to a contingent of the 3rd Armored Division, thousands of American troops were stationed here. Their normal tour of duty could last from one to three years, sometimes longer. The 3rd Armored Division was comprised mostly of tanks, armored personnel carriers and the accompanying infantry. Their mission was to thwart any Russian attempt to invade West Germany through a gap in the mountains in the area of the town of Fulda. This attack never materialized and the troops never had to respond to a real emergency, although almost constant training exercises were conducted for this possible scenario.

Years after detente, the Americans still had thousands of troops stationed in Frankfurt and the rest of West Germany. Although the threat of a Russian invasion had evaporated like a morning fog, the high troop level was maintained for political reasons. If America suddenly pulled all their troops out of West Germany, the impact on the German economy would be devastating. America planned to slowly reduce the troop level to a more realistic size, but it would take years for this to happen. Sleazy and his father hoped it would never happen because the American presence accounted for a large percentage of their business. If the Americans pulled out altogether, shipping home their personal and households effects through Sleazy's father's warehouse would disappear, most likely forcing them out of business. All Sleazy wanted was a couple more good years of business. By then his father would be retired and Sleazy hoped to have enough money to be lying on some sun-splashed beach on the French Riviera enjoying life.

As anticipated, before the month was over, they had enough cargo destined for Boston, Massachusetts to fill a forty-foot sea container. There must have been a lot of soldiers on PCS (permanent change of station) orders because in the next two weeks the army was dropping freight off at the warehouse on a daily basis. Most of the cargo was destined for cities along the eastern seaboard of the United States, Boston being one of the most popular destinations. Sleazy gave top priority to loading the container for Boston, without drawing undue attention. One day they loaded four different shipments into the container and were just a little over half filled.

That night, after closing, Sleazy returned to the empty warehouse. The warehouse was always eerie in the middle of the night, especially that night. But, it was time to carry their plans one step closer to completion. Bringing the C4 from the house with him, Sleazy opened the high value cage at the rear of the warehouse. He approached the steely grey canister with caution. He didn't know why he was so scared. He knew the caesium-137 was harmless; at least that is what they told him. But for some unknown reason, the canister gave him the jitters. Sleazy removed the cover of the canister and gently inserted the four blocks of C4 explosive. No sooner was the cover off than he had it back on. Carefully he lifted the canister out of its wooden container and walked out onto the cargo floor. He set the canister temporarily on the cold concrete floor as he opened the sliding cargo bay door. Then he opened the right door of the container backed into the dock. Armed only with a flashlight, Sleazy stealthily walked into the half filled container, toting the flashlight in his left hand and the canister in his right.

As he approached the cargo, he noticed how well his workers had filled the container. They didn't waste any space. Sleazy put the canister down on the floor of the container, and shone his light onto the boxes. He was looking for space to place the canister. After rummaging around for a few minutes, Sleazy found a large box with "Books" written on the cardboard side. Exactly what Sleazy was looking for. He untaped the box and shone his light inside, revealing what it said on the outside of the box. Attempting to create a space big enough to accept the canister, Sleazy transferred books from this box to some other boxes in the same shipment. He placed the canister into the box and, to his delight, the canister fit perfectly. All Sleazy had to do was put a few books around the outside of the canister to make it more stable. Once he was done, he retaped the boxes.

The box containing the canister was taped shut using bright red vinyl tape. He was making the box easily identifiable for his cousin, Joseph, when he unloaded the container in his Boston CFS. He then rearranged the boxes so the red tape wasn't visible. He wanted to make sure the tape didn't attract the attention of any of his employees that loaded the shipment. Once this was done, he stepped back and looked at the results. He was satisfied that everything looked the same and nothing looked unusual. Sleazy closed the door to the container, secured the warehouse and went home.

In the morning, they continued stuffing the container; they were finished by lunchtime. The container, HLCU 9752469, was owned by the Hapag Lloyd Steamship Line. In the maritime shipping industry, it is standard practice for steamship lines to rent containers to shipping companies. The shipping companies defray their costs by charging the individuals actually owning the freight—in this case the soldiers. It was a profitable industry, but shippers had to be constantly vigilant of their costs or they could lose money. A major concern was the cost of transporting the container from a city in the interior of the country to a port along the coastline. Sleazy addressed this concern by hiring Pakistani immigrants living in Germany to drive the containers from Frankfurt, Germany to Antwerp, Belgium.

Since the distance between the two cities was about 400 kilometers, it was almost an all day drive. Sleazy had his drivers leave on the morning of the first day. Once they arrived in Antwerp, they'd drop the container off at Hapag Lloyd's Terminal at the seaport. Instead of immediately returning, they would sleep in their cabs overnight and return in the morning, hopefully with an inbound load. The Pakistani drivers accepted this practice as a fair deal. If Sleazy attempted this with German drivers, he'd have a strike on his hands. They would want to sleep in a hotel, receive money for meals and get overtime. Thus, Sleazy's costs would skyrocket. However, there were downsides to this arrangement. Pakistani drivers often became lost while navigating the unfamiliar German streets, German drivers never did. It was a trade off that Sleazy was able to deal with over the past several years.

Once the container was stuffed, Sleazy made arrangements for a Pakistani driver to drive to Antwerp in the morning. Sleazy picked a reliable, veteran driver. The cargo was too valuable to have one of the younger, less familiar drivers attempt the trip.

CHAPTER TWENTY SEVEN

Antwerp, Belgium, is the second largest seaport in Europe, only Rotterdam is larger. The container yards are huge, processing thousands of containers daily. The city itself is old, yet young. During WWII, more German V1 and V2 rockets hit the city than anywhere else. They knew how important the port was to the Allies war efforts. After the war, the city and port were rebuilt, converting Antwerp into one of the most livable cities in Europe. The city in 2004 had a thriving economy and its population of 500,000 was increasing yearly.

It was late in the afternoon when the Pakistani driver arrived in the port. He was directed to the main gate of Hapag Lloyd's container yard. There were many truckers in line ahead of him and he had to wait over an hour before he entered the yard. Once the clerks processed his paperwork, they directed him to an area to drop off the container. Luckily, there was a full container to be delivered to Frankfurt, but it wouldn't be ready until the morning. The Pakistani driver didn't mind because he was staying the night anyhow. After he dropped the container, he parked his cab in an adjacent parking area. He used the facilities in the longshoreman's building, and then returned to his truck to have supper. His wife had packed several meals for him, anticipating he'd be gone for at least two days. Once supper was over, he read a bit and then prepared his bed in the back of the cab. He made sure the doors to his cab were locked; he didn't want any unwelcome visitors during the night. Some of the other truckers took advantage of 'the local talent' during these layovers. Prostitutes had a habit of roaming amongst the trucks during the night. Sleazy's drivers were given explicit instructions not to mess with the prostitutes; if they did, they'd be fired. Sleazy knew of several incidents through the years involving the prostitutes and he didn't want any of his guys involved in this activity.

Before first light, Sleazy's driver was in line waiting to pick up the full container bound for Frankfurt. While he was sitting first in line, he saw the other truckers just starting to wake up. Girls were climbing out of a few of the cabs. Dumb bastards, he thought. By 8:30 am he had the container hooked up and he was back on the road headed home. With any luck, he'd be home for supper. He wasn't even out of the city when his problems developed. He first smelled smoke and suspected the odor was coming from the brakes on the chassis carrying the container, but he couldn't see any of the telltale signs of smoke. He was hoping the smell was just in the air and wasn't coming from him. A few minutes later, smoke was pouring out from underneath his truck.

He jumped out of the cab with fire extinguisher in hand to investigate. It didn't take him long to see what the problem was. The brakes on the rear right wheels of the chassis were red hot. The heat transferred to the rubber tire and started a fire. Thick acrid smoke enveloped the rear of the truck. Having experienced this before, the driver knew what to do. He emptied the fire extinguisher on the tire, eventually extinguishing the flames. About this time, a fire engine from a nearby fire house was responding to calls from local residents. Once they arrived, they inundated the rear of the truck with water. The Pakistani driver stood on the sidewalk and helplessly watched. Just an hour ago, everything seemed fine. He had his container and was headed home. Now he didn't know what was going to happen.

Thankfully, Hapag Lloyd sent a tow truck to the scene to retrieve the container and chassis. As the container was towed back to Hapag Lloyd's container yard, Sleazy's crestfallen driver had no choice but to follow. Once back in the container yard, the situation improved immediately. With German efficiency, the container was lifted off the old chassis and put on a new one. In less than an hour, the Pakistani driver was back on the road headed home. This time there weren't any problems, and he arrived at Sleazy's father's warehouse a little after six. The warehouse was closed, but Sleazy was waiting for him. Although Sleazy knew the container had been delivered to Hapag Lloyd's container facility, he wanted to confirm it with the driver. Once the driver told him there weren't any problems, Sleazy relaxed. His plans were proceeding on schedule.

Sleazy gave the driver some extra money for all his difficulties and told him not to report to work until noontime the next day. He had earned the extra time off. Sleazy called Usayd that night and gave him an update. He told Usayd the container was on the dock in Antwerp awaiting arrival of a ship that would carry it across the Atlantic Ocean to Boston, Massachusetts. Usayd, as expected, was pleased. He told Sleazy to call his cousin, Joseph, in Boston and give him an update. Once Joseph had the container number, he could track the container on his own. This way he would know when to expect its arrival in Boston. After calling his cousin in America, Sleazy's role in this endeavor was over; unless, of course, their attempt to send a dirty bomb to America was successful and the triumvirate decided to send more.

CHAPTER TWENTY EIGHT

The Hapag Lloyd Endeavor (affectionately called the Endeavor by her crew) was due to arrive in Antwerp at the end of the week. The steamship agent making up the load plan for the ship assigned Sleazy's container, HLCU 9752469, to a slot amidships on the second level above deck over #2 cargo hold. In layman's terms, that meant the container was located in a row two levels above the main deck and had containers on both sides. While Sleazy's container was being dropped off at Hapag Lloyd's yard in Antwerp, the Hapag Lloyd Endeavor was approaching the sea buoy and entering the harbor of LeHavre, France. The Endeavor had been on the North Atlantic route for the past five years. Her ports of calls were: Lehavre, France, Antwerp, Belgium and Southampton, England. After calling on Southampton, the Endeavor sailed across the North Atlantic and called on the same regular ports in North America: Halifax, Nova Scotia, Boston, Massachusetts, New York, New York, Baltimore, Maryland and Norfolk, Virginia. After sailing from Norfolk, she would head for LeHavre and began the cycle once again. A complete round-trip would take approximately 29-30 days, depending on the weather and any unforeseen delays.

In command of the Endeavor was one of either two captains: Captain Mercer or Captain Holland. Their schedule, along with the rest of the crew, had been worked out years ago and was the same today, with minor alterations due to crew becoming sick, retiring or quitting. Captain Mercer, the senior of the two, would complete two round trips on the Endeavor and then be relieved by Captain Holland. Captain Holland would complete two round trips and then Captain Mercer would replace him. This process had been going on for years and both captains enjoyed the predictability of their work schedule. The rest of the crew had similar schedules, but longer times onboard ship and less at home. The officers, whether mates or engineers, worked three months on and two months ashore on leave. The crew had life the roughest. They stayed onboard six months and went ashore for three. Not only did they have the least amount of time ashore, they were paid the least. Thus, there was a big incentive to study hard and advance through the ranks to become an officer.

The ship was comfortable and pleasant to work on. All the crew did their best to ensure being reassigned back to the Endeavor after their shore leave was complete. The living conditions on the Endeavor were better than most container ships plying the seven seas. Most of the crew had a private room; a few of the lower rates had to share a room, but even that was considered acceptable and reasonable. The food on the Endeavor was the best in the fleet. The Endeavor had some of the best cooks around; cooking all sorts of meals that constantly amazed the crew. The only complaint they had with the cooking was they were always gaining weight. The cooks promised they'd try to do something about that, but in the meantime, they encouraged everyone to eat less and maybe visit the ships gym every once in awhile. This stopped the phony complaining because everyone onboard loved to eat and few worked out in the gym. Granted, their work hours were long and arduous, but the company did encourage a daily regimen of exercise. They knew a healthy workforce was a productive workforce and they went out of their way to provide for the crews welfare. Although the Endeavor did not have a swimming pool (some of the newer ships did) they had a sauna, Jacuzzi and the state of the art weight room. If anyone was out of shape on the Endeavor, it was their fault and not the fault of the vessel's owners.

The Endeavor herself was a well built ship, built in Korea a little over ten years ago. Although ten years doesn't seem that long of a time, banging into ten, twenty, thirty foot seas month after month eventually wears down even the best of ships. Exposure to the elements also takes a huge toll on a ship. Seawater sneaks into the smallest of cracks, eventually creating bright streaks of rust all over the exterior hull of the ship. Daily maintenance by a conscientious captain will help keep the ship in good shape, but regularly scheduled maintenance in a shipyard is mandatory to keep a ship in good working order. Thankfully Hapag Lloyd knew this and insisted on a regular preventative maintenance program, to include visits to a shipyard every two years.

The Endeavor's power plant was run by some of the finest engineers going to sea. They labored over the engines and treated them with a love and passion seldom found on land. The Endeavor had huge diesel engines providing the power to propel the ship through the water. On land, you would only find comparable engines in some of the largest electrical generator plants in the world. A visit to the Endeavor's engine room would also impress the visitor because of the cleanliness they found. Even the bilges of the ship were routinely scrubbed and pumped out. This was a procedure followed by few other ocean-going vessels. Conservatively speaking, the Endeavor was one of the finest ships sailing anywhere in the world, just ask any member of her crew.

The Hapag Lloyd Endeavor arrived at dock # 17 in Antwerp Harbor before dawn on Friday morning. Because of her massive size, it required three powerful tugs to push and pull her alongside the dock. Once alongside, heaving lines from the ship were sent flying through the air, hitting the cement dock with a dull thud. Line handlers picked up the end of the heaving lines and began pulling. Attached to the other end of the heaving lines was thick double braided nylon mooring lines. Once the eye of the mooring line was pulled ashore, beefy longshoremen looped the eye over black shiny bollards, securing the ship safely to shore.

Exactly at 8:00 am, longshoreman began climbing the gangway onto the Endeavor, preparing the ship for unloading/loading operations. The containers to be unloaded had to be released from the constraints of steel cables securing them to the deck, preventing the container from falling overboard at sea. When they were released from their metal shackles, huge shore cranes swung a specially made cradle over the ship. The crane operator attached the cradle to the container and lifted it off the ship and onto a waiting truck chassis ashore. A wave from a clerk on the ground dispatched the driver into the container yard, pulling the container on the chassis behind him. The container would be offloaded from the truck chassis by a yard crane and stored in the container yard until a local trucker came and picked it up. This process continued throughout the day until all the containers scheduled to be offloaded were lifted off the ship. Then the process was reversed. All the outbound containers were loaded aboard the ship in a similar fashion. Container HLCU 9752469 was one of the last containers loaded. After all the other containers were onboard and properly secured, the Endeavor was ready for sea.

Just before midnight, the Endeavor slipped her lines and was pulled away from the dock by the same tugs that docked her earlier in the day. Once she was in midstream, the tugs backed away and left her on her own. Captain Mercer, assisted by a competent local pilot, navigated the Endeavor between the buoys marking the harbor channel and safely out to sea. As the sea buoy marking the entrance to the harbor approached off to port, a pilot boat came alongside to pick up the harbor pilot. After the pilot was safely away, Captain Mercer rang up full speed and ordered the Endeavor on a southwesterly heading. He intended to transit the heavily trafficked English Channel at night and be outside the entrance to South-ampton Harbor by the following evening.

Even though he had been up all day supervising loading operations, Captain Mercer felt obligated to stay on the bridge to help the mate on watch navigate the dangerous waters of the English Channel. Especially dangerous was the body of water called the Straits of Dover. This strait separated Great Britain from northern France and was at the eastern end of the English Channel. Only 21 miles wide, the heavy ship traffic had to converge to squeeze through this relatively narrow body of water. To compound the danger, ships traveling between England and France cut directly across this major ship lane. Even worse, at certain times of the year, heavy fog saturated the area, making the Straits of Dover one of the most dangerous spots to sail in the entire world. Captain Mercer was hop-ing there wasn't any fog this night.

About 3:00 am, the Endeavor was safely through the Straits of Dover and deep, open water lay ahead. Captain Mercer was confident his ship was in safe hands and went below to his stateroom to get some much deserved sleep. He was on his second round trip on the Endeavor and knew he'd be getting relieved in less than a month by his friend of many years, Captain Holland. Captain Mercer, a graduate of Germany's elite maritime academy in Hamburg, had been going to sea since graduation in

1970. Although he was in his mid fifties, he worked out constantly aboard ship and faithfully watched what he ate. Consequently, he looked younger than he was. When ashore, rumor had it that he was quite the ladies man. He was never married and swore he would remain that way; however he was always in the company of a beautiful woman.

When home, he was always taking trips to exotic places; accompanied by one of his many female friends. On his last leave, he went on a safari in eastern Africa. When he returned to the Endeavor after his leave, he had hundreds of pictures to show the crew. Everyone onboard the ship loved the captain because he was so kind and considerate. Probably because he didn't have a family of his own, Captain Mercer treated the crew as if they were his family. As he drifted off to sleep, the captain ran the distances between Antwerp and Southampton through his head. He felt comfortable they would make the evening tide; otherwise they would have to wait until the following morning's tide to enter Southampton Harbor. He hoped this didn't happen because it would throw the ship off schedule and worse, it would make the owners quite unhappy with him.

Two hours before schedule, the Endeavor approached the entrance to Southampton Harbor. Because the pilot hadn't arrived on station yet, Captain Mercer slowed the Endeavor to bare steerageway. He didn't want to drop the ship's anchor because it required so much work for such a short stay. Instead, he decided to drift on the calm sea while awaiting the arrival of the pilot. Shortly, the lookout on watch said he saw a boat approaching displaying a white over red combination light from her masthead. "White over red, pilot ahead," Captain Mercer said smiling, knowing the boat approaching was the pilot boat carrying the pilot out to the Endeavor. After an uneventful transit of Southampton Harbor, the Endeavor was all tied up at Southampton's main container yard by midnight. Captain Mercer was relieved. Since they weren't going to commence unloading until the morning, he looked forward to a good nights sleep.

In the morning, discharging of cargo began at the scheduled time of 7:00 am. Captain Mercer lay in bed and listened to the cranes lifting the containers off his ship. Every once and awhile, when an exceptionally heavy box was picked up, the ship rocked from side to side. Comforted by this rocking motion, the captain closed his eyes and fell back to sleep.

When the captain finally climbed out of bed, he was astonished at the time. It was almost 10:00 am; he didn't know when the last time he had slept so late. As he was freshening up in his bathroom, he heard a gentle knock on his outer door.

The captain yelled to come in and when he looked out the bathroom door, he saw his chief mate standing just inside the door. In mock anger the captain scolded the chief for allowing him to sleep so late. The chief mate told the captain everything was proceeding as planned, and there was no need to waken him. Besides, he said, the captain had been up over twenty four hours straight and must have been exhausted. He needed and deserved the extra sleep. The captain couldn't argue with the chief; he simply thanked him. The chief told the captain he was just checking up on him and when he was done getting dressed they could meet in the officer's dining room to go over the plans for the day. The captain thanked his chief and told him he'd be down in a few minutes.

When the captain arrived at the officer's dining room, the cook had a plate of bacon and eggs waiting for him. The captain was starving and was most appreciative of the cook's thoughtfulness. The chief mate drank another cup of coffee and reviewed the ships load plan as the captain had his breakfast. Once the captain was done eating, he wiped his mouth and turned to the chief. "Okay, Chief," he said, "now that I feel human again, let's get down to business. What do you have for me?" The chief smiled and looked down at his notes. "First of all," he said, "I am glad you are feeling better. You shouldn't stay on your feet so long. It is not good for your health" The captain laughed and waved his hand at the chief. "Okay chief, enough of your patronizing bull. What's up?" They both started laughing and then the chief started his briefing.

Most of the news was good. They should be done with discharging by early afternoon. He had already ordered a pilot for 6:00 pm. Two seamen were taken ashore for a doctor's visit and were back onboard. They were prescribed medicine and were fit for full duty. The captain was happy to hear that the sailors were fit for full duty. If they weren't, he'd have to spend overtime to cover their watch. This always made the owners unhappy. Fuel and water had been taken from shore and all the Endeavors tanks were topped off. Lastly, fresh provisions were received from the ships chandler and the ships reefers were full. "Sounds excellent," the captain said. "Is that it?"

The chief slid a paper from his clipboard and handed it to the captain. "Sorry to ruin all the good news, looks like we're going to be running into some foul weather." The captain looked at the paper the chief handed him. It was a weather map of the North Atlantic that was faxed to the ship not an hour ago. The captain's trained eye immediately saw what the chief was talking about. There were two huge centers of low pressure on the map, one over the Great Lakes and one off the eastern seaboard of North Carolina. From their study of meteorology in school and from real-life experience, they both knew these two lows would come together and form a monstrous storm. They also knew the storm was heading directly in the path of the Endeavor's anticipated route to Halifax, Nova Scotia. But, they also knew these storms often took unanticipated turns and sometimes even fizzled out. The captain and the chief knew there wasn't much either one of them could do. They'd sail as scheduled and deal with the weather as things developed. Hopefully, the lows wouldn't develop or would change course, because if they did come together, they were in for one helluva storm.

CHAPTER TWENTY NINE

The Endeavor sailed at 6:00 pm as planned. The pilot skillfully navigated the ship out of Southampton Harbor and into the open ocean. After the pilot relinquished control of the ship to the mate on watch and left the vessel, the mate put the Endeavor on a westerly heading and rang up full speed ahead, about twenty two knots. Halifax, Nova Scotia lay dead ahead, sailing time should be about four and a half days. As the ship sailed smoothly through the calm seas, the mate stood silently on the starboard wing of the bridge. He gazed upward towards the stars and immediately recognized the constellation Orion the Hunter with the three stars forming the belt pointing directly at the bright luminous star Aldebaran. What a way to make a living. People actually pay good money to go on cruises and enjoy nights like this, he thought. He was lucky enough to enjoy times like this and be paid at the same time. But, he knew, good times were often fleeting, too soon replaced by bad times.

The mate was briefed by the captain regarding the possibility of bad weather in a couple of days. He had been through a lot in his many years at sea, but he always managed to handle anything thrown his way, to include lousy weather. But, the weather system he saw on the fax copy the captain gave him looked pretty ominous. If these two lows merged, he knew they were going to be in for the ride of their lives. But, he also knew, as the captain and chief, weather systems were fickle. Often they would do the unpredictable and fool even the best of them. But, sometimes they did what was predicted. The mate hoped this wasn't one of those times.

For the next couple of days, life on the Endeavor fell into a routine. They all stood their four hours on and eight hours off watches, with nothing unusual happening. Every once in awhile they had a radar contact of another ship, but they never visually saw them. The captain constantly reviewed the updates on the weather and became more concerned as time went on. After two days at sea, the weather began to change. Thin, high clouds developed in the west, a slight wind was perceived and a long ocean swell could be felt on the crew's legs. The last time the captain checked the weather fax, he was convinced they were going to run directly into the storm's path if they maintained their present heading. Therefore, he directed the mate to change the ship's heading to the southwest. The captain was hoping this change in course might bring the Endeavor to the south of the storm and away from the brunt of its fury. The change in course would also delay their arrival in Halifax, but the captain thought the change was necessary to ensure the safety of the ship and its crew.

During the next twenty four hours, weather conditions grew more ominous by the hour. Another check of the latest weather fax indicated the storm had shifted a little to the southeast, directly in the path of the Endeavor! The captain knew there was nothing else he could do but ensure everything on the Endeavor was secured for the strong possibility of heavy weather. He ordered the mate to personally make the rounds with the boatswain and check all the container tie downs. He wanted all the turnbuckles tightened as much as possible to prevent the possibility of containers falling overboard in heavy seas. He also ordered all hatches secured and extra lashings on both anchors. He surely didn't want an anchor breaking loose and thrashing around on deck in heavy sea. Once all the necessary precautions were complete, all they could do was wait and see what Mother Nature had in store for them. They didn't have long to wait.

CHAPTER THIRTY

As the hours progressed, the skies darkened, the wind picked up appreciably and the seas began to build. Eventually, the skies became so dark it looked like they were sailing into oblivion. Some of the crew had the sensation that the darkness ahead was going to swallow the Endeavor, relegating them to the vagaries of the sea gods. The wind began to howl, creating blinding sea spray and a deafening, maddening screeching sound from a loose line in the rigging. Worse of all were the seas. In the beginning, there was a gradual buildup in their height. But suddenly, they became monstrous. Neither the captain nor the crew could remember ever seeing seas so big; some estimated the waves to be over fifty feet high! Immediately, the captain ordered a reduction in speed from the previous twenty two knots to a bare minimum five knots.

This speed gave the helmsman bare steerageway, allowing him to quarter the seas, or to take the seas on a forty-five degree angle relative to the bow of the ship. Consequently, the Endeavor would slowly ride up and then slide down the backside of each approaching wave. This was the safest method in dealing with heavy seas and was taught in all ship handling classes at maritime schools throughout the world. Despite everything Captain Mercer attempted, the conditions on the Endeavor worsened as the night progressed. The seas continued to increase in height and solid water began breaking on deck. The Endeavor rocked violently, but the lady she was, she shook off the water and continued sailing ahead.

In the early hours of the following morning, conditions worsened and the captain ordered all the crew to don their water immersion suits and report to the bridge. Shrill blasts from the ships whistle alerted the entire crew to the seriousness of the situation. As Captain Mercer awaited the crew's arrival on the bridge, he heard a heart wrenching call for help from another ship that was also caught in the throes of this monster storm. After fine tuning the squelch on the marine radio, the captain listened in to the conversation. The name of the ship calling the Canadian Coast Guard for assistance was the Corazon II. She was a bulk ship sailing from New Orleans, Louisiana to Saudi Arabia. The captain notified the coast guard that he was in immediate danger of sinking. The bow of his ship was getting lower and lower in the water, indicating they were taking on seawater in their #1 cargo hold.

Although they had all their pumps working, the bow continued to sink lower into the sea. The captain requested immediate assistance and told the coast guard he would probably have to abandon ship within fifteen minutes. As unbelievable as it sounds, while Captain Mercer was listening to this drama at sea unfold, over the high frequency radio he thought he detected a faint SOS transmitted on 2182 kHz, the maritime emergency frequency. The captain cocked his head and listened intently for another signal. Sure enough, he heard the SOS broadcast once again. The signal was real faint, indicating whatever ship was transmitting the signal was far away or transmitting on weak batteries.

While these two maritime emergencies were unfolding at sea, the situation aboard the Endeavor suddenly took a turn for the worse. Captain Mercer was in the chart room listening to the radio traffic, attempting to plot the position of both vessels seeking assistance. If either vessel was close by, perhaps the Endeavor could offer some sort of assistance, if and when he solved his own problems aboard the Endeavor. Suddenly, he heard the lookout gasp and scream, "Hang on!" The captain, already hanging on to the chart table, looked up in the direction of the screaming lookout. He then looked out the port bridge window in the direction the lookout was pointing. Less than two hundred yards away, a gigantic wave was roaring down upon them. The captain had to look up to see the top of the monster wave; it had to be at least seventy to eighty feet high!

There was nothing for anyone to do but hang on. Within seconds, the monster, rogue wave hit the Endeavor broad on her port side. The Endeavor rolled to starboard and kept rolling. As the captain sailed through the air, hitting hard against the chartroom door, he honestly thought it was all over; the Endeavor was rolling to starboard and would keep rolling until she turned turtle. The helmsman, seeing the rogue wave coming, grabbed the wheel as hard as he could. All his strength was not enough; the force of the wave catapulted him across the bridge deck. He didn't stop until his head hit the starboard radar, blood flowing from his forehead. The sailors rushing to don their immersion suits and get up to the bridge suffered the most; they didn't know the rogue wave was coming and weren't prepared for the impact. They were all thrown against something hard and unmoving, causing bruises, cuts and a couple broken bones.

The captain was lying on the deck in the doorway between the chart room and the bridge. He felt the Endeavor's momentum to starboard slow and then slowly shift to port. He stumbled to his feet and realized the Endeavor was recovering from the horrific roll. But, as he attempted to stand, he saw the ships steering wheel spinning out of control. My god, he thought, where is the helmsman? The captain staggered the ten foot distance to the wheel and tried grabbing one of the spinning spokes. A spoke hit the back of his hand so hard, the captain cried out in pain. Eventually, he was able to get the wheel under control and slowly brought the Endeavor back on her original course. By this time, the mate had recovered from his fall and relieved the captain at the wheel. Others began to stumble into the bridge from down below, their bright international orange immersion suits clearly distinguishable in the dark.

About this time is when they heard the noise. The captain looked out on deck through the bridge window and saw an unimaginable sight. Two forty foot containers were bouncing around above #2 hold as if they were tiny plastic toys. One container smashed into another and then was swept over the side by a monstrous wave, only to be swept back onboard by a second wave. The captain was in a momentary state of shock, he couldn't believe what he was seeing. The rogue wave hit the Endeavor so hard that containers on deck were ripped from their tie downs. As the captain continued to look on in awe, he saw two more containers in the water on the starboard side. They kept banging into the ship as they drifted down the starboard side.

Eventually, all four containers cleared the ship and were lost in the darkness. However, one container remained loose onboard, swinging crazily from the one tie down that remained intact. One moment she veered to starboard, the next second she went to port. The mate yelled to the captain that he was going on deck with a couple of seamen in an attempt to corral the errant container. Captain Mercer, in a firm, commanding voice, told the mate to stay where he was. Only bad things could happen to anyone crazy enough to go out on deck at a time like this; if you weren't swept overboard by a wave, you'd surely be crushed by the swinging container. All of a sudden, the careening container stopped its crazy movement. Peering through his binoculars, the captain could see why. One of the loose tie down cables became snagged between two other containers, temporarily securing the container in place. Thank god, the captain thought, miracles do happen.

Relieved that the container was finally secured, the captain turned his attention to the welfare of the crew. Most were bruised and battered, but a couple were hurting. The helmsman had a nasty head wound and an oiler had a possible broken arm. One of the mates was tending to them and though they would require further medical attention, he thought they could wait until they reached Halifax. Just as their situation seemed to be improving, an audio alarm sounded on the engine room control panel. The chief engineer was the first to the panel. "Shit," he said," fire in the aft steering room." A second later, he and two assistant engineers were bounding down stairs leading to the engine room. They'd be damned if they'd let an engine room fire get the best of them.

Then the helmsman called out, "Captain, I'm losing steerage. The rudder is not responding!" Quickly, the captain realized what must be happening. The fire in the aft steering room had somehow affected the steering pump. In those seas, if this wasn't fixed immediately, the Endeavor was in serious trouble. She would shortly be in imminent danger of broaching. The captain yelled to his first mate to take a couple of seamen and get below. They had to rig up the emergency steering gear in a hurry. He then turned to his boatswain, "Boats," he commanded, "send out a Pan-Pan on 2182. Give our position and status. Tell anyone who is in the vicinity we could really use their help." The boatswain replied firmly, "Yes, sir, captain, right away," and then disappeared into the radio room.

Moments later, the Chief Engineer was calling the captain on his hand-held radio. A hydraulic line for the steering motor had ruptured and was spraying hydraulic fluid all over a hot generator. The smoke was thick but they were all wearing self-contained-breathing-masks. They should have the problem fixed within fifteen minutes. The captain said he was grateful and told the Chief Engineer others were on their way to the aft steering room to rig up the emergency steering gear. The Chief Engineer acknowledged what the captain said and told him they'd assist with the steering gear once they fixed the hydraulic line.

As the captain breathed a sigh of relief, the boatswain mate bounded out of the radio room. "Captain, Captain," he said excitedly, "I made contact. A U.S.Navy ship answered my Pan-Pan. They said they're coming. They're only thirty miles away and they're sending help." The boatswain was crying and laughing at the same time. He knew what danger they were in and it was a huge relief to know help was close by. The captain too was relieved. Maybe they might get out of this mess after all, he thought. But, they still had to contend with the weather. Even though there weren't any more rogue waves to deal with, the seas were still huge. The wind was also continuing to blow, but some swore they thought it wasn't as bad as an hour ago.

Then the helmsman yelled out, "Captain, I have steerage. I have steerage." Just as the helmsman was telling the captain he could now steer the Endeavor once again, the captain's radio began blaring. It was the Chief Engineer; the hydraulic line was fixed and everything was fine once again in the engine room. They were all coming topside. About this time, Captain Mercer thought he was going to collapse. He had fought heavy seas for two days, been broadsided by a rogue wave that nearly capsized them, survived a runaway container, an engine room fire and a steering casualty, all within hours of each other. He couldn't endure one more incident; he was nearing exhaustion.

"Radar contact, Captain," yelled the mate. "Two contacts, Captain. They're approaching from our port quarter at a speed of twenty knots. Distance eight miles." The captain was perplexed. Two contacts approaching at twenty knots? Impossible, he thought. Not in these seas. Then they heard a loud whining noise. Then more noise. The captain ran out to the port wing and looked up just in time to see two jets screeching overhead.

He was just able to make out "U.S.Navy" on their fuselage. Then two more jets roared overhead, or were they the same two? The captain's heart and mind were racing. After all he'd been through, he was utterly exhausted. But seeing these jets brought him back to life. Seeing the "U.S.Navy" on the sides of the aircraft told him everything was going to be okay. He could relax, the U.S.Navy was on scene and they wouldn't let anything happen to him, his crew or the ship.

"Look Captain," the mate standing alongside him said, "just abaft the beam. Look at them sir." The captain turned his head and off in the distance he could clearly see two ships heading in their direction. Seas were pounding off their decks but they still kept coming. In five minutes they were on either side of the Endeavor at a distance of 1,000 yards. Overhead, instead of jets, two large choppers hovered, waiting to render any assistance the Endeavor required, including airlifting the entire crew if necessary. Knowing the Endeavor was now clearly out of any immediate danger, Captain Mercer radioed one of the navy ships steaming alongside. He told them he didn't require any further assistance, but thanked them for their speedy response. After a few minutes delay, the navy ship radioed back. They said they were steaming towards Halifax anyway, so both ships would shadow the Endeavor as she proceeded to port. Captain Mercer thanked them and said he hoped he'd see them in port. He owed them a drink. Laughter could be heard over the radio when the navy responded. They said they too would like to meet in port. Possibly they could oblige him in having a drink.

As the Endeavor proceeded toward Halifax, the seas became less violent and the wind decreased noticeably. Life slowly returned to an acceptable level of normalcy. When Captain Mercer inquired as to the fate of the Corazon II, the Canadian Coast Guard told him they were able to drop enough pumps to her to keep her afloat. She was presently inbound to Halifax, escorted by a Canadian commercial tug. Regarding the other ship sending out an SOS, the Canadian Coast Guard knew nothing about her. Captain Mercer was happy the Corazon II was safe, but he still wondered about the other ship. He promised himself that he was going to do some checking once he got ashore. But, until then, he was going to bed. He was exhausted.

By the time the Endeavor reach the southern approach to Halifax Harbor, the seas had abated. A slight easterly swell was the only reminder of the monster storm that they had just sailed through. The storm did take a toll on the Endeavor, however. Not only did they lose four containers overboard, they had two seamen that would require medical attention ashore. Also, the storm had delayed the Endeavor's arrival into Halifax by almost forty eight hours. Captain Mercer knew the owners wanted to get back on schedule and somehow they were going to make up for the time they had lost.

Slowly the tugs turned the Endeavor around and pointed her bow out, then they gently nestled her into the pier at Halifax's southern container terminal. Captain Mercer had never been so happy to be tied up to dry land. "Terra firma," he whispered to himself. "The more firma, the less terror." As soon as the gangway was safely lowered, a medical unit from Halifax General scrambled aboard. They evaluated both injured seamen and decided they had to be taken to the hospital for further treatment. The helmsman's head wound was going to require several stitches and it was probable that he had a mild concussion. The seaman with the possible broken arm was complaining of numbness in his hand. The doctor feared he had nerve damage and wanted to take him to the hospital for a battery of x-rays.

While the two hurt sailors were being loaded in an ambulance, surveyors from the insurance company were onboard estimating the amount of damage that was caused by the storm. They knew up front that four containers and their contents were a total loss. Another container, HLCU 9752469, was severely damaged with gaping holes in both sides. They estimated the container and contents were probably a total loss, but decided to let the container continue to Boston where other surveyors from the company could make the determination when the container was stripped at a CFS.

This was the container Sleazy was shipping to his cousin, Joseph, at Shawmut Freight Terminal. Unbeknownst to them, their container came real close to going over the side along with the other four containers. Even now, the condition of everything inside the container was in doubt. Possibly, everything was destroyed by sea water. Additionally, the surveyors found extensive damage to the railings on the starboard side. It appeared the two containers that fell overboard and drifted down the Endeavor's starboard side inflicted the damage. The only other damage found by the surveyors was minimal and attributed to the storm.

Trying to make up for lost time, discharging started immediately. Captain Mercer was notified by the ship's agents that a change in itinerary was ordered by the owners. The Endeavor was to bypass Boston and travel directly to New York. All the containers destined for Boston were to be offloaded in Halifax and shipped to Boston on a small feeder vessel called the Yankee Clipper. The owners estimated this change would make up for almost all the lost time and put the Endeavor back close to her schedule. While discharging of cargo was proceeding at a good pace, Captain Mercer remained onboard to take care of the large volume of necessary paperwork.

About dinnertime, two guests wearing United States Naval uniforms came onboard. They were the commanding officers of the two U.S. Navy ships that escorted Captain Mercer and the Endeavor into port. They wanted to come aboard and say hello to the captain face to face. Captain Mercer was most gracious to his guests and asked if they'd stay for dinner. Both declined and asked the captain to come ashore to have that drink they talked about while at sea. Captain Mercer regretfully declined because he had too much work to do onboard to get the Endeavor ready to sail. The two naval captains fully understood and told Captain Mercer he still owed them that drink. Captain Mercer assured them he was a man of his word and someday their paths would cross again, hopefully under better conditions. They all shook hands and then the naval officers left the ship.

Late that same evening, Captain Mercer was back on the bridge of the Endeavor, welcoming the outbound pilot onboard. Because the longshoremen really hustled offloading the containers, they were able to push up the sailing time. Instead of leaving in the morning, the Endeavor was able to leave that night. The crew wasn't happy because they looked forward to a restful night in port. At 11:30 pm the Endeavor was away from the dock and underway for New York Harbor, minus two good sailors and the 112 containers bound for Boston.

CHAPTER THIRTY ONE

The Yankee Clipper was a three hundred foot container vessel of German registry. In the shipping industry, the Yankee Clipper was considered a feeder vessel. Her purpose in life was to shuttle and consolidate containers from smaller ports to major ports allowing mother ships like the Endeavor, to bypass these smaller ports to save valuable time and money. The Yankee Clipper was on the Portland, Maine, Boston, Massachusetts, Halifax, Nova Scotia run. Once a week she would follow this route. Starting in Halifax, she would deliver containers destined for Portland and Boston that the mother ships dropped off in Halifax. As she dropped off these containers, she would pick up any outbound containers destined for overseas and drop them off in Halifax, to await loading on a mother ship heading back to Europe. Similar arrangements like this were performed throughout the world with the advent of containerization. The Yankee Clipper had been on this run for several years to the satisfaction of all parties concerned. Loading the 112 containers from the Endeavor that were bound for Boston was extra cargo for the Yankee Clipper and was much appreciated; it would dramatically increase their revenue for the month.

The morning after the Endeavor sailed, the longshoremen concentrated on loading the Yankee Clipper. Work commenced at 8:00 am and they hoped to have all the containers onboard by late afternoon. The container that was damaged aboard the Endeavor, HLCU 9752469, the one stuffed by Sleazy in Frankfurt and destined for Sleazy's cousin's container freight station in Boston, was stowed below decks. The surveyors made this request because they didn't want the container damaged anymore than she was. Work progressed at a relatively fast pace and the Yankee Clipper was finished loading by 4:00 pm. By 6:00 pm, they were away from the dock and on their way to Portland, Maine.

Most people making a living going to sea would consider the Yankee Clipper's route a "milk run," but most people don't know what they are talking about. Yes, under ideal conditions, it was a milk run, but seldom were the conditions ideal. In the summer months, fog often shrouded their route. Sometimes they would leave the dock in Halifax and not see anything until they reached the dock in Portland. Radar was the only thing keeping them from crashing into another ship. By the time they reached the dock, the crew's nerves were usually frayed. In the winter months, ice formed so thick on the deck and containers that the crew had to break out big rubber mallets to break the ice off. If they didn't, the ship could become top-heavy and flip over or "turn turtle." The one big advantage the crew of the Yankee Clipper had was she was in port almost every night, a luxury deep-sea sailors didn't have.

After sailing into Portland and unloading and loading all their containers, the Yankee Clipper headed south for Boston. Since they weren't due in Boston until the following evening, the captain adjusted her speed so he would arrive at the BG buoy at the entrance to the North Channel at 8:00 pm. No sense burning more fuel running at a higher rate of speed, the captain explained to the mate. The trip proved uneventful until they passed Cape Ann and had Gloucester Harbor on their beam. The mate on watch and the helmsman were drinking coffee and talking about what a fine trip they were having.

Just as the mate put the coffee mug up to his mouth, he saw something move out of the corner of his eye. He quickly looked off to starboard and saw a huge whale broaching the surface of the sea. It wasn't more than 100 yards off the ship's starboard side. Following alongside the whale were dolphins, at least six. The whale and dolphins ran with the Yankee Clipper for at least fifteen minutes, to the delight of the crew who happened to be awake to see them. After the whale and dolphins went on their way, the normal routine returned. A little before 7:00 pm, the mate picked up the BG buoy on radar. About 200 hundred yards from the buoy, he had another solid contact he assumed to be the pilot boat. Fifteen minutes later, he could see both with his powerful binoculars.

As the Yankee Clipper slowly sailed past the BG buoy, the pilot boat came alongside. When the pilot boat was abreast of the Jacob ladder, the pilot reached out, grabbed the ladder and scurried up and onboard. He was escorted to the bridge and took immediate control of the ship. For the rest of the trip into the inner harbor and alongside the pier at Conley Container Yard, the pilot engaged in a running documentary on the history of the harbor. The mate and helmsman enjoyed listening to the pilot's wealth of knowledge and asked many questions. But, they were soon alongside the pier and their tour abruptly ended. It was time to get back to business. In less than 30 minutes, all the Yankee Clipper's mooring lines were ashore and she was safely docked. The crew could relax for the night. Discharging would start promptly at 8:00 am.

PART IV

CHAPTER THIRTY TWO

Because the Yankee Clipper had orders to discharge at 8:00 am, the Customs Inspectors running the x-ray truck had to start work an hour earlier to set up. Larry, the inspector with the most experience on the truck, arrived at the Customs office before seven, with a cup of coffee, a doughnut and a copy of the Boston Herald under his arm. Before he sat down to enjoy his coffee, Larry went outside and started the truck. He wanted the engine good and warm before they started to work. Larry bumped into Russ and Steve in the parking lot as he was returning to the office. Russ and Steve, fellow Customs Inspectors, were going to work with Larry x-raying all the containers coming off the Yankee Clipper. Although they weren't as experienced on the x-ray truck as Larry, they were excellent inspectors.

After having their coffee, the three of them walked out to the truck and began preparing for a full days work. Once they were sure everything was working, Russ jumped in the driver's seat and started backing the truck up, guided by Steve and Larry. When he was in the clear, Larry and Steve jumped in and they drove down to the pier alongside the Yankee Clipper. Longshoremen were already aboard, removing the tie down cables securing the containers to the deck. As planned, at 8:00 am, two cranes rambled down the pier and stopped when they were opposite the Yankee Clipper, one near the bow and the other by the stern. When they were positioned properly, the cranes began lifting containers from the ship and onto awaiting trucks. Once the container was fastened securely to the truck, the driver drove forward where the x-ray truck was positioned. Within two minutes, the x-ray truck ran the length of the container. Larry, sitting inside the truck in front of a colored screen, seeing nothing abnormal, would radio Steve that the container could go. Steve, standing outside as a guide for Russ, would wave to the trucker and tell him he could go. Work progressed in this fashion all morning. By lunch, half the containers were offloaded.

After lunch, Larry drove and Russ monitored the x-ray screens inside. Steve stayed as the outside man. Containers kept coming off and each one was x-rayed before it was taken into the container yard. All the containers on deck were offloaded and the crew opened the cargo hatches so the cranes could gain access to the containers below decks. By afternoon coffee break, only ten containers remained onboard, including damaged container HLCU9752469.

There was a momentary lull in activity, so Steve climbed up on the running board on the driver's side of the truck and started talking with Larry. They were talking about when the next container ship was due when they saw the crane lift the container out of the cargo hold, water pouring out from the bottom and side. "This must be the damaged container they were telling us about," Larry said to Steve. "Shit," Steve said, "what was it, under water?" Larry laughed and said, "No shithead, it was damaged as it was coming over on the mother ship. They ran into some nasty weather. Someone told me they actually lost some containers over the side." "Fuck," Steve said, "that's why I stay on fucking land, there ain't no waves there." They both laughed as Steve climbed down from the running board to take his position at the rear of the truck.

The yard driver pulling the container came to a gentle, gradual stop as he approached the x-ray truck, water was still leaking from the bottom. Slowly, the x-ray truck moved down the length of the container, scanning the contents as it went. Russ was inside, his face glued to the x-ray screen. All of a sudden, he began to see anomalies. The screen was showing two small suspicious areas in the nose of the container, one big area in the middle and one by the door. Russ called Steve over the radio. "Steve, don't let that truck go anywhere. We have something unusual on the screen." Steve in his typical funny style said, "Okay, dude, the truck won't go anywhere." Then Russ called Larry. "Larry, can you come back here please? There's something on the screen I can't figure out." "Okay," Larry said, "I'll be right there." Larry put the truck in park and engaged the emergency brake. As he climbed out of the cab, a loud hissing noise from the air brakes startled him. *What a fucking noisy place*, he muttered.

Larry climbed in the back of the truck where Russ was sitting and looked at the x-ray screen. It was readily apparent to Larry the container contained personal and household effects, more likely than not a consolidation of shipments of soldiers returning from active duty in Germany. Then Larry took a closer look. He saw the anomalies Russ was concerned about and adjusted the tuning to get a better picture. Even after making fine adjustments, the anomalies remained. "Well," Larry said, "I see what you mean Russ. It could be several things. The white patches look exactly like the C4 explosive the ATF (Alcohol, Tobacco and Firearms) showed us in training. But, remember what they said, a lot of other material will look the same way." Russ shook his head and tried to recall what other materials they mentioned because he knew Larry was going to ask him. "Do you remember what those materials are?" Larry asked. Russ felt his face flush as he said, "Fuck, Larry, I'm sorry, I've fucking forgot."

Steve climbed into the back of the truck about this time. "What's up dudes," he said, "You find something Russ?" Larry turned to Steve and asked him the same question he asked Russ. "Steve, what other materials will give you the same image on the x-ray screen that C4 will?" Immediately Steve replied, "Water, any dumb fuck knows that." Steve looked at Russ and said, "You knew that Russ didn't you?" Russ felt like strangling Steve. Steve was right but he was also busting Russ' chops. Steve could tell by the expression on Russ' face when he walked in that Russ was confused and decided to have a little fun at his friend's expense. He couldn't help himself. "Thanks Steve," Russ said, and they all started laughing.

Larry turned their attention back to the screen. He explained to Russ and Steve that it could possibly be chunks of C4, but he didn't believe so. The whiteness on the screen had fuzzy edges; if it was C4 the edges would be sharper. Also, the way the white spots were dispersed throughout the container didn't make sense; they would be concentrated in one area if it was C4. One other factor convinced Larry everything was okay; the radiation detector on the side of the x-ray truck didn't show any presence of radiation. This meant they didn't have to worry about a dirty bomb. Knowing this container was damaged at sea and sea water had obviously saturated just about everything inside, Larry felt comfortable that nothing dangerous was present. It was the sea water causing a false read on the x-ray screen. Larry told Russ and Steve that he had a back up plan anyway. This container was going over to the CFS, Shawmut Freight Terminal, to be stripped. When that happened, they would take a ride over there and inspect the contents of the container to see what was giving them the false read. Knowing this, Russ felt a lot better letting the container go. If they were wrong, they'd soon find out.

They finished x-raying all the containers off the Yankee Clipper and headed back to the office. As soon as Larry arrived, he grabbed a phone and called Shawmut Freight Terminal. Joseph, the lead warehouseman answered the phone on the second ring. Larry and Joseph had known each other professionally for over five years and had the utmost respect for each other. Joseph was always accommodating and respectful with whomever he was dealing with. He also ran one of the most efficient warehouses in the city. When Larry told Joseph they had a container off the Yankee Clipper that had to be brought over to Joseph's warehouse to be stripped, Joseph acted as usual and told Larry he'd send a truck right over to pick up the container. Larry told Joseph they wouldn't be inspecting the container tonight and asked if first thing in the morning was possible. As usual, Joseph told Larry that wasn't a problem and he was even going to bring in an extra man to help strip the container. In the meantime, a truck was on the way over to Conley Container Terminal to pick up the container. Joseph promised Larry he'd have the container backed up to the dock and ready for inspection first thing in the morning.

After cleaning up, Larry, Russ and Steve went down to the Farragut House, a local Irish pub that served great food, to have a quick beer before they went home. When they arrived, there were a couple other Customs Inspectors from the airport already there. By the way they were acting, Larry thought they'd been there for quite awhile. Naturally they all sat together, but Russ was soon bored with the conversation. All the airport inspectors wanted to talk about was how hard they worked and how nobody appreciated them. Russ thought these guys should work the seaport for awhile and then they'd see what real work was. Russ departed, using the excuse he had to get up early in the morning to strip the container. In reality, he wanted to get home to see his wife. She was pregnant and due any day; Russ didn't want to be in an inebriated state when the time came. Besides, the airport guys were getting on his nerves.

CHAPTER THIRTY THREE

When Joseph left work, he stopped by *Patrick's* in South Boston and bought himself a meatball sub and a cup of black coffee. He drove down to Castle Island and parked his car facing Pleasure Bay. As he ate his sub, he bounced a lot of different scenarios around in his head. Now that the container had finally arrived, he had to act and he had to act quickly. With Customs Inspectors coming down to the warehouse in the morning to inspect the container, he didn't have much choice; he was going to have to act tonight. As he ate his sub and sipped on his coffee, he watched husbands and wives with their children walking the boardwalk enjoying the warm September evening. How peaceful he thought. How relaxing. Joseph wished he was with his wife and two year old son walking the boardwalk. Instead, he was sitting in his car eating a sub trying to figure out how to do something he wished he didn't have to do.

He had to do it because of the jam he got himself into. Those fucking loan sharks, he thought. All he needed was $10,000 to pay off the bookies, but then he needed more money. At first it was recreational drug use, but then he got hooked on heroin. Messing with the prostitutes at the local hotels deepened his plight. He had to go back to the loan sharks for more money, but now the interest they were charging was outrageous. He was never going to be able to repay them. They told him if he didn't pay up, they were going to break his legs or worse. They told him they knew he had a wife and two year old son. He didn't want them to suffer for his mistakes, did he? Joseph was considering committing suicide. He had no choice, that was the only way he was going to escape.

Then an angel appeared; his name was Sleazy. When his cousin Sleazy called and told him about their plans to ship a dirty bomb to his ware-

house, Joseph was at first reluctant. He had enough troubles he was dealing with, he didn't need any more. But when Sleazy told him he could
make some serious money in the deal, Joseph was all ears. If he made the
money Sleazy promised, he could pay off the loan sharks and work on
getting his life back. Who knows, maybe he could even kick his heroin
habit. If he did, maybe he could convince his wife to come back and live
with him again. He missed her and he was going crazy not being able to
see his little boy. Like he said, he had to do it.

CHAPTER THIRTY FOUR

After looking out over the water for several hours, Joseph knew it was time. He had to return to Shawmut Freight Terminal, his place of employment since he came to this country from Pakistan over ten years ago. With any luck, he could be in and out within an hour. He had mixed emotions on what he was about to do. Was he betraying his adopted country? Was he being disloyal and unfaithful to his trusted employer? An employer who hired him when no one else would. An employer who treated him as if he was his own son. Enough of this psycho-babble, he thought. He knew what he had to do and that is exactly what he was going to do. If he was successful, he might be able to change his entire life. He might be able to get back together with his young, beautiful wife and their cute little baby. Fuck the loyalty bullshit; he had to think of his welfare first. Besides, the United States deserved being terrorized by a dirty bomb after all the harm and destruction it has caused throughout the world.

He parked in his usual spot. When he got out of his car, he casually looked around to see if anyone else was working. No one should be, but it was possible someone was there catching up on some last minute project. Once he was satisfied he was alone, he walked towards the side door that he'd been walking through ever since he was hired as a janitor so many years ago. Being the lead warehouseman at Shawmut Freight gave Joseph free rein to the warehouse and offices. He had keys giving him access to every room and office in the entire building. As soon as he entered the building, he walked directly to the electrical room, making a conscious decision to stay away from the offices and warehouse floor. After flipping the light switch on in the electrical room, he scanned the circuit breakers in the 200 ampere electrical panel. When he came to breaker # 21, a smile came on his face as he read the sticker on the breaker, *Security Cameras, Do not turn off.* He raised his right hand and with one forceful, assertive move the security camera system for the entire warehouse was deactivated (or so Joseph thought). Now he could roam the building freely, knowing the security cameras wouldn't be tracking his every movement.

From the electrical closet, Joseph walked out onto the main warehouse floor. He removed a bolt used as an improvised lock from the bottom of the roll-up door at Bay 7 and then pressed the 'up' button switch attached to the wall close by. Slowly the corrugated steel door began to rise. During the day, all the other surrounding noises must have masked the noise of the door, because he never realized how noisy it was. He stepped out onto the cargo platform. In front of him were the cold, metal doors to container HLCU 9752469. Using a heavy bolt cutter, Joseph cut the bolt seal securing the doors of the container. He also cut the U.S.Customs seal that Larry had affixed to the container door at Conley Terminal. With the cutting of the bolt and Customs seal, Joseph realized he had crossed the line. He had just committed a felony in the eyes of the U.S.Government. Once the bolt and seal were removed, he opened the right door of the container. Water poured out onto the ground. As the door swung open, a foul, putrid smell hit Joseph. He shone his flashlight into the container and saw nothing but a big pile of broken furniture. Wet cardboard boxes lay in a heap by the door.

Joseph gingerly worked his way into the middle of the sea container. He was getting frustrated because his flashlight kept fading in and out. When he thought he was in the right area, Joseph began moving boxes around, looking for the box with shiny red tape. Suddenly, he saw something shiny in the beam of his flashlight. He looked closer and saw red vinyl tape wrapped around a water-soaked cardboard box. That's it, he thought. He found it! After clambering over a pile of clothes, Joseph reached the box. He took his knife and deftly cut the red vinyl tape. When he opened the flaps of the box, he saw the steely grey canister. His eyes remained glued to the canister for a minute. So this is what it's all about, he said to himself. This is what a dirty bomb looks like!

Joseph reached down and grabbed one of the handles attached to the side of the grey canister. Surprisingly, when he pulled on the handle, the canister slid right out of the box. For some reason, Joseph thought it was going to be real heavy, not the thirty pounds or so that he estimated the canister weighed. Tugging the grey canister with him, Joseph had to fight his way out of the sea container and back onto the platform. Once on the platform, Joseph retraced his steps. He closed the doors to the sea container, closed the roll-up door and then walked to the electrical closet, lugging the dirty bomb with him. After he turned the circuit breaker for the security cameras back on, he scurried out the side door of the building. He put the grey canister in his trunk, and then slowly drove out of the parking lot. He was anxious to get away, but he didn't want to draw any attention. Once he was on Summer Street in front of the Fargo Building, he began to relax and breath normally again.

CHAPTER THIRTY FIVE

As he was driving to his house in West Roxbury, a part of Boston but on the outskirts of the city, he called the contact number Sleazy had given him. When the contact answered the phone, Joseph told him he had the shipment the contact was waiting for. The two made arrangements to meet at Joseph's house at midnight. Once they met, Joseph would give him the grey canister and they'd be on their way. What they planned on doing with it, Joseph didn't care. All he wanted was the money Sleazy promised him. Once he had the money, he could pay off the loan sharks and get himself in some kind of recovery program.

Passing through Forest Hills on the way home, Joseph began getting fidgety. He hadn't had a hit of heroin for a couple of days and he needed it, especially now with all the pressure he was under. He thought of stopping off at the projects and buying a couple of bags, but then decided he better not. He should be straight when he met the contact and gave him the canister. But as he traveled up Washington Street, his car turned down Archdale Road, the entrance to the projects. He couldn't help himself. Buying heroin in the projects was like buying milk at the supermarket. After parting with $200, Joseph had what he wanted and was on his way back up Washington Street. As he was passing through Roslindale Square, he noticed the clock on top of the bank building. The time was only 9:30 pm. Joseph realized if he hurried home, he could take a hit of his shit before his company arrived. He needed something to settle him down and decided a small hit would be exactly what he needed.

It was exactly midnight when they pulled up in front of Joseph's house. The lights were on in the downstairs rooms and Joseph's car was in the driveway, so they knew he was home. Two of them walked up the four stairs to the front porch and knocked on the front door. The other two waited impatiently in the van. Repeated knocks on the door brought no response. Immediately they became suspicious and suspected a set-up. They both fingered their 9mm Glocks and pulled them from their shoulder holsters, holding the weapon at the ready by their side. One of them whistled to the other two in the van. Once he had their attention, he told them to go around back and cover the back door.

After giving them a minute to get in place, they tried opening the door. The door knob easily turned and with a gentle push, the door swung wide open. They stepped over the threshold and cautiously moved forward, one covering the other. The front room was clear and then they were in the study. That room was clear also. As they stepped into the well lighted kitchen, they saw him. He was sitting on a chair at the kitchen table; his head and chest were lying on the table. His right arm was by his side and his left arm was extended across the kitchen table, a rubber tourniquet wrapped around his upper arm and a hypodermic needle dangling from his forearm. Spots of dried blood were splattered across the otherwise impeccably clean tablecloth.

How long he was dead didn't matter to them. This wasn't a social call. They didn't know him and didn't care about him. They came for the grey canister with the dirty bomb and that is all they cared about. After a search of the downstairs, they found the grey canister in a back hallway. A quick peek inside revealed everything was there. The taller of the two picked up the canister saying, "Okay, we've got it, let's get the fuck out of here." They met the other two outside as they were coming from the back yard. Without saying a word, they opened the side door to the van, placed the canister in the back and then they all jumped in. Seconds later the van was on Centre Street traveling towards Route 128. They wanted to get some distance between themselves and West Roxbury before the body was found. While stopped at a red light at the VFW Parkway, two Boston Police cars zipped by them, going in the other direction, blue lights flashing and sirens blaring.

CHAPTER THIRTY SIX

In the morning, Larry and Steve drove over to Shawmut Freight Terminal to help strip the container and determine what was giving them the false read on the x-ray screen. Russ wasn't there; he banged in sick. Supposedly his wife was having contractions and he might have to take her to the hospital. Steve thought he knew different. Russ was up late last night watching the Patriots beat Buffalo. He probably had too many beers, wasn't feeling too good and decided to stay in bed. Besides, he never did like stripping containers. The work was too dirty for him.

They arrived a little before 9:00 am and went directly into the main office. After flirting with the girls for a few minutes, Larry asked one of them where Joseph was hiding. She winced and jerked her head in the direction of the warehouse floor. "You'd better ask George," she said, "We haven't seen him all morning." No problem, Larry thought, and walked out onto the warehouse floor to talk with George, part owner of Shawmut Freight. "Good morning, George," Larry cheerfully said, "how are you this bright, shining morning?" George wasn't in the same cheerful mood as Larry. "Hi Larry," he said, "not too fucking good. I'm swamped with work, got truck drivers yelling for their loads and my fucking lead warehouseman is amongst the missing. Not too fucking good!"

A fork lift sped by with a load of wooden pallets dangling from the two metal blades protruding from the front, "George, where did you say you wanted these?" the fork lift operator yelled.

George looked confused and overwhelmed as he thought for a second and then said, "Oh yeah, Bay 1, the Mayflower driver needs them." No sooner was the fork lift driver gone when a girl from the office was yelling at him. "George," she yelled, "line two is still on hold waiting for you. Do you want me to take a message?" "Oh shit," George said, "I forgot all about him," as he turned and walked swiftly towards the office.

Larry and Steve saw that George was a bit busy so they decided to take a look at the container by themselves. It was obvious to them that they weren't going to be stripping the container that morning, but maybe they could look inside and find some answers to their questions. As soon as they approached the container, they could tell something was wrong; both the bolt seal and the Customs seal were gone! At first Larry and Steve thought that George was thinking of stripping the container that morning and had someone cut the seals. Even though George should have waited until Customs was present, Larry could overlook that infraction. He knew George for years and knew he wasn't up to any hanky-panky. He was probably trying to rush things and forgot he should wait until Customs arrived before he cut the seals. But, when Larry asked George if he had someone cut the seals, George adamantly said no. He knew the rules and he'd never do that. Now Larry and Steve were scratching their heads. If George didn't have the seals cut, who did? Larry and Steve knew the seals were intact the night before, so obviously they were cut here at Shawmut Freight.

CHAPTER THIRTY SEVEN

Larry and Steve walked back to the container wondering what was going on. Steve jumped down from the platform onto the ground to look around. After a quick search, he found what he was looking for. "Hey dude," Steve said to Larry, "look at this shit." In his raised hand, Steve was holding both the bolt seal and the Customs seal. Larry reached out and took the seals. From his back pocket he pulled out a piece of paper, part of the manifest for the Yankee Clipper. Larry checked the numbers on the seals he was holding in his hand against the numbers on the manifest page; they were the same. It was obvious to both of them someone had cut the seals while the container was backed up to the loading platform. But, George said he didn't cut them. So, the question was, who did?

Larry put the seals in his back pocket along with the manifest page. He wasn't feeling good about the situation and wanted to preserve any evidence just in case there was some funny business going on. "Let's pop the fucking thing," Larry said to Steve. Immediately, Steve reached down and grabbed both door handles of the right door of the container. With a firm upward and outward thrust, both door latches were free; Steve swung the door wide open. Larry gagged when he was hit by the foul air from the container. "Let's open the other door too," he said to Steve. "We'll let the container air out before we go inside. Besides, it'll give us more light to see." As they were waiting for the container to air out, Steve went to their car and brought back a couple of flashlights. While they were standing on the platform by the back of the container, Steve asked Larry what he thought was going on. Larry said he didn't know, but he didn't feel comfortable about the whole thing. Obviously the seals were cut while the container was backed up to the platform, but George said he didn't cut them.

As Larry and Steve were talking, George walked up to them. "Oh, you opened the container yourself," George quipped. Larry told him they did, but then he reiterated how the seals had been cut before they arrived. George scratched his head and said, "Larry, honestly, I don't know what the fuck happened. Maybe I did tell someone to cut the seals. This place is so confusing this morning, I really can't remember." Larry and Steve believed George because he had always been truthful to them in the past. Maybe George did tell one of the warehousemen to cut the seals in antici-pation of Larry and Steve coming over. Larry decided to put that mystery aside for a moment. He was anxious to get inside the container to get some answers about those false x-ray images. "Okay, George," he said, "let's not worry about that for now. If you find out who cut the seals, let's us know. In the meantime, Steve and I are going to take a look inside." George thanked Larry and then he was gone. Someone was yelling for him from the other end of the warehouse.

Before they climbed into the container, Larry reached into his shirt pocket and removed a printout of the picture on the x-ray screen from yesterday. Three areas were circled in red ink: two small areas at the nose of the container, one bigger area in the middle and one smaller area by the doors. Using the printout as a road map, Larry slowly navigated his way into the container. About eight feet into the container, Larry stopped and tapped a water-soaked cardboard box. Without looking at Steve he said, "Stevie, according to the printout, this box right here is the first anomaly. Let's see what's inside."

In order for him to get at the box, Steve had to step over a pile of wet clothes. As he did, his foot slipped and he fell over on his back. His flashlight landed in a pool of muddy water. Neither Steve nor Larry said anything; there weren't any of the usual jokes about being clumsy or stu-pid. They were both so focused on what they were doing; there wasn't time for any friendly bantering. Steve regained his footing and climbed over the clothes and stood by the box. He opened his knife and gently cut the tape holding the top of the box closed. When he lifted the flaps back, they both looked inside. The box was filled with seawater-soaked army manu-als and personal papers, exactly what Larry thought. "Hey Dude," Steve said, "Just like you said. You're the man." Larry breathed a sigh of relief. Even though that is what he thought he was going to find, he really wasn't sure. Looking in the box and confirming his beliefs made him feel good.

"Okay, *dude*," Larry mockingly said to Steve, "let's check out the other two areas." Approaching the middle of the container, Steve thought he saw a couple of muddy footprints on the top of a box. He looked at the footprints quizzically and wondered how they got there. When he looked closer, the mud seemed fresh and hadn't hardened yet. Steve wasn't any big game scout, but even he knew this was suspicious. Someone had to have been in the container recently, since the container was transferred to Shawmut Freight from Conley Terminal. Steve felt a chill run down his spine. Knowing someone had unexplainably cut the seals and now the suspicious footprint made him shiver. Something wasn't right, he thought. "Hey Larry," he said with a tone of gravity in his voice, "can you take a look at this?" Larry had to squeeze his body between two wooden crates before he was beside Steve. "What?" Larry said. "Look at this," Steve said, shining his flashlight on the footprints. Larry focused his eyes on the end of the beam of Steve's light. He squinted and looked again. He still couldn't see that well so he shined his own light on the spot Steve was showing him. When he did, he realized why Steve seemed so concerned. Larry could distinctly make out the footprints and he came to the same conclusion as Steve—the footprints were fresh. Someone had been in the container recently. "Holy fuck," Larry said, "there's something going on here and I don't like it."

CHAPTER THIRTY EIGHT

Steve wanted to climb out of the container immediately and call for some other inspectors to come over to help him and Larry. He wasn't scared, but he knew something was amiss. Being in the container under those conditions wasn't the smartest place to be. Someone could close the doors on them and lock them in the container; after that, who knew? Larry could see the concern in Steve's eyes; he tried to settle him down. "Steve," Larry said, "I want to do one other thing before we get the fuck out of here. We have to check out this area first." Larry was pointing at the large anomaly in the middle of the container. "Once we do that, we're history." Steve said okay, but he wanted to do it in a hurry so they could get out of the container. The place was spooking him.

Larry climbed forward a few more feet when he saw the open box. Immediately, he felt his stomach tighten. Now he knew for sure something was really wrong. He continued climbing forward with Steve right behind him. Once he got to the box, he waited for Steve to join him. Together they shined their lights on a cardboard box with shiny red tape dangling from the flaps. Referring to his printout, he confirmed this was the exact location of the second, and bigger, anomaly. Larry pulled back a flap on the box and looked inside, all he saw was a big void. Whatever was in the box was gone! Then the unimaginable happened. Both their personal radiation detectors that they wore on their gun belts started to beep, indicating the presence of some kind of radiation. Now, even Larry had had enough. He was convinced something real bad was happening and it was time to call for help. "Okay, Stevie, my man," Larry said as nonchalantly as he could, "let's get the fuck out of Dodge." They both turned and crawled towards the open end of the container. All sorts of thoughts were running through their heads and none of them were good.

As soon as they were out of the container, Larry looked all around. He wanted to make sure no one was in the area waiting to do them harm and he also was looking to see if anyone was watching them. Once he was sure they were safe, he called Paul, their supervisor, at the Customs office at Conley Terminal. When Paul answered the phone, Larry gave him a brief rundown on what was going on and what their suspicions were. Before Larry was even finished explaining, Paul told him he was on the way over with some other inspectors. Paul told Larry to sit tight and keep Steve with him; he didn't want anything to happen to either one of them. No shit, Larry thought as he hung up the phone.

CHAPTER THIRTY NINE

As soon as Paul, the supervisor, arrived, things started really happening. First of all, he had all five of the inspectors he brought with him form a security zone around the container; nobody was allowed within 100 feet. Next, he had Larry and Steve give him a complete rundown on what had happened, from the unloading of the container off the Yankee Clipper to the present. Once he felt confident that he knew exactly what was going on, he told Larry he wanted to go into the container to see for himself. He asked Larry if he'd go with him and asked Steve to stay outside and keep an eye on the doors of the container.

Once their game plan was formed, Larry and Paul began climbing into the container. This time however, not only did they have their personal radiation detectors (PRDs), but Paul brought from the office the hand-held radiation detector. Although the PRDs were a reliable and invaluable tool, they could only tell you when radiation was in the area and how strong the level was. They couldn't identify the type of radiation; the hand-held unit could. Steve could see their flashlights bouncing off the walls and ceiling of the container as they moved forward. He could hear their muffled conversation as they struggled through the maze. Then the bouncing lights and muffled conversation stopped. Steve assumed they were in the middle of the container at the site of the empty box.

Paul activated the hand-held radiation detector and held the sensor to the suspect box. In less than thirty seconds he was receiving a visual and audio alarm. Paul looked at the reading on the meter; the reading was high and the radiation was caesium-137. Paul's eyes almost popped out of his head. He now realized this was the real thing, it was not a fluke. The usually unflappable Paul now stammered to Larry, "Let's get the hell out of here; we're being cooked as we sit." Larry didn't need any encouragement; he was already crawling his way towards Steve. Paul was struggling his way out of the container right behind Larry.

Now that they were positive there was a radiation hazard in the container, Custom's SOP (standard operating procedure) kicked in. The Boston Fire Department, Boston Police, State Police and a multitude of other city, state and federal agencies were notified. While these notifications were being made, Paul immediately called uptown to let his boss know what was happening. He knew the media would have this incident on radio and TV within the hour and he didn't want his boss to be caught unaware of what was going on. As soon as he hung up, Paul called his buddy in investigations who was assigned to the JTTF (Joint Terrorist Task Force.) Paul advised his friend what was going on and suggested it might be prudent if he got down to South Boston in a hurry. His friend said he was on the way and he should be on site in ten minutes. As Paul closed the flap on his cell phone, he could hear sirens splitting the air in all directions. Holy shit, he said to himself, I hope we know what we're talking about.

CHAPTER FORTY

Uptown in the Tip O'Neill Building, at the district office for U.S.Customs, Paul's boss called the port director, Sebastian Auvil, as soon as he hung up. He gave the port director a full briefing on what was going on in South Boston. Near the end of the briefing, Sebastian's secretary interrupted to say both Leo from the state police and John from the coast guard were trying to get in touch with him. Sebastian asked his secretary to set up a conference call with them and he'd be off the phone in a minute. Soon John, Leo and Sebastian were connected via the conference call. They all agreed they should stay put where they were for now so they could coordinate their different agencies most effectively. However, once things started settling down, all three wanted to get out into the field and see what was going on first-hand.

Sebastian suggested they bring each other up to speed on how each different agency was dealing with the current situation; he volunteered to go first. First of all, Sebastian wanted to tell them what he knew up to this point. Members of the container inspection team, while inspecting a container of personal and household effects of returning soldiers from Germany, detected radiation, specifically caesium-137, in one of the boxes in the middle of the container. When they attempted to inspect the contents of the suspicious box, they found the box was empty. Someone appeared to have already been in the container and removed the source of the radiation. It was a classic "inside job" according to Sebastian. Once the container inspection team realized they were dealing with the real thing, they activated the port's emergency SOP, the exact same one the three of them developed months ago. "Holy mackerel," John said, "it's finally hitting home right here in Boston.

"Guys," he said, "this is what I know and here's how I'm responding to the current threat." Leo said that everything Sebastian had just said is exactly what he knew. Leo told the other two that he had dispatched twelve state police cruisers to the scene to help provide security and crowd control. The bomb team, consisting of seven bomb technicians and two bomb dogs, were mobilizing and should be on scene within the hour. Also, the Massachusetts State Police Commander had called him and promised every asset that the state police had in their arsenal; all he had to do was ask. Lastly, a state police helicopter was being diverted from the Cape to Logan just in case.

John told the other two that he didn't have any new information to add; Sebastian had succinctly and correctly stated all the facts. Regarding his plans, John said more coast guardsmen were already on the way to Shawmut Freight and to Conley Container Terminal. Every one of them was armed with a hand-held radiation detector. His main concern was that there might be more than one container with something bad inside. He wanted to make sure the x-ray truck had plenty of people to address this possibility. They were focusing in on the current situation and hadn't even thought of the potential of another threat. John said he was also in touch with the commandant of the coast guard in Washington. He too promised every asset the coast guard could provide.

All three were gravely concerned with what was going on at Shawmut Freight, but they were also confident in their ability to address the threat. This is what they had been training for and now was the time to put their plans to the test. They all promised to stay in touch with each other and if anything new developed, they'd let each other know immediately As they were hanging up, Leo said something that really hit home. He told John and Sebastian that they had all been through some terrible shit before and they'd get through this shit also.

CHAPTER FORTY ONE

In South Boston, events were unfolding rapidly. The Massachusetts State Police and the Boston Police formed a tight cordon around Shawmut Freight Terminal. Nothing moved within this area without their permission. Boston Fire was standing by with three engine companies, two ladder trucks, Rescue 1 and the Haz-Mat unit. Paul radioed over to Conley Terminal and requested they bring the second x-ray truck over to Shawmut Freight. He wanted to x-ray the container again and compare Larry's printout with a current picture of the container. He felt confident in Larry's assessment, but he just wanted to be extra careful. Additionally, he told them not to let any container out of the container yard unless it was x-rayed and the hand-held radiation detector run over it. There would be no exceptions! The container team at Conley replied they fully understood and told Paul the second x-ray truck was on the way.

Once the truck arrived, they x-rayed the container again. This time, the suspicious area in the middle of the container was gone! They now had conclusive, irrefutable proof that something was there and it was removed sometime during the night. But by whom? One thing kept nagging at Larry but he couldn't put his finger on the problem. Then, all of a sudden, it hit him. The radiation sensor on the x-ray truck was much more powerful and sensitive than even the hand-held radiation detectors. Why didn't the sensor detect the presence of radiation when they first x-rayed the container when it came off the Yankee Clipper? Was there something wrong with the unit? Because they had the back up x-ray truck at Shawmut and the x-ray truck they originally used was still at Conley, Larry placed a call to the office and asked them to test the radiation detector.

Using samples of radiation provided by the manufacturer, they complied with Larry's request. The radiation detector did not sound the expected audio and visual alarms! Something was wrong. Conveniently, a manufacturer representative was on site performing preventative maintenance on some other equipment. He investigated the problem and discovered a blown small in-line fuse, rendering the radiation detector ineffective. Once he replaced the fuse, they retested the radiation detector with positive results. When Larry received the news, he was pissed. Because of a twenty-five cent fuse, the radiation detector failed when it was most needed. If the radiation alarm had sounded yesterday when they first x-rayed the container, they would have taken a whole different course of action. But, there wasn't anything they could do about that now. They had to deal with the situation as it confronted them.

It wasn't until late in the afternoon when everything began to settle down. By that time an impromptu command post had been set up in the office area of the warehouse. Sebastian, John and Leo had arrived and they were impressed how everything was being handled. About 6:00 pm, there was a meeting of all hands to discuss what they should do next. Decisions had to be made because it was impractical to stay at such a high state of alert for much longer. Obviously they were going to seize the container as evidence, but they didn't want to leave it at Shawmut Freight. Leo spoke up and suggested they take the container to Conley Terminal and secure it in an isolated area at the far end of the pier. He promised he would station an around-the-clock security detail until it was no longer required.

The only other major concern was what John mentioned in their initial phone conversation. Knowing how the terrorists work, he was afraid there might be more contaminated containers. He was fearful they might slip through the cracks in all the confusion. Sebastian told his friend not to worry. U.S. Customs had both x-ray trucks working and they were inspecting every container that entered the country through the port. This was only possible because of all the added manpower that was furnished by the coast guard and state police; in fact, Sebastian had also contacted Customs Headquarters in Washington, D.C. and suggested they advise all the other ports to do the same.

Everyone stood down except for the crew transporting the container to Conley Terminal. A contingent of police cars escorted the container through the winding streets of South Boston. Every intersection was blocked in advance and the entire operation was monitored by a state police helicopter hovering overhead. On the water, John stationed numerous small boats to monitor the situation from seaside. He didn't expect any problems, but he wasn't going to chance anything. Finally, about 11:00 pm, container HLCU 9752469 was secured at Conley Container Terminal. After a security detail was posted, everyone began to disperse. Now it was time to find out who was behind this and locate the dirty bomb.

CHAPTER FORTY TWO

Walter Parish had been a criminal investigator for U.S.Customs for almost thirty years. Even at 57 years of age, he was full of piss and vinegar and still had high enthusiasm for the job. A physically imposing figure at 6'2" and 225 pounds, Walter was a relentless and thorough investigator and wouldn't give up until he had the evidence to support a successful prosecution. That is why when they formed a JTTF in Boston, Walter was asked to be the leader.

When Walter arrived in South Boston that morning, Paul gave him an initial briefing. From that point on, Walter was a bulldog in pursuit of the bad guys. Walter began by interviewing some of the key players. He was curious who cut the seals on the container and wanted to clear up this area of confusion. George wasn't much help; he appeared as confused as everyone. But, George did tell Walter something that was quite interesting. George said that if Joseph was around, he might be able to help, but he was amongst the missing. When Walter asked him to explain, George told him he couldn't. Joseph was scheduled to be at work that morning but he never showed nor called. He was pissed and had a good mind to fire him, but he was too good of a worker.

Walter found this 'disappearance' too coincidental. Something was up with Joseph and he intended to find out what it was. He grabbed his cell phone and beeped Cheryl, another investigator on JTTF. "Cheryl," he said, "do me a favor. Come on down to Southie. I need you to do something for me." Cheryl told Walter she was on the other side of the city, but she'd shoot through the Ted Williams Tunnel and would be there in fifteen. Walter thanked her and hung up. He had more questions for George.

"So George," Walter said rather casually, "Tell me, what kind of security do you have here?" George looked confused so Walter decided to elaborate. "Do you have a night watchman, a dog, an alarm system, cameras, stuff like that?" George shook his head emphatically as he said. "I can't afford all that bullshit. I'm running this place on a shoe string. What do you expect from me?" Well, those were the wrong words to say to Walter when he was on the hunt. George was about to see the other side of Walter.

He shifted his feet a bit, like a boxer ready to land a lethal blow, and then looked George dead in the eye. "What do I expect from you?" Walter said. "I'll tell you what I expect from you. I expect a little fucking cooperation from you, that's what the fuck I expect." George saw the fury in Walter's eyes and wished he could take his words back. "Your warehouse has just been involved in a major security threat to this country and you're fucking crying to me; I don't want to hear any of your bullshit. All I want from you is some answers, and I want them pretty damn fast." Walter took a deep breath and continued. "Right now mister, you and your establishment are prime suspects. If you don't feel like cooperating, I'll lock your ass up for interfering with a federal investigation. That's a felony jackass and comes with ten years of hard time. You fucking understand me?"

Well, George understood loud and clear after Walter's berating. He said Shawmut Freight Terminal didn't have a watchman or a dog. They did have an alarm system but it wasn't working. Something happened with the telephone line a couple of months back and they still hadn't fixed it. Walter was sizing up George as he spoke and didn't think too much of him. He ran a real lax outfit and Walter could see why things were screwed up. "But," George said, "We do have a camera system. A couple of years ago we got a real good deal from one of our customers. He installed six cameras and it only cost us a free shipment of electronic parts to the west coast. It was a real good deal."

Walter felt like smashing George in the mouth. At a time like this he was talking about good deals. Walter put his personal feelings aside and asked George to tell him about the camera system. George said the cameras were strategically located throughout the warehouse and office. He was told there wasn't a square inch not covered by at least one of the cameras. But there had been some recent troubles with the cameras. Circuit breakers kept popping and the insurance company told George that if he didn't have the problem fixed, his insurance rates would skyrocket. Therefore, George hired an electrician and the problem was solved within a couple of hours. Supposedly the cameras were drawing too much electricity, so the electrician split the cameras between two separate circuits. Since then, everything has been working fine. Walter was about to pursue this line of questioning regarding the cameras, when he saw Cheryl walk in. He excused himself for a minute and rushed off to talk with Cheryl.

Cheryl had been a criminal investigator for U.S.Customs for slightly more than five years. What she lacked in experience she more than made up with enthusiasm. Walter had other investigators with more experience than Cheryl, but when it came to giving out a dicey assignment, Cheryl was his pick. "Morning, young lady," Walter said. "Good morning," Cheryl replied, "how is it going down here?" Walter's niceties were over and it was time to get down to business. He explained to Cheryl the mystery of the broken seals and the disappearance of Joseph, the lead warehouseman at Shawmut. "It is too much of a coincidence for me," Walter said. "Somehow this guy Joseph is wrapped up in all of this and I want to find out what he knows. But, first we have to find the son-of-a bitch." Cheryl was listening attentively to her boss, a guy she totally admired and respected. While others on the job might treat her with disrespect at times, Walter was always the gentleman. But, don't expect a free ride from him. If you weren't doing your job he'd let you know it in a heartbeat. He didn't care if you were a rookie or a veteran of thirty years.

"So," he continued, "here's what I want you to do." Walter told Cheryl to take a ride out to this guy Joseph's house. He gave her a list of everyone who worked at Shawmut and their home addresses; Joseph's address was highlighted in bright pink. He told her he didn't know what she was going to find. But, after she checked out the area, he wanted her to give him a call. Cheryl told Walter she understood and started to leave. "Do you want to take someone with you?" Walter queried. She kept walking but turned her head sideways saying, "No thanks, boss. I'm not in the mood to baby-sit. Besides, I already have a partner," patting the gun on her hip.

She took the back roads through South Boston and Dorchester. At Neponset Circle, she jumped on the expressway and went two exits. Getting off in East Milton, Cheryl drove through the Blue Hills until she got to Wolcott Square. From there she went down the West Roxbury Parkway until she hit Anawan Avenue; a quick left took her to Wren Street. She drove slowly, as if she was house hunting. Even numbers were on her right so 189 was up a little on her left. As she drove by Joseph's house, she was surprised to see a car in the driveway. She noted the license plate and wrote it down on the pad of legal paper by her side. The house was a pretty looking ranch with an impeccably kept lawn. All the surrounding houses looked to be in the same condition. Cheryl was impressed with the area; it was exactly the type neighborhood she wanted to move to. She turned around at the end of the street and did another drive-by. Nothing struck her as unusual or out of the ordinary. The car in the driveway was telling her Joseph must be home but she didn't see any activity.

Trying to remain innocuous, Cheryl drove down to Mike's Doughnuts on Centre Street and bought herself a black coffee and Danish. While sitting in the car relaxing and enjoying her coffee and Danish, Cheryl called in to her office to have someone run the plate she took off the car in Joseph's driveway. Sure enough, there weren't any surprises; the car was registered to Joseph. Feeling she had accomplished everything she was sent to do, she decided to call her boss and bring him up to speed.

"Hello," Walter said. "Who's this?" Walter was having trouble hearing who was on the phone because of a jet roaring overhead. Finally Walter understood it was Cheryl checking in. He was in the midst of talking with George about the security cameras so he asked Cheryl if he could call her right back. "Okay, George, I'm sorry. Please continue," Walter said. "Well, that's about it, I think," George said. "I think I've told you everything." Walter paused and then asked George if they had a taping system associated with the cameras. If they did, Walter knew this could be a crucial piece of evidence. George told Walter he thought so but he didn't fully understand how it worked. Somehow the cameras were hooked up to a computer and you could view what was on the cameras for the past seven days. Even though he wasn't explaining it properly, Walter knew the system George was talking about. He had taken a computer technology course with Customs and high security cameras interfaced with computers was a major component of the class. Walter couldn't wait to see if the cameras had picked up any suspicious activity.

About this time three more Customs investigators showed up at the warehouse. Walter had a lot of other people waiting to talk with him so he asked two of the investigators to start viewing the taped images on the computer. Specifically, he wanted the time period from 5:00 pm last night to 8:00 am this morning covered first. This is when the container was hit and this is where he was hoping they would find something. He asked Don, the third investigator, to shoot over to West Roxbury and keep Cheryl company. He wasn't overly concerned about her, but he didn't like people being by themselves if they didn't have to be; especially dealing with a high profile case such as they were.

Once everyone was off to their assignments, Walter had a chance to continue his conversation with Paul, the Supervisory Customs Inspector responsible for examining all the inbound containers. Paul explained to Walter that the container in question was not targeted by their intelligence unit because returning personal and household effects of soldiers was considered to be low risk. He also explained to Walter about the busted radiation detector on the x-ray truck. If it wasn't for Russ' sharp eyes, this container could have easily slipped by them. Walter started talking about how big a role luck has in their job when one of the investigators he assigned to view the tapes called him on the cell. "Okay, I'll be right there," Walter said. Then he looked at Paul and smiled, "Come on Paul. They think they have something. Let's check it out."

When Paul and Walter arrived in the office where the two investigators were reviewing the tapes, they could distinctly see on the screen a man moving around in the warehouse. But something was wrong with the tapes. It appeared only half the cameras were working and they couldn't figure out what the problem was. But, regardless of the problem, the tapes showed a male figure walking around the warehouse. At one time he could be seen walking with bolt cutters in his hand and another time they actually had a partial picture of the door to the container wide open. A later screen clearly showed the male figure carrying a metallic looking canister down the hallway by the offices. The time frame for these pictures was between 8:45 and 9:15 last night. Walter was stunned by the pictures. This was their guy, he was sure. He was also sure he knew who this guy was but he wanted to be positive.

Walter asked George where he kept the security badge folder for all his employees. George walked over to a metal file cabinet and pulled out a thick manila folder. "Right up to date," George proudly said as he handed Walter the folder. Walter thanked George and told him that was all he needed. George got the hint it was time for him to leave. Walter riffled through the folder until he found the security badge application for Joseph. Attached to each application was a passport photo of the applicant. Joseph's picture was staring him in the eyes at close range. Walter pulled Joseph's picture out from under the paper clip holding it to the application and held it up next to the computer. The picture on the computer screen and the picture of Joseph were one and the same. They had their guy! All of a sudden Walter stiffened, "Damn," he said, "Cheryl is out on the street by herself. I've got to tell her. She has to be careful."

CHAPTER FORTY THREE

It was late in the afternoon before Walter began to relax. He had one of his investigators up town at the federal courthouse applying for a search warrant to search Joseph's house on Wren St. in West Roxbury. If everything went as planned, Walter hoped to execute the warrant first thing in the morning. In the meantime, he gave Cheryl and Don the responsibility of maintaining constant surveillance on the house until then. He didn't care how they did it or what personnel they used. Using a tactic from a previous surveillance, Cheryl visited a friend of hers that worked as a supervisor for the telephone company in Roslindale Square. She wanted to borrow a phone truck for a couple of days. The supervisor was obliging and worked out all the details for her. Less than an hour after her request, Cheryl was driving a telephone cable truck out of the telephone garage in Roslindale Square. Don was following her in his undercover car.

Cheryl nimbly drove the truck through Roslindale Square and up Belgrade Avenue. At the West Roxbury Parkway, she turned onto Anawan Avenue and then onto Wren Street. When she was in front of the Randall G. Morris School, just opposite 189 Wren, she turned on her flashers and the rotating yellow light on the roof of the cab and jumped out of the vehicle. Dressed in a pair of soiled coveralls, Don almost started laughing when he saw her. He was impressed how natural she looked in her new role. Don and Cheryl spread orange cones all around both vehicles. Then she grabbed an iron hook from a cabinet on the side of the truck and pulled the cover to a sidewalk manhole directly in front of the school. Now she was ready for work. Cheryl had created the perfect cover for a round-the-clock surveillance. They could come and go as they wanted and talk freely and openly on their radios and cell phones without drawing suspicion. All the time, they had Joseph's house under a tight surveillance.

While his troops were spread out all over the city, Walter made plans for an early morning meeting. He wanted everyone involved in executing the search warrant to be briefed. There was an extraordinary degree of risk on this raid and Walter didn't want to leave any chance for a screw up. People from many different agencies planned on being there: Massachusetts State Police, Alcohol, Tobacco and Firearms, FBI, Boston Police, Boston Fire, to name a few of the prominent players. The Boston Police offered Walter their West Roxbury station as a possible location for the meeting and he accepted. The location was ideally located, less than one mile from Joseph's house. After Walter felt that he had addressed any and all concerns for the morning's raid, he decided to rent a room in a local hotel and catch a few hours sleep; driving home to southern New Hampshire would take too long and he was afraid he'd fall asleep on the way.

By 5:00 am, those involved in the search had arrived at the West Roxbury Station. Walter immediately took charge. The first thing Walter discussed was the potential danger in this raid. It wasn't like an ordinary drug raid, even though they were dangerous enough. This raid was much more dangerous and could result in people being hurt or even killed. He said that if Joseph activated the dirty bomb, they could be killed by the initial explosion. Those that survived could be exposed to a lethal dose of radiation. Someone in the crowd, a sergeant on the Boston Police, asked Walter if he could explain exactly how a dirty bomb worked. Walter thanked the sergeant for the question and apologized for not explaining before what a dirty bomb was.

Walter said that a dirty bomb was simply radioactive material wrapped up in some kind of explosive. In this case, they knew they were dealing with the radioactive material, caesium-137 and the explosive was probably C4, about four pounds if the x-ray images were correct. Someone in the audience whistled softly and said, "Sweet Jesus." "Exactly," Walter said. "This shit isn't anything to mess around with. Just the initial explosion will obliterate the house and kill anyone inside. Then we have to worry about the radiation effect, not only for us but the entire neighborhood." Walter saw his audience turning around and looking at each other; the look on their faces reflected the gravity of the situation. Walter knew his words were hitting home and was glad the question came up. He wanted everyone involved to appreciate how serious a condition they were confronted with.

Once Walter thought his explanation hit home, he wanted to continue laying out his proposed plan. The purpose of the raid was to capture and arrest Joseph and seize the grey metallic canister containing the dirty bomb. Hopefully, they could achieve their objectives peacefully, but if not, they still would achieve their objective. Walter wanted to *plan for the worst but hope for the best.* Planning for the worst, Walter wanted the Boston Fire Department standing by with at least one engine, one ladder truck and the Haz-Mat unit. He also requested Boston EMS have a few ambulances on stand-by. Walter was concerned about the neighbors. If things started looking bad, Walter would give the order for everyone to back off and regroup in the school yard. Before they advanced again, they would have to evacuate the neighborhood; for now, he planned on evacuating only the neighbors who lived immediately next door to Joseph.

This plan hopefully was only precautionary. Hoping for the best, Walter intended on calling Joseph on the phone requesting that he surrender peacefully. If Joseph refused to answer the phone, Walter planned to talk to him using a bullhorn. While he was making these attempts to communicate with Joseph, a special team trained in using sensitive high technology telescopic equipment, would be going from window to window trying to see what was going on inside the house. Specifically, they wanted to know where Joseph and the metal canister were.

Walter stressed this was only a tentative plan and he knew he would have to improvise as the situation developed. After Walter answered a few minor questions he decided they were ready to move out. He made sure every team member understood their assignment and then told everyone he'd see them in the schoolyard at the back of the school. Walter wanted to make his first attempt to contact Joseph by 6:00 am, before too many people were up and about.

As the phone was ringing in Walter's ear, the team with the telescopic equipment was crawling up to the side of the house. State police snipers, stationed on the roof of the school, had their every move covered. If Joseph came running out of the house shooting, he'd be dead before he fired off a round. Boston Police had all the roads leading into Wren Street blocked, preventing any cars from driving into the danger zone. Boston Fire had lines hooked up to two fire hydrants and hoses extended on the ground. The Haz-Mat unit was dressed and ready to go on Walter's command. On the fifth ring Walter was beginning to lose hope. He knew Joseph wasn't going to answer the phone. Finally, he hung up in disgust. He waited a few minutes and then grabbed the bullhorn but, before he could use it, the team using the telescopic equipment was calling him on the radio. The team leader, sounding out of breath, told Walter they were on the left side of the house looking in a kitchen window. As unbelievable as it might sound, they could see Joseph sitting at the kitchen table with his head resting on the table itself. He wasn't moving and it looked like he was passed out.

Walter felt his heart beating faster and faster and knew he had to act fast. "Team two," Walter said, calling the telescopic team, "Keep your eye on the subject. Tell me if he starts to make any movement at all. I'm sending a team through the back door." Team Three, laying in wait in the back yard knew Walter was talking about them. Their bodies tensed as they waited for the word. "Team Three, did you monitor Team Two's traffic?" A terse 'roger' was heard over the radio. "Team Three, Walter said, "Enter the house through the back door and take the subject out." The next thing they heard was glass breaking and wood splintering. Then they heard 'Police, Police, don't move.' The telescopic team was watching the entire event unfold before their eyes. They couldn't believe Joseph was sleeping through all the noise and mayhem. Then they sensed something was wrong. Maybe it was the subtle body language of the team members standing in the middle of the kitchen floor, guns drawn but at their side, as if the threat had disappeared. After a brief but distinct lull, the raiding team dispersed and searched the rest of the house, leaving one member in the kitchen standing over Joseph. After a few more minutes, the team leader called Walter on the radio telling him the house was cleared.

Walter radioed all units to remain fast as he slowly walked up the slight incline into Joseph's back yard. Approaching the back door, Walter stepped over the glass and wooden fragments. He was shocked when he entered the kitchen and saw Joseph slumped over the kitchen table. At first he thought someone shot him, but then he saw the needle dangling from his left arm. Joseph's body was ashen, bloated and stiff to the touch; it was obvious he'd been dead for awhile. Even the hardened Walter was affected by the sight of Joseph. He momentarily stared at the body, as in a state of shock, and then recovered his wits. "My God," he said, "what the fuck happened to him?" "Looks like he got his hands on some bad shit," one of the members of the raid team said. "Either that or he got hold of some of that super-duper shit that's been kicking around. It'll blow the top of your head off it's so potent." Walter shook his head and then heard the team leader talking to him. "We've swept the entire house and it's clean. He was the only one here, but we didn't find any grey canister." Walter was confused. *What did he mean he didn't find any grey canister? It had to be here.* "We're going to sweep the house again using the radiation detectors," the team leader continued, "I'll let you know as soon as we're done."

Walter thanked the team leader and stepped outside onto the back lawn. If the grey canister containing the dirty bomb wasn't here, where was it? They knew Joseph took it out of the sea container at Shawmut Freight Terminal; they had him on tape doing so. Did he drop it off to someone on the way home? As he was playing out different scenarios in his head, the team leader approached him. "Walter," he said, "we have a hit in the back hallway for caesium-137. It's a weak hit, but it's showing us the shit was here. Also, we searched the car and didn't find anything unusual. But, when we ran the radiation detector over the trunk area, once again we got a hit for caesium-137. This time the signal was a bit stronger than in the house." Now Walter was in a quandary. The radiation hits indicated Joseph brought the dirty bomb home, but what happened after that was anyone's guess. The dirty bomb was gone, but where was it?

CHAPTER FORTY FOUR

Walter called for a meeting in front of the house of all the team leaders. He wanted to brief them in person on what was going on. As he was running through the chain of events, a Boston Police Sergeant approached. "Excuse me, sir," he said to Walter, "but this guy across the street says he saw something funny the other night and he'd like to talk to someone in charge. I briefly talked with him and his story seems plausible." Walter looked across the street and saw a male in his fifties, with a big beer belly, wearing some kind of a security guard uniform, standing by a telephone pole. Walter briefly thought of telling the sergeant to take a report, but then decided to walk over and give the guy a couple of minutes. "Excuse me for a second," Walter said, and then he crossed the street and walked in the direction of the guy.

Walter's first impression was not positive. The guy was wearing a dirty security guard uniform, smelled of body odor, stale cigarettes and beer, and hadn't shaved in a couple of days. But, Walter wanted to give him a chance and greeted him as he approached. "Good morning, sir, Walter said, "my name is Walter Parish, I'm a criminal investigator with the United States Customs Service. The sergeant said that you might have some information you'd like to give us?" This guy who identified himself as "Bob" told Walter that he indeed might have some information. He told Walter, with obvious pride, that he was a full time security guard at Faulkner Hospital. In fact he was approaching his twentieth anniversary on the job. Walter smiled, acting as interested as possible. Bob told Walter he worked the four to twelve shift, Monday to Friday. Sometimes he worked weekends when they needed him, but he preferred staying home and drinking beer.

About this time, Walter was about to walk away, but remained patient; Bob had to be done with his life history shortly. Then Bob got into the details. Two nights ago when he got home from work, he grabbed a beer from the fridge and took the dog for a walk. While walking the dog, he noticed some activity in front of his neighbor's house at 189 Wren Street. Trying to mind his own business, Bob said he just kept walking the dog up the street and drinking his beer. But, when he was returning home, Bob noticed at least three men putting something in the back of their vehicle. Bob thought that was a bit unusual for the middle of the night so he turned around and started walking the dog back up the street. Just as he turned around, the vehicle turned on its lights and sped off.

Walter was breathing faster now, realizing what Bob saw. "What kind of vehicle was it?" Walter asked. Bob thought for a second and said, "I can't be positive, but I think it was red. It looked like a dark red van, with a sliding door on the side. I think it was a late model Ford." Walter was incredulous hearing this information. Bob was the eyewitness they needed to hopefully crack this case. "Bob," Walter asked patiently, "Did you by any chance get the plate number to this vehicle?" Walter thought hard, "I knew you were going to ask me that. No, not exactly. But I did get part of it." Walter waited with baited breath while Bob collected his thoughts. "They were New York plates. You know, the ones colored orange and black, ugliest plates in the world. I didn't get the entire plate because the lighting wasn't that good, but I think the last four were '9 ISH'. The first two numbers I couldn't make out, I'm sorry."

Walter wanted to kiss Bob. Obviously, the information he provided had huge potential. On the face of what Bob was telling them, this vehicle appeared to be involved in the missing dirty bomb. Part of Walter's conundrum was solved, but now he had to track down the van. Time was critical because they still didn't know what the bad guys intended to do with this weapon of mass destruction. Walter thanked Bob and told him he'd be back in touch. But for now, he had to get back to the office in a hurry. He couldn't wait to contact New York's Registry of Motor Vehicles. They held the key to unlocking this mystery.

CHAPTER FORTY FIVE

Instead of contacting New York's Registry of Motor Vehicles directly, Walter called Brendan Lowell, his counterpart on JTTF in Albany. He figured a little local influence might be able to speed up the process of getting the information Walter needed. Within the hour, Walter received a call back. According to New York's RMV, there were twelve possible matches in the entire state for a late model Ford van with plates ending in '9 ISH.' But, Brendan had done some research on his own and thought he might have targeted the van they were interested in. Doing some computer checks, Brendan whittled the twelve possibilities down to three. Of the three, he thought a girl named Linda McNally, living in Brooklyn, was the best possibility. His reasons were clear once he explained.

According to U.S. Immigration records, Linda married an Algerian seaman who was living in this country illegally. He had absconded off an LNG ship while it was docked in Boston, Massachusetts. Immigration thought it was a marriage of convenience but couldn't persuade a federal judge with the documentary evidence that they had at the time. Could it be legitimate? Brendan asked himself. Of course it could be, but he was suspicious. The only way to get to the truth, he suggested they pay Linda a visit. Walter agreed and asked Brendan if and when he could make arrangements to conduct the interview. Brendan said he and his partner were already on the interstate heading south to the city, he'd call Walter as soon as he had any information.

While Walter was spearheading the investigation into the dirty bomb out of Boston, other parts of the puzzle were coming together in other parts of the world. Because the container that arrived in Boston carrying the dirty bomb contained personal and household effects of returning soldiers, Customs Headquarters contacted the Army's Criminal Investigative Division (CID). Customs didn't think American soldiers were involved in the smuggling of the dirty bomb, but stranger things were known to happen. The call was for informational purposes only and, if the CID wanted to do some snooping of their own, it was up to them.

The CID office in Frankfurt immediately jumped on the case. They called Hapag Lloyd's main office in Berlin and asked them to track the itinerary of the container in question over the past several months. Hapag Lloyd tracked the container (HLCU 9752469) to Sleazy's father's warehouse in Bad Homburg, Germany. It was stuffed with American GIs household goods at that location and then shipped to America through the port of Antwerp, Belgium. Of further interest, there were three more containers in Hapag Lloyd's system that followed the same route at approximately the same time. One container had a bill of lading showing the discharge port to be Newark, New Jersey and the other two had bills of lading showing they were to be unloaded in Norfolk, Virginia.

Paul Sawyer, head of the Army's CID in Frankfurt realized the potential risk this new found information posed. The possibility of three more containers carrying dirty bombs headed towards the United States was a stark reality. Paul picked up the phone and called Customs Headquarters in Washington, D.C. They were flabbergasted with this new information and much appreciative of Paul's conscientious efforts in tracking down this information. Paul told them he was opening an active case in the matter and would keep them informed of the results. Customs Headquarters assured Paul he had their full backing and asked him to call if they could be of any assistance.

That afternoon, Paul and his partner Brian drove up to Bad Homburg and visited Sleazy's father's warehouse. Fortunately for them, Sleazy was working when they arrived. After they identified themselves, Sleazy suggested they go into the office where they could talk in private. Paul asked numerous generic questions about Sleazy's business. Sleazy explained that a good portion of his business was shipping American soldiers household effects back home to America. He also feigned concern that he might be doing something wrong with filing the shipping documents with the Army. He knew there were billing problems in the past, but he thought they were all straightened out. He hoped they were because the army was a great customer of his and he valued their business. He could go under if he lost the contract with the army. Paul and Brian didn't buy Sleazy's line of bullshit. Their years of experience in the investigative field told them Sleazy was lying. But how could they prove it? Surely he wasn't going to come right out and tell them the truth.

While they were concluding their interview, Sonja walked into the office bearing Sleazy's lunch. As soon as Brian saw her, he recognized her from some kind of dealings in the past. He knew it wasn't a pleasant experience, but he just couldn't recall. Then, all of a sudden it struck him. Sonja was involved in extorting money from GIs that frequented the bars she used to hustle drinks in. She targeted married GIs, usually senior non-commissioned officers, and lured them into sexually compromising situations. Once she had the evidence on them, usually Polaroid pictures taken by a fellow prostitute, Sonja extorted her victims for large sums of money. Several non-commissioned officers were so destitute and fearful of being exposed to their wives that they actually committed crimes to get the money to pay her off. A few even committed suicide. Yes, Brian remembered Sonja.

As they stood to leave, Brian told Sleazy they were required to interview several of his employees as a regular annual background check. Since they were already there, they might as well fulfill this requirement before leaving. He told Sleazy it was only a formality and should only take a couple of minutes per interview. Sleazy said he didn't mind—he didn't have a choice—and asked who they wanted to interview first. Knowing Sleazy's father was deathly sick and not available to be interviewed, Brian told Sleazy one of the requirements was to interview a family member besides a regular employee. Paul didn't know what Brian was up to, but had confidence in his partner's ability, kept his mouth shut and looked on with interest. Sleazy told Brian his father was too sick to talk to and the only other person that could be considered family was the girl living with him, Sonja. Brian told Sleazy she really didn't fit the description of 'family' but perhaps they could stretch the definition of the word. Brian looked at Paul for support and Paul, not knowing what was going on, shook his head in agreement. Sleazy said he was appreciative of their consideration and would eat his lunch on the warehouse floor so they could interview Sonja in private. Besides, he said, he wanted to keep an eye on the troops.

At first, Brian went easy on Sonja, but it wasn't too long before Sonja knew she was in some serious trouble. Brian told Sonja she was looking at some serious jail time if she didn't cooperate with them; he intended on arresting and prosecuting her to the fullest extent of the law. At a minimum, he said, she was looking at ten years in jail. Paul still wasn't fully aware of what was going on, but understood more as the conversation proceeded. Sonja, for as tough as she acted, was quite easy to break. She told Brian she was sorry for everything she did in the past and would do anything to make amends. Brian told her that it was about time she admitted her guilt and he expected her full cooperation. Sonja nodded her head and began crying. She wiped the tears from her cheeks with the back of her hands; neither Brian nor Paul would offer her a tissue from a box on an adjoining desk.

"Okay," Brian said, "tell me what you know." Brian was shooting in the dark. He had no idea what Sonja knew or didn't know, but he was willing to find out. Sonja had stopped crying by this time and looked at them directly. "I was suspicious from the start," she said, "but what was I to do? Sleazy takes care of me and I don't have to work in those filthy bars downtown. When his two friends flew here from Algeria, they all acted weird. They were up to something and they never would talk in front of me. They treated me as I was inferior and it made me mad. That's how people have treated me all my life. I thought Sleazy was different, but I guess I was wrong. The only reason why I stay with him is because he treats me so well." She paused, reflected, and then continued. "His trip to Marburg University was part of it. I heard them talking one night when they thought I was passed out from drinking. They mentioned something about Sleazy driving to Marburg University to meet a professor. I was tired and eventually did fall asleep, but I know he was supposed to go to Marburg and pick something up."

Sonja paused, wiped her nose with the sleeve of her blouse and continued. "After his friends left for Berlin, Sleazy acted different. He didn't pay attention to me like he used to. Something was on his mind. Then, after he came home from his trip to Marburg, everything changed. He spent some time in the warehouse that night, but when he returned he acted like the weight of the world was off his shoulders. He was the old Sleazy that I knew from before. Sure I was suspicious that something was going on, but what was I to do? Like I said, he takes good care of me and I sure don't want to go back to hustling drinks."

About this time, Brian had heard enough. He realized he and Paul would have to take a ride up to Marburg to further their investigation. Also, he didn't want Sleazy to become suspicious. When it was time to hammer him, they would. But he didn't want to forewarn him of their suspicions. Brian told Sonja to relax. If she continued to cooperate, he would make sure she stayed out of jail. Regarding Sleazy, Brian told her to act naturally and don't tell him anything. Sonja promised she wouldn't and told Brian she knew how to play the game. She'd been there before.

Paul and Brian rode up to Marburg University early the following morning. They really weren't sure what to expect, but they had to go hunting. They had scheduled a 10:00 am meeting with Mr. Doenitz, the head of security for Marburg University. As soon as they met Mr. Doenitz, both Paul and Brian knew they were going to get along fine. Mr. Doenitz was a no-nonsense, straight–to–the-point type of guy, a reflection of his thirty years working for the federal polizei. Since they didn't want to waste time, Paul decided to come right to the point. He told the head of security that they were investigating the shipment to America of a dirty bomb. They knew where the shipment originated, but they were trying to ascertain the source of the radioactive material. They were given a lead that Marburg University was the possible source, so that is why they came to visit him.

Mr. Doenitz listened patiently, all the while puffing on his pipe. Brian watched as he blew rich clouds of sweet smelling smoke into the air. Then and there, Brian promised himself that he was going to take up pipe smoking. After Paul was done talking, Mr. Doenitz rolled the pipe in his hand, contemplating asking a question. He looked up over the top rim of his glasses and asked, "What type of radioactive material are we talking about?" Paul instantly replied, "Caesium-137." "Hmm," Mr. Doenitz said, "exactly as I thought." Paul and Brian were taken aback by Mr. Doenitz's reply. What did he mean by 'just as I thought?' How the heck did he know what the radioactive material was? Mr. Doenitz decided to explain.

About two weeks ago, one of the professors in the astrophysics department in Heller Hall, a Professor Schwartz, had suddenly come down gravely sick. At first they thought he had malaria or some other exotic disease that he possibly caught on one of his many trips throughout the world. But after days of testing, the doctors said he had radiation poisoning. This was an understandable diagnosis because the professor's main area of research was with radioactive material. Somehow something had gone terribly wrong during one of his research studies. Sadly, the Professor died from the exposure. Mr. Doenitz said they had just buried him two days ago. An autopsy was performed and the cause of death on his death certificate read 'lethal exposure to radioactive material—caesium -137.' "Here," Mr. Doenitz said, "have a look for yourself," as he passed a piece of yellowish paper across his desk.

Paul and Brian were astounded by this discovery. Could this dead professor, Professor Schwartz, have been the supplier of the caesium-137 that Sleazy had shipped to America in the container? If so, why? What was his motive? Money? Politics? Those questions would have to be put on hold for awhile. Right now Paul and Brian were thinking about the other three containers that Hapag Lloyd told them about. Was there caesium-137 in those containers? To find out, Paul asked Mr. Doenitz if there was some way they could track all the shipments of caesium-137, and any other radioactive materials, that Professor Schwartz had had in his possession. Paul explained that he was trying to find out if there was any unaccountable caesium-137, and if so, when did it disappear. Maybe they could match up the dates of disappearance with the shipment of the other three containers from Sleazy's warehouse.

Mr. Doenitz said he understood what Paul was trying to do and he did think it was possible. However, it would probably take a few days and he was going to have to inform the president of the university what they were doing. Paul said he didn't care if the university president knew, he just needed the information. Mr. Doenitz smiled and said they would be hearing from him, hopefully within a couple of days. They all shook hands and soon Paul and Brian were back on the road heading for their office in Frankfurt. Once they arrived, the first thing Paul intended on doing was calling Customs Headquarters to tell them the news.

CHAPTER FORTY SIX

While Paul and Brian were in Germany investigating the source of the caesium-137, who shipped it, and why they shipped it to in the United States, Brendan Lowell and his partner from the JTTF office in Albany were driving down to Brooklyn to interview Linda McNally, the possible owner of the red van in question. Linda was in her early thirties, of medium height and weight and could be considered homely. She lived her whole life in the shadows of the Verrazano Narrows Bridge in Brooklyn with her mother and two brothers. Her father left for work one day and never returned. Linda didn't really mind because when he was home all he did was drink Rheingold Ale and yell at her mother, brothers and herself. For the smallest infractions he would go off on a tirade. Her brothers were gone now; they went into the service and never came home. It wasn't like they were killed in combat or something honorable, they just never returned. Where they were or what they were doing, neither Linda nor her mother knew.

Linda and her mother were still living in the same third floor apartment that they'd been living in since she was a little girl. Only the neighborhood was a lot different now than her childhood. Back then you were either Irish, Italian, Lithuanian or German, anything else and you didn't belong. Everyone spoke English; at least you did after being in the country for a couple of years. Today the neighborhood was predominantly Spanish-speaking. Not that she had anything against them, but she didn't have anything in common. They spoke, ate and thought differently. It was time for her and her mother to leave the neighborhood that they had loved for so many years. But, when they went out apartment-hunting, they were shocked by the rents landlords were charging. Not only the rent, but they also required one month security deposit and two months rent in advance. Linda couldn't afford the rent not to mention the security deposit and the advance rent. So their fate was sealed. Even though they would love to move, they couldn't afford to and there wasn't anything on the horizon that indicated they ever would.

Linda and her mother accepted their fate and decided to make the best of what they had. There was a silver lining to their predicament; Linda worked at a busy Italian restaurant only two blocks from their apartment, an easy walk no matter what the weather was. Fort Hamilton, an old army fort, was right across the street from the restaurant and Linda used to take walks there until the government put the fort off limits in the name of national security. Linda was always perplexed by the term 'national security.' She never considered herself a national risk; did the army know something she didn't?

Working at the restaurant as a waitress allowed Linda and her mother to lead a comfortable life. Even though the neighborhood had changed, people still flocked to the restaurant to eat, especially on the weekends. She made enough money on the weekends she didn't have to work during the week, but her boss made her. It wouldn't be fair to the other girls according to him. The weekdays dragged by for her but, once again, she made the best of it. Then one unusually slow night, one of the dishwashers in the back struck up a conversation with her. He seemed to be a nice guy and Linda had to take advantage of every opportunity that came her way. After all, she thought, the years were ticking by and she never was a beauty queen. After a couple nights of harmless banter, Sami, the dishwasher, asked Linda if she'd like to go out some night after work. Linda, not wanting to seem too eager, told Sami she was kind of busy and perhaps he should ask her again in a week or two. Sami, the gentleman that he was, accepted her reply and patiently waited to ask her again. Linda regretted the words the moment they left her mouth, but she had no choice but to wait. She didn't want to appear too eager.

When Sami asked her again to go out, Linda left no room for interpretation; she accepted his offer. The first date was pleasant. As funny as it might seem, they walked to a local pizza shop and had pizza and lemonade. Afterwards they walked down to the water and watched all the ships coming and going. Overhead, cars and trucks were constantly crossing the Verrazano, a daily reminder to Linda that the world was a vibrant and lively place. While sitting on a park bench watching the ships sail by, their conversation included about every possible subject under the sun. Linda was explaining to Sami how the demographics of Brooklyn really changed in the last twenty-five years. The neighborhood he knew now was totally different back then. Sami laughed and said that was true also where he came from, that is why he left.

When asked, Sami told Linda he grew up in a small town in Algeria called Arzew. In the days past, it was a nice family-oriented town. Everyone knew each other and they all looked out for each other. But in the last ten years or so, the government started cracking down on the people. If you didn't do exactly what they told you to do, they'd throw you in jail or worse. Sami tolerated the oppression until he could take no more. If he stuck around any longer, he'd get in trouble with the authorities. Linda felt sorry for Sami. She thought her life was so bad; it wasn't half as bad as what he had endured. Sami realized, as their conversation progressed, that his plan was working. Linda had a big heart and she was showing a great deal of empathy for him. He hoped he could channel these feelings in a way that could be beneficial to him and his cause.

Sami and Linda dated steadily for the next six months. He always treated her like a woman; no one in her entire life had ever been so considerate of her feelings. Most importantly, Linda's mother loved Sami. He was always coming by the house giving her little gifts, flowers were her favorite. Close to a year after dating, Sami proposed to her. Linda didn't have to think for a moment, her answer was a resounding yes. Their wedding was real small and their honeymoon was put off until they had saved some money. Sami moved in with Linda and her mother and life was bliss. Linda hadn't been so happy in years.

The problems started after about a year into the marriage. Sami would disappear for a day or two, but he always came back. When Linda questioned him as to his whereabouts, Sami told her he was with friends from the old country. Linda loved him and believed him, but she said these mysterious outings had to stop. Sami agreed and promised they would. For a couple of months things were back like they were when they just got married. Then one night Sami asked to borrow Linda's car. That was a week ago and Linda hadn't seen him since. She was devastated and heartbroken.

Obviously he had taken off with another woman. Linda thought of calling the police to report her car stolen, but how could she? She still loved Sami and hoped and prayed for his safe return. But she feared what happened with her father and brothers was happening with Sami. The Irish curse was still with her and her mother. Then one morning she heard a knock at the door. She thought that was strange because Sami had a key. When she opened the door to her apartment, Brendan Lowell and his partner were standing there. When she saw Brendan's badge, she knew something had happened to Sami. She was right, something did happen to him, but not what she thought.

After Brendan introduced himself and Anthony, his partner, he asked if she'd mind if they came in and asked her a few questions. Linda felt sick to her stomach but she allowed them in. She knew it was about Sami and she had to get to the bottom of whatever was going on. Brendan told Linda a crime had been committed and they had a partial description of the vehicle involved in the crime. They were visiting all the owners of vehicles that fit the description to determine if they were involved. Linda was relieved because she knew she didn't commit a crime, but she was concerned because she knew Sami possibly could.

She listened to Brendan and maintained a total blank expression on her face. When Brendan asked her if she owned a red, late model Ford van, Linda nodded in the affirmative. Then Brendan asked her what her license plate was. Linda was so nervous she couldn't think of the number; she tried several times but she kept making a mistake. Finally, from the other room, her mother yelled out "459 ISH." Brendan and Anthony were startled a bit; they didn't realize someone else was in the apartment. Linda saw the look on Brendan's face and explained the voice belonged to her mother.

When Brendan asked where her vehicle was, Linda knew she had to explain; her explanation was about to muddy the waters. Before answering, Linda sat motionless, attempting to compose herself. "My husband borrowed the vehicle about a week ago," she said, "and that was the last time I saw my van. Where it is and where he is, I have absolutely no idea."

Linda couldn't think of anything else to say. She had to tell the truth, which was the type of person she was. Brendan knew he was on to something and decided to press the issue. "I'm confused, Linda," he said, "are you telling me your husband took the van a week ago and you have no idea where he is?" Linda shook her head in the affirmative. "What did the police say when you filed the missing person report?" he said. Brendan was fishing, he knew a missing person report wasn't filed, but he wanted to see what she had to say. Linda started trembling, and then she broke down in tears.

After she composed herself, Brendan asked Linda how much of her husband's background was she aware of. Brendan liked Linda and didn't think she was involved whatsoever, but he wanted to draw out of her as much information as possible. "Not much," she said, "we met at the restaurant, dated for about a year, fell in love and decided to get married. He's really a sweet man and this whole thing must be a mistake." Linda was hoping it was, but deep down inside her she knew there was a possibility that it wasn't. Brendan decided to go for the kill. "Did you know that Sami, your husband, entered this country illegally on an LNG ship in Boston? Did you also know that he has been associated with a terrorist organization for the past five years?" Linda's world fell apart. *So that's why he left Algeria, she thought. Not because he was being persecuted, but because he was a terrorist.* Brendan continued his questions, "Do you also know that we believe he married you because he was trying to stay in America. He married you not for love but for convenience." Brendan knew he was being hard on Linda, but he had to be. Lives were in jeopardy.

Brendan and Anthony were now convinced Sami was their guy. He and two or possibly three others were the ones at Joseph's house on Wren Street. Linda wasn't involved. She was a victim. Sami borrowed her car to commit a crime and couldn't care less that it might implicate her. Their task was far from done, but their trip to Brooklyn was productive. They identified Sami and they also had a complete plate number. As for Linda, the Irish curse had returned.

On the way home to Albany, Brendan called Walter in Boston and gave him the results of their interview with Linda. Walter was most appreciative and told Brendan their efforts tied up a lot of loose ends. As Walter hung up the phone, he was entering the Tip O'Neill Building in Boston's North

End. The port director was having an 'all hands' meeting with everyone involved in the case. He wanted to make sure nothing was left uncovered.

Just about everyone was already there by the time Walter showed up. Sebastian Auvil, the port director, was sitting at the head of the table talking with John Lynch and Leo Williamson as he entered the conference room. A group of investigators and inspectors were bunched up at the other end of the table going over their notes. On the far wall were a pile of pastries and carafes of hot coffee.

Walter nodded to everyone in general as he entered, ignored the pastries and coffee and sat down heavily on a well padded chair in the middle of the table. He dropped a notepad down on the table in front of him and leaned back in his chair. He took off his glasses, rubbed the bridge of his nose and then massaged his temples. Walter was exhausted from being on his feet for too many hours coordinating this multi-layered investigation. His only consolation was they were making headway and he hoped they would soon safely locate the dirty bomb and arrest those responsible for attempting to carry out this terrorist attack.

Sebastian opened the meeting by thanking everyone for their tireless efforts over the past few days. He told them they were making a lot of progress, but the bad guys were still on the loose. They did know the vehicle involved and knew at least one, and possibly all four of the suspects. The problem was, they didn't know where these guys were. The state police had a lookout for the red van not only in Massachusetts but in the entire northeast. However, the likelihood that they were still driving around in the van was slim. Sebastian stressed that now was the time for everyone to tap into their contact pool to see if they could come up with any type of human intelligence. The bad guys were on the move and most likely were planning to pull off some catastrophic event with their dirty bomb. Time was short and everyone had to keep driving hard.

Walter and the others considered this meeting more of a pep rally. But it was important because everyone was throwing their cards on the table letting everyone else know what they were doing. One piece of information provided by Sebastian was startling. He was informed by Customs Headquarters that the Army's Criminal Investigative Division in Frankfurt, Germany had discovered there might be more dirty containers in the pipeline headed for the United States. There were audible groans from everyone around the table. Therefore, Sebastian said, he was reinforcing the container inspection team at Conley Terminal with more state troopers and coast guard personnel. He promised not one container would enter this country through the port of Boston without being thoroughly inspected. He made a suggestion to Headquarters that every port does the same.

Also, the state police and coast guard were repositioning some of their aircraft in the Boston area. Specifically, both agencies were going to position a helicopter at both Beverly and Norwood airports. If something happened to the north of Boston or to the south, they would have aircraft available to shuttle troops or perform others tasks as needed. Lastly, Sebastian wanted everyone to know that the current terrorist threat was a direct result of last year's failed terrorist attempts. Washington had received sensitive information from overseas saying the terrorists were humiliated by their past failures and vowed revenge. It was up to all of them sitting at that table to prevent this from happening.

PART V

CHAPTER FORTY SEVEN

All four of them had been in America for several years. Sami, the de facto leader, had been here the longest, almost six years. They all had quite a lot in common. They came from Algeria, had a deep-rooted hatred for America and were willing to give their lives to destroy everything this country stood for. The obvious question was, why were they here if they hated this country so much? The answer is simple. In their long range plans to destroy America, terrorist groups, in this case a radical sect of the peace loving Salafists, decided to infiltrate America with loyal followers and assimilate into American society. Or so it would seem to the casual observer. When the call to arms was declared, they would already be in place to act. Having lived in the country for several years, they would be comfortable with the American style of life and would not appear to be out of place by their actions.

These groups of people were called "secret cells"; the number of cells increasing in this country after the terrorist's success of September 11th. Members of the most successful secret cells fully assimilated into American society and couldn't be distinguished from a native born American. They often had respected professional positions in major corporations and businesses. They were ticking time bombs within the inner circles of our society, waiting to blow when the opportunity arrived; for these four, that moment was here with the arrival of the dirty bomb. All their training and planning were about to be put to the test. All they had to do was thwart the efforts of America's law enforcement community who were sworn to stop them.

They arrived before the attacks on the World Trade Center. They all came as stowaways on one of the Liquefied Natural Gas ships that arrived in Boston from Algeria twice a month. Without documentation of any sort, they soon acquired driver's licenses, social security cards and often American passports with the aid of fellow Algerians who were living in this country legally. To make the transition into American life as smooth as possible, large amounts of money was needed to buy houses, cars, food and to maintain a standard of living fitting their part in American society. This need was satisfied by the large amounts of hashish and heroin that was smuggled into this country on the LNG ships. The only time drugs weren't on an LNG was because the supplier overseas couldn't supply the drugs fast enough. The Algerians were incredulous at how easy it was to infiltrate the shores of America time after time without being caught. After so long, they became contemptuous of American law enforcement.

Sami led the life of a bachelor in New York until he got caught up in the legal system. He was stopped and detained by the New York City Police for suspicion of robbery. After it was ascertained that it was not him, the NYPD wouldn't release him because he was an undocumented immigrant, an illegal. After a lengthy legal battle, paid for by an unknown wealthy sponsor, Sami was granted a conditional stay because he feared political persecution if he was forcibly returned to Algeria. However, this stay could be rescinded at any moment if the government determined the merits of his case no longer justified such actions. That is why Sami went hunting for an American woman to marry. Having an American wife would tremendously increase his chances of staying in this country. Linda McNally unwittingly fell into his web of deceit and suffered tremendously for her lack of good judgment in picking a suitable mate for life.

Ahmed, thirty three years of age, studied to be a pharmacist in Algeria. When he was smuggled into the country on the LNG almost three years ago, he was taken in by an Algerian family living in Brockton, a city just south of Boston. Ahmed obtained a driver's license and social security card with no problem. Soon he was registered at Massasoit College to study pharmacology. After two years of study he took the boards and passed with ease. He was recruited right after graduation to work in a nationally syndicated pharmacy. He gradually advanced in the company and was soon making a decent wage. Since he still lived in the same house when he first came here and led a frugal, Spartan life, Ahmed was able to send money home to his family in Arzew. He kept a little for himself and gave the rest to Youcef, the owner of the house he was living in, but not for rent. Youcef was a Salafist member and a financier of the movement in America. He communicated with Aadil back in Arzew on at least a weekly basis. Aadil told him where money was needed and Youcef made the arrangements. Youcef played a crucial role in developing, coordinating and organizing a terrorist threat against America.

Yacine and Aziz were outlaws in the eyes of the Algerian government. They were only in their early twenties, but had already been involved in many terrorist activities in Algeria. The Algerian government was hot on their trail and it was only a matter of time before they were caught. The only logical thing for them to do was to get out of Algeria. The triumvirate gave them options of going either to Afghanistan or America; they chose America because they didn't think the war in Afghanistan would last that long. Arrangements were made to transport them out of the country on one of the LNGs going to Boston. As usual, the triumvirate had them take a shipment of hashish to give to Youcef; he would know what to do with it. Once they arrived in Boston, living arrangements were made for them to live with an Algerian couple who had immigrated to America over twenty years ago. He was a renowned psychiatrist and his wife ran a prominent charity in Boston. The wealthy couple owned a beautiful five bedroom, three bath house on a secluded five acre parcel of land in suburban Weston. They were told to sit tight and wait for instructions.

When Sleazy sent word to Usayd that the dirty bomb was on the way to Boston in the sea container and should arrive within seven to ten days, Usayd passed the word to Aadil. In turn, Aadil talked with Youcef and told him it was time. He told Youcef to gather the troops in his Brockton home and stand by. Once the situation developed, Aadil would give him further instructions. In the meantime, he wanted all the players located together so they could act immediately when ordered. By the end of the day, the psychiatrist was driving Yacine and Aziz to Youcef's house and Sami was departing Brooklyn in Linda's red van. They were in Youcef's house the afternoon Joseph called and set up the midnight meeting to pick up the dirty bomb. All went well for them, despite the sudden death of Joseph.

CHAPTER FORTY EIGHT

Youcef and Aadil were prepared to move on to the next step of their plan. In fact they were anxious to move on to the next step. They feared if they hung around too long, someone might get wise to them and drop a dime to the police. Usayd and Aadil had their thoughts on what to do with the dirty bomb from the inception of their plans. However, they kept everything tentative until they were assured the bomb would get into the hands of their compatriots in the United States. Now that the dirty bomb was in their possession, they could reveal the rest of their plans. As usual, they wanted the act of terrorism to be symbolic, easy to perform and to inflict as much physical and psychological harm as possible. After thrashing different scenarios around in their heads, one idea kept popping to the surface. Why not detonate the dirty bomb at a major sporting event? Although they were completely unfamiliar with the game of American football, they had seen it on television numerous times. The crowds that the game attracted amazed them, and they were packed into such a small place.

They once watched a game played between the New York Jets and the New England Patriots. According to the announcers, the game was being played at Gillette Stadium in Foxborough, Massachusetts, less than twenty five miles south of Boston. This is when they started thinking seriously of targeting the stadium where the Patriots played. Logistically, they couldn't ask for a better place. The LNGs that arrived in Boston on a twice a month basis, originated in Arzew, literally their backyard. Smuggling people into the port of Boston would be easy. They also had a strong infrastructure already built up in the area, unlike in other parts of the country. Because of these factors, Usayd, Aadil and Youcef decided Gillette Stadium would be their primary target to detonate their dirty bomb. Secondary targets would be Boston Harbor itself and the hospital area around Longwood Ave. in Boston proper, but they didn't want to spend too much time and effort on the secondary targets. They wanted to concentrate on Gillette Stadium and would only fall back to a secondary target if for some unknown reason the primary target was impossible to hit.

Their plans called for making several dry runs to ensure nothing went wrong on the day of the attack. The Sunday after they picked up the dirty bomb and secured it in Youcef's cellar, Youcef took all four of them for a ride in his Jeep Cherokee. He drove the exact route they would be taking the next Sunday, the day they would execute their plans. Youcef stressed to all of them that they should drive at the speed limit and not to make any erratic moves that might attract the attention of a state trooper. From experience, he knew the state police were all over the roads whenever the Patriots were playing. They were specifically looking for people drinking and driving and driving erratically would definitely get you stopped.

Youcef left his house on Parker Street in Brockton and caught Rte. 123 at the foot of his street. He passed the VA hospital on his left just before he took the exit for Rte. 24. Where Rte. 24 and Rte. 93 merged, Youcef warned them to drive carefully. There were always accidents at the intersection and they had to use extra caution. After they passed through the intersection, they saw three state trooper cars parked in the breakdown lane. Fire apparatus and ambulances were also there. Youcef drove by the accident scene nodding his head. "See what I mean," he said. From Rte. 93 they took Rte. 95 south toward Foxborough. After driving 10 miles, they took Rte. 1 which would take them directly to Gillette Stadium. But they were going to take a little diversion first.

The Wal Mart on Rte. 1 had a huge parking lot. Youcef drove around the parking lot explaining that next Sunday they would be driving three vans. Sami would be driving the red van containing the dirty bomb. Ahmed would drive the white van and Yacine and Aziz would be driving the black van. They would travel together and once they reached Wal Mart, Ahmed would park the white van in the parking lot and jump in the red van with Sami. They would use the white van as a backup vehicle in case they needed it. Then both vans would proceed directly to Gillette

Stadium. Sami would park the red van in the most advantageous location to inflict the most harm, set the timer to the dirty bomb and then he and Ahmed would jump in the black van with Yacine and Aziz and make their withdrawal.

When Youcef was finished explaining the chain of events that would be occurring next Sunday, he left the parking lot and proceeded to Gillette Stadium. On the way, there was a lot of chattering amongst the four. This is the first time that they had actually heard the plan of attack and they were quite excited. They arrived at Gillette Stadium forty minutes after leaving the house in Brockton. Youcef told them the drive next Sunday would be a lot longer, they should allow two hours. The game was scheduled to start at 4:00 pm, so Youcef said they would leave Brockton at 1:00. If they arrived at the stadium around 3:00, there would be plenty of people in the parking lot and entering the stadium. All four of them were awestruck by the sight of the stadium; they had never seen anything so big in their entire lives.

On the drive back to Brockton, Youcef asked everybody if they had any questions. Aziz asked how long the timer would be set for and Youcef said five minutes. Aziz asked if something went wrong, could they bypass the timer and detonate the dirty bomb immediately. When Yousef replied in the affirmative, Aziz sat back in his car seat, closed his eyes and smiled slightly. He appeared to be at total peace with himself. Ahmed asked Yousef about the escape route. Yousef told them that if they could make it back to Brockton, they would. Otherwise, an LPG (liquefied petroleum gas) ship was scheduled to sail out of Portsmouth, New Hampshire the following day. If they could make it to Portsmouth, they were assured a ride home. Ahmed liked that option. He knew if they stayed in America after pulling off the terrorist attack, every law enforcement officer would be looking for them. Sami and Yacine seemed content with the plans and didn't ask any questions. As Youcef drove north on Rte. 95, they saw several state police cruisers with their blue lights flashing pulling cars over to the side of the road. Youcef once again stressed the importance of staying away from these guys. He said they were bad asses and didn't give anyone a break, especially people like them.

CHAPTER FORTY NINE

The day they had been preparing for had finally arrived. Months of preparation was coming to fruition. Youcef had all four up bright and early and made sure they had a hearty breakfast. While they were cleaning up and saying their prayers, Youcef inspected all three vans once again. He surely didn't want one of them breaking down on the way to the stadium, especially the red van. About 12:30 pm, Youcef told them it was time to load the dirty bomb in the red van. This is when Aziz spoke to Youcef. Aziz thought it would be best if he accompanied Sami in the red van instead of going with Yacine in the black van, just in case he needed help for some reason. Youcef didn't see his point, but he wasn't about to argue with Aziz at this crucial point in their plans. Besides, they were carrying out this courageous deed, not him, so why not let them do it their way? Youcef approved the change and told them to load the dirty bomb in the van.

At precisely 1:00 pm, they were standing in Youcef's living room saying their good-byes. All four were confident yet stoic. They had a job to do and they were intent on carrying it out. Youcef was the one that became emotional. He was proud of his fellow countrymen and wished them the best. Hopefully, he'd be seeing them back in his home in a few hours. If not, they knew where they'd be seeing each other.

The red van, with Sami driving and Aziz riding shotgun, led the way. Ahmed followed in the white van with Yacine bringing up the rear in the black van. As instructed by Youcef, they obeyed the speed limit and were careful how they drove. As they approached the merge at Routes 24 and 93, the traffic ground to a halt. Youcef knew what he was talking about, Sami thought. Off in the distance, they could see police cars and fire trucks. As they inched their way forward, they could see a SUV on its side with people standing next to it. Off the road in the woods, there was another car on its roof.

State troopers were standing by the side of the road directing traffic around the accident. As Sami drove by, he made casual eye contact with one of the troopers. He swore the trooper was staring at him as if he knew who he was. He felt his mouth go dry and he had to force himself to act nonchalant. He couldn't wait to get by the accident. Eventually, all three vans did get by the accident scene, but now they were separated. They were no longer in a nice tidy straight line. But, they had trained for this eventuality. Youcef told them if for some reason they lost sight of each other, they should simply proceed independently to the Wal Mart parking lot. They would regroup there and then proceed to Gillette Stadium.

The traffic was heavy as Sami turned onto Rte. 95 south, but it was still moving along at about 40 mph. The further he drove the more comfortable he began to feel. It looked like everything was going as planned. Aziz sat beside him, looking out the window, not saying a word. He looked completely at ease. Sami was about two miles from the Rte. 1 exit when the sound of a siren made him jump. He looked in his side view mirror and couldn't believe what he saw. A state police cruiser was right behind him with its blue lights flashing. Sami wasn't sure what he should do, until the trooper yelled at him over the cruisers loudspeaker, "in the red van, pull over into the breakdown lane and come to a complete stop. Stay in the vehicle and rest your hands on the dashboard." Sami was petrified. Aziz started yelling at him to do what the state trooper told him to do. Breathing heavily, Sami maneuvered the van to the right and did exactly what the trooper said. Aziz adjusted the rear view mirror and watched the trooper as he sat in his cruiser. It appeared to Aziz that the trooper was typing something into a computer that was mounted on the dashboard. Aziz told Sami not to worry. Once the trooper ran the plate and asked them a few questions, they'd be on their way again. As Aziz said this, he adjusted the gun resting in his shoulder holster.

The trooper cautiously approached the van, looking through the rear window as he came up on the right hand side of the vehicle. When he was at the rear bumper walking slowly forward, Aziz jumped out of the vehicle. The next thing Sami heard was at least three loud, deafening explosions.

As he turned to look, Sami saw Aziz's outstretched arms pointed toward the rear of the vehicle. In his hands was his 9mm semi automatic pistol. Sami never saw the trooper, but knew he was back there somewhere. Obviously, Aziz was shooting at him. The next thing he remembered, Aziz was back in the vehicle yelling at him to drive. Sami was in a state of shock and responded to Aziz's yelling without thinking. He drove erratically down the highway and took the next exit, two exits before they should have. Aziz told him to take the exit and told Sami he knew how to get to the Wal Mart parking lot from there. Slowly Sami began to regain his composure. When he asked Aziz what happened back there, all Aziz did was smile and say, "I shot the bastard. What the fuck do you think?"

CHAPTER FIFTY

Trooper Brian Walker had been on the job for almost five years. He worked out of the Foxborough barracks for the last two years. Previous to that, he'd been assigned to the Topsfield Barracks on the north shore. Before joining the state police, Walker was attending college on the GI Bill. He was an army veteran of both the Iraq and Afghanistan war and had seen a tremendous amount of action in both theaters. His last deployment was with the army's elite 10th Mountain Brigade. During this deployment, his company was ambushed by the Taliban and suffered heavy casualties. Walker himself was wounded and was awarded the Silver Star for saving the lives of at least three of his fellow soldiers during an intense firefight.

Walker thought he'd make the army his career but when he was home on leave in Norwood after his last deployment, he met Mary who was to become the love of his life. She encouraged him to pursue whatever career he desired and assured him if he decided to stay in the army, she'd follow him wherever he went. But Walker thought differently. He knew army life was awfully tough on the family, especially being deployed overseas so often, and decided he'd leave the army and pursue a career in law enforcement. They married shortly after and when the state police called him and said they had a place for him in the next class of recruits, both he and Mary were ecstatic. Walker excelled at the state police academy and graduated near the top of his class.

While assigned to the Topsfield and Foxborough barracks, Walker had been cited by the state police on numerous occasions. He received the department's highest award for bravery for single handedly arresting two armed felons wanted for murder. To say the least, Walker was a stellar trooper and had a bright future. While working out of the Topsfield barracks, Walker and his wife bought their dream house in their home town of Norwood. Being reassigned to Foxborough, a town next door to Norwood, meant so much to him because now he could spend more time at home with Mary and their twin boys, Tommy and Billy. That is how Walker found himself working Rte. 95 south that fateful afternoon. He was scheduled for the 4 to 12 shift, but came in early to work a double to help with the traffic heading down to Gillette Stadium in Foxborough for the Patriots-Dolphins game.

All state troopers had been notified the week before to be on the lookout for a red van with New York plates '459 ISH'. They were told to be extremely cautious if they sighted the vehicle because the driver was allegedly involved in a terrorist group and they were suspected of attempting a terrorist act in the immediate future. Troopers received many lookouts during their daily shifts, but this one was different. This one made the hairs on the small of their neck tingle. This one appeared to be the real thing. That is why Walker pinned the lookout on the dashboard right next to his laptop computer.

As he was parked in a rest stop on the side of Rte. 95 south, Walker casually kept an eye on the traffic and an ear to the radio. So far his overtime shift was quiet and he only responded to one minor call. As he was eyeing the traffic, he watched a red van pass by and he naturally scanned the license plate. When he saw the New York plate he looked closer. As he read "459 ISH', he could feel his heart rate increase and the adrenalin pump through his body. He threw his cruiser into drive and pulled out of the rest stop. As he increased speed, he grabbed the mike to his radio and called the desk sergeant at the Foxborough barracks. He told the sergeant where he was and what he was following. The sergeant immediately realized the gravity of the situation and began to respond in the same manner he had in so many other previous situations. But even he felt a tinge of fear in his gut. The sergeant told Walker to keep calling out the location of the van and he would dispatch other cruisers to the location to back him up. Then the sergeant hesitated and did something that he had never done before in his twenty-five years on the state police; he told Walker to be careful.

They weren't sure why Walker didn't wait for the other cruisers to arrive before he made the vehicle stop, but he didn't. For some reason Walker stopped the vehicle, punched the plate number into his computer and then got out of his cruiser. By eyewitness accounts, Walker approached the right side of the vehicle in a defensive manner. One of the eyewitnesses, who were stuck in bumper to bumper traffic, described it as 'the Fourth of July, but only ten times louder.' Another eyewitness described seeing Walker 'flying through the air and disappearing down the embankment'. No one really remembers seeing the red van take off, but obviously it did because it was gone. No one thought to copy the license plate because their attention was affixed to the trooper. Numerous cars pulled to the side of the road and several individuals ran down the side of the embankment in an attempt to help the trooper. Walker was laying there on his side, blood trickling out of the corner of his mouth. In the distance his hat lay in a pool of muddy water.

This is how the arriving troopers found Walker. As a couple of them were giving him medical attention, another trooper was on his radio calling for help. They needed an ambulance and they needed it fast. The sound in the trooper's voice was more pleading than requesting. The desk sergeant in the Foxborough barracks sprung into action. He acknowledged the troopers plea and grabbed the phone by his side. He called the Foxborough, Walpole and Norwood Fire Departments and asked them to send an ambulance to mile marker 198 on Rte. 95 south. A trooper had been shot and he needed immediate attention. He called all three fire departments because he knew the traffic was bumper to bumper and he wasn't sure who would be able to get there the quickest.

As they waited for medical assistance, the two troopers helping Walker assessed his condition. He was bleeding from the mouth and was having trouble breathing so they thought he might have a sucking chest wound. As they ran their fingers over Walker's chest, they felt a rip in his uniform shirt. They looked closely and saw the tear. When they ripped his shirt open, they exposed his bullet proof vest. Right beneath the hole in the shirt was an indent in the vest the size of a quarter. Both troopers realized the vest stopped a bullet from penetrating Walker's chest, but the blunt force of the impact could have broken a rib. In turn the broken rib might have punctured a lung, causing the bleeding from the mouth and the difficulty breathing.

Walker's face was ashen about this time, and they knew they had to do something quick or they might lose him. Luckily, both troopers were combat veterans and had been taught all about sucking chest wounds in basic training. They knew you were supposed to lay a casualty with a chest wound on the side that had the wound. Walker was shot on the right side, but was laying on his left side, exactly the opposite of what they had been taught in the service and at the academy. Praying that they were right, the two troopers gently rolled Walker onto his right side. To their relief, Walker's breathing appeared less labored and his color began to come back in his face. They checked the rest of his body, but it appeared he was only shot in the chest. As they monitored Walker's condition and waited for an ambulance, a civilian offered a blanket from his car to keep Walker warm.

CHAPTER FIFTY ONE

As these events were unfolding alongside the highway, Sebastian, John and Leo were at Conley Container Terminal. They had been there since 8:00 am. They were waiting for one of the three suspect containers that the CID in Germany identified to be possibly high risk for containing caesium-137. The container was supposed to have been unloaded earlier, but the three of them were still waiting, along with the entire container inspection team. They wanted to make sure this container was inspected thoroughly the moment it came off the ship. They didn't want another fiasco like the last container. Even though they were taking extraordinary measures regarding this container, they hoped the container was negative like the other two the CID identified. They had been offloaded from a ship in Newark a couple of days ago and an inspection showed no signs of caesium-137 or any other radioactive material.

The three of them were in the customs office at the terminal when Leo received the call about Trooper Walker's shooting. Leo was visibly upset and cursed the heavy traffic that was slowing down the ambulances racing to the scene of the shooting. He knew the amount of time that elapsed before Walker got to the hospital meant the difference between life and death. He prayed the ambulances arrived shortly. Then John had an idea. "Leo," he said, "we have a coast guard chopper sitting on the end of the runway at Norwood. They can do a medevac. Damn, they do them every day. Why don't we send the chopper over to pick up the trooper and fly him to a hospital in Boston?" Leo looked at John and said, "John, do you think we can do that?"

Without any more delay, John was on the phone to coast guard sector communications in Boston. He told the radio operator to contact the chopper on the ground at Norwood airport and have them respond to the shooting. John gave the radio operator the general vicinity and told him to tell the pilots the state police would have the highway cleared for them to land. As he said this, he looked at Leo and nodded. Leo got the hint and began dialing on his cell phone. He called the desk sergeant in Foxborough and told him a United States Coast Guard chopper would be landing within a few minutes to pick Walker up and transport him to a hospital in Boston. He told the sergeant to make sure the highway was cleared so the chopper could land, he didn't want any delays.

In less than five minutes, CG 65127 was hovering over Rte. 95 southbound. Six state police cruisers formed a rough circle seventy five meters in diameter. The helicopter landed right in the middle of the circle. As soon as the chopper landed, two figures wearing bright blue coveralls, jumped out the side door carrying a stokes litter. They were escorted to the location of Trooper Walker by a burly state trooper. Trained medics, they made sure Walker was stabilized before they put him in the stokes litter and carried him back to the helicopter. State troopers were by their side assisting them the entire way.

Once they had Walker in the helicopter, they closed the side door. The pilot increased the power to the engine and slowly lifted the helicopter off the ground. In a little over four minutes, the helicopter had landed, picked up the trooper and was racing to Massachusetts General Hospital in Boston. Their estimated time of arrival was nine minutes. The state police had already notified the hospital staff of the situation and they promised they'd be waiting when the helicopter landed on the roof of the hospital. Walker's fate would then be in their hands. As the coast guard helicopter was headed north to the hospital, two state police cruisers were racing to Walker's house in Norwood. They were told to pick up Mary and get her to the hospital. She had already been notified and was waiting with her father at her house.

CHAPTER FIFTY TWO

Ahmed drove into the Wal Mart parking lot first, driving the white van. Yacine pulled in alongside him a few minutes later, driving the black van. The time was 1:15 pm. They had 45 minutes to go before their scheduled arrival at the stadium. All three vans got separated while driving down Rte. 95. Luckily Youcef planned for this contingency and had them all meet in the Wal Mart parking lot before they proceeded on to Gillette Stadium. Yacine and Ahmed waited patiently, but wished Sami and Aziz would hurry up. They wanted to keep with Youcef's schedule.

Suddenly they saw the red van approaching from the opposite direction than they came from and it was going much too fast. "What the heck," Ahmed said, "what's going on with these two?" Sami pulled next to Ahmed in the white van. By the look on Sami's face, Ahmed knew something was wrong. "Everything okay?" Ahmed asked. Sami looked straight ahead as if he was in a trance. His hands were gripping the steering wheel so tight his knuckles were turning white. Aziz on the other hand looked relaxed. "Aziz," Ahmed asked again, "is everything okay?" Aziz looked at Ahmed and smiled. "Everything is fine," he said. "We had a small incident with a state trooper, but we settled our differences." He slapped the side of the door with his dangling right arm and said, "Okay, let's go. We have a half hour to get to the stadium. We'll take the white and black vans. They'll be looking for this one."

Ahmed and Yacine were confused as to what was going on, but there wasn't time to get into all the details. They had to get down to the stadium and complete their task. Aziz gently picked up the dirty bomb and transferred it to the white van. Sami walked slowly to the black van and climbed into the passenger seat beside Yacine. He seemed to be disoriented and out of touch with what was going on. After Aziz transferred the dirty bomb, he jumped behind the steering wheel of the white van. Ahmed began to protest, but decided to keep his mouth shut. Even though he was supposed to drive the van, he couldn't see a problem with Aziz driving. He just wished Aziz was a bit more diplomatic on how he did things. Once they were all buckled in, both vans proceeded slowly out of the parking lot. They took a right and headed south on Rte. 1. They should be at the stadium within fifteen minutes if the traffic wasn't too heavy. The red van remained behind. It now became the backup vehicle instead of the white van.

After the shooting, the Massachusetts State Police put out another APB (all points bulletin) for the red van bearing the New York license plate '459 ISH.' This time they added an addendum to the original APB; the van was involved in the shooting of a Massachusetts State Trooper and the occupants should be considered armed and dangerous. The state police and all the surrounding towns flooded the area with police cars looking for the red van. The state police helicopter Leo had on standby at Norwood Airport also got involved in the hunt. Roadblocks were established at key intersections, further slowing down the traffic headed to Gillette Stadium. The media monitored the state police radio frequency and knew about the shooting as soon as it happened. Radio and TV stations were seeking more information as to the status of the manhunt so they could broadcast the information to their listeners and viewers.

WBZ, a local Boston radio station, broadcast the news of the shooting before any other station. Their coverage was complete and accurate. Most importantly, they described the vehicle and license plate correctly. This allowed all the listeners to act as eyes and ears for law enforcement. They were asked to look for the vehicle and, if they spotted it, to dial 911 immediately. They were cautioned not to take any action because the occupants in the vehicle were considered extremely dangerous.

CHAPTER FIFTY THREE

Saturday night, Mr. Hanley had promised his 12–year-old son, Stephen, that they would go to Wal Mart the following day and buy basketball sneakers before his 3:00 pm basketball game in Mansfield. They had just left the store and were sitting in the car admiring Stephen's new sneakers. The car was running and the radio was tuned in to WBZ radio 1030. As Stephen was admiring his sneakers and telling his father he would be able to play basketball much better wearing the new sneakers, a special bulletin came over the radio. Stephen kept talking and Mr. Hanley had to tell him to be quiet for a second. The broadcaster said there was just a shooting of a state trooper on Rte. 95 south in Walpole. There was a massive manhunt for the occupants of a red van bearing New York plates '459 ISH.' If anyone saw this vehicle, the broadcaster asked that they dial 911 immediately.

Mr. Hanley was staring straight ahead through the windshield as he listened to the broadcaster. When he heard a trooper was shot, he paid extra attention because two of his brothers were in law enforcement. When the broadcaster gave the description of the vehicle and the plate number, Mr. Hanley wrote both down on a notepad he had attached to his dashboard. When the special bulletin was over, he apologized to his son and told him to continue what he was saying. Instead of continuing the conversation about his newly bought sneakers, his son pointed out the window and said, "Dad, there's a red van. Do you think that's the one the police are looking for?" Mr. Hanley looked in the direction his son was pointing. Not more than 100 feet away, parked at a weird angle, was a red van. Mr. Hanley looked at the license plate and saw it was from New York. He strained his eyes to read the numbers on the plate and finally made it out; it was '459 ISH.' Mr. Hanley looked at the number he had just written down on his notepad and saw they were the same. He let out a soft whistle and unconsciously said, "Holy shit, that's the vehicle they're looking for."

Mr. Hanley grabbed the cell phone that was clipped on his pants belt and dialed 911. Immediately a voice answered, 'state police dispatcher, what's the nature of your emergency.' Mr. Hanley stammered out the information about the red van and eventually the dispatcher understood. He told Mr. Hanley that if it was safe, he wanted him to stay exactly where he was; troopers were on the way. Mr. Hanley hung up his cell phone and grabbed his son Stephen. He wasn't sure why he was shaking so, probably because of all the excitement, he thought. One thing he did know, he was darn proud of his 12 year-old son Stephen. About that time, they could hear a helicopter hovering high overhead. Then state police cruisers came from all different directions. Troopers exited their vehicles with shotguns in hand; they were all pointed in the direction of the red van.

After the troopers ascertained there wasn't anyone or anything in the van, the Lieutenant in charge approached Mr. Hanley. He began to thank him for taking the initiative to inform the state police about the location of the red van until Mr. Hanley raised both his hands and said, "Whoa, Lieutenant, you're thanking the wrong guy. Stephen here was the one that noticed the vehicle. He deserves the credit." The Lieutenant looked down at Stephen standing next to his father, a smile on his face from ear to ear. "Well, Stephen," said the Lieutenant, "you are the hero of the day. Hang on for one second; I have something for you"

The Lieutenant walked to his cruiser, opened the trunk and took something out. He was back in seconds. "Stephen," he said, "With the powers vested in me by the Commonwealth of Massachusetts, I hereby declare you an honorary Massachusetts State Trooper." With that, the Lieutenant placed an official Massachusetts State Trooper baseball hat on Stephen's head. After squaring the hat, the Lieutenant stepped back and snapped Stephen a crisp military salute. Mr. Hanley was beaming with pride and had to fight back a tear. He was so proud of his son. One thing he knew for sure, Stephen was going to have a story to tell when he went to school. The Lieutenant shook Mr. Hanley's hand and thanked him for all his help.

While the Lieutenant was thanking Mr. Hanley and his son, other troopers were inside the security office of Wal Mart viewing their security tapes. On tape, they could see clearly what transpired. Two vans, one white and one black, with Massachusetts plates, were parked in the parking lot with one white male sitting in the driver's seat of each van. Then the red van, bearing New York license plates '459 ISH' drove up going at a relatively high rate of speed and parked alongside the white van. The driver of the red van, Sámi, climbed into the passenger seat of the black van. He walked as if he was in a trance. The passenger in the red van, Aziz, carried something out of the van and placed it between the front seats of the white van. He then climbed into the driver's seat, the other individual sitting in the passenger seat. As soon as everyone was seated, both the white and black vans carrying two people each left the parking lot at a slow rate of speed. The last shots on the camera showed them heading south on Rte 1.

The Lieutenant called state police headquarters in Framingham and gave them all the information pertaining to the white and black vans. Headquarters was going to relay the information over their statewide net, reaching every state police cruiser in the state and most local police departments. Within seconds, the Lieutenant could hear the information being relayed over his cruiser's radio. Now that he was satisfied that the word was out on the two vans, he wondered where they were headed. Then the logical place popped into his head—Gillette Stadium. He used his cell phone to call the state police captain in charge of the security detail at Gillette stadium. The Lieutenant expressed his fears to the captain and they both agreed they better set up road blocks on both sides of Rte.1. They couldn't let either van get close to the stadium. One cruiser was left behind to secure the area around the red van and await the arrival of the forensics team. The rest took off and headed south on Rte. 1. They had to stop the vans before they reached their objective.

While state police roadblocks were being established on both sides of Rte.1, two state police cruisers were racing through the streets of Boston on their way to Mass. General Hospital. Mary and her father were being rushed to the hospital so they could be by the side of Trooper Walker. Boston Police had been notified of the emergency run and they were stopping traffic at most major intersections. By the time the state police cruisers arrived in front of the White Building at Mass. General, the coast guard helicopter had already landed; the doctors had Brian in the operating room, a priest was with him.

CHAPTER FIFTY FOUR

Both vans were headed south on Rte. 1 in bumper to bumper traffic traveling at no faster then 20 miles per hour. Aziz and Ahmed were in the white van leading, Yacine and Sami in the black van a few cars lengths behind. Sami was still in a trance-like state. As they crested a small rise in the highway, Aziz could see countless police cars about ½ mile ahead. Both sides of the highway were blocked off. Cars were allowed to pass only after they stopped at the roadblock and were cleared by one of the many machine gun-toting troopers stationed there. For the first time since they planned the terrorist attack, Aziz had doubts about the outcome. They would never get by the state police so why bother trying.

For an instant, he thought of blowing the dirty bomb as they sat there amid hundreds of other cars. As these thoughts were flashing across his mind, he noticed a large electrical substation just off the highway. From his vantage point, he saw countless large transformers sitting behind a small chain link fence. It wasn't their primary or secondary objective, but it was better than nothing. Knowing he didn't have much time, Aziz acted quickly. He told Ahmed to get out of the van and go back and ride with the other guys. When Ahmed questioned him, Aziz told him they would never make their objective and they had to turn around; Ahmed had to relay that information to the other two. Then Aziz looked at him and said, "You must save yourself for another day."

As soon as Ahmed left, Aziz felt like a new man. Now he was only responsible for himself. As he inched forward in the heavy traffic, Aziz saw a small road leading off the highway directly to the electrical substation. At the end of the road was a locked chain link fence. Aziz knew he had to act or he would lose his chance to become a martyr. He turned the steering wheel to the right and pushed his foot down hard on the accelerator pedal. The van jumped forward and picked up speed. Aziz was probably going over 50 miles per hour when he crashed through the gate, attempting to keep the van headed directly for the closest transformer. It was hard for him to see because the broken gate smashed the windshield, causing shards of glass to fly into his face, virtually blinding him. Aziz was praying up to the last moment; praying to his god that he would be successful in wreaking havoc and death to the infidel Americans.

CHAPTER FIFTY FIVE

The sound of the transformer exploding was deafening, but things soon became a lot worse. A chain reaction ensued, resulting in more violent explosions. When the fire engulfing the van reached the C4 explosive, a ground shaking, ear shattering explosion resulted that could be heard for miles. Windows of homes over a mile away shattered, causing people to believe an airplane had crashed. Dark black clouds of smoke billowed high into the air, laced with fingers of fire reaching over 100 feet high. The earth rumbled with explosions, one after the other. Mass hysteria resulted on the highway, people scrambling to get as far away as possible from the fire, smoke and earth shattering explosions. The heat from the flames ignited numerous nearby homes and buildings. The shock waves from the multiple blasts could be felt by fans in the seats of Gillette Stadium.

The parking lot of Gillette Stadium resonated with the sound of car alarms blaring, set off by the sound waves of the multiple violent explosions. The sound of fire trucks' wailing sirens could barely be heard over all the noise. Perhaps the most telling moment was when the stadium lost all electricity. The overhead lighting suddenly went out, the scoreboard blackened in an instant; the blaring announcements over the public address system attempting to calm the fans suddenly stopped in mid-sentence. Fans looked to the sky with fear and trepidation. Was this the end? Parents with children by their sides reacted first. They had to get out of the stadium and get to safety. People rushed to the exits, soon blocked by fallen bodies. They ran onto the field, seeking any means of escape possible. Efforts by the police to maintain order soon dissipated in the mass rush of people seeking safety from all the noise and confusion. The rumor of a nuclear attack by terrorists was confirmed, panic consumed the crowd. Those fortunate enough to get out of the stadium had nowhere to go; the roads were blocked. They stood helplessly staring up into the sky as the big plume of smoke continued spreading overhead. Cries for help could be heard everywhere; muffled sobs echoed in the air.

In this state of chaos and confusion, Yacine, Sami and Ahmed attempted their escape. After all, who was there to stop them? Everyone was concerned with saving their own lives and the lives of those around them. Yacine was able to navigate the van to a small side street leading off of Rte.1. From there, they slowly managed to weave their way through the back roads of Walpole. Frequently, they had to move over to the side of the road, allowing room for emergency vehicles rushing to the disaster scene to pass. Ahmed could see a towering black pall of smoke as he looked out the side window of the van. Along with that smoke, he thought, went their plans to wreak death and destruction on their enemies. Ahmed became depressed at the sight; they had failed in their mission. As they neared Walpole Center, two police cars approached the van, blue lights flashing. This is it, Ahmed thought, they were caught. As suddenly as they appeared, the police cars were gone. Ahmed could see them speeding down the street in the direction of the smoke.

Yacine drove through Walpole Center and entered the parking lot for the commuter rail station. Parked on the side of the station was a non-descript green Taurus station wagon. Yacine parked next to the Taurus and said, "this is it guys, our ride to freedom." Unknown to Sami and Ahmed, Youcef had placed this car at the railroad station to act as another 'safe car' in case of an emergency. They all climbed out of the van and jumped into the Taurus. With any luck, they'd be in Portsmouth, New Hampshire just as it was turning dark. If their luck held, they'd be on the LPG ship that night, in time for the morning sailing. Within a week they'd be back in Algeria.

CHAPTER FIFTY SIX

The doctors at Mass. General Hospital were finishing up from the three hour emergency surgery. Trooper Brian Walker's condition was listed as critical, but stable. The doctor's felt his prognosis was good and he should have a complete recovery, but it would take time. The broken ribs did penetrate Brian's lung, causing it to collapse. If it wasn't for the heads up move of his fellow troopers, the doctors said Brian would have died. Mary and her father were able to see him in recovery. He wasn't able to talk because of the tubes in his mouth, but a lot was said with their eyes. Mary was so proud of her husband. He had given so much of himself to keep America safe; first in Iraq and Afghanistan and now on the streets of America. Mary couldn't wait to get Brian home again so she could spoil him with love and attention. Brian couldn't wait either; he longed to see the smiling faces of his little twin boys, Billy and Tommy. As they left the recovery room, two troopers were standing guard by the doors. They would remain there until their fallen brother left the hospital.

In the Wal Mart parking lot, the state police forensics team was poring over Sami's abandoned red van. They were able to get many fingerprint impressions off the doors and steering wheels. As they were working, they monitored their radios as to what was going on by Gillette Stadium. In the distance they too could see the huge plume of black smoke. The situation sounded and looked like a modern day Armageddon. However, they had to put all those thoughts out of their minds and concentrate on searching the van. As one of the investigators was searching the area under the back bench seat, she pulled out a balled up piece of paper. When she unfolded the paper, she attempted to iron out all the creases. After she did the best she could, she looked at the paper and could tell it was on line directions from Google for an address in Brockton to Gillette Stadium in Foxborough. Immediately she knew that she'd found something significant.

The intelligence unit worked with the Brockton Police Department to determine who lived at 10 Parker Street, the originating address on the Google search. Using town records, the police identified the owner of the home at that address as Youcef. Also, they said he owned two vehicles, a Jeep Cherokee and a Ford Taurus. They said they never had any trouble at that address, and it was in an upper class neighborhood. The state police initially thought of seeking a search warrant for the address, but reconsidered. They decided to do a 'knock and talk' instead. If that failed to produce any positive results, they felt like they had enough probable cause to seek a search warrant, but the first method was faster and easier. While they were gathering units to conduct the 'knock and talk', the state police asked if Brockton could send an unmarked unit to conduct a covert surveillance on that address until they arrived. Brockton readily complied.

It was early that evening when two state police detectives and Walter, the customs investigator leading the case, knocked on Youcef's front door at 10 Parker Street in Brockton. They knew what they were doing was risky, but obviously they thought the possible benefits were worth the risk. In case something went wrong with the 'knock and talk' two SWAT teams were stationed at both ends of the street. At the least sign of trouble, they both had orders to respond immediately to the house. The trooper was knocking on the door for the second time when, all of a sudden, the door flew open, startling all three of them. Youcef was standing in front of them with a quizzical expression on his face. "May I help you?" he said. Walter stepped forward and identified himself and the two state troopers and then said, "Yes you can sir. We are conducting an investigation into a possible terrorist plot. A piece of evidence has been uncovered that implicates you. We'd like to talk to you about it." Walter was a sweet-talker but, over the many years he'd been conducting investigations, he realized you really did get more out of people by sweet talk than by being a hard ass with them.

Surprisingly, Youcef said he didn't mind and invited all three into the house. Walter was taken aback by Yousef's cordiality. He thought either Youcef was a great con man or else he really didn't have anything to hide.

Youcef escorted them into a room off the kitchen that appeared to Walter to be a TV room. He offered them a seat and asked if they'd like something to drink. As Youcef was acting as the gracious host, one of the troopers called the units outside on his radio and told them they were inside and everything was fine. Once they were seated, Youcef eyed Walter and said, "Now, what would you like to ask me?" Walter cleared his throat and began.

He told Youcef that without going into specifics, they searched a vehicle earlier in the day that was involved in some kind of terrorist activity. The search uncovered many promising leads, Walter told Youcef, and then he pulled a copy of the Google search out of his shirt pocket. "We'd like to ask you about this," Walter said. Youcef looked at the paper for a few seconds and then looked back up at Walter. "This appears to be a Google search for directions from my house to Gillette Stadium," he said in a calm matter-of-fact manner. "I have been going to see the Patriots play for years. I don't understand what the problem is." Walter was listening to Youcef's words closely. His reply was plausible, but it didn't answer the question how this piece of paper wound up in the red van, especially when the paper showed it was printed only the day before. But, the content of Youcef's words didn't concern Walter; it was how he said the words. Walter had been interviewing people for years and he felt he was pretty good at detecting when someone was lying to him. Walter knew Youcef was lying. He detected a crack in Youcef's nonchalant carefree attitude.

Before Walter could pursue his questioning, one of the troopers spoke up. "Sir," he said, "how many cars do you have registered in your name?" The trooper spoke in a harsh no nonsense manner, quite unlike Walter's subtle mode of attack. "One," Youcef quickly replied, "the Jeep Cherokee you saw in the driveway when you walked up the walkway." They already knew he had two cars registered in his name; why was he lying about the Ford Taurus? Again, Walter was more concerned about how Youcef answered the question than the answer itself. For the second time, Walter detected in Youcef's mannerisms and body language that he wasn't telling the truth, something was amiss.

The trooper looked at Youcef and unceremoniously said, "So, the registry is wrong, is that what you are telling us?" Walter didn't exactly like the trooper's direct, harsh type of questioning, but if it worked, so be it. Youcef looked a bit stunned, and then he regained his composure. "Oh," he said, "you're talking about the Taurus. That was stolen almost a month ago. I've been so busy lately I haven't had the chance to call my insurance company and report it stolen." The trooper knew he was lying and went for the jugular. If he pulled it off he could break Youcef and be a hero. If not, he could blow everything. "Is that so?" the trooper sarcastically said, "then either your neighbors are fucking liars or you're the liar. They told us they saw the Taurus in the same fucking driveway as your Jeep Cherokee just yesterday." The trooper was lying, neighbors never told him that, but Youcef didn't know. The trooper sensed he had Youcef on the ropes and was going for the knockout punch.

All of a sudden, Youcef's face turned pale and his fingers began trembling. He attempted to say something to the trooper but his lips just quivered. Walter was stunned. The trooper's harsh interrogation methods appeared to work. Youcef was definitely shaken. "Well, what is it?" the trooper continued, "Who's the fucking liar, you or them?" Youcef looked at Walter, his eyes appealing for help. Walter turned his head away in the direction of the trooper asking the questions. "Are you going to answer the question?" the trooper asked. "It's simple enough, isn't it?" Youcef's entire body began to shake. "I never wanted anything to do with them. They made me do it. If I didn't, they said they'd hurt my mother. She's in her nineties. Oh God!" he cried. His words were unintelligible after that. Walter looked at the trooper that was asking the questions and smiled. The trooper remained stone faced, looking directly at Youcef as if he was waiting for a reply. Walter decided to give Youcef a minute or two to calm down, and then he planned on reading him his Miranda rights. After that, either he'd waive his rights and cooperate or he'd 'lawyer up.' Either way, they had him, only difference was, one way was faster than the other.

After Youcef settled down, Walter read him his Miranda rights. Youcef wanted to cooperate and promised he'd tell them whatever they wanted to know. Like he said, he was forced into the situation he was in and didn't have anything to hide. Walter encouraged Youcef to begin recounting his story from the beginning and if they had any questions, they'd interrupt him. Youcef spoke of how he longed to come to America since he was a little boy. Finally, in his early twenties, he obtained an immigration visa to come and live in America. The first few years were wonderful. He landed a well paying job and met a girl he fell in love with. He still had the job, but the girl ran off after a year or two, after emptying Youcef's bank account of more than $25,000.

It was shortly after the girl disappeared when he was contacted by members of the Salafist movement in Algeria. They asked him to be their financier in America, to distribute and oversee payments of cash to different people. Youcef said he vehemently refused to take part in any nefarious operation, but soon changed his mind. They told him if he didn't cooperate, they'd kill his mother who was still living in Arzew. Youcef thought of going to the FBI, but what could they do? Things operated differently in Algeria than they did in the states. Initially, his role was bearable. They would send him money through a bank and he had to distribute it to different individuals. Then they wanted him to board people in his house for extended periods of time. He could feel himself getting sucked deeper and deeper into their spidery web, but he had no alternative. It was either do what he was told or his mother would die.

Youcef was telling a believable and convincing story, but it was all bullshit. He was a willing participant in these activities; in fact he initiated contact with the Salafists and not the other way around. Now he was in way over his head and was finally caught, a fate he said he deserved. His attempts at self pity fell on deaf ears, Walter and the troopers had heard it all before. They didn't buy it then and they weren't buying it now.

The same trooper who was previously questioning him looked at Yousef and said, "So where's the Taurus?" Walter chuckled to himself. He loved the trooper's approach, full steam ahead and take no prisoners. Youcef said his four 'guests' took it earlier in the morning, along with the red van. He had no idea where it was. Once again, Youcef was lying. He knew where the Taurus was because he was the one who left it at the Walpole train station. He also had a good idea where the Taurus was going. If the guys felt coming back to Brockton was too risky, they decided they'd head for Portsmouth, New Hampshire and try to hitch a ride back home on the LPG. If Yousef had told Walter and the troopers the truth, they could have captured all three before they left the country. Instead, he continued to betray their trust and kept feeding them lies. He would soon pay for his transgression.

While Walter and the troopers were interviewing Youcef, messages were being transmitted by fax, email and over the radio to every law enforcement agency in New England to be on the lookout for the missing Ford Taurus and the black van. The message was crisp and clear; the vehicles were involved in a recent terrorist act and the occupants should be approached with extreme caution. Officer Lutz of the Walpole Police Department heard the message over his car radio. He vaguely remembered seeing an abandoned green Ford Taurus at the commuter rail station parking lot last night while he was on patrol. He decided to shoot over there to see if the Taurus he saw was the one they were looking for. When Lutz arrived at the parking lot, he was disappointed to see that the vehicle was gone. But, sitting right next to where the Taurus was, Lutz saw a black van. It was the black van everyone was looking for.

Lutz called his dispatcher with the news and five minutes later the parking lot was filled with police cars. Luckily, as in the Wal Mart parking lot, the commuter rail parking lot had twenty four hour surveillance cameras covering the entire parking lot. So many cars had been vandalized in the past; the railroad felt they had no other alternative. A review of the tapes, starting from the most recent time and going backwards, revealed some extraordinarily incriminating evidence. First of all, they had excellent footage of the black van pulling alongside of the green Taurus. Then three males jumped out of the van and into the Taurus. Seconds later, the Taurus was driven out of the parking lot. A further review of the tapes showed Youcef dropping off the Taurus in the parking lot the day before. They now had documentary evidence that Youcef was intimately involved in the entire terrorist plot.

As soon as they had this information, one of the troopers at the scene called Walter on his cell phone. Walter was pissed. He knew Youcef was playing with them, but he couldn't prove it. Now he had Youcef by the balls and he intended on doing some squeezing. The trooper was still questioning Youcef about incidental bits of information when Walter interrupted. "Excuse me, Walter said, "but may I interrupt?" Youcef looked at Walter and said, "Well I was just…" Walter interrupted him. "Fuck you!" Walter said. Both troopers looked at each other in amazement. So much for the subtle approach, they thought. "Fuck you, you fucking lying son of a bitch." Walter wasn't holding anything back. He was frustrated and tired, and Youcef's antics were the last straw. "You don't know where the fucking Taurus is, isn't that what you said?" Youcef wasn't even thinking of answering. He knew more was to come. "Isn't that what you said?" Walter repeated. "You were forced to help because they'd kill your mother. What a ration of bullshit. You were involved from the start and we've got the evidence to prove it. Maybe your comrades got away, but we've got you and we're not going to let go."

Walter was spent. It had been a long, hard investigation and he was burned out. Now he had to deal with the possum-playing Youcef. It was too much for him. Walter walked into the kitchen and turned the cold water faucet on. Once the water was good and cold, Walter washed his face and then gulped handful after handful of water. He wiped his face on the sleeves of his shirt and then returned to the other room. Walter felt and acted like a new man. "Okay, Youcef, thanks for your cooperation," Walter said in a less than sincere voice. "These gentlemen," he said while waving his arm in the direction of the two troopers, "they'll take care of you now." Walter hesitated for a second, thought of saying something, thought again and then said what he wanted to say. "Oh, by the way my friend, you are under arrest for aiding and abetting an act of terrorism against the United States of America." As the troopers were handcuffing his hands behind the back, Youcef was sobbing softly. Walter couldn't care less. He had other things on his mind. He had to find the Taurus. If they found the Taurus, they'd find the terrorists.

CHAPTER FIFTY SEVEN

Over the next several days information trickled in to the office about the whereabouts of the Taurus and the three missing terrorists. The New Hampshire State Police were the first to call Walter. They had some information for him, but they also had an apology to offer. The toll station in Hampton, New Hampshire had a record of the green Taurus passing through the quick pass lane the evening of the terrorist attack in Foxborough. They even had a picture of the vehicle because it went through the quick pass lane without a transponder affixed to the car. The system is designed to automatically take a picture of the scofflaw. No one realized the car was wanted in Massachusetts until a computerized bill was generated. New Hampshire's billing system is interfaced with their registry of motor vehicles. If scofflaws have any other outstanding warrants, the state police are notified. This should have happened within a couple of hours after the car passed through the toll. But because people were out sick and no one was manning that position for several days, the discrepancy wasn't discovered until several days later.

This information was cold by the time Walter received it, but it told him the terrorists were headed north after the attack. They were probably headed for Canada. Walter was about to contact the Royal Canadian Mounted Police when more news regarding the Taurus came in to the office. This time it was from the Portsmouth, New Hampshire Police Department. They received a call from a fisherman on a boat that a car was half submerged along the banks of the Piscatagua River. Portsmouth Police and Fire responded and found a green Taurus with Massachusetts plates in the water along the banks of Freeman Point. Running the plate number through their system revealed the car had a national lookout on it for being involved in terrorist activity. The lookout requested anyone who had any information regarding the car contact Walter at his Boston office. When Walter received the call from Portsmouth Police, he became suspicious. Why would the terrorist go to Portsmouth? Walter thought. What was there that could help them? The next phone call Walter received answered most of his questions.

A customs inspector assigned out of Portland, Maine read a little blurb in the Portland Herald about a submerged car found in the Piscataqua River in Portsmouth. As he read further, the article said the car was possibly linked to a terrorist attack in Massachusetts by Algerian radicals. The inspector had just been in Portsmouth the other day clearing a ship from Algeria. He began to wonder if there was any connection between the car and the ship. He wasn't sure, but just in case there was, he decided to give the Boston investigators a call. This third piece of information tipped the scales for Walter. He now thought he knew what happened. The three terrorists fled the scene in Foxborough, swapped vehicles in Walpole and drove to Portsmouth, New Hampshire. In Portsmouth they attempted to ditch the car in the river before they boarded the LPG ship that was tied up at a nearby dock. The following morning, the LPG ship sailed and headed back to Algeria. The three terrorists were onboard hitching a ride out of the country.

To confirm his beliefs Walter took a ride up to Portsmouth with Cheryl. After stopping by the Portsmouth Police Department to get a copy of the police report regarding the car, Walter and Cheryl drove over to the LPG facility to talk with their security people. After an exhaustive review of the gate guard's visitor log book, they realized three people entered the facility that night but never left. They were signed in at 9:15 pm but never signed out. It could have been an oversight on the guard's part, but Walter didn't think so. He knew the bastards had given him the slip. But he wasn't done with them yet.

When Walter returned to his office in Boston, he called his state department contact in Washington, D.C. Walter related the whole story about the terrorist attack and his beliefs that the three terrorists were onboard the LPG ship headed back to Algeria. Walter wanted to know what the possibility was of having the U.S. Navy or the U.S. Coast Guard board the ship at sea and search the ship. Walter's contact was less than helpful. He told Walter the ship was the sovereign territory of a foreign country. Boarding the ship on the high seas by the U.S. Navy or Coast Guard would cause an international shit storm. America would be perceived by the international community, especially the Muslim community, as a bully ignoring all the basic concepts of international maritime law. Needless to say, Walter was less than pleased with the state department's lackluster response. Walter asked his contact if he'd mind kicking the question up to his superiors. Maybe they could suggest a more productive response to Walter's question. However, Walter's contact would not budge. He couldn't justify bothering his bosses; his decision was final.

Walter couldn't control his emotions any longer. "Listen moron," Walter began, "if you ever got your fat lazy ass out of Washington, you'd realize there's shit happening out here in the real world. All I wanted was a little help and guidance from you; not your stonewalling, bureaucratic bullshit." The state department contact started to interrupt, but Walter wouldn't have any of that. "I'm talking," Walter said, "maybe if you'd listen instead of flapping away with your bullshit rhetoric, maybe you'd learn something." Walter continued his ranting and raving but suddenly realized no one was on the other end of the line. The guy in the state department hung up on him. Walter went ballistic. The phone bouncing off the wall sent a piece of plaster sailing across the room. The secretary in the outer office heard the commotion but pretended not to hear. As quickly as Walter flew into a rage, he was back to his calm, stoic self. He wasn't about to give up his quest to capture the terrorists and had one more card stuck up his sleeve.

Next, Walter called CIA Headquarters in Langley, Virginia. He talked with the agent in charge of Mideast operations. When Walter briefed him on what was going on, the agent had a simple answer. "No problem," he said. "Fuck State. They look for ways to be obstructionists. But, boarding the ship on the high seas will cause a whole bunch of shit; not that I mind, but why not do it an easier way if it's possible?" Walter was all ears as the CIA agent continued. "Here's what we'll do. When the ship arrives in Algeria, I'll have a couple of my guys board the ship with the Algerian authorities. We'll snap the sons of bitches up and have them on a plane back to the states before they know what hit them." Finally he was dealing with someone who knew how to operate instead of a bureaucrat that was always looking for excuses instead of solutions. With any luck, within a week, all three terrorists would be back on American soil. Walter was looking forward to introducing them to the legal system of the United States of America.

CHAPTER FIFTY EIGHT

Because the ship hit some heavy weather as she transited the North Atlantic, it wasn't until a week later when she sailed into Arzew Harbor. As promised, two CIA agents along with at least twelve members of the Algerian National Security Forces were standing by on the dock. As soon as the gangway was secured, they jumped onboard to find and arrest the three terrorists. As in all boardings by government officials, the crew is mustered on the mess deck to be inspected. Once the CIA saw that the three individuals they were looking for were not present, it was assumed they must be hiding somewhere on the ship. But after a four hour search, no one was found.

The Algerian authorities questioned the captain and all the officers at length. Their story was the same; no one was onboard but the crew. They did not have any stowaways. Neither the CIA agents nor the Algerian authorities could come up with any evidence that indicated they were lying. Somehow, the information from the states saying there were three terrorists onboard was wrong. Having no other alternative, the CIA agents left the ship with the Algerian authorities.

When the CIA agent in charge of Mideast operations called Walter with the bad news, he was not happy. All the evidence indicated they were onboard the LPG when she sailed. He wasn't sure what was going on, but he just knew he was right. Somehow they had given them the slip. How, Walter did not know. But he knew they were on that ship. Then Walter got mad once again at the guy in the state department. If Walter had done what he wanted to do from the beginning and board the ship on the high seas, he'd have the terrorists in custody by now. But because of that idiot at state, Walter felt they lost them. There wasn't anything else Walter could do, it was over. Maybe some day he'd learn the truth, but for now, Walter had to drop it.

In fact, Walter was right. The three terrorists did sail onboard the LPG ship out of Portsmouth, but they pulled a classic move that the Salafists had used in the past. It was a little after midnight on their final night at sea. The radar had a contact fine on the port bow at a distance of ten miles. Gradually the distance closed. When the contact was two miles away, the captain ordered all engines stopped. Three shadowy figures on deck were lurking around the Jacob's ladder that was hanging over the port rail. Suddenly a shape appeared out of the darkened night. It was a fishing vessel, running with all her lights extinguished. The boat maneuvered alongside the ship, directly under the hanging Jacob's ladder. Out of the dark a voice could be heard calling, 'It is okay now. Let's go, we must hurry. Please climb down.' One by one, the three figures on deck disappeared over the side of the ship. Moments after they were all gone, the boat pulled away from the ship and disappeared into the night. If someone with good eyes was standing on deck as the boat disappeared into the inky blackness of night, he could make out the name on the stern of the boat. It was the Pegasus, captained by Captain Papadopoulos.

EPILOGUE

At the same time back in Arzew, Aadil was saying good bye to Usayd and his niece, Sameenah. Things were getting too difficult for the Salafists in Algeria. The new government, a staunch ally of the United States, promised a severe crackdown on anyone who was remotely sympathetic to a terrorist organization. Aadil was afraid if Sameenah stayed, she'd be arrested by the authorities and imprisoned. Aadil wasn't going to wait to see something like that happen. He gave her and Usayd a good amount of money and set them up in a house in Bern, Switzerland. Aadil had plenty of friends there and they'd make sure Sameenah and Usayd were well treated. Aadil promised he'd visit. Perhaps, he said, he'd be invited to the wedding. They all laughed at that because Usayd and Sameenah never mentioned anything about getting married.

At the airport, Aadil couldn't help himself; he cried like a baby. After all, Sameenah was all he had left. Everybody else was dead. Even Waqas was teary eyed. As they gave their final hugs and kisses, Usayd shook Aadil's hand and thanked him for all he had done for him throughout the years. Aadil didn't want to hear it. Aadil said he owed Usayd for all he had done for the movement. Finally, they had to leave. As Sameenah and Usayd walked towards the plane, Usayd stopped suddenly and turned towards Aadil. "Six months," he said. Aadil looked confused and said, "Six months for what?" Usayd started laughing. He told Aadil that in six months they expected to see Aadil and Waqas in Bern; that is, if they wanted to be part of the wedding party. Aadil beamed with joy. "I'll see you then," he yelled as Usayd and Sameenah disappeared into the plane. Sameenah was crying as she wrapped her arms around Usayd.

Aadil, Mubid and Sabir decided to stay in Arzew. They were too old to start a new life in another country. Although there was a new regime in Algeria, Aadil wasn't too concerned. He'd made enough contacts through the years that he felt he could weather any storm. As for Waqas, he'd remain by Aadil's side. He couldn't imagine being anywhere else; besides, they had a wedding to go to in a few months.

Mubbaligh and Correntine remained in New Zealand. Mubbaligh was doing well at work while Correntine stayed home raising their son, Mubarak. Lately, she'd been doing a lot of shopping. That's what you did when you were expecting another child. Correntine was due in a couple of months. They were expecting a little girl.

In Boston, Walker was discharged from Mass General. His ribs were healing and his lung was functioning again, but he still had weeks of recovery before him. Brian didn't care. He just wanted out of the hospital and to be home with Mary and the boys. Once he was fully recovered, Brian wanted to get back on the job. Bad guys were still out there and Brian wanted to make sure he did his part to prevent them from doing harm to his country. As always, he was a proud, patriotic American.

-

LIST OF CHARACTERS

Ahmed—one of the four main characters in the 2004 terrorist plot

Aldebaran—First ship to be boarded by newly formed ship search team.

Angus—New Zealand Salafist operative helped Faarooq in assassination attempt on Mubbaligh and Correntine

Anthony—member of JTTF out of Albany, New York

Dr. Assad—psychiatrist who treated Usayd for PTSD

Sebastian Auvil—U.S.Customs, Port Director, Boston, Massachusetts.

Aziz—one of the four main characters in the 2004 terrorist plot

Bashir—Childhood friend of Usayd, living in Beirut and working in the import-export business

Bob—security guard and neighbor of Joseph on Wren Street, provided invaluable information to U.S.Customs

Brian—Army CID agent in Frankfurt, Germany

Cheryl—criminal investigator assigned to JTTF

Correntine—Ex-CIA operative and Mubbaligh's current partner.

Dieter—man Usayd and Sameenah met in Rex Café in Berlin

Mr. Doenitz—head of security at Marburg University

Don—Customs investigator assigned to Boston JTTF

Elias—assumed name Mubbaligh and Correntine gave themselves

Faarooq—loyal Salafist member enlisted by the triumvirate to find and kill Mubbaligh and Correntine

Mr. Farah—National Algerian Telephone Company executive that helped Faarooq

Flynn—New Zealand Salafist operative helped Faarooq in assassination attempt on Mubbaligh and Correntine

George—part owner of Shawmut Freight Terminal in South Boston

Gus—Owner of No Name Restaurant in Boston

Hanifah—Bashir's girlfriend

Mr. Hanley—Mr. Hanley and son, Stephen, spotted red van in Wal Mart parking lot

Harvey—German shepherd, Massachusetts State Police K-9

Captain Holland—One of the two Captains of the Hapag Lloyd Endeavor

Joseph—lead warehouseman at Shawmut Freight Terminal in Boston. Cousin of Sleazy

Kheazai—better known as "Sleazy". He was Usayd's closest friend on the battlefields of Afghanistan.

Mr. Laham—CIA officer Mr. Yasir met in park in Arzew

Lambros Y—name of ship that tool Usayd home to Algeria from Beirut, Lebanon

Larry—United States Customs Inspector, chief operator of x-ray truck

Linda—wife of Sami

Brendan Lowell—JTTF Albany, New York

Captain John Lynch—United States Coast Guard, Captain of the Port, Boston, Massachusetts

Maisa—waitress at Dominique's

Manuel—steward on the Lambros Y, befriended Usayd

Matilda—cook in New Zealand safe house

Captain Andrew Martell—Commanding Officer of United States Coast Guard icebreaker 'Southwind'

John McDonough—Team leader for the ship search team. He holds the rank of Boatswain Mate 1/c, U.S.C.G.

Captain Mercer—One of the two captains of the Hapag Lloyd Endeavor

Mubarak—infant son of Mubbaligh and Correntine

Mubbaligh—Salafist in charge of July, 2003 American terrorist attempt that went wrong. He is currently on the run from the triumvirate and Algerian authorities

Nick—Waiter at No Name Restaurant in Boston

Captain Papadopoulos—Captain of fishing vessel Pegasus, boat that took Usayd home to Algeria from Malta.

Walter Parish—United States Customs Service Special Investigator. Head of Boston JTTF and lead investigator in case dealing with the dirty bomb in the container.

Paul—Supervisory Customs Inspector stationed at Conley Container Terminal

Pegasus—name of fishing vessel taking Usayd from Malta to Algeria

Russ—United States Customs Inspector assigned to x-ray truck

Sameenah—former lover of Mubbaligh, before Correntine

Sami—one of the four main characters in the 2004 terrorist plot

Paul Sawyer—head of Army's CID in Frankfurt, Germany

Professor Schwartz—Marburg University professor, recipient of package of caesium-137 from Minsk

Sonja—Sleazy's girl friend

Special Air Service (SAS)—New Zealand's elite anti-terrorism unit

Corporal Spellman—in charge of Massachusetts State Police dive team

Steve—United States Customs Inspector assigned to the x-ray truck

Tom—Massachusetts State Police K-9 handler

Triumvirate—leaders of the Salafist movement in Algeria—Aadil, Mubid and Sabir

Usayd—ardent Salafist member, chief architect of 2004 terrorist attack

Waqas—bodyguard for the triumvirate

Brian Walker—Massachusetts State Trooper shot on Rte. 95 by Aziz

Mary Walker—wife of Brian, two children: Tommy and Billy

Major Leo Williamson—Commanding Officer of Troop F, Massachusetts State Police, Logan Airport

Yacine—one of the four main characters in the 2004 terrorist plot

Yasir—embassy employee that helped Faarooq, eventually became a CIA informant

Youcef—financier for Salafist movement in America, lives in Brockton

Mr. Youssef—code name given to Mr. Yasir by the CIA